Copyright

All Rights Reserved.

StarScout Rising, First Trail

Library of Congress Control Number:

2010926611

ISBN: 978-0-9823017-2-2

Published in the United States

by

Kayto Communications Incorporated
P. O. Box 34682
Juneau, AK 99803
www.kayto.org

Cover Art by Sharon Ennis

info@galleryennis.com
www.galleryennis.com

StarScout Rising

First Trail

by

Gary Darby

Dedicated to all those who dream of what lies "Out There."

Special Thanks

If there is anything of good report or praiseworthy in my life, it lies within my family, and especially with my sweetheart of 35 years, Pamela. She is my source of encouragement, my sense of stability, my sense of what is right in the world. To our seven sons, our own little band of Stripling Warriors, good men all, thanks for believing, thanks for never giving up hope that we could bring this work to fruition.

A special thanks to author and copy editor Marty Johnson, whose writing guide "Write or Wrong" was always nearby to help sort out where those pesky pronouns and adverbs really fit within a sentence.

Thanks to cover artist Sharon Ennis, not only for her great artwork, but for her patience and perseverance in helping us decide what we really wanted for the cover art.

And to Tom Nelson of Kayto Communications, thanks for making it all work. Gary J. Darby

Table of Contents

Chapter		Page
1	Simon Bolivar Parque Nacional Del Sur America Star Date 2433.056	1
2	Geneva, Switzerland, Seat of the Terran Confederation Star Date 2433.056	30
3	Mystery Stalker	59
4	StarScout Command, Cheyenne Mountain, Terra	87
5	XT Attack!	139
6	Everglades Historic Sanctuary	162
7	Treachery Unleashed	180
8	Kidnapped	189
9	Cobras and Mongoose	219
10	Attack of the Garther Ape	242
11	The Queen Bee Crash Dives	272
12	Gadion Faction	293
13	To Swim with Human Sharks	320
14	Omega-Epsilon	337
15	Finger Lakes of Acid	355
16	Acid Maelstrom	407
17	Luna, Armstrong Bay Naval Station	428
18	Gadion Faction Lair	438
19	Great White Shark	450
20	Deep Space Distress Message	456
21	The Hunter is Hunted Down	461
22	Ambushed in the Double Helix	466
23	ALPHA PRIME...	484
24	Footprints in the Forest	510
25	"I will Return with Honor"	537

Chapter 1

Simon Bolivar Parque Nacional Del Sur America Star Date 2433.056

Snake strike! The mottled brown serpent head, wicked fangs extending from a milk-white mouth, stopped its lunge just short of Del's Blue-Lipped Dragon leather boot.

Before the muscular viper could recoil to thrust again, Del flung his tall, lean frame backward out of the wispy golden-green fronds where he had just knelt. The mushy soil bordering the tropical waterway softened his landing but not enough to prevent an "umph!" when he landed on his backside in the streams' wet muck.

Del crab-legged backwards, his feet slipping on the wet ground, as the aggressive snake slithered toward him. That the serpent missed on its first attack was near miraculous, but Del knew his luck might not hold a second time. He struggled to regain his footing in the slippery ooze and instinctively raised a boot toward the viper. The tough dragon skin might provide some protection.

The snake curved its body into an "S" shape,

exploded outward and sank its needle sharp fangs into Del's right boot. In reflex, Del kicked at the shiny v-shaped head, only to gape wide-eyed as he watched the meter-long snake struggle to free its fangs that were caught in the tough leather!

The snake lashed back and forth, fighting wildly to get loose, its mouth repeatedly clamping down on the leather that held it fast. Del pushed his foot down as hard as he could against the boot's inner sole, afraid that the fangs would penetrate the boot and puncture his skin. Del realized that the snake was truly caught and couldn't get free. He reached down to his hip scabbard and whipped out his scout long-knife. In one flashing motion the sharp blade sliced through the snake's thin neck. The beheaded serpent curled in on itself as blood and yellowish mucus spurted out the severed end.

Del watched the serpent body slowly unwind from its tight coil, as he shook off the green colored muck that caked his hands. The ooze stank of decomposing vegetation and rotten eggs. "Snakes, slime, and stink," Del muttered to himself. He inhaled deeply to slow his racing heart, and eased his right boot close. The snake's unblinking eyes stared accusingly up at him. In a curt tone, he said, "Don't blame me; you're the one that started this fracas." Careful not to touch the venom that pooled on the leather, he cautiously dug the fangs out of the boot with his knife.

Digging a small hole in the ground, Del speared the snake's head and buried it in the mossy earth. He looked at the twisted body, its patterned hide glistening from roiling in its own life fluid. He would leave it for the scavengers of the jungle.

Del examined the two punctures in his boot. He didn't understand how the fangs had caught in the leather, but felt for a certainty that if they hadn't, the snake would have delivered a life-threatening bite. And that would take a very embarrassing explanation to the ScoutMaster, who in one nano-second could turn a good day into a very bad day with "the look."

In the mission pre-brief before the exercise, I.M. Tarracas, the retired and much decorated StarScout who served as the school and program ScoutMaster, warned of "highly poisonous serpents in the exercise area." And, "if a junior scout allowed a snake to bite him or her, and self-aid was ineffective, the support team would provide medical aid, but the Instructor

Scouts would not accept a debilitating bite from a venomous snake as grounds for failure to finish the mission. It would merely indicate stupidity on the part of the scout for not getting out of the snake's way."

Besides vipers, Tarracas warned of "large land and water carnivores that could and would hunt human prey." So far Del had seen nothing larger than small monkey-like creatures that skittered treetop high and kept him company before losing interest in the dull human. But he took the injunction quite seriously regarding meat-eaters.

Del strode over to a small pond to wash his hands. The water's reflection showed a tall, lanky 18 year-old young man with a tanned narrow face, topped by light-brown hair that curled at his brow. His face had the usual assortment of pimples and freckles for youth his age. His physical appearance was fairly non-descript. Unlike the majority of his generation who dyed, clipped, sculpted, banged, toned, or star-dusted their hair, Del wore his completely natural. It was in deference to his mother who repeatedly said, "it wasn't what was on top of your head that was important . . . what really mattered was . . . what was between the ears of that head . . ."

His green eyes mirrored the unpretentious intelligence of a young man who took life seriously, but humble enough to know not to take himself too seriously. The smooth water also showed the greens and browns of his field uniform. His breast tag said "Baldura" and on the left collar were the four insignia bars of a fourth semester junior scout, with the letters "TL" on the right collar.

Del was currently the "TL" or team leader of Team Three of the Denali Vista High Academy Junior StarScout program. As a fourth-semester scout, he was near the end of his training program and this latest field mission would be among the last he would do as a junior scout . . . if he passed . . . if his team met "mission complete" criteria . . . if the team found the extra-terrestrial they were searching for . . . if they didn't run out of time . . . if he didn't do something really stupid and have one of the Instructor StarScout's relieve him of command . . . The list of "ifs" ran on and on and fueled the worry flames of his mind.

Del wiped the excess water off his hands, and looked around at the dense vegetation. The jungle was still and silent in contrast to his heart which still beat wild and loud from the snake's near miss. He shook his hands again and muttered, "Why do I do this?"

Even as he said the words, he knew the answer. He looked upward and just for a moment could see a speck of blue through the tree tops. A blue sky that led to the blackness of deep space where billions of stars blazed bright and hot. And among the sweeping firmament of suns lay one star in particular: Froma. And circling her was Froma IV, a planet enshrouded not only in swirling gray clouds and but also deep mystery.

Froma IV, where Del's father, a renowned StarScout, disappeared under bizarre and unexplained circumstances some seventeen years ago.

And with that vanishing came the rumors. Del's father deserted his team, left them to die a horrible death, that he found and stole a cache of priceless Kolomite ore. And the worst of all, he became a crossover, a turncoat who joined the infamous terrorist organization, the Gadion Faction.

The awful weight of the allegations caused Del to

bow his head in shame. Then he raised his head as he thought of his mother. She never lost faith in his father's innocence or that he was still alive. Neither of which she was ever to prove, though she never lost hope even to her dying day.

Del believed that the StarScouts were the key to unlocking the answer to the bizarre circumstances surrounding his father, and only from within the organization could Del hope to ever turn that key. So to his mother he promised to make the attempt, though he hadn't revealed to her his serious doubts that he could do what she asked. Nevertheless, he would try, and he promised himself that he at least, wouldn't shame the family or bring further dishonor onto its name.

With a start, Del realized that he had spent too much time sitting and not moving. The hot mid-morning sun was climbing to its zenith and he lagged behind in the stalk. It was time to contact the team. Del reached down to the small communicator pack and keyed open the trans-comm device. The minuscule audio receivers implanted in his ear canals allowed him to hear both outside sounds and audio transmissions from distant transmitters. The tiny microphone affixed to his right cheek picked up his words and sent them to the torso-vest's transmitter.

In quiet tones, Del said, "Path . . . this is Team Lead." Sami Lenz, the team's current Pathfinder, sarcastically replied, "'Bout time, lead."

"Still true to your azimuth?"

Sounding a little exasperated, Sami snorted, "Of course. 070 degrees. Steady and dull as she goes. Where've you been, you're late checking in. Taking a nap?"

"You bet. Local Milky Way Inn. Had to catch today's episode of 'As the Galaxy Turns.' The hot shower was the best though . . . any XT contact?"

"Lucky you. Negative on the Xee," the other youth replied. "I think they've got us chasing the Phantom of the Jungle." Del grimaced as he answered. "Feels that way, doesn't it?" He pulled at his chin with his hand and looked at the moss-covered earth at his feet. Still the same. This was certainly not going like it was supposed to!

Five days earlier the troop deployed from campus for a typical Search, Locate, and Catalog, or SLC, mission in the deep reaches of Amazonia's Simon Bolivar National Park. Mission: Locate the extraterrestrial animal that was their target quarry and meet catalog criteria at or greater than the ninety-five percentile level. Normal . . . routine . . . typical . . . standard.

But after five days of stomping through the steamy jungle tracking their alien quarry, they had nothing to show for their efforts but a few fleeting contacts. Two very brief visuals and three faint LifeSensor readings did not a successful hunt make. As he looked up through the leafy overhead and mulled over what to do next, Del saw puffy biscuit-like cumulus clouds push across the light blue sky. Already the clouds were clumping together as the midmorning tropical sun boiled their innards. Soon the clouds would expand, swell together, and then with lightning and wind, pelt the jungle with brief but intense heavy rain.

Del needed to get his team moving to a new search area before the rains came and make their quest that much more difficult. As the Team Leader, he had the responsibility to orchestrate the movements of the team. And so far, he thought to himself, he was doing that about as well as a first-semester junior scout or "toady" as seniors called incoming junior scouts.

It wasn't that he and his teammates weren't good scouts. On the contrary, during solo missions, the five junior scouts, Sami Lenz, Tala Janair Utlander, Nase Ahren, Shanon Hsu, and Del, were all at or near the top of their class in the basic scout subjects. The word among the Instructor StarScouts was that these particular JS's from the Denali Vista High Academy Junior StarScout Troop (The Fightin' 288th DegaBeasts) were "very promising" candidates for enlistment selection.

What was unusual was that this was the third time in the last two months that the ScoutMaster placed these particular junior scouts together. Del and the other scouts wouldn't dare ask why of course. They obediently accepted their assignments and carried out their missions. But so far, on every field exercise, this particular combination was woeful in execution. For some reason, they simply could not, or would not, jell as a team.

In a test area working a Seek, Locate, and Catalog Mission against a pre-programmed SimLife, or a flesh-and-blood creature, based on individual abilities, they should be the best in the troop, a fluid synchronization of five moving parts. But the chemistry needed to be that stellar team hadn't developed in the previous two exercises and was again missing this time around.

Del ruefully recalled IS Tosind's sour observation as they trudged out of the field on their last out-trek, "Circuses have clowns . . . Aussie's have roo's . . . Kallorians have dippy-dogs . . . and we . . . have . . . you . . ." The message in the ditty was clear enough. Kallorian dippy-dogs were renowned for their hilariously wild antics that defied reason and logic.

Del didn't socialize much with the junior scouts in the program but he did know a few things about his current teammates. There were whispers that Nase was "blue blood." His family had deep connections in the financial world and was very wealthy. Del didn't know for sure as he had never asked the quiet, tall, dark-skinned youth about his family as he didn't want any questions in return. But he did know that Nase was very intelligent, very observant, but kept to himself. On solo missions his ratings were always near the top in all categories, but for reasons that Del didn't understand, working within a team was a struggle for Nase and for the team he was on as well.

Sami on the other hand was temperamentally and physically the opposite of Nase. Short and a bit on the stocky side, Sami was definitely an extrovert. Outspoken, quick to smile but easily angered, often sarcastic, with a sharp wit that matched his tongue. He was the troop's unofficial prankster and there wasn't a JS who hadn't been the target of his practical jokes, including Del.

During one sixty-kilometer solo trek through the Kalahari Desert, to Del's embarrassment, he discovered that Sami replaced his water vest with one filled with heavily carbonated water. Del tried the Bushmen technique of finding fresh water by digging plant bulbs out of the sandy earth to squeeze their pulp. He failed miserably and had to drink the "fizzy water" that Sami provided.

Not that Del was in any danger of dehydration, but it was fortunate that the trek didn't require any silent sneaks as his stomach foamed and distended from the carbonate and caused Del to belch almost constantly. It was no wonder that he hadn't seen a single animal on his journey either —without doubt they heard him long before they saw him and fled the area.

Of course he couldn't report his predicament to the Instructor Scouts, who not only would've busted a gut laughing, but more importantly given him a demerit in "Equipment Check, Prior." And Del couldn't afford the loss in points.

He had a few choice words for Sami when he got back to base camp, to which Sami grinned, tossed him a water flask saying, "Welcome back. Have a drink sans carbonate on me." He flipped Del a packet of "nogas tabs," snickered loudly and walked away.

Del considered reporting the incident, but didn't. The truth was that Sami was a very good junior scout and he never, ever pulled a prank that could hurt a teammate. In the bush, he had incredible natural instincts for trailing life-forms; the best in the troop. Del asked him about it once and Sami just shrugged and said, "Not much different than the barrios. You run with a gang that spends most of its time hunting down other members of a rival gang . . . you get pretty good at it . . . or . . . you get pretty dead."

Tala was hard to fathom. The pert, dish-water blond was full of energy, quick on the draw, not hesitant to make snap decisions and to speed ahead at full throttle. Other times she was melancholy as if something heavy weighed her down. There was a saying in the troop that if you were charged up and full of energy, you were having a "TJ day." On the trail, no one was steadier or had more endurance to keep at the task. She drove herself hard, and her teammates as well, which often left them grumbling and agitated with her.

Shanon was steady as a rock but fiercely competitive . . . she really hated not being in charge. Having someone else make the decisions grated and it took a great amount of effort on her part to not speak up or try to take command. Her natural beauty made her a magnet for the young men in the troop, but behind the beautiful face was one very smart scout who had a penchant for quick thought, quick conclusions, and quick action.

A few weeks into the course, she found Del playing a game of rac-ball by himself. "Aren't you getting tired of beating yourself?" She asked as she walked onto the court and flipped a ball to him. "Volley for serve?" Del had just stood there unsure of himself.

She pointed with her racquet, "Front wall is over there mister. The ball goes that'a way." When Del still didn't move, she placed her hands on her hips and asked teasingly, "Are you waiting for me to spot you points and the serve? That's not very gallant."

Del shook his head and said, "I've never played against a girl before . . . are the rules the same?"

An astonished look crossed her face, "Are the rules the same? You're serious? You've never played racball against a girl before?"

"No. Sorry. Where I come from the girls didn't play."

With a little snort, Shanon replied, "Same rules. Serve gets the point. Serve has to hit the octi-wall and then two walls and the floor after that."

Del tried to be gentlemanly as he said, "Back home, I was pretty good at this, so to make it even, I should spot you points." He shrugged while saying, "I think that's why the girls didn't play, they weren't any good and we always beat them."

Shanon looked at him, raised her eyebrows and said, "Well, things are a little different round here. Tell you what, let's play it straight up for now." She gestured with her racquet while saying, "And forget the volley. You serve Mr. I'm Pretty Good at this."

Thirty minutes later Del collapsed to the floor in a

heap, sweating profusely, gasping for breath, and totally pointless in three matches. Shanon stood at mid-court, barely breathing hard, a few drops of perspiration on her forehead. She shook her short brown hair and said, "You need to practice your serve, your slap shot, taking the ball off the back wall, watching the angle on the octi-wall, digging the ball out of the corner, playing the three-wall return, and your back-hand."

She started to walk off, but then she pivoted and laughed lightly. "Oh, but I must admit, you're pretty good at diving out of the way when somebody scrams the ball at your head."

Later, Del discreetly asked around and learned that Shanon held a 4th-degree Master's Rating, one level short of the top rung among rac-ball champions. Del immediately made two vows, one, to always remember that the way things were done on his home world didn't necessarily equate to Earth ways, and secondly, never, ever, to open his big mouth about girls again, especially when he was around a girl.

So, while Del knew that his teammates in every case were top-notch in the field, Del practically groaned when he saw the team list for this exercise.

He couldn't believe his eyes when he saw the five teamed again. And his anguish wasn't based on anything personal; rather it was based on something very practical.

Without doubt, Del knew that this was probably the last training mission the troop would have before each junior scout received 'Mission Alert' for their No-Notice Final Exam field test. The No-Notice was the decisive crucial field test of the program. It determined if a JS was qualified and worthy for an enlistment offer in StarScout Command.

Del desperately wanted to finish in top form so as to be ready for the No-Notice. But when the ScoutMaster posted the team manifest for this stalk mission, Del felt a deep uneasiness that once again they would come out worse than when they started. Now they were into the fifth day and Del's fears were coming true for they were no closer to pinpointing, observing, and cataloging the XT target than they were on the first day. Not only was the sun hot, but so were tempers as the frustration mounted. Their brushes with the XT target were too brief. Each time they tried to close, the creature slipped away, forcing the team to restart the stalk-and-fix sequence. Worse, they did not have a clear idea of what they sought, except that it was a large, furry OutLand beast with extraordinarily oversized ears, able to move through the jungle faster than they.

Arching his back, Del worked the kinks out of his neck. Another short night. Or rather, a short night for sleeping. Not wanting to spend the dark hours on the ground, the team took to the trees. Precariously draped over a tree limb or scrunched into a v-notch was not the most comfortable resting conditions. Del knew the lack of sleep, the hot, muggy weather, and the ever-present jungle dangers would take a toll on the team. A few more days and they would lose their sharp mental and physical edge. If they were bad now, they would get worse, leading to a real fiasco.

Del set his jaw. It was time to finish the mission. To find and catalog the XT, get his team out of this jungle and back home to prepare for the No-Notice that would surely come in a few weeks or even days after they returned. And being ready for the No-Notice was of supreme importance.

Del knelt in the lush undergrowth, and unfolded the plas-map that the instructor scouts provided just prior to the team jumping off. According to the map, to his right was a medium-sized river the team paralleled most of the day. Upstream the river made a wide sweeping loop to his left before emptying into a large lake. Studying the map, Del had the gleaming of an idea. He keyed his trans-comms, "Team 3, this is Team Lead, net call."

In sequence, the other four team members responded to the call for a comms-conference. Del instructed them to open their own maps, and said, "Coordinates 612 by 300. See the river and lake? We'll use them as two sides of a triangle. We'll form the third side with a search line from the lake to the curve in the river at 610 by 385. I think the XT is somewhere between the lake and the river and if we do this right we'll pin it against the water and get our mission complete data."

He paused to let his teammates mull over the map and get the same picture as he. "Pathfinder is the northern end point in the line," he went on, "Flanker One, Shanon, you're on Sami's right. Nase, center. Flanker Two, TJ, you're on Nase's right, and I'm the southernmost point. Once we're in position I'll start the Grand March. Everyone set?"

For a long moment there wasn't anything over the

trans and then Sami said, "Understand the plan, TL. But we're spread pretty thin. The XT might be able to slip through the holes."

"I totally agree," Shanon firmly chimed in, "We're way too far apart, the intervals are so wide that a bison herd could stampede through and we'd never hear or see them. TL, I strongly recommend that we rethink this because you're not going to get total sight and sound coverage."

"Maybe," Del replied, almost sighing in his response, "But I think it's the best we can do for right now and we don't have time to 'rethink this' Shanon . . . so let's do it! Scouts Out!"

Del didn't feel like arguing and besides, if one of their earlier LifeSensor registrations of the star creature was correct, Del felt fairly confident that the alien was between the river and the lake. He would spread the team on a more or less straight line, less than a kilometer long, and on order, move forward, attempting to drive the creature. Using the water as a backstop, the team would form a loop from the juncture of the river and lake to a point a kilometer or so up the lake shore.

Once they formed the loop-screen, the team would

close the net until one of them had a visual sighting of the XT or a positive reading on the LifeSensor. From there they could hopefully get one or two of them close enough to do the cataloging. Del knew there was no guarantee it would work, but it was better than the floundering around of the last several days.

Since he was now tail-end Charlie with the longest distance to go, Del traveled rapidly but carefully through the dense underbrush. He closely watched where he put his hands and feet, not wanting a repeat of his meeting with the venomous serpent.

As he moved through the jungle, Del kept on a bearing that should lead him to the river and his jump-off point. With few landmarks to go by, he depended on his geo-compass for direction, having determined a bearing off the map. It was not the most accurate of methods, but for this mission it was all the JS's had to navigate through the jungle growth.

The ScoutMaster had not seen fit to issue one of the sophisticated global-Nav units to the team members for this exercise. Without it they were unable to use Luna laser grid which could pinpoint a person's geo-grid location to within half a meter on the globe's surface.

Since this test was under "Field Conditions 1-Uniform" the scouts could not use any man-made mechanical devices other than a compass for navigation. Even a geo-compass was a luxury of sorts since most exercises were done strictly by using terrain landmarks, solar navigation and the always steady and reliable constellations and individual stars in Terra's night sky. However, the luxurious plant canopy of the dense jungle made it extremely difficult to navigate by the stars and so the instructor scouts grudgingly issued the geo-compasses for use in the test area.

After an hour of slogging through the jungle Del stopped to check his bearings and take a short breather. The aroma of lush plant life filled his nostrils as he stood next to some tall bamboo-like grass shoots. On his march he had noticed narrow, open areas but avoided those, surmising that hunting predators would frequent those trails in their search for game.

An eruption of squawking ground birds flying up

from a nearby patch of tall grass caused Del to freeze in place. Del felt the hairs on the back of his neck rise up. His "jungle radar" was broadcasting loud and clear. Danger! And very close. He knew instantly he was being stalked. The hunter had become the hunted.

Controlling his initial urge to run, Del recalled a lesson from ScoutMaster Tarracas. "To flee from an unknown danger only makes that danger loom larger and more frightening to the mind. A known danger provides knowledge of itself and therefore opens up possibilities for its defeat."

In a slow arc, Del surveyed his surroundings. He didn't see anything amiss but there was no doubt in his mind a deadly something crept closer and he only had a few moments to act. He'd have to use the frantic birds as the most logical place from where the danger emanated . . . but to move forward and meet the danger or try to escape and evade?

Del started to step toward the slightly waving grass but stopped in mid-stride. No, this wasn't right, he thought. This called for evasion until he could find a place and time of his own choosing to meet his nemesis. To his right rose a small, jagged ridge of fissured rock that split the jungle. The rocks would give him some protection from seeking eyes and a chance to evade detection.

Twisting between two vine-covered trees, Del scampered through a brushy meadow and into the rocks. For several seconds he stopped to scan his back-trail but didn't spy his pursuer. Keeping low, he quietly made his way up the ridge to its craggy rock crown and hunched down behind a clumping of rock boulders and looked down into the jungle expanse below. Nothing moved on his back-trail and he puzzled over the identification of his stalker. He thought his hunter was probably a natural denizen of the jungle, a jaguar perhaps, shopping for its lunch.

He considered if his pursuer were a Sim-Life, one of the sophisticated robots the instructor scouts used as training devices. Del discounted that thought since all the Sim-Lifes he was familiar with were clumsy and slow. Beautifully crafted to look and act like alien life, and remotely controlled by instructor scouts, the Sim-Life imitated the most basic and primitive of alien life-forms. But they lacked speed and finesse, so he seriously doubted it was a Sim-Life that lay in wait.

There was another possibility. It might be one of the instructor scouts making the exercise more challenging by adding the element of an unknown stalker. In two of the last four exercises the instructor scouts were the antagonists, ardently chasing and in some cases catching the unlucky JS.

And in the last exercise where the IS's stalked and chased the junior scouts, it had been a "do or die" exercise. The JS's, acting solo, had to outwit, outrun, and outmaneuver the StarScouts. The penalty for getting caught: you were done. Out. Finished. Expelled from the course. Just like that.

Del clearly remembered the grueling chase through the steep canyons of the Bitter Root Mountains. He almost shivered in the tropical heat as he recalled the biting cold sleet and the harsh, knifing wind. The agonizing battle up the precipitous sides of the mountain where each breath was like a laz-gun shot to his chest.

The last night was the worst. He had to stay hidden and uncaught for only six more hours. Then two instructor scouts flushed him out of his hidey-hole and penned him in a narrow box canyon. His only escape route was to scale a 20 meter-high sheer rock wall without climbing gear. As he looked up at the almost vertical gray rock barrier, and then at the advancing StarScouts, Del came very close to quitting . . . very, very close. Near physical exhaustion, he knew that he might not have the strength to maintain hand-and-footholds on the rock face. It would be a desperate gamble, one that could cost him his life.

Like most, Del feared death, and the rock wall scared him to his very core. But the act of giving up was more terrifying for him than losing his life. Not after coming so far and working so hard . . . and there was too much at stake for himself and his family. To give up would forfeit any chance he had of finding the answers to the questions that harried his mind and haunted his soul. Questions that aged his mother far beyond her youthful years and day-by-day drained her full-of-life spirit.

That thought surged new energy into him. He turned, leaped onto a nearby small boulder, reached up to grab hold of an angled piece of rock that jutted out from the cliff and centimeter by centimeter pulled himself up the rock facing. When he finally levered himself over the top, he knew that climb would forever remain a benchmark in his mind of what he could do when desire and motivation were so powerful as to overcome physical, emotional, and spiritual fears and doubts.

That mission was a turning point for him in other ways as well. A day after returning from the Bitter Roots, IS Oburra ordered Del to report to ScoutMaster Tarracas's office. This was Del's first visit to the "holy of holies" and it frightened him almost as much as that rock climb.

Straightening his uniform as he walked to the SM's office, he rapped on the outer wall with the prescribed three knocks. A gruff but firm voice said, "Enter, Junior Scout." Del smiled at that, while the other StarScouts called the JS's by their last names, but never by their first names, to ScoutMaster Tarracas, they were always, always, "Junior Scout."

Del entered the ScoutMaster's office, strode forward, stopped and did a brisk right facing movement to place himself directly in front of Tarracas's desk. The SM had his head down over several plas-papers and didn't look up as Del stood ramrod straight. Del waited, without moving; while he let his eyes wander around that part of the office that he could see.

To his left were numerous 3-D photo plats. Their exotic backgrounds were of Tarracas and former StarScout teammates on starside missions. Behind Tarracas was a large Terran Confederation flag suspended from the ceiling, with the StarScout and school colors on its right and left, respectively. What really caught Del's attention, was a beautiful painting that covered the entire right wall. Del dared to turn his head a fraction of a centimeter to see more of the work of art.

The magnificent mural depicted a wonderfully detailed forest with a mountain landscape in the background. The foreground showed a large, lightly armored, but heavily muscled man astride a magnificent black steed, holding aloft a flowing bright green and yellow banner. The horseman led an army of handsome bare-chested young men who carried spears and short swords.

The face of the large copper-skinned leader seemed sad but very determined, while the countenances of the young men were eager, almost hopeful in their expression. They strode confidently below snow-capped mountains. It was obviously an army marching to battle.

To find such a painting in the ScoutMaster's office fascinated Del. He would have thought that with Tarracas's exploits in the StarScouts, a painting of a ferocious alien beast on a strange OutLand world would be more appropriate. He surmised that the scene was from Terra, though Del was unfamiliar with the event it depicted. Del was so engrossed in the painting that he missed the ScoutMaster's initial words, " . . . customary when a junior scout begins Phase 4 to review the scout's training and personnel record to ensure that all is in order."

As soon as the ScoutMaster mentioned his personnel file, Del stiffened and brought his eyes straight forward to stare unblinking at the wall directly behind Tarracas. "Your birth record was not in the file, which is not unusual, unless the names of both parents are not listed, which they were not. Since you were in the field, I chose not to disturb your training cycle and contacted your district recorder on your home world for your record, only to discover you were not born on Randor, but on Terra."

"I have your birth certificate," he paused before continuing, "You came to us under the name of

Baldura, but your birth record says that you are not who you say you are. You are not Del Baldura."

[Handwritten: ↗ first time it gets interesting]

Chapter 2

Geneva, Switzerland
Seat of the Terran Confederation
Star Date 2433.056

[Handwritten: – why do only the first 2 chapters have stardates?]
[Handwritten: ↳ should be 17 yrs. before]

The soft chime from Adiak Peller's wrist communicator interrupted Peller's forced laugh at his dinner partner's old and tiresome joke. Peller purposefully programmed the device's minuscule brain to accept only a limited number of callers, so he knew that it was a very important message. He tapped the little communicator and instantly a 3-D hologram appeared over his wrist. He quickly read: "*The Alpha Centauri delegation left the negotiating table,*" and wrinkled his Romanesque nose as he grasped the hidden meaning behind the text.

He eased his thin body up from his high-backed dinner chair so as not to appear too excited about the message. He extended his half-filled glass toward the perfectly groomed and elegant woman at the other end of the long dinner table. She wasn't his contract spouse of course, but a very well-paid professional hostess who would expertly tend to his guests while he was gone. He flashed his guests a polite smile from perfectly formed teeth, made his excuses and strode out.

No one found this unusual of course, since a man of his position in the Terran Confederation often received urgent messages that needed attention. Besides, if anyone at the party had inadvertently seen the communiqué they would simply assume that he was being updated on the negotiation situation. Of course, the Centaurians were *always* leaving the bargaining table and had been for years so the message was innocent enough.

But the true message was that he had an urgent call waiting for him in his private, sophisticated, and utterly secret hideaway. And the call would have nothing to do with endless negotiations of squabbling starsiders like the Centaurians.

Entering his study, Peller strode to a far wall where a world-class painting hung mid-wall and touched three distinct places on the painting's textured frame. A dark line creased the nearest corner as the wall separated from the adjoining partition and glided back to reveal a high-tech security door. Peller stepped forward, entered the security code on the control panel, and placed his eye against the retinal scanner. With a soft *whish* sound the heavy silver and black door slid open.

As he stepped inside, bright lights revealed a room full of communication and computer consoles. Not even his closest advisors, staff, or aides knew of this room, and Peller had made sure that those who built it were no longer alive to divulge its location or contents. The ultra-sophisticated consoles gave Peller the ability to confer with almost anyone on any of the inhabited worlds of the Confederation and provided unlimited access to the Confederation's voluminous data files. More importantly, the concealed room held his deepest and darkest secrets.

He moved to the hyper-transmitter console and punched in the transmission code that correlated to the Alpha Centauri message. He didn't engage the visionome program to hide his identity since the man he was about to speak to knew who Peller was. He was one of the very few who did, and it would remain that way. Peller had ways to ensure that it did. For now the man was useful. When his usefulness ended, there would be one less who knew Peller's true identity.

In an instant, a wearied and drawn face appeared on the holo-view. With a cold stare, Peller addressed the StarScout. "I was in the middle of a very expensive dinner. This had better be worth the interruption." Peller didn't add that two of his guests were members of the Lydorian Delegation whom he was slowly, but surely, ensnaring in his league of lies.

He eyed the man and sniffed, "You look awful, you really need to take better care of yourself."

The man ran a hand over his eyes before replying in a deep baritone voice, "Haven't slept . . . going to bed soon . . ."

"Good," Peller said, growing stern, "but you didn't call for us to chat about your health or bedtime habits. Let's have it."

The man's dark face grew darker as he leaned forward. "The mission failed."

Through clenched teeth, Peller ordered, "Go on."

"No Kolomite." The man stated in a flat tone, "Nothing there."

The scout looked at Peller and dropped his eyes. "And we lost one whole team . . . ."

Peller's body went rigid. The words, the look on

the man's face, for one second the whole scene took Peller back seventeen years to another time, another conversation.

Then too, this same scout had started . . . "We lost one whole team . . . "

He'd hesitated and then went on, "It was Kavon's team. They . . . found his . . . and Beth's remains two days ago . . . I've been waiting for the confirmation. It just came in."

Peller's normally icy demeanor had boiled to hot anger. He slammed a palm down on the console surface as he leaned forward, his face mere centimeters from the holo-screen. "What happened!" he hissed. "Your slime-birds were supposed to be watching him!"

"They were! We had him clearly up to the drop-off point. His body-tracking sensor was working, we had good audio and his beacon was on the grid from base camp until approximately twenty-four hours into the mission. Then . . . nothing. Everything went dead. At first we thought it was us, but the communication diagnostics checked out, plus we had comms with the other teams."

After a slight pause, he continued, ". . . a very

localized area with disruptions of electronic emissions. The comm-tech said it was like the transmissions either bounced off some obstacle and went who knows where, or they were just totally absorbed—nothing going in, nothing coming out."

Peller pulled himself from the mental blankness that momentarily enveloped him. He almost hadn't heard the man's last sentences. As he regained his emotions, Peller remembered what part he had to play. The man was a fool but he still needed to . . . use him. But for this, there would come a day of reckoning with this man—that he promised to himself.

He glanced away for a moment and then gave the senior StarScout a hard look that belied the almost uncontrollable rage he felt. "And the Kolomite?"

The man blinked several times and looked surprised. Peller could see that the StarScout officer expected questions about his son's death, not the Kolomite. But Kavon was dead and Peller coldly reasoned that the details of his death could wait. The Kolomite was more important.

"I managed to get the extraction team to the site. They found microscopic traces but nothing else. The ore was gone. Taken."

Peller sat straight up, his face, cold, hard, with a voice to match. "What do you mean taken?"

The man licked his lips. Peller could see that the scout knew he was on dangerous ground but it would be even more deadly if he didn't disclose everything he knew.

"We found minute particles of Kolomite scattered over at least a hectare." He inhaled deeply. "The ore was just below ground surface, and based on the total area, there was at least a thousand kilograms, maybe more. But totally mined out, and very recently, too."

As he ran his hand through his slightly wavy hair, the man said somberly, "Your information was right, it's just too bad that we had to lose Kavon . . . and Beth to prove it."

Peller took his own deep breaths, clamping his jaw tight as his mind jolted by the size of the ore bed. A thousand kilograms! For a moment he was almost giddy with the thought of how much wealth and power a thousand kilograms of the rarest substance in Confederation space could bring.

Practically in his grasp until someone beat him to the site, robbed him of the ore. But who? Outside of the Confederation itself, there were few that dared offer challenge. And he was making sure that those few were getting fewer. Harshly he asked, "Were there any reports of anyone else in the vicinity, any signs of who might have gotten there first?"

The man squeezed his mouth with his hand, obviously knowing that his master wanted answers . . . but if he had little to offer, that of itself could lead to dire consequences. "No, nothing," he began, "Tracks of a large, non-cataloged quadruped covered most of the area and their movements obliterated any signs of tracks or machinery." He stopped for a moment as his own face grew hard and cold. "There is one possibility, incredible . . . but possible."

Peller nodded for the man to go on, but the scout hesitated. "For you to understand, I need to describe the events leading up to Kavon's death and it's not . . ."

Peller cut him off. "Get on with it. *All* of it."

The man clinched his fist in front of his face, "A hunting pack of carnivorous flying creatures attacked Kavon's team. Its presence and hunting techniques on Froma IV weren't documented. There was nothing in the database on the animal, so the team wasn't out-briefed before the mission.

"From what we can tell, they beat off an initial attack, took refuge in a cave. I don't think they knew that the cave was actually a part of the creature's underground lair. The beasts attacked en masse." The man's jaw muscles tightened and he swallowed hard. "We found the . . . bodies . . . of four of the team in a small outer room of the cave. There was a side tunnel that went back several hundred meters to a rather large cavern.

"We found your son's remains there. But there were two sets of boot prints. The other set of prints led from the tunnel opening, across the cavern to an outer exit. Some forty meters past the opening was the Kolomite ore field."

Peller leaned closer, his eyes fixed on the man. "Who? Who do the prints belong to?"

"Dak McCarel, the team leader," the man answered.

"Dak McCarel . . ." Peller breathed out.

Peller's underling exploded in a venomous tirade, "Dak McCarel! Supposedly one of the best StarScouts in the Corps. He and his twin brother, Jak. Between them, the McCarels have probably half-a-dozen

LionHearts, twice that many First Landings. But in reality one of them is a coward, deserted my Beth, and your son."

There was a look of sheer hatred on the man's face. His emotions were barely in check. "Explain," Peller demanded.

The scout was silent for a moment, his face contorted as he fought some inner struggle. "The two sets of boot prints lead from the inner tunnel into the cave. They're obviously Kavon's and McCarel's. It's clear what happened.

"When the creatures attacked, McCarel and your son ran into the tunnel to escape, left the others. They made their way to the large cavern but must have thought the things followed and tried to make it across to a far opening." The man stopped to compose himself before going on. "We positively identified the remains of the team. None of the equipment and pieces of clothing found in the smaller cave was of Kavon or McCarel.

"The two sets of boot prints separate near a wall outcropping in the large cavern where we found your son's . . . body, so we know that McCarel was with Kavon. It looks like Kavon walked right into a nest of the creatures. McCarel's tracks split off and went through a cave opening and outside. About forty meters past the opening, the prints stop in the middle of dozens of the creature's claw tracks and at one edge of the Kolomite field. But the search team didn't find his body.

"Another thing. This was McCarel's Last Trail. StarScout Command approved his request for release from active exploration pending his last outworld assignment. He had the option of going to Antares 9—a milk run, virtually hazard-free, or Froma IV. He turned down Antares and went to Froma IV instead. To a non-cataloged planet where he knew the danger would be high."

His pent-up emotions exploded again and he slammed a fist down on his desk. "No one turns down non-hazardous duty for a last assignment! No one! But he did! He went to Froma IV for a reason and I think it was the Kolomite. Somehow he knew the ore was there. And to get it he sacrificed your son and my Beth!"

Frustrated, Peller snapped, "Stop! This Beth, what does she have to do with this?"

The senior scout visibly controlled himself before

he spoke. "Beth was a member of McCarel's team and . . . and . . . my wife. We married secretly a few years ago and she kept her family name. I never told anyone, I don't think she did either. We had . . . problems, especially after our daughter was born. She left me a year ago—but I never stopped loving her . . . never will . . . she was the only one who ever . . ."

Peller started to cut the man off since he didn't care for personal drivel, but then let him ramble. This was a hidden side that he hadn't known before and it was always good to know the secrets of underlings. It made them much more malleable later when he needed to bend them to his will. Feigning compassion, Peller said, "I am sorry. Together we will share our grief. Go on."

In despair the man shook his head. "That's all there is . . . about Beth I mean."

Peller placed his fingers in a pyramid and considered the man's analysis. Would a renowned StarScout willingly desert his team? Leave them to die? Yes. After all, for all their public preening about honor, duty, The Oath and so on, in reality StarScouts were simply human beings, no more, no less, and possessed of the same frailties as the common citizen. Yes, he thought, very possible if the scout knew that the richest deposit of Kolomite in charted space was his for the taking.

Kolomite. A hundred grams could power a starship for years. Ten kilograms could buy you the governor of a planet. A hundred kilograms and the governor would throw in the planet. What could a scout do with a thousand kilograms?

The same as he . . .almost anything.

Peller looked hard at *his* StarScout. "Removal of a thousand kilograms requires a large operation. McCarel couldn't have done it alone. Any sign of a ship on the ground or leaving the surface? Who else was on the ground—and able to get to the ore?"

The man ran a hand over his tanned face. "We only had one support vessel in synchronous orbit at the time and the cave site was at the extreme edge of its line-of-sight. It's possible a ship was just over the horizon and used the backside of the planet to mask its run-in or boost-out.

"None of the other teams were anywhere near the site. The recovery team reported was that there were several dead carnivores outside the cave's exit. But our energy weapons didn't kill them. The wound sites don't match what our laz-guns and other heavy arms do to living tissue."

He looked meaningfully at Peller and said, "And the wounds don't match the weapon parameters of your organization either."

His organization. Peller's eyes grew hard. The man had just told him that it wasn't a Gadion Faction weapon that destroyed the creatures. So if it wasn't StarScout or Faction, then who? Who would dare challenge him? There were other possible organizations, but he seriously doubted they would know about this particular ore site. He had made sure of that before putting this plan together. No, Froma IV was a very closely held secret.

Another thought began to shape in Peller's tortuous mind. He glanced sideways at the scout, suspicion growing hard the more he thought. Peller hadn't told the man all beforehand, just enough to shape the plan. Was it possible that his accomplice would dare betray him? Though the pips on his uniform said he was a senior officer, Peller knew that he had long ago lost any self-will to attempt anything against Peller. He knew the consequences were . . .

lethal.

But for a thousand kilograms of Kolomite the man might make a pact with Beelzebub himself - after all, he *was* in league with Peller.

Peller reasoned that the man's convoluted emotions were causing him to overlook other possibilities that explained Kavon's and McCarel's actions. But though it was a simplistic answer, nevertheless, the explanation was probably correct. And that implied that either McCarel and yet unknown accomplices stole his ore, or this man had conspired with McCarel and was covering for the renegade StarScout.

Of the two, it was almost certainly the former. So, until he knew differently he would assume that this supposed hero Dak McCarel was alive and with help extracted the Kolomite—his Kolomite! And he *would* get it back . . .

The answer to retrieving the ore was simple, find McCarel and you find the Kolomite. To do that he would use his formidable Faction organization, but he would also use this man and through him the StarScouts, to find McCarel.

So—either way, the trail led to McCarel, He would

find McCarel and when he did, if this man had a part in the betrayal, his end would be as ghastly as his beloved Beth's.

He carefully chose his next words, as he didn't want this man to even get a glimmer of his real suspicions. "Kavon's body?"

The scout shifted his weight slightly. "I'm sorry. The predators didn't leave much. We interred your son's and the other . . . remains on Froma. We normally transport bodies back to their families and home world," he went on, "but in some circumstances it's not . . . practical."

Peller raised his head to look at the ceiling and took a deep breath. He ran his hand through his own slightly wavy hair. "That will be very hard on his mother." He leaned forward again, "Equipment?"

The man shook his head, "Bits and pieces. We did find . . ."

With a slash of his hand, Peller cut him off, "Kavon's LifeSensor!"

"Missing. They didn't find it."

"Was the search thorough?"

The man nodded and said, "Very. It's possible the creatures swallowed the device as they were, uh, feeding. We don't have much information on the animal; they could've flown a hundred kilometers from the cave area."

Peller persisted, "Are you absolutely sure? Is there any chance it's still in the cave?"

"Yes. I'm sure, it's not there."

Peller considered for a moment. Kavon's assignment was to search for the Kolomite deposit, with the promise that he would share in the wealth and power it would bring. His equipment had been . . . modified, specialized . . . and as such might have provided more clues as to what really happened. More importantly, it was possible that there were other ore sites in the area and Kavon's altered equipment would hold that information. But without it there was no way of telling now.

The scout shifted uncomfortably in his chair. It was evident he knew more but was afraid to speak. In hard tones, Peller ordered, "Go on. Spill it."

The man gestured nervously as he began, "I've done what I can on my end, but you need to be aware that it appears that Kavon might have used his real name during the mission."

Peller bolted upright in his chair. "What!"

The man held up his hand as if to ward off Peller's explosion. "Don't ask me why, I haven't a clue. He had the false identity documents when he left the staging area. But I found a reference in a mission log to '*Kavon Peller.*' How it got in that log I don't know."

"Can you get his name off the mission records?" Peller demanded.

In low tones the man the replied, "I've already taken care of all that I can. But I have no way of knowing who Kavon talked to on Froma IV and what name he used."

Peller controlled his anger as his mind raced. This was too dangerously close to him. They needed to hush this up before anyone started asking questions. His mind caught on a thought. If they couldn't cover it up completely, at least change the focus dramatically to something else, away from Kavon— and particularly away from Adiak Peller.

He stared hard at the StarScout; the man was enraged from the thought that McCarel deserted his wife—left her to die. Peller was a master at controlling others, either by force or guile. A dark scheme began to shape in his mind, one that would serve several purposes; perhaps find McCarel, test the loyalty of this minion, and divert any attention away from Kavon and his idiotic mistake.

He silkily asked, "I am sorry about your wife . . . you mentioned a daughter?"

The man nodded numbly. "Yes."

"And now she is left without a mother." The man placed his hands over his face. For a moment they stayed there and then he said, "I'm sorry. I—"

"Oh no, no," Peller gently replied, "There is no need of apology. This is a great tragedy for both us. This obviously shouldn't have happened. There is no one to blame but . . ."

"McCarel!" the man exploded as he once again pounded a fist down on his desk.

"Yes, McCarel." Peller softly replied, "He's taken much from both of us."

The man clenched and unclenched his fists. Peller knew he had him now. "Yes," the man hissed, "And he is going to pay . . . "

"By all means," Peller replied, "But let us reason together how . . ."

"Reason! There is no reason! I am going to find McCarel and when I do, he's . . ."

"Stop!" Peller commanded. "*We* are going to find

McCarel. And he will pay. Terribly. But I want the Kolomite first! Then you may do with McCarel what you will." He pointed at the man and icily demanded, "Is that understood?"

Peller and the StarScout locked hard eyes for just a moment before the man nodded and said, "Yes—but McCarel is mine . . ."

Peller leaned back slightly; this was going well, now to the next piece. "You mentioned that McCarel had a brother. Are they close?" Peller asked.

The senior scout frowned, puzzled by the question. "Close? I don't have any idea . . . why?"

"Would it be possible that the brother was on Froma?"

"Impossible. I have the duty roster of every scout who planeted. Jak McCarel wasn't assigned to this operation."

"Is it possible that he was covertly on the planet, say to rendezvous with his brother?"

The man hesitated and shook his head, "Possible but highly improbable. I'll check the command-wide personnel assignment log to make sure."

"Good, and while you're at it, if this Jak McCarel wasn't on Froma, I suggest we keep a very close eye on his personal movements. After all, brothers often share traits; perhaps they both have a propensity to acquire power as well." Peller could see in the man's eyes that this was a totally new thought for him, one that he hadn't even considered. But that's what made him slow and stupid.

"And family? Did McCarel have immediate family—wife, children?"

The man turned, picked up a plas-paper and quickly scanned the writing. "His personnel record lists a wife and a son. The child was born about two years after my daughter, so he's a year old."

For a moment Peller considered the kidnapping of child and mother to use as bait to flush out McCarel, but he quickly dismissed that idea. No, there was no need and there was always the slimmest of chances that the trail would lead back to him.

"So . . ." Peller began, as if thinking aloud. "McCarel has a son. You have their address?" He quickly tapped in data to the computer and pressed the transmit button. "Send the information to this site. The person on the other end will know what to do." The man started to speak but Peller quickly held up a hand, "You watch the brother; I will take care of the others. They are no longer your concern." He went on, "Now, I assume that there will be an investigation."

The man nodded in reply. "Standard procedure," he replied.

"And who appoints the investigating panel?"

Obviously confused at the question the man answered slowly, "The senior on-site officer. In this case, the brigade commander on Froma."

"That's not going to happen," Peller ordered, "You will be the investigating officer."

The man sputtered, "But that's not . . ."

"I don't care what it is!" Peller almost shouted, "You will conduct the investigation and this is what you are going to put in your findings. McCarel deserted his team when the creatures attacked. My son held his ground with the others but when it was obviously hopeless he retreated into the cavern for a last-ditch fight. You will of course, use the false identity we provide.

"Your report will state that a large deposit of Kolomite ore was illegally mined at the same time by unknown persons but that there is strong reason to believe that McCarel may well have been a part of the mining operation. You might also suggest that since Froma IV was so dangerous that the only ones who could survive in that environment and take the ore were StarScouts."

"You . . . you . . . want me to acknowledge the existence of the ore?"

"Oh yes," Peller smoothly answered, "Most definitely I want the existence of the Kolomite to be in your report. The location, the quantity, everything."

"I don't . . ."

"Understand? It's simple. Everyone thinks StarScouts are nothing less than goodness personified. Brave, shining knights roaming the star lanes for the good of humanity. Let your High Command get even one whiff of scandal and they'll have every scout from private to the General himself on the lookout for McCarel. No one will want him caught worse than your sanctimonious pie-in-the-sky StarScout Corps."

Peller allowed himself to laugh, "The name of McCarel, once known for good, will soon be synonymous with bad. And if Jak McCarel is clean, he'll want to find his brother most of all and clear the family name."

Peller leaned forward as if he wanted to reach out and grab the man. His hard eyes, full of deadly menace, held the man fast and still. "You ensure that report shows that Dak McCarel deserted his post, ran like a coward, left his comrades to die a horrible death, and he did it for the love of money. I don't care how you do it, you just make sure that there is no safe harbor for him anywhere in StarScouts!"

"I'm not sure that I can—"

"You can and you will! A slight twist of a fact, the adding of a few subtle phrases and terms in the report, the loss of evidence. It can be done. It will be done. See that I have a copy of that mission report when it's ready. The full version. And remember, Kavon's name is expunged from everything associated with this. Understood?"

The man bleakly nodded and rubbed his forehead. His crestfallen demeanor revealed that he fully understood the tangled web that ensnared him, with no chance of escape. "I understand. Anything further?"

"No," Peller replied. "I will let you know when to set up the next operation." Peller reached over to his control panel to end the transmission. Peller sat for a few moments as a small smile played across his face. He had once thought of being a politician. After all, politicos were simply better actors than everyone else and had the innate ability of making a falsehood appear close to the truth or even as the truth. But while his morals were the same as most politicos he could act so much better than any politician he knew.

His mind came back to the fact that Kavon was dead.

Several parts of his Froma plan were chancy from the beginning; to send Kavon and to use the unsuspecting StarScouts to search for the Kolomite. But Kavon had wanted his own share of power, and was willing to take the chance, given the potential reward far outweighed the risk. Peller had other sons and his anger was not at Kavon's death but that someone dared to take something away that belonged to him. That was unforgivable, and McCarel would soon join those who tried before, had failed, and payed the ultimate price.

As for using the StarScouts, in the past Peller and his cohorts had tried civilian mercenaries to carry out this part of his grand plan, but those missions were disasters, with no results and a waste of resources and precious time. After repeated failures, Peller devised a scheme to use the one organization that had all the skills, training, and equipment to do the job. The StarScouts.

They were the Confederation's explorers, the modern-day Lewis and Clark, Jeve Voghn, EmmaLee Elstrom and the other great adventurers. The scouts were the best when it came to exploring and surviving on alien worlds. So, Peller began to use them as unwitting accomplices. Through nefarious schemes he entrapped the senior scout and others to become his co-conspirators.

But the plan on Froma had gone awry and Kavon was gone, and there was nothing more he could do. Cold logic entered Peller's thoughts. Kavon had taken his chances, had known the risks but still demanded that he be included in the operation. The lure of overwhelming power had been strong in Kavon. Like father, like son.

Peller mentally shrugged; he had sacrificed others to get to this point. He couldn't change course. He was getting that much closer to the final goal. If sacrifices had to be made to capture the prize, including this son . . . so be it.

* * *

Peller brought his mind back to the present. Seventeen years and the memory of that day were still sharp and crisp in his mind. The cold hate almost overwhelmed him when he thought of Kavon's death, the loss of the Kolomite, and Dak McCarel's treachery. He would never, ever forget, nor did he want to forget.

And now, seventeen years later, there was still no sign of McCarel or the stolen Kolomite. As the years passed, his hatred transformed from a burning fire, into a cold consumption that slowly and surely wasted away what little humanity he had left.

With a stone face he ordered the scout, "Prepare another team. The same location."

"But . . ." the man sputtered.

"No buts!" Peller stated, "The Kolomite is there. Your team was ill-prepared." He leaned close to the vu-screen. In a menacing tone he stated, "This time make sure they're ready or . . ."

The scout threw a hand up as if to ward off Peller. "No, no, I'll personally see to it. No mistakes this time."

Peller nodded and practically hissed as he said,

"See that you do. See that you do."

With that he turned off the vu-screen. For a moment he sat, calming himself. Another failure at the hands of this man. If the man weren't so highly placed, he would . . .

Purposefully he walked over to his computer console and tapped in a series of commands. Moments later the computer imaged a large three-dimensional galactovue in the room. Each pinpoint of light within the spherical holographic image represented a star, some with planetary systems, and others barren.

Peller gazed at the hundreds of lights and thought of how far-flung his organization had grown over the years. He had operatives and agents in virtually every inhabited star system that fronted the unexplored OutLands. Peller smiled sardonically. The fool he had just spoken to probably thought that he was in the upper echelons of Peller's grand scheme. Almost laughing, Peller thought of how amazed the man would be if knew just how low he was in Peller's overall organization.

He sent [set] in another set of commands and his Faction display disappeared from the galactovue followed by another set of red, glowing lights. As he gazed at the display, he picked up the alien artifact that lay on his desk and almost lovingly held it in his hands as he ran his fingers over its strange cold metal. Its curved silver-blue sheen seemed to absorb the light in the room, leaving a dark smudge instead of his facial image on its surface.

He knew the hand-sized orb was the only one in humanity's hands, the only real proof of Their existence. He knew it was a device of some kind, but its true purpose eluded him. His finger quivered slightly as he held it mere centimeters above the first of three tiny indentations that pocked the ball's surface. So many times he almost gave in to the almost irresistible urge to press the notches, but his keen sense of self-preservation, then and now, caused him to withdraw. Someday he would know exactly what the blue orb did, but that time was not now.

Gently, he placed the extraterrestrial device in its velvet lined receptacle and turned to the galactovue image that represented the work of a lifetime. The various colored lights and symbols in the holographic star-fields represented every sliver of information, every tiny scrap of evidence, painfully and carefully collected over the years of their existence.

He put out a finger and traced the series of red lights that started from the edge of the celestial image. Their trail wove through hundreds of star systems to end interestingly enough near Froma IV. For several moments he thought long and hard about another possibility of the missing Kolomite. He had too little evidence to make that fantastic connection. No, McCarel was the answer of retrieving the ore. Find McCarel, and the Kolomite would follow, of that he was sure.

His eyes narrowed to slits as he studied the star path. There was absolutely no doubt that they were marching closer and their trail was leading them to this part of the galactic spiral arm where an unsuspecting and vulnerable Earth glided peacefully along in its orbit around Father Sol.

This suited Peller perfectly.

Chapter 3

Mystery Stalker

Del's heart beat fast and hard, loud enough that Tarracas certainly heard. His hope of no questions regarding his family's past was obviously doomed. The fact that he stood in this office could only mean one thing. The ScoutMaster had serious doubts about Del's worthiness to remain in the program. For Del, the past, present, and future now merged into this one moment in time.

Normally Tarracas's light-brown face displayed little emotion, but now held a deep question as he held up a sheet of plas-paper, "Baldura is not your birth name, it is your mother's maiden name."

Though slight in build, Tarracas had a commanding presence, held in great respect by his fellow StarScouts. As the Instructor Scouts often reminded their charges, "You may grow physically taller than the ScoutMaster, it's doubtful you will ever reach his stature." Del couldn't agree more. What Tarracas lacked in physical attributes he more than made up for in spirit, valor, and moral courage.

"Why have you chosen not to use your recorded last name?" Tarracas now demanded. Del stood ramrod straight, his knees locked, his eyes fixed. He knew this was a test as critical as the "do or die" in the Bitter Roots. The ScoutMaster was more than the titular head of the school program. He was *the authority* on whether a person stayed or was dismissed. He had the final word, and he didn't have to justify his actions—to anyone.

He would be totally honest with the ScoutMaster; there would be no shading of the truth, no lies, even if it meant expulsion. Del knew that if he made it into the StarScouts he would meet this issue again, and again. Like the harrowing climb up the cliff, it was something he had to face and conquer on his own. His fervent hope was that the ScoutMaster would understand.

"My mother raised me as Del Baldura," he began, "Yes, I was born on Earth, but we emigrated and on Randor, a person's last name is not important nor do the authorities much care what you go by." He stopped for a moment to settle his thoughts. "My mother didn't tell me about certain . . . aspects of our family's past until I decided, on my own, to enter the junior scout program."

Del shrugged and went on, "She felt it best for me that I didn't know until then . . . and I decided that I would use the name I've always gone by . . . and not by . . ." he took a deep breath but didn't finish the sentence, didn't utter the name the ScoutMaster waited to hear.

The silence stretched on for several moments as Tarracas stared at the plas-paper in his hand. Almost to himself he said, "Teach a child in the ways he should go . . ." and then seemed to gather himself as he looked up at Del to ask, "What would your mother say if she were here now?"

Del felt a lightning bolt sear his mind. What a totally unexpected question from this man, and a personal arrow through a very tender part of Del. But the ScoutMaster didn't know or he wouldn't pose such a question. Del answered in a hoarse voice, "Tanom's Plague swept Randor. We lived in a very remote community. My mother died before the medical authorities could reach us."

There was a long moment of silence. Somehow Del felt a sense of sadness emanating from Tarracas and his reaction surprised and puzzled Del. Del allowed his eyes to follow Tarracas as the ScoutMaster rose from his chair and walked over to a large picture window. That in itself was a bit of an enigma. A real window instead of the usual pic-grams. Del turned to his head just a fraction to see the StarScout gaze out at the hot and still Arizona desert. Tall Saguaro cactus marched across the rocky landscape. He seemed deep in thought which caused Del to assume the worst.

Tarracas turned and walked back to his desk. When he spoke, it was the question that Del dreaded but knew would come and there was no avoiding. "And what do you know of your father?"

Del swallowed hard before answering, "ScoutMaster, I believe I know some of the story, but not all." He hesitated then continued. "Before she died, my mother told me how and why we went to Randor. I hadn't known any of it before and at first I didn't want to believe it was true."

Tarracas nodded for Del to continue. Del took a deep breath, "She told me that after my Father's mission to Froma IV, he was listed as missing and presumed dead. But, then came ugly rumors and insinuations concerning his conduct on Froma. At first she stayed on Terra, to try and fight the allegations. She loved my father very much, and didn't believe there was any truth to the charges. But, she just didn't have the means or resources to fight back and the only other family she really had was my father's brother, but he had an accident and was in a coma and not expected to live.

"The rumors grew much worse, that my father sold out to a criminal organization, became a crossover. She stayed and took it for a while. But one day she finally realized he wasn't coming home, the allegations weren't going to stop, and she really didn't have any way to disprove the accusations. And there were . . . other things . . . sinister things. She felt watched constantly . . . and became very afraid for our safety. She was totally alone and had no one to turn to for help.

"She became so frightened that one night we left our home, as if to go shopping. Didn't take anything with her but me, the clothes on her back and a few family digi-photos that she hid in her shoulder bag. Left everything and just kept going until we ended up on Randor.

"Randor's not high on an emigrant's list. It's backward and not a lot of people choose to go there, so the planetary authorities don't ask questions like who you are, or where you're coming from or why. If you want to get lost and leave a life behind, it's just about perfect.

"I was about one when we got there. We lived on a

small farm in one of the frontier farming communities. Ever since I can remember, I would watch the night sky and dream of what was Out There and when I was old enough, I told my Mother that I wanted to be a StarScout."

He paused for a moment and cocked his head, "Funny, I didn't realize it until just now . . . but when I told her, she didn't seem surprised at all, she just nodded her head as if my decision were absolutely normal. Which it wasn't, not for someone from Randor."

He shook his head as if clearing his thoughts. "She then set me down and told me about my father, what happened, the unfairness . . . the charges. At first I wouldn't believe her, and then I guess I became angry, really angry. Deep inside. My mother was . . . is, such a wonderful person . . . she didn't deserve the treatment she received. As far as my father is concerned . . ." Del stopped for a moment before going on, "I never knew him, only really know him through my mother's memories. And I just can't . . . won't . . . believe or accept that he did any of what they said he did."

Del bit down on his lower lip as he struggled with

the emotions surging through him. "So . . . after my mother . . . left . . . I thought long and hard about . . . well everything. At first, I said no, I was not going to devote myself to an organization that was capable of doing such things. At that's the way it stood before . . ." Del stopped as tears welled up and his words caught in his throat.

Del gathered himself and said, "A few weeks after the funeral, I was going through my mother's things. She didn't have much, and I found a small box with several e-letters from my father to her. I felt a little guilty but I couldn't help reading them." A small smile crossed his face as he said, "They were mostly romantic, but every once in a while, my father would speak about being a StarScout.

"In his last e-letter, my father said, 'after I've walked my Last Trail with StarScouts, I hope that someday, Del and I might walk a trail together . . . father and son . .'." [not likely to have elipses in the letter]

Emotion gripped Del again, causing him to stop for a moment. "My father loved being a StarScout. I know that. He couldn't have done those things. After that I decided that I wanted to be a StarScout . . . to prove . . . well, it was I needed to do.

"My high academy counselor helped me with the paperwork . . ," He dared to turn his head to look straight at the ScoutMaster. "I didn't put down . . ." He stopped and brought his head back to the front before he stated, "I didn't put down his name, because I wanted the StarScouts to judge and accept me on what and who *I* am. Del Baldura. Not Del . . ."

The stillness in the room was almost palpable. Neither spoke for several moments before Tarracas broke the silence. "You mentioned that your father had a brother . . . a StarScout as well."

Del shook his head. "Yes, but he's dead. My mother told me that she believed he died from his accident." Tarracas stared at Del for several long seconds. He opened his mouth as if to speak then stopped as he folded his arms across his chest and brought one hand up to his mouth. Del had the distinct impression that the ScoutMaster mulled over something very important and he had no doubt what it was. Whether Del stayed or was summarily dismissed from the StarScout program.

The minutes stretched on while the ScoutMaster pondered over Del's fate. Del let his eyes wander back to the mural. Del found the hope on the young men's faces oddly comforting as it mirrored his own feelings just then. Del was so engrossed in the painting that he almost didn't hear Tarracas. "You find my two thousand stripling warriors interesting, Junior Scout?"

Del snapped his head forward. "Uh, yes sir, I do. It's . . . beautiful artwork." He found the change in topic disconcerting. He remembered thinking that some day he hoped the ScoutMaster would teach him how to read minds. He knew the SM had taught the Instructor Scouts, since they always seemed to know what the junior scouts were doing and thinking at any given time.

Tarracas walked over to stand before the painting and turned toward Del. "It is a depiction of a remarkable event from an ancient book about my native people and homeland. The man on the horse is a great warrior-king. The army he leads is of two thousand young men, mere striplings, who left their families to defend their homes. They march to war, but are hopelessly outnumbered against a ferocious enemy who gives no quarter in battle."

He raised his hand toward the painting as if to reach out to those pictured there. "Before these young men were born, their fathers were a bloodthirsty people, having no respect for the inherent right of human beings to life. Their way was to kill, and kill again. Then a miraculous event changed their hearts. Completely. In consequence of that they took a sacred oath and covenanted before their God to never take up arms again or to kill any human being."

"Even to defend their families and homes?" Del asked, daring to interrupt.

Tarracas nodded as he answered, "Even to defend their families and homes." The ScoutMaster went on, "The mothers of these young men taught them from their earliest youth of the faith of their fathers. And, they were taught that a promise, a covenant, whether made to God, or to another person, or to yourself, should be held as a sacred trust."

Tarracas paused and then continued. "When war came, these young ones, not wishing for their fathers to break their sacred oath, and not having made the same promise, left their homes, their mothers and fathers, and enlisted with the warrior-king to defend their people and loved ones."

Tarracas turned from the painting, went to his desk and sat down. Del patiently waited for him to continue. When he didn't, Del overcame his natural resistance to question the SM and asked, "Sir, begging your pardon, but what happened to the striplings?"

The ScoutMaster hesitated, raised his head, and looked into Del's eyes. In a still, quiet voice he answered, "An oath, taken as an inviolable promise by the oath-maker is a mighty thing. It becomes the hallowed ground of a person's mind and character and elevates the individual's mental, physical, and emotional powers so that he can perform great deeds that under ordinary circumstances he would not be able to accomplish."

Tarracas dropped his eyes to the documents and seemed lost in his own thoughts before asking, "Junior Scout Baldura, what does the StarScout Oath and Covenant mean?"

The question caught Del off-guard, as well as the fact that the ScoutMaster used 'Baldura' and not 'McCarel' in addressing Del. Had he passed the test? Was this the ScoutMaster's way of telling him that for now, he was still in the program? Del considered questioning the ScoutMaster, but thought better, and reflected on the SM's inquiry.

IS Jorgenson in his 'Scout Ethics' class drilled the junior scouts on the oath and its associated covenant in Del's first semester. The class bored him and he often nodded off during Jorgenson's lectures. One such catnap cost him a ten-page essay on the question, "Which guarantees the success of a team, or culture, nation or society; personal free agency or the survival of the fittest?"

Del received a mediocre passing grade as he crammed the pages with voluminous quotes and little original thought. Jorgenson filled the margins with comments such as, "Really? What about the Donner Party, or Marsten's Colony? Recheck your use of Ulan's Leadership Index Equation; you've inverted the wrong coefficient in the second clause. See Sten's article in last month's *StarScout Review*. He would say you're in a double corkscrew orbit."

Del hadn't slept for two days as he prepared his paper. He'd wondered if Jorgenson was testing his mental faculties under sleep-deprivation or did he really want Del to answer the question. Del admitted that the exercise made him reconsider his beliefs concerning the nature of free agency and personal commitment to the survival and advancement of the team, or even of society.

But he did come to understand that the exercise of free agency propelled nations forward in terms of personal liberty, thought, and enlightenment, whereas the savagery inherent in the survival of the fittest, at least for human societies, brought a loss of personal freedom, decay of personal responsibility, and the debasement of the human spirit and condition. He also concluded that just as water seeks its own level, there were individuals whose natural instinct was to protect, embrace, and promote free agency, just as there were humans who would, if left unchecked, deprive every human being of their birthright to choose their life's course.

Del recalled being jolted awake just as he was about to fall asleep with a sudden understanding of what Jorgenson was really teaching . . . that the Scout Oath and Covenant had to be entered into, followed, and obeyed freely . . . without coercion or force of any type or it became nothing, of no consequence. . . but if accepted in that spirit it emancipated rather than enslaved the Oath Taker.

Del wasn't sure that that was what the ScoutMaster wanted so he began to recite a simplified version of the instructor's explanation of the Oath and Covenant;

Of my own free will and choice, I solemnly pronounce this oath and do covenant that;

I will do my best to do my duty at all times, in all places, in all climes, and with all people.

"Upon taking the oath, I am bound by personal honor and integrity," Del began, "To perform all lawful tasks and assignments to the full extent of my capabilities."

I will obey all lawful orders of the Terran Confederation and StarScout command.

"As directed by my superiors in the Confederation and Scout Command," he went on.

On whatever star paths I stride and worlds that I visit, I will respect the sanctity of life, taking life only in the defense of my own or for those I hold responsibility.

"That I am a commissioned explorer and representative of the Confederation, sworn to find, investigate, report and most of all to respect life of any form, and that the indiscriminate taking of life is strictly forbidden."

I will safeguard the lives of my teammates,

holding their lives as sacrosanct as I do my own.

"Except as called for by mission requirements, to never endanger the lives of my fellow scouts through negligence, complacency or criminal conduct, respecting their persons and rights."

I will magnify my abilities by keeping myself physically fit, mentally alert, and morally just.

"And that I must increase my ability to do my duties by mental and physical exercise, to be fair and impartial, and to respect the laws, culture, and beliefs of all societies."

From my First, to my Last Trail, I will Return with Honor.

Del choked a little before finishing his last sentence as it hit so close to home, "And that I will never do anything that will disgrace the StarScouts or dishonor the Oath and Covenant."

Tarracas snorted, and fixed his eyes on Del. "An excellent class recitation, Junior Scout. Now tell me what the oath really means to you."

A little confused at the ScoutMaster's continued insistence on an explanation, Del tried again. "I believe the Scout Oath embodies a general and specific set of principles for the conduct and actions of all StarScouts and ..."

"No, no!" the ScoutMaster exclaimed, "A book answer! I know you know what the textbooks say. Your test scores tell me that. What I want to know is what you believe, what—"he pointed to his head and then to his heart, "what this ... and this, together, say to you about the oath."

For a long moment, Del was silent. No doubt the senior scout was testing him, as if it were very important to the SM to understand Del and his motivation to be a StarScout. Del thought of what he could say that he hadn't said. To be honest, he had never given the oath much thought except for class-time requirements. It was just something he accepted as part of the entrance standards. Like StarScout Command laws and regulations, it was just there. To obey and follow. Not to think about!

Del's heart quickened and his eyes swept over the mural. He gazed at the young faces, and recalled one of his last conversations with his mother. She'd brushed his hair back with her hand and said, "Your father believed that it didn't take perfection to become a scout, and there are no perfect people in the StarScouts. But what the scouts have in common is an intense curiosity to see what's *Out There* and to do it so that the rewards are shared among all humankind, not just the few.

"So, they are willing to place their individual and personal desires aside to work within a common organization for the benefit of all." Looking at Del she paused for a moment and said, "That's what he believed and so do I. And if you ever decide to follow in your father's footsteps, carry that in your heart, just like your father."

He looked at the mural and thought over what she had said. He lifted his hand toward the painting and looked squarely at Tarracas. "ScoutMaster, I'm not entirely sure I know what the Scout Oath means to me at this moment, but for now, I choose the conviction and works of my father, who I believe was a just and honorable man and who lived the Scout Oath."

For the tiniest of moments Del regretted bringing his discredited father's memory into the conversation, but discarded the thought because the words felt right and good. The veil of embarrassment lifted, though Del knew it wasn't permanent and wouldn't be until the Terran Confederation cleared his father's name.

The older man stared at Del for a long moment, and his hand went down to his desk drawer as if he meant to pull something out, but stopped, straightened and looked deep into Del's eyes as if wanted to sear into his mind with what he said next, "Your father's name is known for both good and evil in the StarScouts. But if you live the oath as your father did, you will live well and do well. And perhaps in time, you will know for yourself what it means."

The ScoutMaster's response regarding his father shocked Del to his core, but without allowing Del to speak, the ScoutMaster ended the moment with, "Dismissed, Junior Scout!" and turned away. Del's elapsed time from desk to door was in milliseconds as he didn't want to spend any more time with the ScoutMaster right then. He didn't know how close Tarracas had come of dismissing him from the program but he didn't want to push his luck.

He was three-quarters across the school's central courtyard when he pulled up and looked back at the cream-colored domes of the office complex. Tarracas hadn't answered his question; what happened to the Stripling Warriors? For some reason he really wanted to know their fate. Del had never known the ScoutMaster to do anything without good reason and he felt certain this experience was no exception. Tarracas gave Del a message, but darn if he knew what it was.

※ ※ ※

Now as he sat among the rain sculpted rocks, Del brought his mind back to the present. His conversation with the ScoutMaster raised as many questions as it brought answers, but that was for the future, right now he had a more pressing question to answer. What or who was stalking him and how was he going to lose his pursuer without getting caught? As he mused again on the nature of his personal predator, he recalled another conversation with Tarracas.

There was a break in the training, another hound and rabbit scenario in the hot Sonoran Desert where the IS's were the hunters, and the junior scouts, the almost defenseless prey. As the JS's rested, one of them, unaware that Tarracas was nearby, muttered aloud, "Why are we always getting chased? Why can't *we* do the chasing?"

Overhearing, the ScoutMaster walked over to the group. There was instant silence. Tarracas fixed the complainer with a piercing, cold stare. "A StarScout performs many missions where he or she is the hunter, the seeker . . . You cannot hunt well unless you . . . have been hunted well!"

Del seized on Tarracas's words. Yes, his pursuer might well be one of the Instructor Scouts, teaching his young charges how to hunt by being hunted. And that would make the most sense, but Del didn't think so. Not this time. *Still confused! Which is the present?*

No, it was either a jungle hunter or maybe an alien predator that the IS's brought in for this exercise. Either way, since they were unarmed except for their long-knives and shorter field knives, it made for a dangerous situation. With that in mind, Del came to a decision and keyed open his transmitter. In a whisper he said, "This is Lead. I have a stalker. Breaking off to deal with the threat. Continue with the mission. Succession of command is in effect. Shanon has operational control."

"Whoa!" Sami instantly replied, "That's a definite no-go. You can't flop out now, you owe me a rematch when we . . ."

"Oh enough Sami," TJ growled, "Del, you got an ident on your playmate? We should link-up and take this on together."

"Stop the chatter," Shanon ordered in a no-nonsense tone, "Listen to his voice, his stalker is too close and he doesn't have time for this! Del, you sure you don't want us to force-march to you?"

"Yes." Del whispered.

There was a moment of silence before Shanon spoke. "I don't think this is a sound decision Del, but you're the boss." She paused before ordering, "Let's move, the order is given. Scouts Out."

Del nodded in thanks that Shanon didn't buck him on this one. He knew on the surface that his decision seemed rash but the last thing he wanted was for one his teammates to walk into whatever lurked in the jungle. No, Del, thought, *I will safeguard the lives of my teammates, holding their lives as sacrosanct as I do my own.* He would do his best to stay ahead of his stalker, leading it further away while the other four searched for the XT that was the goal of their mission. With no movement below, he crept away to begin his run through the jungle to escape his unseen pursuer.

An hour later, with him playing mouse and his pursuer playing cat in the thick steaming jungle, his antagonist was still on his tail. Del had second thoughts about his decision to go it alone. Maybe Shanon was right and he wrong. He had tried every trick of field craft he knew, quick double-backs, silent ground sneaks, even tree hops to lose his nemesis. Nothing worked.

On this exercise neither Del nor his teammates carried weapons such as stun- or laz-guns. Trained to find, observe, and catalog life-forms, StarScouts avoided killing as much as possible. Out There, in galactic deep space, StarScouts carried weapons, but they were strictly for personal defense, used only as a last resort. To instill that attitude, junior scouts were seldom allowed to carry weapons on training exercises even when the test area contained dangerous animals.

Del recalled the ScoutMaster's reply to an unwitting junior scout who challenged the no-weapon policy. He fixed his piercing dark eyes on the scout and patiently explained, "We do train you in how to use weapons. At the proper time. Anyone can learn to aim and shoot; that is simply a matter of eye and hand coordination. Hopefully though, we train you to master the art of when to shoot and when not to.

Why? Because as a practically defenseless bipedal humanoid you must learn to rely on your senses, instincts, and the weapon under your scalp for survival instead of a piece of metal sitting in your holster. If you cannot or will not master that . . . then . . ."

He left the unspoken thought for the junior scouts to finish. *You're dead.* Or washed out of the program due to serious injury or an unfit rating. Just as he turned to leave, he gave a final thought, "Learn to use the mind in order to live and live that you might learn how use the mind."

Bringing his thoughts back to the here-and-now, Del knew that so far, he was very, very lucky, for whatever or whoever stalked him had shown an amazing ability for moving unseen and unheard in the jungle thickets. And he had to admit a darn sight better at it than he. His one consolation was that he was still one step ahead of the danger.

With sweat running in tiny rivulets down his tanned face, he knelt beside a clump of bushes that branched over a nearby stream-fed pool. He took a quick drink through his mouth tube and cupped water from the stream onto his hot face and neck.

The liquid in his vest was warm and stale and he badly wanted to drink from the stream. Though the fresh water at his feet was clear, Del assumed it contained harmful parasites. While he'd had the usual series-22 inoculations, this was not the time to take a chance. StarScout medicos were known to be wrong before. Hu Mikso's perforated intestines from Zon-amoebas were proof enough.

He eased himself back into the multicolored foliage and used the large interlaced branches to shield himself from view as he puzzled again over the identification of his stalker. He was convinced that his hunter was a natural denizen of the jungle out shopping for its lunch.

Del looked over the nearby pool and decided to try one final trick to evade his stalker. He broke a water reed into a one-meter length. Holding it in his mouth, he slipped into the water and submerged himself among some tall reedy stalks in a deep recess of the pool. For fifteen minutes he lay just under the smooth surface, breathing through the open canal of the long water reed. He wrapped his legs around a moss-covered log to anchor himself to the pebbly bottom.

Finally emerging, he waded out of the water and climbed a tall tree to watch and listen. After a while he slid back down to the jungle floor, having decided that the jungle felt "normal" again and that his near-invisible hunter had lost interest. That suited him just fine as he'd had enough of being the hunted for one day. He much preferred being the hunter.

"Team," he stated through his trans-comm, "This is lead."

"Del!" Shanon practically yelped, "Are you alright?"

"I'm fine, thanks. Whatever it was gave up . . ."

"Or maybe it equated your body odor to week-old rotten meat." Sami interjected.

Del ignored the jibe and said, "Any luck on the XT?"

"None." Shanon returned, "Nase and TJ have had some tough slogging. We've been a little ragged in maintaining the line."

Del raised his eyebrows slightly at that . . . it was almost unheard of for Shanon to admit less than perfection while in command. Heat must be getting to her, Del thought. "Ok, everyone take a break. I'm going to hustle up to where I should be and we'll restart the drive when I'm in place."

Minutes later, with the sun beating down, he pushed through a last stand of broad-leafed plants, his breath coming fast and hard. His goal was the bank of the river that formed the search backdrop and he felt sure that the open water he sought was not more than a hundred meters away, but hidden by the dense brush. As he wiped sweat from his brow, he turned, and noticed to his left a narrow open area leading in the general direction of his intended march.

He crinkled his forehead in thought. The track would save him the effort of pushing through or around the dense foliage, and it was only a short distance. The chances of meeting a large predator on the trail were slim, and he was hot and tired. It would be cooler and faster to walk along the open trace. The possibility of being cooler even for a few minutes made the decision for him.

He stepped out onto the path-like opening. A breeze coming up the trail felt good on his sweating body. For the moment all thought of danger passed and his confidence soared. Overhead he could hear the thin screeching of small primates and other tree-living animals, along with the exotic calls of multicolored birds as they flew through the high green canopy. [? You just said they were making noises. Now all of a sudden they are quiet.]

The ominous quiet shattered Del's reverie and alerted him that danger lurked near. [and then loud again?]

Like the explosive bellow of Fagar's RocBeast, a group of small apes erupted in a cacophony of shrieks and high-pitched howls in the tree limbs overhead. Del froze where he stood and turned in a tight circle to take in the surroundings. What was agitating the small mammals? Del didn't believe it was him. No, something nearby frightened the little animals into a frenzy of fear.

Continuing his tight radius, Del focused his eyes on the dense underbrush, but though the sun was midmorning bright, deep shadows covered the unknown danger hidden somewhere in the lush growth. [thought it reached its zenith earlier?] He listened intently, tried to drown out the screeching but gave up. His ears were of no use, he would have to rely on his eyes. He scanned the gently swaying vegetation and let his mind digest what his eyes saw, tried to pick out any anomaly in the normal background of the jungle.

With a start, his mind registered a disturbing

difference in a clump of tall bushes nearby. With a jolt, his head snapped back as the image became crystal clear.

Eyes! Two large dark eyes stared unblinking back into his. Using them as a focal point, he outlined the head of the beast.

Jaguar! The identification of his mystery stalker was solved and he wished mightily that he'd been dead wrong in his earlier guess.

With a burst of speed that would do justice to a starship going into hyper drive, he spun away from the great cat and sprinted toward the water. Behind him, he heard an ear-splitting roar as the powerful predator sprang from the bush in a giant leap to pursue her prey . . . Del.

Chapter 4
StarScout Command
Cheyenne Mountain, Terra

StarScout Jak McCarel's mind was in a hurry, his feet were in a hurry, and the rest of him tried hard to keep up. The click-click sound of his brisk steps echoed down the wide corridor deep in the granite heart of Cheyenne Mountain. He didn't want to be here, didn't like being here, and didn't understand why he was here. At that moment, here, was not a pleasant place for him.

He turned a sharp corner and saw a trio of StarScouts guarding this entrance to the StarScout Command Intelligence and Operations Center. McCarel smiled thinly as he thought that seeing a senior grade officer in the mottled tans and greens of a field uniform in the underground labyrinth would no doubt raise the Sergeant-of-the-Guards eyebrows to an all-time height.

McCarel hadn't taken time to grab garrison garb from the post shop and change uniforms after his shuttle craft docked at Lincoln Field. His orders carried the general's personal chop and instructed him to go immediately to the IOC and report to StarScout's intelligence chief, Colonel Shar Tuul. All during his transit to Terra, McCarel worried and wondered over the orders. There was no rhyme, no reason to them but when the general said *git*, you got and asked questions later.

This was the "back door" to the center and it had been years since McCarel was at "the mount" as the StarScout Command headquarters was jokingly called. Most used the main entrance, five stories above and a full 180 degrees on the other side of the complex. McCarel had his reasons for using this portal, reasons that had to do with looks, whispers, and hated questions about the past.

As McCarel approached, the sergeant got a glimpse of his insignia and rank and ordered, "Scouts, atten-shun! Port . . . arms!" In perfect synchronization the two StarScout privates brought their stun guns to the correct prescribed military angle and locked their heads and bodies forward in a rigid stance. At three paces the sergeant snapped McCarel a sharp salute. "Good evening, sir!"

His own return salute was crisp in respect. "And to you, Sergeant."

McCarel handed the trim-looking scout his thumb-sized security card. She took the badge and inserted it into a slot in the multi-lighted console as McCarel pressed his face against the retinal viewer. Seconds later the sergeant read the alphanumeric display.

A rueful smile lifted McCarel's thin lips as he watched the sergeant's dark eyebrows rise. He knew why. The display said that McCarel held the highest number and level of clearances possible in StarScout Command and all personally approved by the commanding general. It wasn't the first time that General Rosberg had jigged the system for him; he knew it wouldn't be the last.

The sergeant handed McCarel his security badge. "You're clear, sir." Massive security doors slid open to reveal a lighted tunnel. With a wave, McCarel headed for the door, "Thanks Sergeant. Your team's lookin' sharp!" The sergeant raised herself an inch taller. "Thank you, sir!"

A brief assignment in the IOC many years ago had made him familiar with most of the turns and twists of the "mystery mansion" [don't use quotes unless it's clear this is an often used nickname] and the duty officer had told him that Colonel Tuul was still "on deck." McCarel had a pretty good idea where he would find him.

The tunnel, twenty meters long, cut through solid mountain rock. It was the by-product of an earlier age when the complex served another purpose, but now the passageways and interior rooms housed the headquarters of StarScout Command. The tunnel led him into a large, circular room lined with computer consoles and glowing display mounts. The subdued lights showed several StarScouts, a handful of Confederation Navy, and a few civilian technicians working at various stations. There was a low murmur of voices and a slight humming noise in the background.

A giant holographic three-dimensional galactovue dominated the center of the room. Nav personnel and civilians hovered around the perimeter of the starfield inputting observations into their palm computers and then going back to their work stations for further analysis. As he watched, the galactovue changed views to a different set of starfield images.

He nodded in understanding. This galactovue displayed the locations of dozens of StarScout operations in progress in the known part of the galaxy. In addition, the J2 Intelligence Operations team kept track of other pieces of information such as space-time anomalies, worm hole locations, stars reaching potential supernovae stage, rogue asteroids wandering into interstellar shipping routes, and gravity wells. Those, and a hundred other categories that the organization needed to know in order to plan where, when, and how to send the StarScouts on their missions.

As he glanced away from the galactovue he saw branch tunnels leading to other parts of the Ops Center. For a moment he hesitated, his memory faltering as to which led to Tuul's office. He was about to ask one of the nearby technicians when he heard, "Jak!"

McCarel turned at the hail and saw a figure wave from the galactovue pit. With a little reluctance, he raised a hand in reply. The figure yelled, "Stay there, I'll come up to you!" The StarScout hustled over to the turbo-lift and a moment later stepped out onto the circular ramp.

A smile cracked his face as he offered a hand. "Dang, Jak," he started, pointing at McCarel's uniform, "No need to get all gussied up to come visit us, we're just plain folks down here."

McCarel glanced at the man's nametag, 'Shar Tuul, Colonel, StarScout' and smiled. "Sorry, sir, I didn't take the time to change to garrison uniform."

Tuul chortled out loud, "Jak! No need for 'sir', I know it's been almost twenty years but we're the last two members of Rakin's Raiders, so none of this rank business between us, okay?"

McCarel shrugged his shoulders as he said, "Sure.

Whatever you say."

"Great. You look terrific, little less hair, a bit of gray on the sides but otherwise . . ."

"Thanks, um, you too. For twenty years older, you look like you're in great shape."

Tuul's smile dropped just a bit as he replied, "uh . . . thanks . . . Jak." For a moment there was an awkward silence and then Tuul asked, "Any problems with the security post?"

"None. The CG's signature still counts for something around here.'

Tuul laughed, "I would hope so. Did you contact the Old Man when you grounded?"

"I did. He was a bit grouchy. Something about having to get ready for some ball he had to attend. Told me to hot-jet it over here, said you've proven that the Asteroid Belt is Lost Atlantis and the Atlanteans want to join the Confederation."

Tuul shook his head with a light laugh. "Naw, everyone knows that Atlantis is inside a volcano at the South Pole. It's the Lost Ten Tribes that inhabit the belt . . ." He stared at McCarel for a moment. "Wait, what did you say about a ball? What ball?"

"I believe he said something about the

Confederation Jubilee."

"The Jubilee," Tuul began in a perplexed tone, "Say . . . what day is this?"

McCarel took Tuul by the shoulder and turned him around. He pointed to a large calendar displayed above the galactovue. "Well, your ops calendar says 2433.056."

Tuul looked at McCarel as if he couldn't believe what he was seeing. He brought his hand to his forehead and scratched. "056 . . . that means the Jubilee ball is . . ."

"Was, you mean," McCarel responded, "This evening."

Tuul started laughing. "Son of Seti!" he said, "Jak, my orbit is about a week out of synch. I thought the Jubilee was next Friday! And me with a personal invite from the general too!"

McCarel grinned, "I'm sure you'll have a more than suitable excuse of why StarScout Command's ranking intelligence officer ignored the Old Man's invitation to attend the Grand Ball."

Tuul returned McCarel's smile, then his face and tone grew very serious. "I do, Jak," he said. "I do. Come on, there's someone I want you to meet. After we talk I suspect that you and I are going to be seeing quite a bit of the Old Man . . . and not talking about Jubilee cuisine either."

"Lead on, but this is pretty mysterious. A week ago I'm starside worrying about beans and bullets for my troops, now I'm here talking to the J2 of the whole StarScout Command."

"Sorry Jak, I know this is pretty fast, but time is not our friend here. You'll get the picture in a few minutes." Tuul gestured to his right and motioned for McCarel to follow. "Over here."

With quick steps Tuul led McCarel a quarter of the way around the walkway. A young StarScout lieutenant came around the corner and in polite terms greeted the two. She glanced at their nametags and upon seeing 'McCarel' her step faltered. Noticing her misstep, Jak glanced sideways in question, but continued on as Tuul gave a warm response to the young officer.

"LT's in the mount?" McCarel questioned.

"Yep. Part of the General's new training initiative; wants them to understand that there's more to StarScouts than the wild Out There . . . or as he puts it, 'let them see the dark side of scouting' meaning the tedious and humdrum life of a staff officer.

"They go deep space for six months or a year fresh out of the Academy and then a select few come here." A lopsided smile cracked his face. "The Old Man sends some to my shop, since he thinks we literally live down here and rarely go outside into the daylight." He paused for a second and chuckled, "Actually, he hits pretty close to home . . ."

Tuul stopped in front of a secondary security door and started to wave his access card in front of the reader. For just a second he paused and then turned to McCarel.

"Jak," he began, "Before we get started, there's something I want you to know." He swallowed for a moment and went on. "To clear the air between us. That business with your brother, Dak . . . on Froma . . . deserting his team, becoming a cross-over , all of that stuff . . . I, uh, I just wanted you to know that I for one, didn't believe a word of it then, don't believe a word of it now."

Their eyes locked for a moment as he finished, "The brother of the Jak McCarel that I know wouldn't be capable of such things."

McCarel's heart rose in his throat. It was just as

he feared. He hadn't made a half-hour in the mount before Froma IV raised its ugly head and old, hurtful memories came flooding out. He hadn't wanted to come to the mount. Too many senior officers with too long memories of a very painful and distasteful moment in StarScout's otherwise illustrious history.

A moment in which the name of McCarel would be forever linked in infamy.

McCarel rubbed his forehead, he had to admit it was the rarity for anyone to offer verbal support, usually it was quite the opposite, or at the very least a hard stare and stone silence. Still, it wasn't in his nature to be effusive in gratitude so he gave a curt nod, "Thanks, I appreciate that."

A smile creased Tuul's face as he nodded back and with a flick of his security card against the reader, ushered McCarel into a large, but rather plain office. The outer wall held large windowpanes that allowed Tuul to look out on the activity in the operations well. Inside was a short, dark man with close-cropped black hair. He stood as Tuul and McCarel stepped through the portal.

Tuul stepped to his desk, which held a large built-in computer console. With quick strokes he punched in several codes. The windowpanes went opaque and McCarel felt and heard the background humming noise disappear. It was obvious that Tuul had damped the room sound and vision-proofed the windows to outside observers. McCarel's eyebrows rose and he pursed his lips. Why add another layer of security in the most secure facility in StarScouts?

"Jak," Tuul began, "this is Teng Rhee. He sits on the Overview Board of the Confederation's Security and Operations Group."

McCarel's surprise was evident on his face as he shook Rhee's hand and exchanged greetings. Seeing McCarel's reaction, Tuul smiled wide and said, "Relax Jak, the Old Man knows Rhee's here. Like you, he has personal clearance from the CG."

"Sorry. Not my place to question; it's your show."

McCarel's hesitation was due to the fact that the Security and Operations Group, or *SOG*, was the Confederation's prime intelligence-gathering organization. Its main purpose was to provide planetary and interstellar information and Intelligence Estimates, Outlooks, and Forecasts to the top decision-makers in the Confederation. It was a politically charged establishment beholden to whoever was in power at the moment. To an apolitical, neutral organization like StarScout Command, to deal with the SOG was almost anathema, and to have one of its movers and shakers in the midst of their own intelligence unit was close to heresy.

"Colonel," Rhee began, "I understand your feelings. Let me assure you that we . . . I, wouldn't be here unless it was imperative."

McCarel opened his mouth to speak, stopped, and then said, "Sir, I'm just a plain simple scout, if General Rosberg wants us here, well . . ."

Tuul interjected. "Speaking of the Old Man, he wanted me to get him on the horn at about this point." He turned to his console and within seconds the wall in front of Tuul's desk held the image of a mature-looking woman in a StarScout uniform.

"Major Tomas," Tuul greeted the woman. "The general wanted us to notify him when we were ready to begin our meeting."

The woman nodded. "He's expecting your call." She glanced down at her console. "I'm reading security lock-in as Baker Charlie Orange."

"And matched at Delta Zulu Yellow," Tuul replied

as he locked in the secure communications link between the two. Major Tomas looked up and stated, "Link confirmed. Green mode, Colonel. Transferring you now."

A moment later the wall framed the image of General Rosberg, Commanding General of StarScout Command. He was elegantly attired in the silver and blue dress uniform of a StarScout officer. He looked at the three and then said, "Shar, you're not dressed for the ball."

Tuul opened his mouth just as the General said, "Forgot the Jubilee was tonight, didn't you?"

Tuul sheepishly nodded. Rosberg shook his head in despair. "I'll make your excuses to the missus, something about you're out saving the universe from the plundering pirates of Philo Three. But remember, you promised to teach her the Flanova at the ball. She's gonna be grumbling at me all night, telling me how I can't manage my own people."

Tuul mumbled his apology, "Sorry, sir. Won't happen again."

Rosberg winked at Jak, as he obviously relished Tuul's discomfort. "Jak, good to see you. Sorry to have to bust into your battalion ops and chase you down here, but you'll understand why in a moment. Mr. Rhee, thanks for making yourself available on short notice."

Without waiting for a reply, Rosberg launched right into the business at hand. "Jak, as of this moment I'm relieving you of your command."

Startled, McCarel started to speak when Rosberg held up a hand. "It's not for poor performance. Your efficiency report from your commander will give you top marks . . . as usual. You've done a great job and earned them. But now, I need you for something much more important.

"We've got a pretty serious situation on our hands, one that we've watched for some time . . . but the time for watching is over. We need answers and we need action. That's where you come in.

"With the latest intelligence provided by SOG and after Mr. Rhee finishes his comments, I think you'll understand the urgency."

The general hesitated as a look of frustration, almost disgust crossed his face. "This matter has political overtones and you know that from its inception StarScout's charter requires neutrality. If I could handle this in-house I would, but we don't have the resources . . . and SOG does. The Select Committee for StarScout Operations of the High Council knows about this and they've provided formal approval for this temporary association.

"You and Shar are to form a special task force as my personal liaison with SOG, and Mr. Rhee will be your counterpart at SOG. Because of the deep, sensitive nature of the information, for now it will be just the two of you on the task force from StarScout. And because of SOG's involvement I'm ordering both of you to keep everything, and I mean everything, under your hats. No discussion of this with anyone without my specific approval. Mr. Rhee is under similar orders at SOG."

The general glanced at McCarel as he said, "That includes my Chief of Staff, Colonel Romerand." At the mention of Ri Romerand's name, McCarel shifted in his stance and for the briefest of moments locked eyes with the General.

Rosberg returned the look and continued, "You've got information or an idea that you think I should hear, contact Maggie Tomas. She'll have you on my priority call list. If you need resources beyond our capabilities, I authorize you to confer with Mr. Rhee, but only with Mr. Rhee."

He looked straight at McCarel. "The reason you're here, Jak, is that this concerns the *Gadion Faction*." McCarel's eyes hardened at the mention of the notorious terrorist organization. One too many run-ins with *Faction* henchmen had left nothing but anger and loss for him.

"You've got five times the experience with the *Faction* than anyone in StarScout," the general continued, "and I need to draw on your expertise to help us counter these Sagittarian cutthroats." His intense anger was evident for a moment before he concluded. "That's enough from me. Shar, Rhee, the floor is yours. Shar and Jak, I'll see you in my office, 1300 hours."

"Yes sir," replied Tuul and McCarel as the vis-screen went blank. Tuul turned to Rhee and said, "Why don't you start first."

"Alright." Rhee replied and directed McCarel to another of the wall-sized screens as a 3-d starfield image slid into view and asked, "Do you recognize that?"

McCarel took a few steps and raised a hand upward. "Sure," he said, and pointed out interstellar features. "That's the Eagle Nebula, the Cat's Eye Planetary Nebula, and Virgo's Cluster." He shrugged. "Alpha Quadrant, Sector Ten."

"I'm impressed," Tuul quipped. "Gold star. Know anything unusual about that sector?"

McCarel laughed out loud. "What's *not* unusual about Out There? Ask me something I can answer. Besides," he said as he pointed at the map, "Been there . . . scouted that."

Rhee stepped forward. "Permit me to share a few things that I know about this sector. I apologize if some of my information is redundant, but I want to paint a full picture for you."

He pointed at the multi-starred display. "For years your service ignored Sector 10 because the exploratory reports showed an almost barren sector with few stars, a handful of planets, most of them either devoid of life or large gaseous Jupiter-like worlds. About twenty years ago one of your robot seekers penetrated the Eagle Nebula. The information it returned was almost unbelievable."

He tapped a few commands into the input device he held and another image sprang up. The 3-d picture glowed with multiple yellow suns of varying luminosity against a dark backdrop. McCarel recognized the scene as being deep within the Eagle Nebula. "Inside the Nebula were dozens of Sol type stars and almost each one had at least one Earth-like planet orbiting. It was an incredible bonanza for the Confederation. Our scientists believe the Nebula is, you might say, a birthing ground for suns like our own Sol, and for M Class or Terra-like planets."

McCarel looked over at the intelligence chief with a questioning face as if saying, 'this is old news.' Tuul motioned for him to be patient.

Not seeing the unspoken exchange between the two StarScout officers, Rhee continued. "Over the years since that drone went in, your scouts have been very active in the Nebula. They've found more Class M planets in this sector alone than in the previous thirty years in all the other galactic sectors combined. And most of them are rich in animal life, in mineral resources, in water and oxygen, and of course potentially habitable by human beings. It is a mother lode."

Rhee turned from the star images and saw McCarel with a bored look. He smiled thinly and continued, "Great discoveries sometimes require great sacrifices. We are aware that your StarScouts have, and are, paying a high price for this . . . as you are prone to say 'prime piece of real estate.' We've seen your reports. You've lost a great number of scouts in this part of the sector. In fact, according to our analysis you've lost scouts at nearly ten times the rate of your normal star side operations." He pointed at the Nebula. "Red indicates planet ops where you've lost StarScouts."

McCarel looked again at the display. It was freckled with several hundred glowing red spots. McCarel personally knew too many of those ovals [dots]; he'd been there when the bodies were brought back to base camp . . . some from his own unit.

McCarel looked at Rhee and cautiously said, "Yes, we've lost a high number of scouts there. But when you run our type of operations at an increased tempo . . . you sometimes get a high casualty rate." He frowned and spread his hands. "It's the nature of the beast. And I remind you sir that our mission priorities come from the Assembly High Council. [stop with the LDS stuff!] They want us in there with maximum effort, so we go full-bore." McCarel turned to Tuul. "You know the score. . ."

Tuul nodded, understanding that although McCarel expressed it in professional terms, a human tragedy lay behind each of the red dots.

Rhee began again, "Normally, my associates and I would agree with your assessment. The greater the rate of operations, the duration, intensity, yes, those factors lead to more injuries, more fatalities in your operational units. But, you may not be totally correct this time. There may be more at work here than just a high ops tempo."

McCarel came to full alert. "What do you mean?"

"Let me show you," Rhee said. He punched more commands into his handheld remote. "About the time StarScout Command increased ops in Sector 10, we began to notice a sharp rise in civilian comm traffic coming from the same area. At first we thought it was one of the big interstellar corporations moving in before the Confederation released the sector for private development.

"With all those Terra-like planets your scouts were turning up, the Confederation knew it couldn't keep the news secret for long. And, knowing how deep space corporations do business Out There, it was an easy assumption to make that they would try to sneak in their teams to stake out the best claims and get a jump on the competition. As I'm sure you're aware, it's pretty typical.

"Those," he said, pointing at a multitude of green dots appearing on the screen, "represent our communication intercepts of civilian traffic in the sector." Studying the picture, McCarel saw that many of the emerald-like spots clustered in the same general area as the red dots.

Rhee continued, "As I said, we thought the intercepts came from corporate development teams. CDTs operate their communications on secure channels, so we didn't try and decipher their transmissions when they started popping up because we, uh, had other missions of higher priority.

"We simply didn't have the resources to spare on what we considered to be commercial enterprise." Rhee had caught McCarel's attention and he listened intently to the intelligence operative. Interrupting, he pointedly asked, "What do you mean you *thought* they were CDTs?"

Rhee shrugged. "Just that. Initial analysis was that based on location, frequency and other signatures it matched the profile we had on corporation operations when they send in their development teams. Overtly or covertly for that matter." He pointed to the image, "To SOG they walked like a duck, quacked like a duck, so . . . it was a duck."

Rhee stopped to rub his chin. "But then the 'duck' started quacking like something else entirely."

McCarel gave Rhee a sharp look, but refrained from saying anything. The SOG official turned and sternly said, "Colonel, the information I'm about to give you is on a need-to-know basis. I want to emphasize what your commanding general stated about sensitivity. If this information falls into the wrong hands, it could have disastrous, even deadly consequences to members of my organization and possibly to yours."

McCarel somberly nodded. "I understand."

"Good." The dark man took a few steps toward Tuul's desk and turned to the two StarScouts. "A year ago SOG managed to tap into a highly secure comms link that the *Faction* leadership used to pass message traffic from Terra to their OutLand cell groups.

"We had very sketchy information that indicated that the *Faction* might try to sabotage Navy starships, or Space Marine transports, or even possibly StarScout troopships. We were trying to get the jump on them before they actually did." Rhee definitely had McCarel's attention now. He gave Tuul a sharp look and said, "Never heard that."

Tuul returned McCarel's stare. "Very, very close-hold. Darn few in the Confederation knew, and only two of us in the Command, the Old Man, me . . . and now you."

Rhee interrupted, "The reason for the high level of secrecy is quite simple. In the past the Gadions stayed away from targeting military and quasi-military units such as yours. We always assumed it was because they didn't have the resources or organization to tackle strong groups like the Confederation Fleet . . . or StarScout Command.

"For years they've conducted low-level terrorist operations on a small scale. Hit-and-run assassinations, bombings, extortion, bribery, political kidnapping, that sort of thing. The military and your organization have had some run-ins with them, but comparatively speaking they've been minor."

McCarel glared. "I wouldn't call the death and injury of a number of StarScouts *minor* Mr. Rhee."

"Sorry. I'm not making light of those incidents and I understand your feelings. When I said minor, I meant in comparison to what we now know. Now our intelligence indicates that not only do they have the capability, the organization, but also the *will* to carry out operations on a wide scale.

"The information and our analysis, lead us to the conclusion that the *Faction* is going to seriously challenge the Confederation along a broad front . . . including your organization. In fact, it appears that those operations not only started but are increasing."

He paused for a moment as if considering his next words. He looked at both men. "The politicos don't want it to get out that the *Gadion Faction* has the strength to tackle Confederation military or other major organizations. It wouldn't look politically . . . good . . . if a group of *Faction* terrorists blasted apart a Fleet capital starship or Marine troopship in deep space or in dry-docks."

"Or a commercial liner," McCarel muttered under his breath, "Let's never trust the common people with the truth. Rhee glanced sideways at McCarel but ignored the jibe as he continued, "It would play havoc with interstellar transportation, the media would have a field day with it, and the general public would demand a military escort for every freighter, passenger liner or private yacht that left Luna StarPort for star side."

To a simple StarScout like McCarel, this was pretty heady stuff and he knew he was seeing into some of the Confederation's secret workings. McCarel was no fool and he clearly understood that the *Faction* was a dangerous organization . . . Rhee didn't have to convince him of that.

He also understood that what Rhee described would mark a major shift in *Faction* operations and abilities. It would thrust them to center stage of Confederation politics and cause politicians to clamor for someone, somewhere to do something. Would they look to the StarScouts as that 'someone'? Jak prayed not.

Tuul continued the conversation. "I won't bore you with the heavy technical details of how we got this information. In simple terms the *Faction* use a very unique comms system to transmit local and deep space messages. They employ an extremely high-speed algorithmic syntax technology to transmit each message which is then buried or piggybacked on a private or commercial link.

"This incredibly sophisticated code is layered, with a base code forming the foundation for what we call add-on codes. The base code stays the same but they switch out the add-on codes on a random basis, sometimes daily, sometimes every two or three days.

"Hard to intercept, almost impossible to decode. In fact, statistically, you would have a better chance to hit one particular 10-centimeter-sized pebble in Saturn's rings while standing on her moon Prometheus using a slingshot, than to break a *Faction* code. Pretty difficult proposition, even for GERTRUDE."

McCarel snapped, "Whoa, who's Gertrude?"

Rhee raised a hand in apology. "Sorry, shop talk for SOG's premier computer. Gigahertz, Encrypting, Receiving, Transmitting, Researching, Underground, Decrypting, Encyclopedic SY 9000 Omega computer. Does about everything but burp the baby."

McCarel let out a big puff of air. "Thanks – now back to these codes. Sir, I'm certainly not an expert in such things, but what you're describing . . . well, you're talking about huge amounts of capital, the ability to obtain state-of-art technology, and first-class scientific and technical know-how."

Rhee actually squirmed a little as he replied. "And more, sir. We've tried to find out who's selling them the technology, and as of right now, nobody. They're making this stuff themselves. That means high-tech labs, sophisticated machine shops, access to logistics and supplies, and . . . they've got all this secreted away so well that . . ."

"For all of your own secret and advanced intelligence collection capabilities, they've got you running in circles." McCarel stated bluntly.

"Whoa, Jak," Tuul started, "That's a little . . ."

Rhee held up his hand, "It's okay, colonel, he has a right to an opinion here." Rhee half-snorted, "Besides, he's not that far off from the truth. The reality is that in at least this instance, their expertise matches, and in some cases, exceeds Confederation capabilities."

Rhee worked his mouth as if he'd bitten into a sour hósi-grape from Alderan. "Colonel, frankly, I'm not sure any of us really know the depth of their organization, or their abilities, but the deeper we dig, the more convinced I am of how dangerous these characters are.

"They've gone far beyond the typical homespun

variety of terrorist or rebel group that we've seen before either on Terra or on the colony planets. I'm beginning to think they're something much more."

McCarel looked down at the floor and then up, "Ok, this was all very educational. But just exactly where does StarScout come in?"

"Fair question," Rhee replied, "Bear with me for a few more minutes.

"A few months ago we got a tremendous break through a HUMINT—human intelligence operation. One of our agents got her hands on part of a computer drive that contained an ops key for one of their add-on codes. It was an old code but when we fed the program into GERTRUDE, it began to decipher parts of encrypted *Faction* transmissions that we previously stored in her memory banks. Including some from Sector 10.

"GERTRUDE couldn't spit out much because we only had a tiny fraction of one key, in fact we could only see only 1 or 2 percent of any one message. In other words, from one whole paragraph you might get a letter in one sentence, maybe a whole word in another, and that would be it. Not much to go on. But it was more than we'd ever had before.

"Reid Lofsen, one of my associates, pulled together a task force of intelligence analysts from throughout SOG to try and fill in the blanks. Some of the brightest and best, in fact. Our priority was to find references to the *Gadions* targeting a Fleet starship or similar objective. We didn't find anything of that nature in the decoded messages . . . instead, we found something else entirely and it was almost pure luck that we did.

"One of Lofsen's analysts had a set of messages that appeared to have some common wording, but she wasn't making much headway. She asked GERTRUDE to take the few deciphered letters and words on the message, and using statistical probability assign the most likely words that the letters might be associated with. Got gibberish.

"However she noticed that GERTRUDE spelled out the phrase *Oden's cell* several times. She ran the phrase through the database cross-referencing it against *'Gadion Faction'* and got zip. She then put it through the *sounds like* program and got about a million hits of unusable data.

"She then cross-referenced it against fifty other likely categories and still nothing. Then she had another idea, which is what we pay these folks for. Maybe *Oden* and *cell* weren't complete words. So she asked the computer to take *Oden* and *cell* and extrapolate what other complete words could be created using those two as the base. The computer gave her a number of words for each. She took those words and asked the computer to match them against anything in its database.

"Got two hits. Ogden, Utah, and *Ogden's Cello*. Ogden, Utah is a large city that might have *Gadion Faction* cells, but not likely. So, back to GERTRUDE and *Ogden's Cello*. The computer brought up a topographic map from a deep-space terrain-mapping satellite. There was a geologic formation labeled 'Ogden's Cello' on the map."

He pointed to the screen where a new image formed. "That formation is on Cyron 5. It's a massive plateau that from a thousand kilometers up looks like a giant cello. Those river channels run down the plateau's center, just like the lengthwise strings on a cello. The name of the galactic topographer who did the survey was Mandy Ogden, a researcher out of Cal-Tech who had the naming rights. Thus, *Ogden's Cello*."

He changed the screen back to the star field image. "Cyron 5 is a newly found planet in Sector 10. We assumed the plateau was a reference point and using the analyst's technique as a guide, we soon discovered half a dozen more reference points . . . all on planets in Sector 10."

He paused for a moment and looked McCarel square in the eye. "This is where the StarScouts come in, Colonel.

"On a hunch, we asked GERTRUDE to pinpoint by location any comms-link band that used that partial deciphered code we had. And just to spice things up a little we asked for a five-year analysis by star side sector. What she gave us showed some activity in other galactic sectors, about the norm for what we know of the *Faction.* But when we matched it against Sector 10 . . . well, as they say, a picture is worth a thousand words. Watch the display. Orange is for *Faction* code transmissions."

McCarel turned his head to the brightly lit monitor. His mouth opened in amazement. The image with its tiny orange and red spots indeed spoke a thousand words. Almost all the green dots were now orange, and they all clustered where the corps had lost StarScouts.

McCarel stood statue-still for a moment and then turned to Rhee in astonishment. "You're not suggesting . . ." Seeing the look on Rhee's impassive face, he turned to Tuul. "Do you know what SOG's postulating here? This . . ." he sputtered, pointing at the screen image, "this is crazy!

"The *Faction* has never had a quarrel with StarScout Command. We've had incidents, yes, but they were just bad luck and bad timing. What you're suggesting is that the *Gadions* are intentionally mounting operations in the same locales and at the same time that we are.

"That smacks of some deliberate plot against StarScout. It doesn't make sense. As the general said, we're an apolitical, neutral organization. We don't support any political party or even planetary government!"

As McCarel finished his outburst, Rhee spread both hands outward. "All of that may be true Colonel, but the evidence is substantial. The *Gadion Faction* has multiple operations ongoing in and around the Eagle Nebula and throughout Sector 10. So do your StarScouts.

"We have hard data showing the *Gadion Faction* actually on the ground on the same planets as your StarScouts, and you've lost scouts at more than ten times what is normal. I believe this is a little more than circumstantial evidence."

"But to murder . . . assassinate StarScouts!" McCarel began hotly. [handwritten annotation: "Assassinated — technically, they aren't"]

"Hold on!" Rhee countered, holding up a hand, "I didn't say anything about the *Faction* killing scouts. It may be something else."

"But," McCarel said as he pointed at the image again, "You—"

"I said 'lost scouts,'" Rhee replied. "Since taking on this assignment, I've gone back and read all your operations reports for the last several years where you've reported a fatality. Colonel, you've spent most of your career Out There. How many of the 'lost scouts' reported were actually found dead?"

McCarel pursed his lips and rubbed his forehead. As he looked at the star-studded map he thought rapidly. "Maybe two-thirds," he ventured. Rhee nodded in approval. "Close enough. Sixty-eight percent according to my statistical analysis of the mission reports. That other 32 percent represents true missing scouts . . . no bodies, no remains."

Tuul interjected softly, "One hundred forty-two StarScouts."

"So . . . are you suggesting," McCarel asked almost rhetorically, "that the *Faction* is into kidnapping StarScouts?"

"Colonel," Rhee spoke in a tired voice, "Obviously there are a number of possibilities, including murder and kidnapping that I . . . and SOG believe the *Gadions* are capable of. What exactly happened to your missing scouts? Frankly, we don't know."

He rubbed the back of his head and said, "Have we caught a *Faction* agent on one of those planets, or decoded a *Faction* message that unquestionably says they're targeting your StarScouts? No. What I am suggesting is that the intelligence is too solid for StarScout Command to ignore. The correlation . . . the direct link . . . is there . . . and you're going to have to deal with the hard fact that the *Faction* is playing in your backyard, in your sandbox, and kicking sand in your face."

McCarel walked over to the wall monitor and stared at it for a long time before turning to say, "No offense intended Mr. Rhee, but Shar, do you really

[margin note: Don't use italics for terrorist group name. for example: Taliban isn't italicized.]

buy into this?"

Tuul folded his arms across his chest. "Jak, I realize that to you this may be stretching things, but the Old Man wouldn't have brought you in from starside if he didn't think there was real substance to this."

He nodded his head toward the multicolored image. "The intelligence business is not an exact science. We get a piece of information here, a piece there, we put them into the jigsaw puzzle and where there's missing pieces we add our own best guesses to try and plug the holes. Sometimes we're right, a lot of times we're not."

"But," he said as he strode over to the star-studded map, "this goes beyond the coincidental. I've checked the analysis myself, looked at the probability indices. Compared to other sectors, *Faction* activity is off the scale in Sector 10." He shrugged, "The *Faction* is there Jak, and you've got unexplained deaths and disappearances of StarScouts. From where I sit, that's the picture the intel paints. SOG is correct and I think the Old Man's right for sounding the alarm."

Tuul looked uncomfortable for a moment and then said, "There's one other thing that you need to see and know."

He went to his desk console and slid his hand over the display. A bright, yellow sun appeared next to the star map. "That," Tuul began, "Was Alpha Cyron approximately two years ago."

McCarel turned with raised eyebrows and asked, "Was?"

"Was." Tuul returned. "Alpha Cyron was a G-type star in Sector 11, but we hadn't paid too much attention to it because its planetary system was devoid of M-Class planets. The SciCorps Deep Space Survey Ship *Galileo* was headed out to a neighboring binary star system when it slipped out of n-space, why we're not exactly sure of, and started using its double-H telescope to start recording images of Alpha Cyron, and beaming those images to the nearest SciCorps Station, which was on Hadon 3 in Sector 10."

He stopped and said, "Watch the video stream."

McCarel fixed his stare on the star image. Tuul's description of events left him with a bad feeling as his words seemed to portend disaster.

With a blinding burst of red and orange plasma energy that caused McCarel to shade his eyes, Alpha

Cyron exploded. In a few seconds, the energy wave loomed on the screen, heading directly at the viewers. McCarel's natural instincts kicked in and he was about to bolt into action when he suddenly remembered where he was, just as the screen went dark.

McCarel turned to Tuul and in a low voice asked, "The *Galileo*?"

Tuul shook his head no in answer. The room was silent for a moment before McCarel asked, "Ok, are you saying that I just saw a G-type star go nova? G-stars don't go nova."

"You're right," began Tuul, "At least according to all the science we know about star lives, but there's the evidence that one did explode . . . and maybe not as a natural star nova."

McCarel's head jerked as he said, "Say that again . . ."

"You heard right Colonel," Rhee interjected, "And let me explain why."

He nodded at Tuul who caused the star image to reappear pre-nova and magnified the left center of the image. Rhee turned back to McCarel and asked, "Colonel take a step or two closer and tell me what you see center screen."

McCarel walked forward two steps, stopped and shrugged as he turned, "Looks like maybe a small planet or planetoid."

"That's what SciCorps originally thought too," Rhee said, "But not after a more in-depth analysis. In fact, what they found caused the local SciCorps station leader to put this whole scenario under the highest clearance classification and send it directly to the SciCorps Commander. She in turn, after her review, sent it immediately to us."

McCarel waited expectantly, almost leaning forward to catch Rhee's next words.

"It's a rather large asteroid and it's headed directly at Alpha Cyron . . ." Rhee said and stopped as McCarel gave out a small laugh.

"That's it? A rather large asteroid?" McCarel asked a little sarcastically.

"Hold on Jak," Tuul directed, "Let him finish."

"My apologies again, Mr. Rhee." McCarel stated.

"No apology needed," Rhee replied, "But what might interest you is that there are a few anomalies about this particular asteroid.

"First, you can't see it by the naked eye, but the light waves hitting this asteroid curve around its structure in such a way as to suggest that some type of energy field surrounds the asteroid.

"Second, it's traveling just under light speed, third, it is well into the corona of the star and still intact, fourth, given the velocity of the asteroid against the time of the nova event awkward and it appears that the asteroid's impact into the star and the nova event are one and the same.

"And last, Alpha Cyron is approximately 100 light years from the area in Sector 10 with the highest Gadion Faction activity. As they say in the vernacular, a mere hop, skip, and a jump."

McCarel looked at the two intelligence men. The silence was so deep he could hear the others breathe. McCarel massaged the tight muscles in the back of his neck as he looked at the image and grappled with Rhee's revelations.

"You're suggesting that the Gadion Faction has a weapon powerful enough to cause a star to nova," he began, "That would mean that they could literally blackmail the Confederation into capitulating on whatever terms they demanded . . it would mean . ."

"Hold up, Jak," Tuul interrupted with, "We're all very aware of the implications of such a device, but remember what I said, this was two years ago. If indeed the Faction has such a weapon, we've not seen any further use of it, nor has the Confederation received any demands linked to a weapon of this magnitude.

"So, what we're operating under is that this is a supposition . . . and all the evidence we have is what we've shared with you."

McCarel shook his head and somewhat in anger hooked a thumb toward the two images. "It's not enough that we have to worry about hostile life-forms, virulent micro-organisms, and a thousand other things that can rise out of the ground and bite you, now we have to worry about some pipsqueak secret society that wants to take over the universe."

He caught his breath and muttered, "Politics" as if it was a dirty word. "How much of this does the general know?"

"Everything," Tuul said, "The general thought that you needed this additional information as well to give you the broadest sweep of intel that we had." He looked squarely at McCarel. "He too believes SOG's analysis on both counts."

McCarel shook his head back and forth and was silent for a long moment. "Okay," he began, "I guess the big picture is why? In all frankness, I can actually buy more into the doomsday weapon scenario than the one with the Faction going after StarScout. I mean why? Why would the *Faction* target us? We're not their enemies, we're not police or military that would mount any force-type action against them. That's not what we do."

Tuul rose and paced a bit before answering. "Good question. Don't have the answer. Could be a dozen reasons but right now, it's anyone's guess. Suffice it to say, the *Faction* sees a threat and they're reacting by targeting StarScout."

McCarel tapped on the back of the chair for a moment before he nodded and asked, "All right, given that this is all true, just why am I involved? This is stratospheric stuff, way out of my league. I'm just a grunt StarScout now temporarily on staff duty."

Tuul smiled and clapped McCarel on the back. "C'mon Jak, give yourself more credit than that. You're one of the best tactical StarScouts in the Corps. And like the boss said, you've had more than your share of contact with the *Faction*. You've seen how they operate, their weapons, their organization when they make planet-fall. We need to develop counter-measures, our own tactics against theirs.

"Don't worry; the Old Man will handle the political stuff. He needs answers, ideas, to help our scouts deal with this and still do our real mission. That's where you and I come in. We'll put the intel picture and your tactical experience together and take a good hard look at everything. Hopefully we'll find some answers for the CG."

Rhee scratched the side of his temple before saying, "There's one other piece of information that you need to know. It came out of the decrypt team about twelve hours ago so that means the actual message is dated."

He opened his portfolio satchel, pulled out a piece of plas-paper and handed it to McCarel. At the top McCarel saw a series of innocuous phrases, each quoting prices and states of various common commodities. In the middle was a cryptic two-sentence analysis of the message.

McCarel read the two sentences and then reread them. He looked unbelieving at Tuul and then at

Rhee. His voice choked as he asked, "You're not serious." He looked from one to the other. Their stone-faces said it all. "You are serious . . ."

"We ran the data, did the analysis a dozen times through the computer." Rhee stated, "Analytical accuracy index came out to 90 percent, margin of error less than 2 percent."

McCarel's eyes focused on the plas-paper and then up to Tuul's own grim face. "You're telling me that the *Gadion Faction* is going after Junior StarScouts? To . . ." McCarel practically sputtered. "This is insane!"

Tuul nodded in agreement. "At first I thought it was too. I went over the report myself. Several times in fact. Trying to convince myself that SOG had missed a beat. I don't think so. Let me show you." He pointed to one of the sentences on the paper.

Seneca or Maldish melons to Cyngus 6; take no less than eight credits for each unit.

"*Seneca* and *Maldish* refer respectively to two specific political families." Tuul began, "That's locked in the database and verified through several independent intel sources, but, SOG hasn't got enough to go on to identify which families. However, SOG's verified through a highly classified source that

Cyngus 6 is a *Faction* reference to the JS program.

"The rest of the message is ordering someone in the *Faction* to start a specific operation. Exactly what we don't know, but SOG was able to decode similar messages linked to at least five different *Faction* hits. So the probability is very high that the message is directing a *Faction* mission against a JS team, or perhaps teams, in the very near future. Neither the computer nor SOG's analyst group can tell us what team, or who is targeted, or what the operation is specifically.

"However, acting on the premise that the *Faction* isn't in the business of general mayhem, but rather executes its missions for specific purposes, I think we can narrow the who down." He reached over to his desk and brought out another folder. "This is the finalized No-Notice list for this cycle. I pulled it off the database a few hours ago. Take a look at the front page, it's an interesting piece of reading."

Quickly McCarel scanned the paper which held a list of all the Junior StarScouts that were due to begin their No-Notice Exam sometime during the current eight-week test cycle. Highlights covered several names. He looked up at Tuul with a questioning look.

"Daughters or sons of senior Confederation Assembly members," Tuul began, "Two are siblings of ranking members on several critical committees. One is the son of the Planetary Governor of Vega V." Tuul leaned over and pointed at one name in particular. "And she is the daughter of . . ."

". . . the President of the Assembly." McCarel finished for him. "I recognize the name." He pursed his lips in a soundless whistle as the far-reaching implications of the list became clear.

McCarel clamped his jaws tight and felt hot anger build up. These were children! He thought. No, he corrected himself, these were young adults, not children, though in comparison to his age they were almost children. Young adults who worked and fought to earn the right to become StarScouts . . . if they passed their No-Notice.

The No-Notice Final Exam, the most arduous, and dangerous test that they would experience, but it was the one test that every junior scout had to pass, had to survive, in order to win an enlistment into StarScouts.

McCarel's mind digested Tuul's information and

raced ahead. If the intelligence chief was even remotely right, and the *Faction* was going to hit a JS team, it would make sense to do so during the No-Notice. There would be one or more periods when the team would be out of comms-link for a specified period of time, and regrettably there were *always* injuries and though rare, fatalities did happen during the exam.

But still, for some cold terrorist political organization to plot against the junior scouts was unfathomable. He balled one hand into a fist. He wanted to reach out and—with a start from a sudden thought, he turned to Tuul, "Wait a minute! If you're saying that the *Faction* is targeting these particular scouts, that means they had access to the list!"

"And the man wins the prize . . . "Tuul said, cocking his own head slightly sideways.

Taking the next step in the logic, McCarel said angrily, "And that means the *Gadions* have someone inside StarScout Command . . ."

"And the man wins two prizes . . ." Tuul quipped.

McCarel almost slammed his fist on the desk surface in utter disgust, but stopped, saying in despair. "Well, I guess we have no choice, we tell the general to yank these JS's from the list and reschedule them at a safer time. Maybe spread them out over several different times so that we can protect them somehow. Change some of the procedures to. . ."

"No, Colonel," Rhee quickly interrupted. "You can't do any of that."

"What do you mean *we* can't? We've got to protect. . ."

"Jak, de-orbit and calm down," Tuul interjected. "I know how you feel. First inclination is to safety-wrap these kids. But Rhee is right. We can't change our modus operandi now because if we do, we'll alert the *Faction* that we've broken their codes.

"Those *Seneca*, *Maldish*, and *Cyngus 6* codenames in particular came from one of those algorithm syntax add-on codes that Rhee told you about. One of the very few that SOG's managed to get enough to have a pretty good idea what the message says.

"Remember, we're dealing with the most sophisticated code ever devised. The mind behind its development is a super genius. SOG's devoted literally millions of computer hours to decrypting and what they have to this point is equivalent to about the first five paragraphs of one of our field manuals.

"What we just showed you comes from one, just one add-on code. The *Faction* probably has a thousand of those. And the big-daddy of them all, their base code? Forget it. SOG hasn't even gotten one letter decrypted from that monster.

"Jak . . . think for a second! If SOG can continue to break their codes, then we might get a handle on those operations in Sector 10. Really find out what they're up to. Why we represent a threat. And find out for sure if they're really going after junior scouts and who are the targets.

"But if they even get so much as a whiff that we're reading their mail, they'll change the encryption sequence faster than hyper-light speed. And we'll start from ground zero again."

Rhee spoke up. "We might even be able to use what we learn to back-trace and find your mole. Turn him, or her, to our advantage."

Tuul took a deep breath and let it out in a rush. "This is tough Jak, and not an easy choice, but when we go see the Old Man, I'll buck you on this one if you try to get him to pull those JS's or touch that list in any way."

McCarel looked at Tuul, saw the man was dead serious, and leaned back against a chair. Right now he'd rather be facing a raging mon-Panther on Epsilon 3 than this. But, he had to admit, what Tuul said made perfect sense and he clearly understood the ramifications. Still, it was one thing to let junior scouts face dangers on an alien world; it was another to place them in harm's way because of political intrigue.

"Even if it's the Assembly's President's daughter?" he asked, holding up the folder with the No-Notice list.

There was a long drawn-out moment of silence before Tuul stated emphatically, "It sounds cold, but it's the right thing to do." He pointed at the nebula. "The *Faction* is growing Jak. Like some cancerous tumor Out There, they're growing. Reaching into places and doing things that we've never seen before, exercising power that we didn't know they had.

"If they're behind our 'lost scouts,' Jak, we're going to have to know our enemy, get inside his mind, his organization. If we lose this one small advantage . . ." He stopped and squarely faced Jak. "We may never recover, and StarScouts, the Confederation . . . well, the empty, cold darkness between the stars may be more welcome than what we're facing."

"Quite a speech Colonel Tuul," McCarel said, and sighed. He knew Tuul was right. But he couldn't let go of the mental picture of those young scouts facing not only alien beasts but also unknown brutal human foes on some far-distant exotic planet. It was not what they were trained or prepared for. He felt like he was sending unprotected youngsters into the fiery maelstrom of a comet's tail.

"What if," he began, as if thinking out loud, "we held a surprise medical exam, and we 'flunked' at least some of these scouts, not completely out of the program of course, but just until their medico physicals were 'back' within standards. Meaning until we could figure out some way to protect them and still let them take their No-Notice."

In determined fashion Rhee shook his head. "Won't work. The minute that list gets touched in any unusual fashion, your mole is going to report it to the *Gadions*. They'll add two and two and come up with five. I've seen it before. The slightest deviation from the norm, and just like that they're off the scope again, leaving us in the dark trying to pick up the pieces."

Tuul looked sadly at McCarel as he asked, "Besides, Jak, how would you pick which scouts to pull, and which to leave?"

McCarel nodded, "I know, I had that same thought as soon as I said it." McCarel shrugged in resignation. "All right, you've convinced me. Where do we go from here?"

"Well," Tuul started, "We send Mr. Rhee on his way and we find you a place to bunk. Then we see the Old Man tomorrow and get to work."

Taking his cue, Rhee bowed slightly and said, "Safe trails to you both. We'll obviously be in touch." Quick handshakes around and Rhee was through the doorway portal.

McCarel stood with head down, hand on chin. The discussion about young people had struck him hard because of his own heart-wrenching loss that still weighed so heavy on him even after all these years.

Looking at the plas-paper, he closed his hand tight enough to cause the filmy paper to crinkle. A cold anger enveloped him, and he thought that if something were to happen to one of these youngsters at the hands of the *Faction*, he would personally become their avowed enemy and nemesis.

That, he silently swore to himself.

Chapter 5

XT Attack!

Del sprinted through the jungle, the Jaguar in fierce pursuit. He could think of only one thing: get to the water, dive in, and out-swim the hungry hunter. It was no use trying to climb any of the nearby trees, before he could get a good handhold and shimmy up the trunk the ferocious feline would pounce and bring him down.

Dashing between trees, he could hear the meat eater growling behind him as it closed the distance, and wished that just this one time the ScoutMaster had removed the no weapon restrictions. He understood Tarracas's rational of using the mind first rather than firing first, but right now the only thing his mind was learning was sheer irrational terror. *[margin: really? irrational? I think it is perfectly rational to be terrified]*

With the Jaguar squalling just behind, Del knew it was only a matter of seconds before the great cat raked him with one of her deadly claws, sending him sprawling to the ground and vulnerable to its ripping attack. Just ahead Del could see a shimmering through open spaces in the brush. The river! He put on a burst of speed and crashed through the bankside bushes. He took two giant strides across the muddy bank and leaped into the air; only to frantically contort in midflight and reach out to grasp a long, thick tree limb that jutted out over the water.

Moments later he swung helplessly above several, black, three-meter long caimans floating motionless in the green water. Their fang-lined snouts and nostrils barely protruded above the river's roiled surface.

No sooner had Del grabbed the tree limb than the Jaguar burst through the brush. Unable to stop its headlong dash on the muddy embankment, the muscular feline slipped and slid down the steep slope into the water. Spitting and squalling, the animal tried to leap out of the river only to stumble in its initial spring to safety from the aquatic carnivores.

Before the angry cat could jump again the closest of the massive reptiles snapped shut its fang-lined jaws on the feline's rear leg and dragged it further into the muddy water. Another leather-coated reptile, aroused by the thrashing, swam to the struggling cat and viciously clamped down on the unlucky animal. As the water rolled into a dark brown and red mass from the agitated churning, the two water carnivores dragged the unlucky predator to the bottom of the slow-moving river.

With arms and legs wrapped securely around the sagging tree limb, Del looked at the bloody water. There was no sign of the fearsome cat except for a few shredded pieces of fur floating on the swirling surface. Holding tight to the branch's underside, he crawled slowly, hand over hand, towards the bank and the trunk of the large tree that had sent its life-saving limb over the river.

Soaked with perspiration and breathing heavily, Del could feel the adrenaline pumping through his body as he finally reached out to grab the tree trunk that sat solidly in the river's muddy bank. Thanks to the cat's demise, his under-limb travel went unnoticed by the aquatic reptiles. As he eased himself into a v-notch at the base of the tree's large trunk, he scrutinized the immediate area, not wanting to go to ground until he was satisfied that none of the hungry caimans lurked nearby.

After a few minutes, confident that none of the

reptiles were close, Del clambered down from the tree. Taking one last quick look around, he rapidly pushed through the tall brush bracketing the river. Del wanted nothing more than to put distance between him and the river beasts, and sprinted back up the trail that initially led him to the water. Fifty meters further, feeling secure that none of the water predators would venture this far from their natural habitat, he slid into a patch of leafy dense foliage and allowed himself a good shake from the narrow escape.

He had faced death before, but nothing quite so personal. His cocky laxity almost cost him his life. And he had forgotten for a precious few moments that even on gentle Terra there were real dangers, and death was still a frequent companion of the unwary, the foolish, and the careless.

He sighed and took a deep breath. Okay Del, he thought, you're supposed to be one of the best JS's in the field, and you almost became somebody's midday meal. Pay attention! He silently vowed that he would never again forget where he was and what he was doing. He keyed his trans-comm, "Team-Lead to Team Three, net-call."

His teammates responded in the affirmative to his

call. "Team," Del said, "Predator warning. There are caimans in the river near my start location, and there may be others in the area. Take appropriate precautions as you close on the water."

Sami snorted. "What did you do, step on someone's tail?"

"No, just routine observation, Pathfinder."

A new voice chimed in. "Del, TJ. Did you hear the cat squalls? They sounded like they were coming from near your location."

Del smiled to himself. "Yeah, he was just mad because someone woke him up from his nap. Enough chatter. Keep moving. Acknowledge when you're in position to begin the drive. Lead out."

Del followed his own directive and started moving again in the general direction that would place him near the river's curve. He prudently paralleled the river and the now known haunt of the huge reptiles before turning back toward the water again.

Pushing through chest-high undergrowth, Del again saw sunlight sparkling on water. As he eased through the tall grass, Del searched for any signs of the reptiles. Quietly, he stepped out on a pebbled beach of the sluggish river and searched the water for any signs of the fanged carnivores. Finding none, he slipped back through the foliage and opened his transmitter.

"Team, this is Lead. In sequence, what is your status?" In rapid succession came the answers.

"Path's in position. Let's either get moving or take another siesta."

"Flanker 1. Ready. Time to get this done and go home."

"Flanker 2, positioned, let's do it."

"Center's ready."

"You know the plan," Del instructed. "Heads up and watch your sensors. Check the setting; remember it should read 6.5 on the Beta Scale. Let's get the X this time and make it Mission Accomplished for Team Three. Scouts Out!"

Their response deepened Del's feeling that the team didn't appreciate the fact that their antagonist had outsmarted them for several days now and they were ready to turn the tables. Del took his LifeSensor out of its carrying pouch, checked the setting and activated the device. The Enser-Taylor LifeSensor was an essential StarScout tool and it was rare for the junior scouts not use the small hand-held device on their mission stalks.

Developed after years of painstaking research by the genius biophysicist team of Sterling Enser and Sheila Taylor, the sensor was essentially a supersensitive energy detector. It worked on the principle that all life-forms radiate energy into the surrounding medium. And each life-form, based on genus and species, radiated its bio-energy at specific wavelengths. On Terra, the higher the life-form on the evolutionary intelligence scale, the higher the radiated frequency of energy.

The StarScout could manipulate the device and focus exclusively on the known wavelength of the target life-form. If the tracker sought a panda bear, it was easy to tune out the frequencies of birds, insects, and so forth that coexisted with the bear in its habitat. The trick was to determine at what frequency the life-form radiated. The frequencies of Terran animals had long ago been cataloged and so presented no challenge, except to the novice, to track with the LifeSensor.

In general terms most exotic life-forms on far distant star worlds followed the same pattern found on earth. However, there were worlds where evolutionary patterns differed radically because of their non-terrain environments, and it was very difficult to determine if an extra-terrestrial equated to a mammal, reptile, or fish, on the evolutionary life scale.

One limitation of the LifeSensor was its detection range. The denser the medium the bio-energy had to pass through, such as rock or ice, the shorter the LS's detection range. Under the best Terran atmospheric conditions, the LifeSensor could detect human beings, who projected the highest radiated energy output of all known creatures, at a distance of around a hundred meters.

At the exercise start, just before the JS's pushed out into the jungle, the ScoutMaster provided them with the only clue as to the nature of the creature they sought. He described the beast as a "large extraterrestrial near-ground-dwelling hybrid mammal with evolutionary characteristics similar to the Terran animal order Chiroptera."

As they sat down to draw up their initial stalk plan, the team compared notes and puzzled over the nature of their quarry. They were stumped as to what frequency range to set their LS's to, and were afraid they would have to do a free search stalk until Shanon remembered that Chiroptera had something to do with bats. Using the Enser-Taylor frequency for Terran bats as a starting point the team settled on a frequency point in the middle range of the beta scale and began the hunt.

Their search area was a tiny slice of the vast preserve in the southwestern corner of the park. The preserve was an enormous nature and animal sanctuary in the Amazonian jungle, enclosed and protected by a towering barrier known as the Domingo Fence, and patrolled inside by professional park police. Besides its luxuriant animal and plant life, the park had a most unusual feature. In certain carefully protected and enclosed zones it contained numerous oxygen-breathing extraterrestrial creatures transplanted from their home worlds and allowed to roam at will.

Because of that, the area was a natural training ground for the JS's. It was not the only place where the scouts trained of course, but its high level of challenge and adversity was exactly what StarScout Command wanted for junior scouts. Just as importantly, the scouts could pit their field craft skills against exotic star-beasts without ever leaving Terra.

The first time that Del ventured into the park, at the very beginning of his fourth-year StarScout course work, he was sent on a simple 20-kilometer straight-line march from point A to point B. Along the way he made a visual record of specific plant life through his camcord. A routine mission, two days and two nights, and then home.

His second mission, a month later, was to track and record Wood's Bespectacled Lizard and Frote's Protosaur, two sluggish reptiles from the Vega IV system. Thirty-six hours in the bush. Another routine mission.

Since then, his scout class trained in the preserve several times, each mission progressively more difficult. There were other missions in other locales as well, such as the troop survival trek across the Punjab desert and the climb of Alaska's Mount Foraker in a howling blizzard. And just last month, the 50 kilometer solo trek across the arctic wilderness in the dead of winter.

That last one had cost them dearly. Eli Cho. Caught in a whiteout by one of the few Terran carnivores that actually stalks and kills humans. Ursus Thalarctos Maritimus. The great white polar bear of the northern climes.

When the team walked through the fence's access portal to begin this mission, they knew it would be the hardest mission so far, a grueling train-up for their final junior scout mission, the No-Notice Field Exam.

Toward the end of their first day in the bush, they'd discovered that the initial setting on their LifeSensors was close to the mark when Shanon, acting as Pathfinder, started receiving a faint registration on her sensor. Carefully watching the display indicating the direction of the energy emission, she silently moved through the jungle forest. When the signal strength appeared to peak, she stopped at the edge of a clearing and scanned the area.

Unable to see the creature, but still receiving a strong signal, she keyed her communicator to report. Just as she did, a large, furry, almost man-size creature, with huge accordion-like ears burst from the bushes less than ten meters to her right. On all fours it sped across the clearing into the brush on the far side. Watching it disappear, Shanon estimated that it could run faster than a human.

After she reported her sighting to the team she crossed the small clearing and followed the broken foliage the creature had left behind as it moved through the underbrush. However, after a few hundred meters the physical trail diminished to the point that it was useless to follow and they were forced to rely on the LifeSensor again to seek the creature.

Twice more, one of them got close enough to the creature for sensor activation. But each time the spotter tried to call in the team, something alerted the beast and off it sped through the jungle, leaving them empty-handed, and with no other choice but to restart the stalk. The one good thing that came from their encounters was that they fine-tuned the frequency band of the creature's radiation, which allowed them to negate other background radiation noise from the life-rich jungle.

Now as Del moved his team forward to try and snare the XT, he once again, for the umpteenth time, wondered why he put himself through all of this. But he knew the answer, and knew that it would keep him slogging no matter what, all the while dripping sweat while blood-sucking insects used his face as their personal breakfast table. *well past lunch by now.*

The high-academy course catalog listed 'Intro to StarScouts' as: "Introductory course. Instructs the student in the basic skills, techniques and standards of StarScout Command. Course requirements include fieldwork at Terran and Solar System locales. Requires coordination with other faculty departments to make up missed schoolwork. Successful completion awards student one-half credit toward physical training requirements for graduation. Final exam is No-Notice deployment star side. Prerequisite for acceptance into StarScout enlistment."

A half-credit in physical training was all well and good, and at this particular moment Del half-wished that he were back in Mr. Crain's zip-ball class or even Mrs. Graden's Old Style Dance course. Dodging a high-voltage conductor ball that jolted you with electrical shocks when touched or getting criticized by Mrs. Graden's sharp tongue for being out of step in a waltz seemed preferable to sweating through this jungle.

Del had made it this far and wasn't about to give

up now. Besides, it was that last sentence in the course description that really mattered. To be a StarScout you had to satisfactorily complete the Junior StarScout course. Failure to complete the course or a down-check from the Instructor Scouts meant no enlistment in the StarScouts, no matter what your accomplishments were in other areas.

Not everyone had what it took to be a StarScout. The criteria were stringent, the standards tough, and the entry requirements set purposely high. Perhaps one in ten met the test. Del's class started with almost two hundred fourth-year academy students, and now numbered less than thirty. Of those who dropped out, some left the class for personal reasons, some due to serious injuries or illness, but most for just not being able to handle the grueling demands of the course.

So now Del and his team, having endured all that the IS's had thrown at them knew that they just had to get successfully through this one last exercise and then wait for the call for their No-Notice. Passing that, they could opt for the next phase of their training to become full-fledged StarScouts. But first, they had to pick up the spoor of the elusive deep-space creature and this time hope the thing would cooperate instead of being so stand-offish.

Three hundred meters away from Del, edging close to a giant moss-covered tree, Tala Janair Utlander, TJ to the team, was about to step around the tree when the alert display of her LifeSensor began to blink. Swinging the instrument in an arc in front of her, the perky dish-water blonde watched the display register the greatest signal just to her left.

As TJ peered along the bearing the detector indicated, she slowly sidestepped in that direction, keeping low to the ground and moving as silently as possible. Five minutes and a little less than thirty meters farther, the signal was stronger and remained on a steady bearing. TJ hoped mightily that since the bearing was constant, it meant that the beastie wasn't moving. If the star creature was sleeping or eating, then TJ's goal of initial observing and cataloging would be a lot easier.

She was about to move forward again when the signal strength shifted slightly-the beast was moving, albeit slowly. She decided to stay put and watch which way the creature moved. She braced her back against a tree trunk and eased down to the ground.

She might as well rest for a few moments as she waited to see what the creature would do. She looked at her mud-splattered uniform. Her fingernails and hands were dirty and grimy and she knew that her body odor was such that even she wouldn't want be downwind of her.

She glanced up at the almost cathedral-like trees that towered into the sky; the brilliant green of the sky canopy that crowned each trunk. She wasn't at home in this jungle, would never be; the very real perils kept her continually on edge. Still, even in the midst of danger, the rain forest's beauty was a little mesmerizing.

She smiled ruefully as she thought of how this jungle was such a far cry from the ornate halls and luxurious spas of her far-off home. Her smile broadened as she considered how wonderful a deep plunge into the crystal clear waters of her personal bath would be about now. Followed of course by a total body massage by her family's full-time masseuse. Followed of course by an all-out raid on the luxury treats found in their constantly stocked pantry. Followed of course by . . .

TJ felt warm wetness splash on her tanned face.

With a start she jerked up, acutely aware that she'd almost dozed off in her day-dreaming. The raindrop hitting her face brought her to back to the moment at-hand. She wiped the wetness off cheek. Her dreams would have to wait.

Glancing up, she could see through openings in the tree canopy that the daily monsoon rain clouds gathered to pour out their deluge on the tropical forest. The daily rain cycle provided the copious amounts of water needed to keep the foliage lush and growing. The rain cycle was rarely broken and today wasn't that day.

Though TJ quite clearly understood and appreciated the rainmaking process, right now it presented a distinct nuisance in her stalk. The sound of the rain pouring onto the leaves of the forest growth would drown out any sound her prey made. But in addition, the dense gathering of clouds and rain turned the jungle into a dusky twilight that made visual sightings difficult and elusive.

TJ grimaced in mild frustration at having the rain come at just this moment when she knew she was close to their quarry. She reached into her front-pack and brought out her snooper goggles. TJ didn't like wearing the eyepieces, but under the limited visibility conditions it made sense. The eye apparatus operated both in ambient light and the infrared, or IR, spectrum. During nighttime operations the device gathered the subdued light from the stars and moon and magnified it thousands of times, turning darkness into light for the wearer.

But that wasn't what TJ needed now—what she needed was the IR capability. She knew from experience that the goggles would help her see the animal's radiated heat in the intense rain. She programmed the device to register only heat sources from mammal-like creatures. With a practiced hand TJ pulled the device on her head and powered up the goggles.

The rain became torrential and TJ's camouflaged clothing was soon soaked through. She wryly thought of the uniform's clothing tag that pronounced it 'water-resistant' which actually meant water-resistant in a parched desert. She stepped from the bushes and moved forward. Her goggles showed no mammals in her immediate area so she continued through the now rain-drenched jungle.

As she moved deliberately through the tall

strands of rain-bent grasses and brush, the LifeSensor display signaled that the creature was not moving and that TJ was probably within meters of the animal, and it was somewhere directly in front of her.

Or above her . . .

TJ went dead-still as that thought popped into her head. The previous sightings placed the animal on the ground but that didn't necessarily mean the brute wasn't a tree-climber. Ahead was a stand of tall trees whose leafy green cover spread and blended with the canopy from neighboring hardwoods. She edged forward to take advantage of the cover provided by several large and verdant bushes and knelt in the soggy mud.

TJ peered upward into the branches of the forest as silvery raindrops pelted her face. She didn't see anything through the splattering rain so she flipped the visor-like goggles back to her eyes. She panned across the swaying trees, eyeing as much of each tree from top to bottom as she could. As she rotated her face to the right, the IR viewpieces blossomed in a burst of vivid red-orange. She reached up to fine-tune the device and the image wavered, and then sharply focused into view.

It was the XT!

The beast sat on a large branch, protected by an overhang of leafy criss-crossing branches. It didn't move and appeared to be dozing. As TJ kept her eyes on the extraterrestrial's location, she brought her eyepieces up and visually inspected the area. In the heavy rainfall she couldn't make out the beast clearly, so she began to slip closer to the tree where the star creature sat.

Confident that the splattering raindrops on the foliage would mask her movement and any noise she might make, TJ eased through the wet growth. She did a careful low-sneak until she was some five meters from the animal's tree and completely hidden in the dripping plants.

Carefully rising, she cautiously moved her head back and forth, peering through the leaves, trying to get the best view of the creature. She finally had to settle on a small opening where she could see the creature's head and upper torso but not it's lower body.

TJ reached into her torso pack and removed her palm-sized cam-cord. She turned it on, and pointed its tiny focal eye at the creature and its perch. In less than a minute, the diminutive camera's miniature recording brain blinked a red light at TJ indicating that its canister was full. She inserted a new button-size film-pac in the camera and began to film again. She keyed her trans-comm to speak with her teammates and report her situation. Before she could speak, the creature bolted upright, wide-awake as if suddenly startled. As it sat up TJ got a really good look at the creature.

Its head and face reminded her of an oversized mouse, except that its nose was squashed in and no mouse ever had long needle-sharp fangs. The creature was close to being two meters tall. Hunched on all four legs, it now sat upright on two powerful hind legs while small, muscular forelegs dangled in front of its gray hair-covered body.

Most striking about the creature were its ears. When she first saw the exotic animal the ears were folded behind the head and rested somewhat on its back. Now the ears snapped forward and unfolded completely. They reminded TJ of small elephant ears. Along the edges of each auricle were tubular projections that jutted out several centimeters.

[handwritten note: the thesaurus is not your friend — with "limpid brown" circled]

As she watched, the creature turned until it faced her, its large limpid brown eyes centering on the clump of bushes were TJ crouched. Its ears twitched forward until TJ could almost imagine that they formed a cone to listen for her. In her excitement at watching the creature awaken, TJ forgot to stop pressing the send button of the trans-comm and the communicator continued to operate.

In one fluid motion, using its powerful hind legs, the alien beast launched off the branch to the ground, and sped through the jungle opposite TJ. In her fleeting glimpse of the creature before it disappeared, TJ could clearly see its ears, fan-like, folded behind the head and along its back.

TJ rocked back on her haunches and smiled. Obviously, she couldn't match the creature's speed. It was also clear that the creature was very sensitive to its surroundings, particularly to sound, which partially explained why the team was having such a difficult stalk. She re-keyed her trans-comm and spoke quietly. "TL, Flanker 2. I have a visual sighting and recording event of the target."

"Good job!" Del enthused, "What are your coordinates?"

"616 by 302. The creature left my area on a bearing of 243 degrees true. Running pretty hard so he's a hundred meters from my position by now."

"Understood, do we meet exercise cataloging criteria?" Del asked.

TJ looked at the camcord recording she had and shook her head. It wasn't enough; they would have to get at least two or three times that amount to meet the criteria for Mission Accomplished.

"Negative, I only have sixty seconds of observation on the camcord."

"Check. Follow the trail and we'll close the loop around you."

"Sami," Del said, "See if you can fast-pace and head the XT off and herd him back towards us."

"I'm way ahead of you," Sami answered. "Started my intercept as soon as TJ gave the bearing."

"Good," Del replied. "Nase, Shanon, swing slightly westward and then return to your original bearings. TJ, anything else on the XT?"

"Yes," TJ replied. "This thing's got a nasty set of fanged teeth. Large canine incisors, upper and lower. Probably dangerous if cornered."

"That is certainly good to know," Del said,

sounding very surprised at the news. "Everyone use extreme caution when approaching our target. Lead out," Del replied.

TJ began to put away her mini-camcorder when she heard a sharp cracking sound to her immediate right. Tearing through the underbrush at full speed, the OutLand creature that moments before sped away, now bore down on her, fanged mouth wide-open. She spun on the balls of her feet and came up with her arms and hands in the Sung-Tu defensive posture to ward off attacks, but she knew it was too little and too late against the claws and teeth of the onrushing monster.

Chapter 6

Everglades Historic Sanctuary

The senior StarScout squirmed his way between two rotting logs, the smell of decaying wood thick in his nostrils. The small sharp blades of wet grass clung to his face and occasionally poked him in the eyes as he crawled toward his goal. The merciless sun and oppressive humidity caused him to grind his teeth as pushed through the saw-grass.

He was at that point in his StarScout career that he truly hated these annual evaluations. But every member of StarScout Command staff had to certify their overall fitness by passing these once-a-year tests, and even his lofty status was not enough to warrant exemption.

The week-long exercise in the swamps took him away from his senior post at StarScout Command, which caused him great mental agitation which was only getting worse with each passing day. Plus, he knew that the Evaluator StarScouts were taking great pleasure in giving him the most innocuous assignments, a deliberate swipe at his rank and prestige. They could have their fun now, he darkly thought, but he would have the final laugh when he personally chose their next Outworld assignments; each of which would make Hades seem like Eden.

He would make sure they got a personal note from him with their outbound orders. He already had the words framed for the note, "I appreciated your personal touch in the Everglades. In turn, I hope you'll appreciate my own personal touch in selecting this assignment for you. Good hunting."

His body hidden by the crusty logs on each side,

the scout crawled to the end of one and brought his LifeSensor out to the front to take another reading. He edged forward just a bit more and extended his hand out into the open.

The strike to his hand was so fast and hard that the scout had no chance to avoid the bite. He yanked his hand back to look at the two pinpoint welts that quickly turned red. A stinging sensation radiated outward from the back of his hand. He dropped his LS and gripped his wrist in a tourniquet grasp as he stood. He needed to see what type of snake had bit him so that he received the proper anti-venom. He started to lean over the log to look for the snake when he came face to face with the giggling, animated face of his daughter.

"Gotcha, Pop," she laughed as she held up a short stick with two sharpened thorny ends. "Not bad, huh" she continued, "Oh, the stinging sensation is Cayenne Pepper, wash it off and it'll stop." Stunned, the scout stood immobile for a moment as he first looked at his daughter and then back at his hand. Embarrassed he looked around at the surrounding tropical foliage.

His daughter laughed lightly as she stood. "Don't

worry. All of the evaluators are off having chow. Nobody's watching or within hearing distance."

"What are you doing here, and what's the meaning of this?" pointing to his hand.

"Looking for you, obviously. And oh by the way, you're lucky it was just me and not the viper that's in the other log."

"What . . ." he began as the young woman walked around to the end of the other decayed tree and with a long, hooked branch pulled out a large, puffed up snake that opened its angular mouth to reveal two large and wicked fangs. It was obvious from where it received the name, cotton-mouth. [reword]

There was a moment of strained silence between father and daughter before the older scout said, "Alright, point proven. Now, exactly why are you here, Alena?"

Tossing the snake aside, she brushed leaves out of [her] short, coal-black hair. "Waited as long as I could for you to get back, but couldn't wait any longer." In a rush she said, "Dad, he's on Earth! In the mount! I saw him!"

"Who? Who's here—what are you talking about?"

With clenched fists she snapped back, "Jak

McCarel! I've seen him, down in Ops."

At McCarel's name, the StarScout stiffened. For a moment his mind whirled as old memories flooded back, and the pain and loss stabbed deep. He clenched his hands in a tight fist before he regained control and looked at his daughter. Her face was a mirror of his own fury, hurt and hatred.

He shook his head. "McCarel's battalion is in Sector 9. He can't . . ."

"Then we've warped to Sector 9," she sarcastically interrupted, "He's in the mount I tell you. He and Tuul the Fool are spending a lot of time down in ops and intel. I think they're working on something together."

He hesitated, then snapped, "Impossible. I'm the only one other than the CG who approves in-bound postings to the general staff." The utter disgust on Alena's face was her only reply.

Her silence and disdainful look was enough. With a slap at his trans-comm he snapped out, "Ops officer!"

"Ops, go ahead sir."

"Patch me through to the personnel duty officer at command."

A few moments later another voice answered, "Personnel, Captain Banson."

"Banson, give me the current duty status of Lieutenant Colonel Jak McCarel."

"Standby, sir."

Father and daughter balefully glared at each for a few moments before the answer came, "Sir, my duty roster is showing Colonel McCarel assigned to the J2 section."

"By whose authorization?" he tersely asked.

"The orders came out of the CG's office sir. Posted seven days ago."

"Roger." With a start he realized he needed to come up with some excuse for this highly irregular communications. "Good. Just making sure that General Rosberg's orders were carried out. What duty rotation is McCarel assigned to?"

"None sir. Colonel Tuul assigned him internal duty within the J2, and exempted him from watch status."

Slowly, the scout replied, "Very good, Captain Branson. Everything appears to be in order. Carry on."

He took a few steps and then looked back at his

stone-faced daughter. Grudgingly he admitted, "You're right. He's been assigned to the command!"

Her voice heavy with sarcasm, Alena replied, "Well I guess that proves I can read a uniform nameplate, doesn't it?"

"Enough Alena. You were right; you can turn off the attitude now." For a moment he looked upward at the hazy blue sky and said to himself, "Why? I wasn't notified of his transfer and I haven't seen any orders or paperwork come across my desk." He rubbed the back of his neck, "This doesn't make sense!"

"What?" she asked.

He half-turned to speak to her over his shoulder, "McCarel's made a career out of remote assignments. Practically stays in exile. He's maybe spent 3-months grand total at the mount, unlike other officers who usually get several years on staff. So by rights he should be put on the operations watch-list and take his turn at the duty rotation. By being exempt from any watch stander posting and instead assigned as a J2 supernumerary means he's free to come and go as he pleases. Very odd for a staff officer, even one with McCarel's senority."

He paused for just a moment, "The fact that his

orders didn't come across my desk relieving him of his battalion command and assigning him to the J2 staff means they were never published to the whole organization. The orders were cut by the general's aide and placed in McCarel's file and on the ops roster. That means that only about 3 or 4 people in all of StarScout Command would know of McCarel's assignment."

"And you weren't one of them until I told you," she dryly replied, "So two questions, who transferred him here and why."

"Actually only one. This came straight from Rosberg."

"And the general didn't tell you."

Annoyed, he replied, "In case you've forgotten, the Commanding General doesn't have to tell me. But . . . this is the first time he's ever done anything like this. Normally he tells me everything."

"So it's also obvious that he didn't tell you the why." He was about to angrily reply when she said, "Before you snap my head off, I might be able to help you on that one, or at least possibly point you in the right direction."

He slowly took a breath. "Sorry. Go on."

"I had early stand-to this morning. McCarel was in Tuul's office working. He came out several times to the galactovue work stations. I pretended not to notice but I was able to see that he was working on several tactical training scenarios. He set down his plas-papers once and as I walked by I was able to read several assignment codes.

"Later, when he left, I tried to bring up the codes to see what they were, but I couldn't. The security level was higher than I have clearance for."

"What? That can't be right. Your clearance level should be more than sufficient for training scenarios."

She nodded. "To make sure, I checked on some other training exercises and was able to read them just fine. But of the three codes I was able to see on McCarel's list, the computer wouldn't open any of them for me. Access denied every time."

"And he was using the galactovue you say? Anything about . . ."

"Froma IV?" she finished for him. Both shifted uncomfortably for a moment as the hurtful name was mentioned, but then she continued, "Not that I could see. Different sectors, various planetary systems, and they weren't of anything I was familiar with."

He furrowed his brow for a moment. "Did the computer state the access level needed for those codes?"

"Yes," she replied and stated the alpha-numeric code word.

He looked at her sharply. "Say again." She repeated the security code word.

He inhaled a deep breath before asking, "And you're sure that he was working on some sort of training operations?"

"Absolutely. He pushed aside his privacy screen once and I saw 'training rotation forecast' at the top. I've seen that before, it's a J3 resource planning document."

He nodded his head in agreement, "Yes, it's a comprehensive database used to forecast what teams are due for training, where the training will occur, and who is being pulled in as the training cell."

He stood stock-still for a moment as his mind digested the information. "McCarel is assigned to the J2, he's working on a routine training database, and has security access as high as mine? Doesn't make sense."

"And you didn't know about any of it," she

brusquely replied.

Her tart comment was uncalled for and he was about to snap a reply when he whirled around and ordered, "Give me those assignment codes. Stay here but don't let yourself be seen!"

Twenty minutes of quick-march brought him to the exercise "head-shed" where the Evaluator Scouts monitored the various evaluation lanes. Startled heads turned as he stomped into the room. He pointed to an adjoining office that held a computer workstation, "That room empty?"

"Yes, sir, but . . ." one of the scouts began, then stopped in mid-sentence as the senior scout shot him a dark look as he pushed into the room and slammed the door behind him. A minute later the senior scout scrolled through the various documents that McCarel's assignment codes opened for him. But none of it made any sense, it was all routine, lower level stuff. Any junior staff officer could handle it and there was absolutely no need to assign the information the level of security it held.

And why had General Rosberg kept him out of the loop on whatever-this-was. The fact that McCarel was in the mount was mystery enough, but to have the brother of his hated enemy involved with something that he was not aware of was almost asphyxiating. The more he read the more frustrated and angry he became.

His heart pounded and he kept tightening his hands as the flood of emotions surged through his body. He stopped and leaned forward in his chair so that his face was mere centimeters from the screen. He reached out a finger to touch the screen as if to make sure that what he saw was actually there. He read and re-read it several times.

He bolted into action and slapped several commands into the computer. Almost instantly new documents appeared on his screen. With flying fingertips he searched the documents until he found the exact document he needed to see. Hardly breathing, he scrolled down... stopped... stared hard for what seemed like minutes.

He couldn't believe it... but there it was. For a moment a sense of numbness filled his body before he shook it off and went back through the entire file. For twenty minutes he studied the documents before finally signing off. He rose from the chair and left the office. As he stepped out, he found the Senior

Evaluator Scout waiting for him.

The look on his face must have prompted the scout's question, "Sir, are you alright?"

He blankly looked at the woman for a moment before mumbling, "What? Yes, yes, I'm fine."

She stepped close, "Sir, you realize that you shouldn't have broken off the evaluation without my authorization. This is highly irregular; I'll have to enter a note into your evaluation report."

He looked at her for a moment and then back at the computer and started laughing. He waved a hand as he turned to walk out. "Oh, by all means Major, enter a note on my fitness report . . . but make sure you also put in there that I haven't felt this fit in years."

He retraced his steps to the small clearing where he'd left his daughter. The open space was empty so he sat on a log and pretended to check his equipment, "Where are you?" he quietly asked.

"Bushes at 9 o'clock," she replied.

He stood and entered the brushy thicket to face his daughter. The look that crossed his face caused his daughter to state, "You know something."

He nodded and explained in detail what he'd

found. She listened intently until he finished and with her own stunned expression softly exhaled, "No . . . I don't believe . . . could it really be him?"

The senior StarScout shook his head from side-to-side. "It can't be . . . but it must be. The name, the age . . . it has to be him."

Alena licked her lips before she replied. "First Jak McCarel arrives unannounced and now . . ." She vigorously shook her head. "This can't be sheer coincidence; it's too . . . too . . ."

"Timely?" Her father darkly finished for her. "I agree."

He walked several steps in a tight little circle while his daughter watched. Finally she demanded, "What are you going to do?"

He ran a grimy hand over his forehead as if mulling over his options before he looked straight at his daughter. "For now . . . nothing, I . . ."

"Nothing!" Alena practically yelled as she cut him off, "But we know exactly where . . ."

"Yes, exactly!" he testily replied, "We know where he is and he's not going anywhere that we won't know of . . ."

"But, now's our chance, what we've waited for.

They've come out of hiding and all we need is to . . ."

"Do nothing!" he angrily snapped, "This is too pat, too simple . . . There's more here than we see or understand. People who've been hiding for all these years just don't suddenly walk out into the open. So until I know more, we stand down until I say how and when we move!"

His daughter looked at him with an open mouth as if she couldn't believe what she was hearing. A look of cold fury crossed her face, and she practically hissed at him, "All my life you've pounded into me of what happened to my mother and who was responsible, and how, when the time was right, we would take our just due, and now you're telling me that when both are practically in our grasp, you are going to . . . do . . . nothing?"

Controlling his own pent-up emotions, the scout firmly said, "Alena, you don't understand . . . there is so much more here that you don't know about . . ."

"Understand! Understand? No, I understand all too well. I understand that because of them all I've had are a few digi-photos . . . and . . . and . . . a death certificate . . ."

She stopped as the emotion swept over her, "I can

still see her . . . hear her . . ." With a visible effort she regained her composure and in a deadly cold voice went on, "And I've had the memory of her being deserted, left to horribly die by a coward of a McCarel! And now you want me to do nothing!"

Her flood of emotions caught him off-guard for a moment, but when he stepped forward as if to embrace her she raised her arms as if to ward him off and turned away. Furious, she took several steps away before turning and angrily stating, "By the way, just like you're now missing this target, your exercise target is 100 meters in the other direction, you passed it twice in the last hour!" With that she angrily punched through the surrounding greenery and disappeared into the greenbelt.

The older scout stood still, the core of his own anger and hurt barely abating in the aftermath of his daughter's outburst. Finally regaining his composure, he made a quick decision and opened his transmitter, "Ops officer, I'm headed back to base camp, have my strato-cruiser standing by and tell them to file a flight plan back to command."

"Excuse me sir," the startled scout replied, "You're quitting the exercise before mission complete?"

"That's right mister. Tell the crew to be ready for jump off as soon as I get there."

"But sir, this is irregular, no one . . ."

His voice was a snarl as he responded. "Listen, and listen carefully. If someone uses that word 'irregular' to me one more time today, they'll be doing 'regular' permanent duty in the ammonia soup on Titan. Now I have more important things to do than checking on 2-week old alligator eggs in this stinkin' swamp. I'm heading in and you simply tell the senior evaluator to put me on the next rotation. Is that clear or do you want me to come in and spell it out personally?"

"No sir," the chastened officer replied, "Understood perfectly."

The senior scout stood stock-still for several seconds, thinking of . . . her. Alena had so many of her fine qualities... intelligence, beauty, courage, decisiveness. He wouldn't admit it to his daughter, but the anger and rage she got from him, not to mention the almost uncontrollable need for revenge. It was like a habit-forming stimulant that coursed through his veins, overpowering and controlling . . . and he did absolutely nothing to reduce its effects. He wanted it with him every waking moment; always there so that he would never, ever forget what the McCarels had done to him . . . what they had taken from his life.

He ran his hand over his face and leaned up against a smooth-barked tree to think. It was an incredible stroke of fortune that they had stumbled across this but he knew he had to be very careful and patient.

His thoughts came back to Alena. He dearly loved his daughter but there were times when he didn't like her—like now. In a way, he understood her outburst but knew that she didn't realize the deeper and more sinister considerations. If he didn't go at this the right way, the consequences could be disastrous. For both of them.

He looked down at the red welts on his hand. Alena's little prank had more realism that she intended because what he was about to do would literally push him deeper into a human viper pit. Up to now, he had been on the edge, but now he would have to actually step-off into the abyss. But there was no turning back, he was snake-bit any way he went and the poison of hatred that coursed through his body was killing off what little conscience he had left.

He stepped out of the thicket, and lengthening his stride, pushed through the foliage, his hatred building with each step he took. There were a few things he needed to check on when he got back. Once he had the information, he would make the comms-call that he'd waited so long to make, the one that would start the McCarels on their road to a final, deadly destiny.

Chapter 7

Treachery Unleashed

In an incredulous voice, Adiak Peller demanded, "There is no doubt?"

"None. I checked the records personally. It's him all right," the StarScout officer replied.

Peller sat back in his chair and ran his fingers through his perfectly sculpted hair, of which not a single grey strand showed to the world. The news stunned him to his core. It wasn't the same as finding Dak McCarel, but it was practically the next best thing. After all these years he had almost given up hope of settling the old score.

McCarel's treachery had been a constant irritant to him, a mental barb that with each passing year augured its way deeper into his psyche. His power had grown to the point that McCarel's deed was literally the last to go unpunished and that meant someone had bested him. Him! There was no forgiving or forgetting for that!

When he found out about the disappearance of McCarel's wife and child, he ordered his organization into a frenzied search. He even covertly used Confederation means to seek them out. They looked—how they looked, but with absolutely no results. The failure to find the two was like salt poured into a bloody, deep wound. How the McCarel witch vanished without leaving a trace was astonishing, but now he would have the satisfaction of finally getting what was rightfully his.

"Anything to connect him to Dak McCarel?" Peller demanded.

"Nothing that I can see. But we now know where they've been. It's the logical place to start looking for him."

"And McCarel's wife? Is she still there?"

The officer shook his head. "The transcript

indicates she died some months back."

"Hmmm," Peller mused. "That might be a false record. We'll need to verify. McCarel could be using it to cover her disappearance just as he faked his own death."

Peller was quiet for a moment as his mind raced through the implications. Then he said, "You're sure you know where the boy is and can keep close tabs on him?"

The officer vigorously bobbed his head. "Oh yes. As if he was in my hip pocket."

"Good. I'll need some time to set things up; you make sure you know where he is at all times."

"That's not a problem; this couldn't be more perfect for us. You have a plan in mind?"

Peller scowled, "I swore a long time ago that if need be the son would pay for the transgression of the father. It looks like that time is now here." He eyed the StarScout. "And if I remember correctly, you have a matter to settle with Dak McCarel as well."

A look of hard hatred crossed the StarScout's face. "That's right, and I intend to collect on that debt."

Peller chopped him off with a wave of his hand. "And so you shall. But, remember, it's Dak McCarel that we want, and more importantly what he stole. Don't let your emotions get out of hand and you lose sight of that!"

"I won't!" the man retorted. There was brief silence and then he asked, "How do you know he still has the Kolomite after all these years? He must have sold it on the market by now."

Peller firmly shook his head, "No, he hasn't. I would've known if he had," he said confidently. Peller realized his mistake as soon as he spoke. He had just told the man that Peller practically controlled the Kolomite market. There were few if any transactions in Kolomite that he didn't know about and the amounts in those deals were minuscule. The officer blinked a few times at the revelation but wisely kept his mouth shut.

Peller changed the subject by saying, "What about the uncle? You mentioned that you have some misgivings about his presence there?"

"More than just misgivings. He and Tuul are apparently meeting with Rosberg regularly. I think they're up to something but I don't know exactly what yet. But I intend to find out."

Peller's always suspicious mind was mulling over

Jak McCarel's mysterious comings and goings that his operative described. It naturally led him to his next question. "Is there any possibility that they are working on anything to do with the organization?"

The man cautiously shook his head. "Possible, not likely though. I wouldn't have been kept out of the loop on something that significant. They need my experience, my abilities." He didn't say it but Peller knew the man' thoughts: I'm too important for them to leave me out of anything major. Peller knew from experience, however, that that wasn't always true.

By the man's own admission they were keeping something from him. He knew they were but didn't want to admit the fact. That made him an even bigger fool than Peller originally thought. Peller made up his mind. He had sources that this man didn't know about inside StarScout. He would use them to find out if Rosberg was planning something against the *Faction*.

And if StarScout was moving against him, and this man couldn't provide him with the information he needed, it was time to think of his permanent departure. That was Peller's ultimate plan anyway.

He scowled as if making a decision he didn't like

but needed to make. Pointing his finger at the scout he ordered, "First things first. Use any means necessary, but find out if Rosberg is moving against our organization. I want to know anything that you find out as soon as possible. Rosberg isn't a fool; he knows he needs allies on the High Council for StarScouts to survive. It may be that he's offering his services to them to use against us, which would raise the worth of StarScouts highly among to the assembly . . . and the council."

His look penetrated the man as he went on, "If you're not capable of this, then I'll find someone who can . . ."

The scout gave a start as Peller's words trailed off, the meaning perfectly clear. "No, no," he hastily responded, "I have a resource that may be very handy in this matter."

"Good," Peller coolly replied. "Now to this other matter." He sat back and observed, "Most things don't happen by accident. It's too coincidental that McCarel shows up at the same time that his nephew is about to begin this special operation."

With a deep frown he directed, "Briefly describe for me what happens during these missions. The information may be useful later."

The man outlined the protocol and major events. Peller stopped him before he finished. "So what you are saying is that there is a great deal of flexibility in travel route and mission areas, plus they're not monitored closely, nor are they under a strict chain-of-command."

"That's a broad generalization, but close enough," the StarScout muttered.

"Sounds perfect," Peller curtly replied.

The StarScout waited for Peller to continue. When he didn't the man asked, "Perfect for what?"

"To bring Dak McCarel and his Kolomite home."

The StarScout sat completely immobile, stunned by Peller's announcement. "I don't understand. How—"

Peller impatiently waved him into silence. "As far as the Confederation is concerned, the cloud of suspicion hangs over Dak McCarel, not his brother Jak, nor his son. Jak is a renowned scout, the son just beginning his career. Squeaky clean, completely above board, the two of them.

"So what better way to get the goods safely home, without suspicion, than the uncle arranges for the transportation, and the son picks up and delivers the package."

"But," the man sputtered, "They could've done something like that years ago and with far less trouble. Why go through such an elaborate charade?"

"Simple. If the word got out that a ship carrying that much Kolomite was transiting known space, what do you think the chances are of it making port call? Not only would we go after it, but every pip-squeak gang between here and the center of the galaxy would be lying in wait. This way, they have the perfect cover to bring it into Terran space and get it legally bartered at the government trading docks on Luna. Neat, simple, above-board."

The scout ran his hands through his graying hair. "I see your point," he said slowly. "But if what you're saying is correct, that would implicate—"

Peller shrugged indifference, "It doesn't matter who it implicates, what matters is that you stay on top of what is going on. This may be the very break we need to find the Kolomite."

Peller took a deep breath and slowly let it out. "And if it is, then we're going to be there waiting for Dak McCarel. And when he makes his appearance, then we'll close the trap shut around his neck and we'll both get what we want."

He thought for a few moments more and then said, "And just where is this son of a McCarel currently located?" The scout quickly gave Peller the Terran coordinates. "Good," Peller answered, "If the mother is truly dead, McCarel won't want to see his son follow his wife so quickly."

"You're going to use his son to . . ." the senior scout started, "Of course!" Peller snapped, "Just as he used my son!" Peller took a deep breath and rose from his seat. He paced for a few moments as if lost in thought, then said slowly, "We'll use a team out of the southern hemisphere to do what's necessary. They'll need a cover story of course, something simple and not too complicated." He looked around at the rare and priceless Amazonian hardwoods that covered the walls of his hidden lair, wood that was verboten to legally own. "Smuggling, perhaps," he mused.

With that he snapped out of reverie and coldly ordered, "Make sure that there are no changes to his immediate schedule . . . understood? I'll take care of the rest."

The StarScout merely nodded as Peller went on,

"One final thing. I will be out of touch for a while. A personal matter. I will notify you when I return."

Peller closed the transmission between the two and sat back in his chair. He brought his fingers together in front of his face as he stared at the blank screen. He had two plans to set in motion. One to finally entrap Dak McCarel, the other to eliminate this doddering fool who was becoming a millstone around his neck.

A cruel upturn of his lips appeared as he thought of how much pleasure he would derive from both.

Chapter 8

Kidnapped!

As Del listened to TJ's report, he felt a momentary sense of gratification and relief that the plan apparently worked. He keyed his communicator and ordered the other team members to close the loop in the area indicated by the creature's flight. If TJ failed to locate the extraterrestrial again, maybe one of the others would. "If we can nail the XT one more time," Del told his team, "We might be sleeping in our own beds tonight."

"Yee haw!" Sami replied. "A real pillow instead of a rock to lay my head on!"

Smiling at Sami's enthusiasm, Del said, "Flanker 2, give us a readout on the X's bearing every hundred meters so we can adjust the closure loop," and waited for her reply. There was none.

"Flanker 2, this is Team Lead, did you copy my last transmission?"

Again he waited, but there was no reply. Puzzled, Del transmitted to Sami, "PathFinder, did you hear my transmission to Flanker 2?"

"Roger, but I did not copy a reply from Flanker 2."

Del grew a little concerned over TJ's lack of response. Loss of radio contact with a teammate occasionally happened, though it was highly uncommon. And, since on this exercise their transmissions were sent through the overhead COM-SKY global network of communication satellites, distance and line-of-sight were not considerations.

However, TJ's report on the star beast greatly concerned Del. TJ was smart and wouldn't do anything foolish. Still, death or serious injury were variables that did enter the equation without warning. Standard operating procedures called for the non-communicating scout to remain at her last known location and wait for the team to search her out and regroup.

Del quickly gave new orders to the team, redirecting them to converge on the grid of TJ's last transmission. Glancing at the jungle terrain for bearings, he quick-marched through the dense growth and periodically tried to rouse her on the communicator.

As Del closed to TJ's last location, he pushed through a stand of rain-soaked foliage and found himself in a large clearing. Hearing a rustling to his left he turned to see Nase and Shanon step through a large clump of greenery and stride over. A few moments later, Sami appeared and gave the scout signal for *close on me*. The three junior scouts rapidly teamed up with their Path Finder.

"Over here," Sami said as they walked up to him. Following his lead they came into another clearing, this one smaller than the previous. Del could see bent and trampled grass and foliage. As he walked through the short grass he saw something metallic in the mid-afternoon sunlight. He reached down and picked up TJ's hand-sized camcorder. He held up his find so that the others could see. They gathered around, concerned by this evidence that something serious had happened to TJ. ~~Not needed~~

Nase voiced the unsaid fears. "Doesn't look like it's just a communications failure."

Del nodded in agreement. "Ok, gang," he ordered, "give me a three-sixty." The others fanned out in a 360-degree outward search pattern. A few minutes later, Del heard Shanon say over the transmitter, "TL, you'd better come see this."

At a half-run through the slippery foliage, Del came to where Shanon knelt over something on the ground. She stood as he approached and pointed to a muddy trail that led through the grass and dripping brush. Del knelt to get a better look. What he saw caused him to look sharply at Shanon. The signs said that something had dragged a large mass through the mud and wet grass. For a moment the thought flashed through Del's mind that their extraterrestrial quarry had seized TJ.

Shanon, who had moved slightly further down the muddied trail said, "Del, over here." He stood to see at what she pointed.

Tracks! Boot prints! Several sets that led off

through the jungle along the crushed grass track. Studying the impressions, Del began to get that prickly feeling in his gut that he had had just before the Jaguar attack. XT animals didn't wear boots!

Del glanced at Shanon and spoke quietly. "This doesn't make sense. What gives?"

For a moment she didn't say anything. "You're right. Doesn't make sense. From this it looks like TJ was grabbed by someone and dragged off. But why and who? This place is supposed to be off limits during field exercises."

"Supposed to . . ." he replied and nervously looked around. Shanon was right, the preserve was a protected, enclosed area vigorously patrolled by specially trained rangers. Only they and the Instructor StarScouts were allowed in the exercise area, and they certainly wouldn't kidnap TJ! But the evidence said that someone, a human someone, and not an off-world creature had taken TJ.

Del opened his trans-comm and directed Sami and Nase to regroup with Shanon and himself. They needed to talk this one over before going on. As the two came up, Del knelt and showed them the tracks and the trail leading off into the jungle.

"If we can believe this," Del began, "TJ found the XT, but someone in turn went after her."

Sami whistled off-key. "Not good, folks. Not good at all."

Nase knelt to study the tracks. He looked up at Del. "Change in modus operandi."

Sami snorted, "And just exactly what does that mean, oh Wise One?"

"It means," Del said, "that we change our mission. Someone's snatched TJ and we're going to go find her."

Shanon looked around and asked in pointed terms, "And our mission target?"

"You know the answer," Del cryptically answered. "The beastie will have to wait."

Shanon asked, "Emergency call-out?"

"Yes," said Del, "But we're not going to wait. TJ's in trouble and we need to find her. Shanon, you start the emergency call after we move, but stay behind us, I don't want anyone to hear you."

For a moment Del considered his decision. By abandoning their Seek and Find mission, the scouts chanced Failed Mission on their report cards. But their friend was in danger and each knew that none of them would be worthy to wear the Scout Arrow if they left her in harm's way.

He looked around and asked, "Everyone okay with this?" Seeing the agreement in their eyes, Del went on, "As I see it, we now have two missions instead of one. First priority, we locate and extract TJ from whoever has her and turn them over to the authorities. Second, if we can, we still do our job and locate the XT for observation and cataloging."

Sami, who had gone back to inspecting the tracks, spoke up. "Could be that in doing either of those, we accomplish both."

Puzzled, Del questioned Sami. "What do you mean?"

"Look," Sami said as he pointed at the slushy mud, "These prints here, they sink into the ground deeper than the other set. Either this fellow is one hefty banana, or he's carrying something heavy."

"Like TJ maybe?" Shanon asked.

"Like TJ maybe."

"Then what's this other flattened area where someone is obviously being dragged?" Del asked.

No one said anything for a moment, as Sami slyly smiled at Del and Shanon as if he knew something that they didn't. Then it dawned on them what he was driving at and almost in unison each said, "The XT!"

"Kudos, my friends," Sami rejoined, "I hope that didn't frazzle your brains too much. It is a bit of a warm day."

"Okay, okay, nice deduction," Del said approvingly. "So these guys grabbed both TJ and the XT. We're still going to have to change our modus operandi to go after these people, and I am more than open to suggestions and recommendations."

"Modus, schmodus," Sami piped up. "What the heck are you talking about?"

"Latin, Sami," Shanon patiently explained, "Means mode of operation or how you do business."

As she pointed down to the boot-prints, she went on, "In our case, changing our modus operandi means we alter our methods because we now have a different type of target. Humans. And humans, I might add, who aren't afraid to hunt and bag other humans."

"Thank you too much for the explanation," Sami replied. "Are you saying that these people have been hunting us ever since we walked in?"

"Don't think so," Del frowned in answer. "Why would anyone want to hunt us? We're just JS's on a field exercise; we don't have anything that anyone would want. Or at least I don't think so."

Nase, who had been examining the broken track and listening to the conversation, spoke up, "TJ apparently did. And I think I know what."

All three turned to look at him as he looked down the trail. "They're XT poachers or hunters," Nase began, "TJ got between them and the XT, or more likely saw what they were doing. Before she could trans and report, they stunned her." The team went silent as they considered Nase's observation. It was chilling to consider that TJ was in the hands of outlaws.

Shanon looked at the others as she commented. "Makes sense. A witness is evidence. But why kidnap her? Assault gets you jail time, XT poaching gets you a penal moon for several years, but kidnap someone and you atone with your life."

"All right, all right," Sami said testily. "Let's assume that it's starside poachers that grabbed TJ. The why isn't important. We need to get going. Daylight is burning and TJ and her playmates are probably moving further away. I strongly suggest that we not try to follow that trail in the dark. Even with snoopers it would be very slow and we need to beat feet."

"You're right," Del acknowledged, "We need to move."

Del quickly gave instructions. "Sami, you're Pathfinder, directly on the trail. Nase and I will flank you by ten to fifteen meters on the left and right. Shanon, cover the rear and keep up the emergency call-out." Before they moved out, Del cautioned, "They probably have at least stunners, and maybe heavier hardware. Long-knives against laz- or d-guns aren't exactly fair odds."

"Not to worry, TL," Sami quipped. "We know it's not fair, but we'll go easy on them!"

Seeing Del's dark glare, Sami shifted his torso-vest and began to stride down the beaten trail. Motioning to the others to take up station, Del trotted to the side of his Pathfinder.

Around him the jungle felt even less friendly than before. Somewhere near, there were renegade human beings who had stunned and kidnapped a junior scout. Del was angry at that, but he was also afraid for TJ's sake. Only desperate individuals, knowing what the penalty was for kidnapping, would take such drastic action. And someone who was willing to risk the ultimate price was willing to do most anything to cover up the crime.

For half an hour, the now reduced team warily edged through the jungle following the trail. Though their LifeSensors could register human beings, the LS's limited range wasn't much use against a sniper sitting two or three hundred meters away with a d-gun scoped on them. They would use the LS's anyway, but depend mostly on their eyes and ears.

Del queried Shanon, "Anything on the emergency call-out?"

"Nothing! Not a peep. You sure we got the right frequency?"

"I'm sure. Keep trying."

A few minutes later, Del heard his trans-comm click open. "TL got a hit on the LS. Human. Really faint, at the extreme detection range, ten degrees to my left," Sami said.

"Understood," Del softly replied. "Nase, investigate the reading. Stay out of sight. Path and I will continue on the trail."

"Copy," Nase transmitted back.

Del turned to Sami and instructed, "Ease up another ten meters and wait. I'll parallel you."

"Roger." Sami whispered. Del leaned low to the ground and silently moved through the jungle. A few meters on, Sami stepped purposefully out so that Del could see him. His hand-signaled Del to join him. The fact that he hadn't used the trans-comm told Del he didn't want to be heard. Del turned to Shanon and signaled her to stay put.

The trail had followed a series of small clearings and Del could tell by the break in the trees ahead that they were coming to another large opening in the jungle forest. This one, however, looked much larger than the clearings they had crossed earlier.

Just as Del was about to step around a bush, he saw Sami hand-signal, "Take cover!" and point to his LS. Looking at his own LifeSensor, Del could see the device's tiny read-out window blinking. Its digital message indicated that the human target was almost directly ahead.

Del stepped back behind the bush and went to ground. Cautiously peeking through the foliage, Del saw Sami squirm ahead on his stomach through some stringy brush and then disappear into greenery. Several anxious minutes later, Del heard Sami whisper through the trans-comm, "Nase, freeze! TL, ten meters ahead. Burned tree."

Del understood Sami's message. Sami had seen something ahead and he didn't want Nase to run into it, and he was telling Del to meet him ahead near a burned-out tree.

The mossy earth felt soft as Del slid onto his stomach to begin his creep. Carrying his field-knife in one hand, Del crawled from bush to bush, trying hard to blend in with the natural foliage. His camouflaged scout uniform helped, and so did the dirt and leaves that now clung to him.

Del spotted the burnt shell of a forest giant that had fallen victim to a lightning strike. Easing forward, he crawled underneath a clinging bush and was about to raise his head when a human hand grabbed his ankle. In a flash he brought his knife up only to feel his ankle squeezed twice rapidly in the scout recognition pattern. Looking around, he saw Sami smiling at him. Del had to admire Sami's woodcraft; he had crawled right past the camouflaged youth and hadn't seen him.

As Del nodded acknowledgment, Sami pointed with his chin to a jutted-out shoulder of the burned tree that provided a place for them to kneel unseen. He signed to Del that there was something on the other side that Del needed to see. Del crawled up to the splintered tree and carefully eased himself up till he could see on the other side.

His eyes widened in amazement. An off-planet ship! A gleaming gray space cruiser, resting on its landing pods, sat in the large jungle clearing. And the trail they followed led right to the craft!

It definitely looked like Nase was right. XT poachers or hunters had set down in this clearing, gone hunting for an XT, and had run into TJ instead. Del would bet his fourth-semester bars that TJ was in that cruiser! Alive, he hoped.

Sliding down, Del let out a small expulsion of air and looked at Sami. The question now was how to get TJ out of the ship without any of the scouts getting hurt. They would also need to lose the poachers long enough in the jungle for the JS's to contact help. The spacecraft didn't look like it was getting ready for take-off, but Del knew that could change in a matter of minutes. He had to assume that time was not on their side and that the spacer could lift at practically any time.

Considering that, Del decided to take a chance and contact Shanon and Nase on the trans-comm. He assumed that the poachers would have sophisticated communication detection devices that allowed them to eavesdrop on unsecured transmissions like theirs. But they probably had those devices tuned to the park ranger frequencies. What he was gambling on was that it would take them a while to figure out StarScout frequencies and that they hadn't yet. If they were listening in on scout comms, then he would be broadcasting their plans. But he really had no choice.

He keyed his communicator open and softly whispered, "Shanon, anything on the call-out?

"Negative, TL."

The no-reply to their call-out was very puzzling. Del didn't understand why the IS's or Park Rangers hadn't responded, as the call-out frequency was supposed to be constantly monitored. But he didn't have the answer and they didn't have the time to find out.

"Stop transmitting. Slow sneak to Nase . . . Nase,

where are you? Do you see the cruiser?"

Nase whispered back, "Roger. I'm twenty meters due west of the craft. Saw it just before Path grounded us. I have two targets near my location. One male, one female. Walking towards the craft. They've netted what looks like a small Insul-Tyger. Orders?"

"Stand by," Del replied and leaned his back against the tree-wall. Not much in the scout manual to cover situations like this. And they certainly hadn't done any fieldwork on this sort of thing. Running his hand over his sweaty face, he considered their options, which weren't many.

Sami, who had been peering over the shoulder of the tree to keep a lookout, reached down and squeezed Del's shoulder. Del carefully poked his head up and looked into the clearing.

Two figures, an older man and a young woman, were just coming out of the forest carrying a web sling between them. They obviously were the two humans that Nase had reported. Coming from around the far end of the vessel were two more adult males who stopped to wait for the incoming party. Both men were short and swarthy, with a menacing look about them. Del assumed that these two were the humans that Sami's LS had registered.

As the young woman came up to the two men, one of them started gesturing into the jungle towards Del and Sami, and then back at the ship. The other joined in and both were talking quite animatedly but were too far away for Del to clearly hear their words.

Putting her burden down, the lithe female listened intently for a few moments and then in great agitation obviously began giving orders. Del wished mightily that he could hear what she was saying because it was quite clear that she bossed this crew.

As she finished, two of the men picked up the I-Tyger and carried it into the ship. Moments later they jogged back down the ramp again. All four carried laz-guns and their manner indicated that they were practiced in their use. At a quick walk, the young woman led the party towards the trail that Del and Sami had followed. Seeing them approach, the two scouts melted into the bushes and waited tensely, their knives drawn as the renegade poachers came closer.

"Geez, Bianca," Del heard one of them say as they neared the charred tree, "How wuz we supposed to know that she was part of a team? Mitch and I don't know nuthin' about StarScouts. The only time we wuz even near 'em was when they chased us off Franson's Planet."

"Shut up, Gunter!" the young woman snapped and turned on the man, stopping the others dead in their tracks. "If you couldn't get the others then you should've just stunned her and left her there! Now we've probably got her teammates and park rangers scouring the woods for her!"

"But boss," the target of her wrath said, "we couldn't just leave her. I think maybe she saw us. If she did, she could identify us to Confederation Police!"

"Maybe! Maybe she saw you! You turtle-brain, she definitely saw you and the ship when you brought her back here. You dosed her again, right?"

"Yeah. We dosed her good. She's out," the man hastily replied. The men stood silent as the woman vented her wrath. Finally one asked, "What are we going to do now?"

For a moment it looked like the woman was going to backhand him. She coldly replied, "This is what we're going to do. You two are going to check the three traps we set this morning. Lel and I are going to check the one just to the east. Then he and I will put the ship into ready configuration for flight. As soon as your skinny tails are in-board we're going to zip this place."

"And the . . . uh, young lady?" one of the men asked furtively.

"She's got to go with us until I can figure out what to do with her."

"But, that's . . . kidnapping!" one of the men said.

The woman rolled her eyes and answered as if she was speaking to a child, "And what do you call it when you stun someone and drag them through the jungle to this ship? A polite invitation to a party? You idiot, you've already kidnapped her! Now get out there and check those traps!

"Remember, the fix is in for only two more hours and then our stooge goes off-duty at SATCOM. If we don't lift by then, the spy-sats will pick us up, so we sit here until Imelda makes another payoff. But I'm not going to sit in this stinking hot jungle another hour with our *guest* on board! So the *Jigger 2* lifts with or without you in twenty minutes! Now move!"

The two mumbled replies as they hurried away

from the fury of the ferocious young woman. Del and Sami watched as the two pairs split and patiently waited until they were sure that the poachers were out of earshot. Del spoke quietly over the trans-comm, "Nase, Shanon . . ."

"Go ahead," Shanon responded.

"We're on the south side. Rendezvous. Careful, at least four poachers in the area."

"Understood," she replied, "We saw them."

Del didn't know if there were more poachers in the ship or in the jungle besides the four they had seen. He suspected there weren't, but he couldn't take a chance. Especially not with laz-guns in the hands of their adversaries. He couldn't believe their luck that the poachers had practically stopped on top of them and argued. But he wasn't going to complain. It was just about the first stroke of good fortune they had had on this mission.

Minutes later, Del heard a soft click-click like the sound of a bird tapping its beak against wood. The signal repeated itself. Del said over the communicator, "Got it. Bushes two meters from burnt-out tree." In a few moments, Shanon, and then Nase poked their heads out from under the bushes and silently crawled to face Del and Sami.

The young scouts put their faces together and Del quickly recounted the poacher's conversation in muted tones. As he concluded, Shanon asked, "At least we know she's alive. Okay, what now?"

With a slight shrug, Del said, "Obviously we can't wait till they get back. No one's answering the emergency call, so . . . I've got to go in for her."

"Hey!" Sami whispered. "What's this *I* business, did my lousy hearing not catch the *we* part?"

"Look," Del began, "these are bad people with bad weapons. They're playing for keeps. I lost TJ. I certainly am not going to risk losing the rest of the team. I go in. Alone. You go to ground and keep watch. If they space, and TJ and I don't get out, or if something happens to us, well, follow procedures and contact the authorities as soon as you can."

The three listening scouts looked at each other in turn, arched their eyebrows and nodded. Sami said to Shanon, "Do you want to do the honors?"

The petite brunette tilted her head slightly to Sami and Nase. "With pleasure."

Shanon turned to Del and said formally, "Junior StarScout Baldura, under StarScout Regulation One-

Alpha dash Three, sub-paragraph 6, I formally relieve you of duty as Team Leader. Justification: Mental stress that has adversely affected your decision making. Do the other team members concur in this matter?"

Nase nodded his head and quietly replied, "Yes," followed by Sami's, "Indubitably!"

"Wait a minute," Del countered strongly, "I'm not overstressed, and what regulation is that? I don't remember any such regulation that covers relieving a team leader. You're half-cocked."

Shanon sniffed delicately and replied, "We studied it the two days you were in the hospital with your broken leg. Your fall off Old Baldy. Remember? You were very stressed then, too. Forgot to set your grav-' piton' deep enough in the rock fissure."

"I did set my piton' deep enough," Del said darkly. "The rock fractured under the weight. And I wouldn't have broken my leg," he continued, turning to Sami, "if someone had been paying attention to my belay line and slowed me down before I hit the ledge."

Sami looked sadly at Shanon. "Selective memory. Stress does that, you know. Short-circuits the neural synapses, causes a dysfunction in the recall region of the right hemisphere of the brain . . ."

Nase reached out to stop Sami and sternly said, "TJ . . .cruiser . . ."

Del shook his head and quietly smiled to himself.

"Okay, okay," he said, shaking his head. "I recognize a conspiracy when I see one. I give up."

"A conspiracy? Please," Sami quipped, "It's more of a democratic mutiny."

"Fine. Call it what you want," Del said. "Enough chatter. I'm going in for TJ. You want to come? Okay. Let's assume there are no poachers in the ship. Shanon, rear-guard on the ramp. Nase, you and Sami with me. We'll figure out the rest when we get in. Questions? No. Scout's Out."

With that, the four junior scouts sprinted low across the clearing, hoping that Del was right and there wasn't anybody left in the cruiser or the poachers outside wouldn't spot them. Hitting the ramp at a dead run, Del, Nase, and Sami sped up the incline and threw themselves through the open airlock hatchway that led into the ship.

Del turned to see Shanon fling herself to the ground, makes herself small against the foot of the metal ramp. He frowned, but it was the best she could do. She would have a really good look at anyone approaching the ship from this side but the large landing strut-pylons blocked a good portion of her view to the other side.

Inside the ship, Del and the other two found themselves in a short entrance corridor that led to a larger passageway. They listened intently but only heard the metallic clicks and whirrings of ship machinery. So far there didn't appear to be anyone else in the ship.

As the three crept silently forward they came to a corridor intersection and stopped. Del poked his head out and looked both ways. The passageway was empty.

Del signed to the other two that they were to go forward and search, he would head to the rearward part of the ship. If they found TJ, they were to get her out of the ship as quickly as they could. Use the trans-comms only in a life-threatening emergency.

The two nodded that they understood and headed forward. Del did likewise on the other side and moved silently along the deck plates. The ship was so quiet that Del could almost hear his heart pounding in his chest. Del eased up to the first bulkhead door and stood to the side as he pressed the release button. The door recessed into the bulkhead wall. As he peeked around the corner, Del found himself looking into a tiny stateroom, obviously the sleeping quarters of one of the poachers.

And by the looks of the cuddly stuffed Womba Bear on the narrow bed, it was the female poacher's room. Somehow, Del thought, the soft texture of the stuffed star beast did not match the rough and tough character the pretty young woman presented out in the jungle.

Del stepped back and pressed the button to close the door. He silently continued down the corridor. Two more doors found two more empty rooms. At the end of the narrow corridor Del found a transverse bulkhead door which led him to a series of cargo compartments.

As he came up to the first cargo door, he had a strong suspicion of what he would find behind the entrance. As the door slid open, a soft red light filtered out of the compartment. Inside, Del found exactly what he thought he would find.

Two stasis chambers each held a sleeping star creature wrapped in soft plasfoam. Del didn't know if these XT's were from the Natura Preserva or were captured star side. He only knew that they weren't supposed to be here.

He stepped out of the compartment and opened the second. He had just entered it and found an empty cargo-hold when he heard his trans-communicator key open, "TL, Searcher 1," said Sami.

"Go ahead,"

"Found her! She's forward in a small infirmary. Unconscious but looks okay otherwise." Del nodded his head gratefully, "Okay. Stay there. I'll come forward to help."

Del backed out of the compartment, pressed the panel button to close the door and was about to sprint to the main passageway when his trans-comm exploded to life. "TL! This is Rear-Guard and we've got trouble!" Shanon said, not trying to keep her voice down, "Bad guys inbound!"

"Do they see you? Can you get away?" Del asked as he raced toward the main passageway.

"No to both, TL. If I try to sprint through the clearing, they'll have a clear bead on me, and I don't think I can outrun their laz-guns!"

Del made the only decision he could think of. "Get

in the ship, Shanon! Stop at the first intersection. I'll meet you."

As he slammed through the transverse hatchway into the main passageway, Del continued, "Nase, Sami. Can you wake TJ?"

"That's a negative, TL," Sami answered. "We tried. I think she's either been stun-gunned or sedated. She's really out."

As he ran up the passageway, Del tried to think of what to do. Jump the four poachers when they got in the ship? Risky business against laz-guns in a close-quarter fight.

The entry air-lock hatch! Could they seal the hatch and prevent the renegades from getting in the ship? Might be a back door to the ship that the scouts didn't know about, but Del doubted it. Most space-cruisers this size had only one main cargo or passenger hatch.

"Shanon," Del spoke urgently, "stop at the hatchway. See if you can retract the ramp and seal the hatch so that those poachers can't get in!"

"Understood!" Shanon crisply replied.

"Sami, Nase," Del continued, "leave TJ for now. Meet us at the hatchway intersection. If we can't seal the hatch, then we're going to have to either jump these guys when they come in, or find a quiet hideaway on this ship. Fire it up, guys, we don't have much time!"

"Roger!" Sami replied, "Hyper-speed!"

Del mentally flogged himself. He should have thought of bringing Shanon in and closing the hatch when they first went inboard, but he instinctively didn't want to close off their one escape route. Now, not only were they trapped, but they really didn't have a way to fight back. Del skidded around the intersection corner and sprinted up to Shanon who was desperately trying to code the hatchway pressure door to close. And not succeeding.

As Del rushed up, Shanon said, "No good, Del. They've pre-programmed the door to a secure code. We're not going to be able to decipher it."

As he looked at the tiny computer grid, Del knew Shanon was right. "Okay," he said, grabbing her elbow, "Back to the intersection."

Both spun on their heels and raced for the t-section where they almost ran head-on into Nase and Sami. The adrenaline pumping through their veins made their breathing rapid and shallow. Nase, Sami, and Shanon looked at Del. He was the Team Leader. They would follow his decision.

Looking at his teammates, his friends, Del made the only choice he thought he could.

"Okay, gang. I once heard the ScoutMaster say that only the foolish die a foolish death. Let's not be foolish. We'll choose our own time and place to take these guys. But not right now. Let's see if we can hide on this rust bucket. This way."

Shanon grabbed Del's arm, "What about TJ? Are we going to leave her?"

Before Del could answer, Sami interjected, "Shanon, TJ's okay. We saw her. She had a cut on her head that someone had taken the time to bandage. If they were going to hurt her, or do worse, they wouldn't have given her first aid."

Shanon gave a quick nod of acceptance. With that, Del led them back down the passageway to the cargo compartments. Just as they reached the transverse portal they heard voices behind them. The poachers were coming up the ramp, angrily and loudly arguing among themselves.

Quietly closing the hatch behind him, Del motioned for the team to go into the second cargo compartment. As they entered the hold Del pointed up to a large metal grill set high in the joint where bulkhead wall met ceiling.

The latticed opening led to the service ducts that ran the entire length of the vessel with several off-branches to port and starboard. They carried the ship's numerous electronic microcables and computer filaments as well as providing the ship's air ventilation system.

And, because ship innards needed occasional repairs, the ducts were large enough for an adult to crawl through, though not comfortably. Fortunately for Del and his mates, he had spotted and remembered the access hatches to the duct during his earlier search. For better or worse, the channels would provide the team a place to hide.

Del motioned for Sami to give him a boost up. With a quick jab Del pressed the release button to activate the small entrance hatch. He hoped mightily that the overhead grills weren't patched into some monitor board on the flight deck. It would be just their fortune to have some flashing peewee light give away their location.

With Sami's help, Del leveraged himself through

the hatch into the duct and then reached down to help the others. One by one the three climbed through the metal portal. When they were all inside, Del closed the hatch and leaned back against the wall. He took a deep breath and looked at his teammates. Sami lay on the floor, while Nase and Shanon sat wearily against the wall. They were all bone-tired, drained by the constant exertion and adrenaline rushes of the last several days.

Del felt and heard a rumbling vibration through the metal walls. The vessel's propulsion engines were powering up. Del reached over and pushed Shanon and Nase to the floor. Without grav-seats to ride out the heavy gravities of lift-off, it was all he could do to lessen the agony of what was coming next.

Seconds later, Del felt as if someone, no, several someones, were sitting on his chest as the space-cruiser blasted off from the jungle and headed into deep space.

Chapter 9

Cobras and Mongoose

Agonizing minutes later, the ship powered down, and Del and his teammates roused themselves from the conduit's metal plates. Del rubbed the back of his neck where it had painfully pressed into a c-bar during the power out-run from the surface.

"Ugh," Sami wheezed. "What ran over me, a crazed Fuji Beast?"

Del grimaced as he raised himself. He agreed with Sami, the analogy of a thousand-kilo Fuji Beast sitting on one's chest was about right. Shanon muttered, "Someone was in one big hurry."

"Yeah," Del replied. "That felt like at least five, maybe six g's of acceleration."

"Short power run," Nase observed. "Close destination." Del nodded in understanding. The poachers' punch through Earth's atmosphere at high acceleration but for a short duration meant they weren't going very far, but wanted to get there in a big hurry.

"Any idea where we're headed?" Sami asked.

"Somewhere in-system," Shanon answered.

"How do you know that?" Sami sharply questioned.

"Didn't you check the engines on this heap?" Shanon replied. "No external gravity disrupters, no hyperspace enfold conductors. She doesn't have hyper-light capabilities, Sami. Strictly a Sol system ship."

"Oh," Sami said in a meek voice, aware that he should have checked for the elemental devices that, when attached to the Hartbeld StarDrive, gave a space-faring vessel faster-than-light speed.

"Okay," Sami agreed. "So if we're not going far, what do we do—hide here and pick lice out of each other's hair?"

"Sounds like good clean fun," Shanon replied, giving Sami a disdainful look.

Del looked at the three. "I've got a better idea. We need to figure out what the human lice in this ship are up to. I think we can use these internal conduits to check up on our playmates and TJ. They run the length of the ship. If we do careful slow-sneaks, they won't even know we're here."

Del motioned with one hand. "Shanon and I go forward. Nase, Sami, head aft and poke around. We'll meet back here." He pointed to a plate on the bulkhead. "Okay, we're at Main Conduit, Bulkhead 36 Starboard side. This is base-point until we find something better."

Sami glanced at Del. "What if we can jump a

couple of these *banditos* and take them out of action?"

Del chewed his lip. Sami's question had merit. The scouts hadn't hidden in the ship for the ride; they were going to have to make a move against the poachers sooner or later. Sometime in the near future there would have to be a showdown with the renegades, perhaps a violent one. But first they had to know more about the poachers and especially about TJ.

Del shook his head. "Not yet. We need information. Especially about TJ. She's our primary concern. No heroics. No rough stuff until we know the odds and nothing that would possibly get TJ hurt. Understood?"

"Spoilsport," Sami replied surly, but nodded in agreement as did the others. "Let's go," Del said, as Nase and Sami scooted off towards the ship's aft section where the engineering spaces lay. Shanon rolled to her hands and knees and joined Del in crawling forward.

Every few meters, the metal channels had small, slatted ventilation openings. Though their observation holes would be small, making for limited visibility into a compartment, Del's hopes were that they could move silently through the conduit system and spy on their kidnappers.

Ten minutes later, having crawled through most of the forward part of the ship, Del and Shanon heard voices coming through the next ventilation grill. Easing his head over the grating, Del peered through the slits and saw the head and shoulders of the young woman called Bianca. She stood in the center of what looked like the ship's medical infirmary speaking to someone, but Del could barely make out her words.

"She'll still be out when we rendezvous. That's good. Easier to ship her across. Go aft, and tell Mula to check the sedation drip on the Garther Ape. Make sure the dosage is right. One cc per hundred kilograms. Remember, too much and you'll kill the beast. Too little and it'll go on a rampage when it wakes up, and I'm not sure the stex-glass will hold it. I'll be forward in nav-plot."

Someone mumbled assent and Del saw a shadow cross the room to the hatchway. He wasn't sure but he thought it was the poacher named Mitch. A few seconds later, Bianca followed the male poacher out the hatch into the passageway. Turning to Shanon,

Del signed to stay put for a few minutes. Shanon nodded yes.

After several minutes of patient waiting and listening, and hearing nothing from the small space below, Del gingerly opened the entry hatch. He poked his head through the ceiling and peered into the tiny dispensary. Against the far right bulkhead lay a sleeping Tala on a narrow ship's bunk.

Del pulled his feet under him and quietly dropped to the sickbay floor. He crept over to TJ, keeping a watch on the door. Her blond hair partially hid a flesh-colored medico-bandage over her forehead. Her round face with its almond-colored cheeks and slightly upturned nose didn't seem to have any other wounds. Her breathing was light and normal as if she were asleep. Following the basic first-aid techniques taught to the scouts, Del looked for other injuries but found none.

Del rapidly checked out the tiny infirmaries equipment and medicines and let out a deep sigh. It would have to do for now. Giving his friend's hand a last pat in parting, Del slid over the floor, making the barest of noises, stepped up to stand on the edge of a small desk, and reached up to grab Shanon's outstretched hands.

Bracing her feet against the sides of the hatch, Shanon leveraged Del far enough up that he was able to grab the lip of the conduit and pull himself in. "Well?" Shanon demanded in a whisper.

"No good, Shanon," Del whispered back, "There isn't any way we're going to bring her around any time soon. Looks like she's in a stun-gun coma." He stopped for a moment, "TJ will have to sleep it off, let her nervous system reset itself."

"We can't leave her!" Shanon hissed.

Del shook his head, "Shanon, think about it. That little sickbay is strictly for the simplest of medical needs. We need a medical facility with neural-synoptic restorers and nerve fiber regeneration medicines and we certainly can't drag her through these conduits."

He reached out and squeezed Shanon's arm, "She's safer and better off in the dispensary for now. And it looks like they're taking care of her." Shanon's look said she wasn't entirely buying into Del's argument, but finally she shrugged and gave the ok sign. Re-seating the access hatch, Del and Shanon continued crawling forward, peering and listening through each of the ventilation slits they came across. But each space they looked into was silent and empty.

Since the ship was fairly small they soon reached the most forward part of the ship, which housed the piloting and navigation spaces. Looking through the small lattice of the overhead vent, Del could see that this was the astro-bridge, from where ship's captain piloted the vessel. Off to one side he could barely make out Bianca's form reclining in one of the grav-cushion seats. She seemed to be monitoring the pilot's console.

For long minutes, Del and Shanon crouched in the ventilation duct above the poacher, waiting for something to happen. Finally, the female renegade got up from her chair and walked across the oval room and then out the hatch, leaving the room empty.

As Bianca rose, Del had a better view of the young woman. She had a tanned complexion, with chin-length lightly brown hair parted in the middle. Her lithe body suggested she was athletic by nature and her crisp movements indicated she was confident and professional in her abilities.

Del figuratively scratched his head. The young

woman did not exactly meet his mental picture of a renegade poacher.

For a few more minutes the two scouts sat in the semi dark watching and waiting. The temptation to unseat the access hatch and explore the instrumented room grated at Del as he thought that maybe he could learn the ship's destination and when it would get there. But he had seen Bianca lock down the console before she left and he knew that without the pre-set computer code he wouldn't be able to access the navigation plot console.

Finally recognizing that there was nothing for them to gain here, he signed to Shanon to return to aft. Squeezing through the narrow spaces, the two slowly made their way back to their rendezvous point where Nase and Sami waited.

"What did you find?" Del asked.

"Got to engineering, no one in the spaces, must be on full-automatic. In between are cargo spaces. Might be where they've stashed the XTs but couldn't really see inside very well," Sami began, "Heard two of our low-lifes talking in one cargo hold but couldn't see them or make out their words. Maybe something about port call on Evon 2. Nothing useful. That's it.

You?"

"Saw TJ," Del answered. "Still out but okay. Overheard the Bianca female talk about a rendezvous. Think it must be a spacer-to-spacer linkup for transfer of the XTs. Sounds like they plan to trans-ship TJ, too. And I think the get-together is going to be pretty soon."

"Hit'em now before they link up!" Sami adamantly stated.

Del was thinking exactly that as he and Shanon retreated to the rally point. It made sense. The poachers would be preoccupied with navigational needs to match orbits and then with the cargo trans-shipment. And, they would be separated from each other, maybe even working alone.

He looked around and observed, "If we can pick them off one by one, capture the ship, we could get on the ship's communicator and alert the authorities. Since the ship isn't going into hyperspace, it could be easily found by the inter-system patrol."

The three nodded in agreement. "Okay," Del sighed. "We'll strike just after they begin their approach to the other ship. Our cue will be when they start maneuvering. They're probably going to do some deceleration and vectoring. That should keep them busy while we make our move."

He thought for a few more moments and said, "When the time comes, Sami and Nase, you'll go forward and grab TJ. Shanon and I will try to ambush one or two of the poachers and then head for the astro-bridge. Somehow we'll have to force one of them to pilot this rig for us or it might be a short ride to nowhere. Especially if their inbound friends catch up with us and try to board."

"Maybe we should try to find their armory now and grab their weapons." Shanon suggested.

Del thought that was a good idea and was about to say so when Nase interjected, "No good, saw what looked like the armory. Empty. Think they're still totin' their hardware."

At that Del raised his head to look at Nase. He hadn't seen Bianca carrying a weapon, but he'd only had a really good look at her head and shoulders. "Are you sure it was the armory?" he asked.

Nase shrugged his shoulders and said, "Weapon racks. Empty. Re-charger packs still operating. Weapon repair kit out on a console bench. But no weapons."

"Interesting," Del mused. "No weapons in the armory of a poacher's ship. Wonder why. There's no reason to carry charged weapons on your own ship."

"Check," Sami replied, "Doesn't make sense. It's silly to carry that stuff around. What are they gonna zap out here? A meteorite? One discharge from a laz or d-gun on the right setting, you've got a hole in the ship and you're pumpin' oxygen into deep space. Not to mention you'd soon be breathing some of the thin stuff yourself."

"Both are fairly powerful energy weapons," said Shanon. "They say you really mean business. Remember what the ScoutMaster used to say, *the threat determines the weapon and the weapon determines the threat.*

"You carry a weapon to counter a specific danger. But sometimes you think that the menace is bigger than it really is. The proverbial bogeyman takes on outrageous proportions. What are they frightened of?"

They looked at each other, before Del said, "Do you think they know we're aboard?"

Shanon shook her head, "Even if they did, I doubt our knives pose much of threat."

"Each other." Sami said firmly. "No love lost between *banditos*. Sleep with one eye open and one hand on the fire button."

For a long moment there was silence while each considered the question. Finally Nase spoke. "Perhaps. But I don't think so. Not from the way they acted. And if they thought we were aboard, I don't think they would allow us to go crawling through these overheads. I think we've got a mongoose-and-cobra scenario."

Sami practically sneered in reply. "All right, my genius friend—what exactly does that mean? Haven't seen any mongooses, uh, mongeeses—whatever, on this grungy bucket, or cobras either."

Shaking his head as if exasperated with Sami's choice of words, Nase patiently explained, "Cobras and mongoose are adversarial predators . . . venom versus razor-sharp teeth, striking distance versus lightning speed. Offsetting weapons based on enemy abilities.

"If the poachers know that we are aboard, then they know who and what we are. They would know our weapons are nonexistent, and our technical abilities on a space vessel extremely limited. In practical terms we are neither cobras nor mongoose in comparison to their abilities."

Obviously irritated at Nase's patronizing tone, Sami retorted, "You know, you really surprise me . . . for a high-falootin' blue-blood you sure got a lot of trivia packed in that rich kid's head of yours."

Nase's eyes grew hard. "Listen. Who and what I am is nobody's business but my own and it's especially not *your* business. Got it, amigo?"

Sami leaned toward Nase, his own face tight, jaw clenched, "Oh yeah? Maybe I make it my business . . . you . . . "

Del looked from Nase to Sami, surprised not only by the sudden flare of temper between the two, but also by Nase's scathing reply. He had never seen Nase so close to losing his composure. There was a real tension between these two that he hadn't seen till now . . . and one that he needed to watch or it could blow up in his face and drastically hurt the team's ability to function properly.

He looked over at Shanon who returned his look with wide eyes; this had caught her off-guard as well. "Enough," Del said firmly, "We've got more important things to consider than who's who or what." He reached out and pulled Nase around. "Go on with what you were saying."

Giving Sami a curt look, Nase continued, "In simple terms, they're not wearing weapons because of our threat; they're wearing weapons because of another, greater threat."

With a start Del remembered the conversation between Bianca and her poacher companion. *Check the sedation drip on the Garther Ape—too little and it'll go on a rampage.* Del quickly grasped Nase's point. "They're armed to the teeth because they think they have a cobra aboard!"

Nase gave Del a thumbs up as Sami said, "Huh? You mean they're out-shipping a cobra? But why carry a d-gun for a cobra?"

"No, no." Del furiously answered. He chopped the air with one hand. "Not a literal cobra—they've got something on board that's so dangerous that they're willing to take a chance on a d-gun discharge in a small ship."

Shanon snapped her fingers. "You mean one of the XT's in the cargo holds?"

"Exactly," Del said and repeated the conversation he'd heard between Bianca and the unseen poacher.

"Okay, so what the heck is a Garther Ape?" Sami asked.

There was a long moment of silence as they each tried to remember if a Garther Ape was one of the numerous species taught in Instructor Smythe's XT Identification and Characteristics class. As Del saw the stumped looks on their faces, he knew that they had drawn a blank. Either it was a species whose characteristics they'd forgotten, or it hadn't been taught in class, or more likely it was a totally new species to them. Which was entirely possible, considering that StarScout Command daily added an average of ten new species to the Galactic Extraterrestrial Encyclopedia.

Del shook his head slightly in frustration. There were just too many species to learn! Even if he and his teammates did nothing but study extraterrestrials all their waking moments, there were too many to memorize even in one lifetime.

When humankind finally burst the bounds of Father Sol's planetary system, one of the great exploratory surprises was the immense wealth of life Out There. Just in the small sphere of explored space that the Terran Confederation claimed there existed literally thousands of new species of alien life-forms. Most of the known star creatures were benevolent to humans, but others evoked a virtual instantaneous enmity. Some of the discovered star creatures were deadlier and more vicious than any known Terran predator.

The Garther Ape could be one of those murderous alien predators – and the d-guns that the poachers carried were their counter to the beast.

There had been one other surprise in humankind's venture into Deep Space, and one that was beginning to become a deep disappointment. During the initial decades of exploration, among all the hundreds of star systems visited and the myriads of planets where humans had trod, not once had Homo Sapiens met Alpha Prime. Humankind had found life among the stars, but not one species whose intelligence scale matched or surpassed his own.

However, there were faint whispers of other civilized societies. The massive hive-like ruins of Anthor Bay, and the wispy, curling Towers of Numercon that seemed to exist in an ethereal other world. But they were the only two pieces of evidence of long-vanished civilizations. At least in this corner of the galaxy, as an intelligent race of beings, humans appeared to be alone.

No extraterrestrials to make First Contact with. No alien star cities to explore, no advanced new technologies to learn, no larger-than-life alien starships moving through interstellar space, no Galactic Empire for humans to join. But that hadn't stopped the star rovers of Terra. The galaxy was wide and deep. It would take literally thousands of years to explore just the spiral arm of the galactic Milky Way to which Terra belonged. Sooner or later Alpha Prime would be found.

But right now Del and his fellow scouts, future world discoverers in their own right, had a smaller problem than exploring the galaxy. Their world was now the confines of the small space cruiser that apparently carried a deadly alien creature, of which they had exactly zero knowledge.

Sami eyed Del, "Obviously we four don't know what a Garther Ape is. But why do I have this idea that you want us to go out and give this thing the once-over?"

"You're right. We're going to because we need to." Del paused for a second. "Look, it makes sense that we find out what a Garther Ape is, just in case something goes wrong and it escapes. Besides, this is what you wanted to do, remember? To explore new worlds, see exotic creatures . . ."

Sami let out a deep breath. "Okay, okay. Hold the propaganda please. I already signed up. What's your plan?"

"Easy. You and Shanon hightail it forward and hide in the duct above the infirmary. I want you there in case the poachers start to match in with the incoming ship. If they do, lock yourself in sick bay. I'll contact you over the comms with instructions. If I don't, chain-of-command succession procedures are in effect and Shanon becomes TL."

Del thought for a second. "Nase and I will do the search. We probably can't reach all of the cargo holds through the main duct and the cross-ship conduits are too small for us to slide through. One of us will have to do a sneak through the corridors but that's a chance we have to take."

The three nodded in agreement. Del ordered, "Okay, let's do it. Scouts Out."

Del remembered the three small cargo spaces that he'd seen when they first came on the ship. The ape probably wouldn't be there. If he were bossing the ship and its crew, he'd have the dangerous creature in the furthermost recesses of the ship, away from the living quarters, astro-bridge and similar spaces where the ship's crew spent most of their time.

With that in mind, he and Nase headed aft toward the engineering spaces. From Sami and Nase's report, the larger cargo holds were back there, and it was those compartments Del wanted to get a close look at. In one of them he figured to find the alien beast that posed such a deadly problem to the renegade crew and now to his JS team.

Del and Nase had just finished navigating a tight squeeze in the conduit caused by some bulky machinery when Nase reached out and touched Del's shoulder. Pointing ahead, Nase signed that there was an upcoming ventilation grille that opened to a cargo hold. Del signed his understanding and cautiously moved forward to peer through the metal slotted opening.

Del couldn't tell if the cargo hold was empty or not, but it was as good a place to start the search as any. Reaching down, he undid the seating mechanism of the hatch, swung it away and poked his head out into the compartment. A small extraterrestrial creature lay wrapped in a small stex-glass chamber in the far corner of the cubicle. Jutting his legs through the access hatch, Del pushed himself through the conduit opening and dropped cat-like to the metal deck.

Del looked up at Nase's face framed in the hatch and signed he was okay. He quietly walked over to the XT. As he peered intently at the creature through the slightly shimmering curves of the stex-glass that encased it, Del immediately recognized a Splena Cat of Durbon 2.

Del's eyebrows rose as he looked at the rainbow-colored marsupial. Odd, he thought. A Splena Cat was a common mammal whose chief virtue was that they readily adapted to Terran temperate and tropical environments. While exotic in that the cat came from a far-off star system, he wasn't aware of any other distinguishing features that would make them worth a XT-poacher's time.

Del bit his lower lip in thought. It didn't make sense for these renegades to be transporting a Splena Cat. Unless—unless they were using it in some fashion to cover their real activities. Del shook his head in bewilderment. Too many pieces of the puzzle were missing, and he didn't have time to try and figure them all out. Not now anyway. There was a more important piece of the puzzle they had to find— the Garther Ape. *[language? sygnols? All these signs, is it like sign]*

Leaving the cat to sleep peacefully, Del signed to Nase that he was going out the hatch. Nase was to stay put in case Del needed help. Del crossed over to the hatch and placed his ear to the metal door to listen. When he heard nothing he pressed the access button and watched as the hatch recessed into the bulkhead. He hoped that the hatch door wasn't tied to some shipboard monitoring system. If it were, Del would soon have unwelcome company.

Del poked his head out through the hatch and scanned the short transverse passageway. It was empty. As he stepped out, he pressed the button to reseal the cargo hold behind him and swiftly moved to the opposite side where another hatchway indicated a second cargo space.

Del opened the hatch; saw that the compartment's deck had thick white padding covering it. He stepped in — only to jump back out just as fast. Coiled near the door was a giant Alger Python. With a quick swat, Del hit the hatch-door close button, Del looked around, fearful that his noisy exit might have alerted the poachers.

He listened intently but heard nothing as he walked down the corridor and turned the corner. At the far end of a small lateral passageway, he could see another hatchway. Del assumed it would open into another cargo hold. He would go a little slower on this one as he was a bit shaken from his brush with the huge python. His assumption that any XT he found would be unconscious and restrained by stex-glass enclosures was obviously wrong.

Alger's Python was a misnomer as the creature was not a true snake in terms of a Terran reptile. In biological category it was more like a giant worm. It had the unsavory characteristic of seizing its prey, wrapping its coils around the unfortunate creature and then, through pores in its body, oozing out a tissue-melting fluid that literally dissolved its still alive and struggling victim. The worm then fed on the liquefied remains of its prey.

Upon reaching this new hatch, Del stood to one side with his field knife out as he pressed the release button, his hand poised above the button to quickly re-press. As the hatch door slid open, Del could feel a gentle puff of air on his face. The atmospheric pressure inside the cubicle was set slightly higher than in the rest of the ship. Seeing nothing immediately in front of him, Del cautiously looked in. His eyes widened as he looked at the sleeping creature held in the stex-glass cubicle. The small tubing leading from the intra-venous machine into the creature's lower leg convinced Del that this was almost certainly the Garther Ape.

Coming closer, Del sucked in his breath. He knew this creature! The brown shaggy hair, the huge accordion-like ears jutting out from its head; it was the XT the junior scouts had tracked in the Amazonia Preserve on Terra!

Chapter 10

Attack of the Garther Ape

Del edged next to the stex-glass enclosure, carefully examining the star beast and getting as close a look at the creature as he could. He didn't know how much time he had before the poachers returned. Del assumed that they would be checking the deep-space animal frequently.

The large, sculpted muscles and sinews in torso, arms and legs indicated that its home planet had a surface gravity greater than Earth's, hence the need for the large skeletal frame. That would make it extremely fast and agile on a one-g world such as Terra, or on this ship for that matter.

Without seeing the star creature in its natural habitat, Del had absolutely no idea what purpose the large ears served. Maybe they were for hearing, maybe not. If they were for hearing, the creature would be supersensitive to sound. And the frequency spectrum at which it heard sounds might be greater than that of any Terran animal.

As he inspected the further, Del spied something about its elongated paws that made him look closer. At first Del had thought that the beast's paws were ape-like in appearance, but as he pressed his face against the stex-glass to get a better look, he noticed that there was something odd about its hands. But try as he might, the slight distortion from the curve of the stex-glass prevented him from clearly seeing into the cubicle. He needed to get a better look at the creature!

Frustrated, Del stepped back and thought for a moment. He could raise the curved cover and examine the creature, but that might alert the poachers. He looked around but couldn't see anything that indicated the poachers had the pod-lid wired to alert the crew if it were opened. Del decided to take the chance and open the pod. It was the only way he could see the star animal up close.

The young scout reached over to the control panel and pressed the button that raised the pod lid. Silently, the curved panel popped up and away. A tiny acrid smell wafted up from the chamber; obviously the creature's home world atmosphere contained just a hint of ammonia.

Del bent over and gingerly touched the creature's hairy hand nearest him. The hair was coarse and rough, the filaments large but fairly short. The top portion of the hand felt fairly soft, but Del could feel a steely hardness in the long slender fingers. As he turned the hand over, his beating heart quickened its pace. Within each finger was an embedded, recessed claw. Del could see that this was no ordinary claw. It was obsidian black, sharper and more finely pointed than anything Del had ever seen on a living creature.

It was a cruel slashing weapon that could maim or kill in one blow.

Del glanced upward at the stex-glass. Fine, deeply etched scratch marks serrated the lid . . . scratches that could only have been made from the inside. And it was apparent what had made them. At some point this creature clawed the glass, leaving the almost invisible, finely carved lines.

Del was genuinely amazed. Stex-glass was the normal choice for XT carry-alls because of its tensile strength features. Del couldn't believe that something organic, like the creature's claw, was stronger. But with the scratches on the glass clearly visible, the evidence was unmistakable that this creature had the strength and means to slice super-hardened stex-glass.

Similar to a Terran cat, the creature's claws retracted, which gave it the advantage of being able to grasp things without tearing, and of moving silently on surfaces where an unsheathed claw would make noises. Del gingerly raised the mouth lip folds and found what he expected. Cruel, half-recessed long fangs, which swung forward from a hinged jaw as they sank into prey.

Del rocked back and let out a breath, making a small whoosh sound in the hold. Incredibly fast on the attack, claws so sharp that they would rip through organic tissue like a razor-gun through sim-butter, and deadly fangs that could sink through several centimeters of hardwood. If this thing had half a brain, Del thought to himself, this beastie would be the stuff of StarScout nightmares.

Then another thought struck him and he scowled darkly. This was an extraordinarily dangerous beast. Why were he and his team sent up against something like this with only long-knives! Together the five of them probably wouldn't have stood for ten seconds against the likes of this. Del ran his hands through his hair. This didn't make sense. He and his fellow junior scouts had faced deadly life-forms before, but nothing anywhere close to the sheer lethality of this thing.

It almost looked like the poachers had done the junior scouts a favor. If they had really closed on this thing back in the jungle—Del hated to think what might have happened. As it was, they could thank their lucky stars that TJ was still alive. After all, she had gotten close enough to the beast to cam-cord . . .

and that appeared to be way too close.

Well, Del thought, what now? For a moment, he fingered his field knife. One well-placed stroke and the threat would be over. But, a dead beast from a cutting blade would be a clear advertisement that someone else was on the ship. The poachers would turn the ship upside down looking for them.

Del fingered his knife again and raised it slightly. Just as he did so, the words of the Scout Oath came to mind . . . *On whatever star paths I stride and worlds that I visit, I will respect the sanctity of life, taking life only in the defense of my own or those I am responsible for* . . .

The knife hung suspended in mid-air before Del finally brought it down and slipped it back into his scabbard. It wasn't just the Oath; Del had a natural aversion to destroying life without just cause. And though this beast presented danger, he could not bring himself to kill it in its unconscious condition. Del took his hand off his knife scabbard and stepped back. He would let the creature live. He knew it was a decision he might later regret, but for now it was the right choice.

Del reached up to close the XT's sleep-chamber. As

he brought the curved panel down, a sharp horn blast from the ship's intercom shattered the silence. Startled, Del lost his his grip on the hinged plas-door. Before he could recover, the door slammed hard into its locking mechanism.

A loud voice said, "All hands. Stand by for space dock and transfer. Man your stations!"

Del snapped his head up. The poachers were maneuvering their ship for the linkup with their comrades. Soon they would be down in the XT cargo holds transferring their ill-gained catches to the other poacher ship. It was time for the scouts to make their move against the renegades.

Del took one last look at the sleeping star-beast before rushing out of the compartment. He closed the hatch behind him, and retraced his steps through the corridors to the first cargo space. As he entered the compartment, someone tackled him hard. For the briefest of moments he and Nase wrestled trying to get a sleep-hold on each other before finally realizing who their opponent was.

As they let go of each other, Del was about explain what he had found when his communicator keyed open, "TL, this is Rescue 1 and we got a big problem,"

Sami whispered.

"Go ahead," Del replied.

"She's gone! TJ's not in the infirmary!"

"Say again!"

"Open your ears! I said TJ's not in sickbay. When we dropped into the dispensary we found her bed empty. They've moved her and we don't know where!"

He turned to Nase, "They must have moved TJ in just the last few minutes. But why? The linkup with the other ship can't be complete! We've only had two small maneuvering episodes! Surely that couldn't be all!"

They stared at each other before Nase snapped his fingers, "The other ship Del!"

Del pounded a hand on his thigh. "Of course! They did the bulk of the piloting! And that means they have the ship-to-ship trans-link established!" Del was not a swearing person, but right then he felt a few expletives were in order. One part of his mind admired the superlative piloting job of the poachers. It was first-class astro-navigating to maneuver two ships together with so little vectoring.

They had not foreseen this and now their plans were in shreds. Del keyed his communicator. "Sami,

Shanon, back to the conduit. Meet us at the main passageway T-section where it meets the air-lock corridor. They've dealt us a new hand and we need to relook the cards."

"On our way."

Del grabbed Nase and boosted the slender scout up the access hatch. Nase helped pull Del up into the conduit. A few minutes later, the four scouts met at the T-juncture where a small transverse conduit ran above the corridor leading to the air-lock.

Del hurriedly whispered a description of the Garther Ape and then said, "They must have taken TJ over to the other ship. Looks like we have two options. We can jump them here, while they're occupied with transferring cargo. Same deal, take over this ship and put it on a tangent back to Earth, and notify the authorities. It means we'd have to leave TJ on that other ship and hope the Confederation Navy can intercept them before they boost into hyperspace.

"Or, we can try to sneak across to the other ship and try to jump them there. But we'll probably be dealing with at least double the number of poachers." The four junior scouts exchanged glances. Their chances against armed and hostile poachers were somewhere between none and zero. But still, that was TJ, their teammate, over there in the hands of very bad and unpredictable outlaws.

In hesitant tones, Sami said, "If the poachers had me over there, I'd want you guys to bug out. Get away safe and sound and alert the authorities. But since I'm not over there, my vote is to get TJ. I don't like the idea of bustin' up the gang." He looked around and snarled, "For no other reason than to get mission complete from the ISs . . . which we have to do as a team!"

Del looked at Sami and smiled. For Sami that was quite a noble speech. He looked at Nase and Shanon. "The same?" he asked. They nodded and Del whispered, "Okay, it's unanimous. Another charge of the Light Brigade. Let's go."

"Light Brigade?" Sami asked, "What the heck is a Light Brigade? Dolkien's Brigade, Mouftasa's Conger Brigade I know, but Light Brigade?"

"Later Sami, I'll explain later . . ." Shanon tiredly replied and reached over to help Del lift the access hatch. Del pulled up the hatch, squeezed through the portal, hit the deck, rolled, and was up in the High

Ka-Ra-Te attack stance, his knife drawn.

The corridor was empty.

Shanon landed almost next to him, rolled, and came up in the same position. She put her spine to Del's back, forming a two-person defensive box. In succession, Nase and Sami landed on the metal deckplates, their knives drawn.

With the main corridor empty, Del trotted over to the smaller passageway that led to the air-lock and peeked around the corner. The inner and outer airlock hatchway doors were open and unguarded. Del was looking down a long, gray, airtight tube that was attached to the side of the ship and covered the open portal. It was the trans-ship shaft that linked the two ships.

Shanon craned her neck around the corner and surveyed the situation. "Almost too easy, don't you think?" Del took a deep breath. He too hadn't expected the gate to be open and unlocked.

Del motioned for Sami and Nase to stay put and scout-signed for Shanon to follow. Half-trotting, they entered the plas-sylcron man-sized tube and sprinted to the other side. As they entered the access corridor of the other ship, Del immediately guessed from the size of the corridors and the feel of the ship that this was a much, much larger vessel than the one they had just left. It was quiet but there was a distinct humming in the background.

Del keyed his comms-link, "Sami, Nase. Hustle up. It's clear."

Seconds later, the two burst through the tubing's open end and skidded to a halt next to Del. "What now?" Sami asked.

Del looked at the ceiling to see if this ship had the same conduits that served them so well in the other craft. Not seeing an access hatch, he said, "Stick together, and see if we can find a hidey-hole."

With Del leading and Nase as rear guard, the four edged down the passageway towards a T-intersection with a larger corridor. They were just a few meters from the intersection when they heard pounding footsteps and shouting coming from the other ship. In seconds, whoever was making the frantic noise would be upon them. Del spun around trying to see a hatch that hopefully led to an empty compartment. There were none. However, just a short distance ahead there was a cutout in the passageway that contained large heavy machinery sitting on the deck-plates. Del had no idea what the machinery was, but it was just large enough for them to hide behind.

"There!" He whispered and pointed to the bulky, chromium-plated implement. "Get behind it!" With a quick dash down the corridor, the four scouts literally dove behind the machinery and flattened themselves on the dull-gray metallic floor. Moments later, Del heard shouting and dared to peek out from behind one edge of the metallic wall.

One of the poachers half-pulled, half-dragged another poacher into the corridor. From the blood stains covering his tunic coveralls, it was obvious that the second renegade was badly hurt. Just then, Bianca and two other poachers came around the intersection.

"What happened?" Bianca shouted at the poacher who supported the injured man.

"It's out of the cargo compartment! Ripped Mitch up and I think it got Mula!"

"The I V-sedation! Didn't you have it hooked up?" One of the other renegades asked. Del had the impression that this man was one of the crewmen on the new ship.

"We did!" the poacher yelled back. "But Mitch said

that when he and Mula went to check, the needle-tubing going into the stasis compartment was pulled out. They were trying to reattach it when the beast ripped open the pod. Slashed poor Mitch here and chased Mula out of the cargo-hold. The only reason I knew the thing was loose was from the most gosh-awful blood-curdling screams I've ever heard. From Mula. I'll never forget those terrible sounds for as long as I'll live."

Del squirmed slightly sideways to get a little better look at the poachers. Didn't take a whole lot of guessing to know what *thing* meant. The Garther Ape was loose on the other ship!

"Get him to sick bay!" Bianca commanded, and then turned to the other poachers.

"Let's go!" she said. "We'll split up when we get to the other side."

"Hold it," said a new voice, "What're you planning?"

"To capture the ape of course!" There was a brief moment of silence and then the crewman of the new ship said, "Bianca, you know what it takes to stun one of these things. You were awfully fortunate the first time. Let's cut our losses and just d-gun it before it kills someone else!"

"Are you out of your mind?" Bianca practically screamed. "Don't you know what that thing is worth? One G-Ape on the Artron Market is worth a hundred times what we can get for all of the rest of our flea-bitten XTs! I'm not going to give it up!"

"Now look, Bianca," the man started, but before he could finish, another poacher screamed, "It's coming across the tube!"

Del heard shouting as the small group of poachers started scrambling wildly to get away from the shaft portal. Amidst the shouting came the characteristic *ping-ping* sound of stun guns going off, but only a from a few while the rest of the poachers got out of the creature's way. As the renegades rushed back down the other transverse corridor, Del leaned his head out to look. What he saw made him instantly jerk his head back.

The Garther Ape was half-standing, half-squatting in the corridor, its head pitched forward with ears cupped open. If the stun-gun emissions had hit the creature, there was little if any effect. And there wasn't a poacher in sight, all of them having dashed to the forward part of the ship.

Del leaned back against the wall and signed to his companions what was happening and for them to be completely silent. They gripped their long-knives a little tighter and tried to get their legs underneath them in case they had to spring up to attack.

Del dared not poke his head out to look, though he desperately wanted to see what the creature was doing. For the moment this was to be a listening game. In the silence of the corridor Del strained with every ounce of his being to shut out all other sounds and listen just for the ape. Del could almost feel the deathly quiet as if it were a physical thing pressing down on him. It seemed as if the whole ship was waiting and listening.

He wondered why the poachers hadn't come back with their stunners or even d-guns to take on the Garther Ape. Del closed his eyes, tried to hear where the beast was, and tried to somehow reach out with his consciousness to feel the creature's presence. Something told him that the thing had stopped in the intersection and was just sitting. Listening.

Del thought of the ape's huge ears . . . maybe it could hear his prey's heartbeat! If that were so, Del thought, the ape could certainly hear his thudding heart. Del snapped his head to the right as he heard the tiniest of sounds, like a claw tapping on metal. Then he heard it again . . . nearer to the four nervous youth! Was the ape edging closer to the crouching scouts before springing on them?

The sound came again. Closer.

Del looked at his field knife, and turned it over to grasp the bladed end. Many practice hours of hand-throwing this knife might pay off now.

The tapping was barely a meter away . . .

He glanced over at his teammates and signed what he was going to do. He would leap up and throw the knife, aiming for one of the beast's eyes. If his aim was true, then the other scouts were to try and finish off the ape with their own knives.

Del modified his grip slightly on the knife to get a better hold. He took a deep breath, leaped out into the corridor, drew back his arm to throw . . . and stopped.

The corridor was empty! The Garther Ape was gone! *how did he drop?*

Del dropped into a fighting stance, and crouched low while his teammates gathered on each side of the machinery. Del listened intently but couldn't hear anything except for the slight sounds of their muffled movements.

After waiting a few moments, Del slipped forward and jutted his head into the main corridor. It was empty both ways! He waved his ~~the~~ team forward and they briefly huddled together. "What do we do now?" Shanon quietly asked. Del jerked his head toward other ship. "It's probably empty, or maybe only has one or two poachers. We can still take it over and boost away. Or, using the ape as a distraction, we may be able to find TJ and then get back."

From the looks in their eyes, Del could see that his teammates didn't think much of his first suggestion. "Okay," he contritely said. "We find TJ and worry later about getting away."

"What about the ape?" Shanon half-demanded. Del shook his head. "We avoid it and the poachers. They were made for each other . . . we use it as the diversion we need to find Tala."

"Which way do you think it went?" Sami asked.

Del and the others paced the deck for a short distance but couldn't find any evidence of the ape's direction of travel. There were bloodstains on the metal deck from the bleeding poacher that led forward, but that didn't necessarily mean the star-ape had followed.

In the past, Del's hunches usually paid off, and he had a feeling now of where the creature had gone. Pointing down at the blood, he said, "You three follow the blood trail forward. It should lead to the dispensary. It'll take one of you to carry TJ and the other two to provide overwatch. "

For a moment he eyed the others and then continued, "If this is a typical cargo-type ship, the sickbay is forward, with the living spaces and astro-navigation as well. Try to use a side corridor off the main way. Might reduce the chance of running into the poachers.

"Find the infirmary and TJ. Hole up there. I'm going aft. We need to know what's to our rear. I'll trans you if I find anything. Keep off the comms unless it's important. The LifeSensor is going to be practically useless with all this metal around, but try it anyway. Might get lucky. Got it?"

Nase and Sami soberly nodded and with a half-wave moved off. Shanon hesitated, shaking her head and giving Del a clearly quizzical look that said, *What are you up to?* She frowned, reached out and touched his arm. "TL, this is not a good decision. You can't go up against that thing alone."

Del wet his lips, as he replied, "I don't have a death wish and I'm not trying to be a hero. But, we've got to keep tabs on it, especially with TJ down and out. I'll be okay. Now, you have a job to do, and so do I. Scout's Out." Del gave her a small crooked smile in parting and lightly pushed her towards the waiting Nase and Sami.

Del turned towards the aft corridor, half-laughing to himself. He hadn't fooled Shanon one bit. She knew that he thought the G-Ape had gone aft, and was sending his team forward toward the lesser of two dangers. He gripped his weapon deftly and shifted the knife handle as he edged closer to the bulkhead. He cautiously began making his way down the quiet corridor.

As he slipped down the passageway, he thought how ludicrous this had become. He joined the StarScout program to search out new life on exotic planets, not to go skulking about in a poacher's ship trying to find an XT! And a highly dangerous alien at that. Getting his mind back to business, Del crept further down the corridor. He still didn't understand why the poachers hadn't come back. But now they were a secondary worry.

Del passed several hatches but since they were sealed, he ignored them as he didn't think the star beast had the intelligence to figure out how to open a security-coded door. He knew that in a typical space freighter the main cargo holds and engineering spaces aft would have lots of nooks, crannies, and closed spaces for the ape to hide in, waiting to pounce on its unfortunate prey.

Coming to an intersection, Del cautiously poked his head around the corner and looked both ways. Empty. Something caught his eye at one end of the transverse passageway; a ship's turbo-elevator doorway.

Del immediately understood. This ship was split into two or more levels aft. The lower level was almost certainly engineering spaces, the upper for cargo. Del stared at the control panel for the elevator for a moment and then turned back. He was quite positive the ape couldn't operate the controls for the elevator, simple though they were, and therefore he wouldn't have gone to the engineering spaces on the lowest level.

That left the cargo spaces, which probably began just ahead.

A noise made him immediately stop and crouch against the wall. It came from further down the corridor but he could see the passageway was empty all the way to the next closed hatch. There must be an open hatchway ahead that led to a compartment, and something was in the cubicle making noise. Del hoped it was a poacher, but something told him that it wasn't a human being.

Del lightly chewed on his lower lip and brought out his LifeSensor. The display panel showed the right frequency level but the indicator panel was dark. He was quite sure that the specialized, super-hard and condensed metals of the ship were blocking the creature's signature frequency.

Del edged toward the open hatch. He knelt as low as he could and looked around the corner into the cubicle. From the huge size of the compartment, Del guessed it was the main cargo hold, full of unrecognizable pieces of machinery and stacked plas-containers. From the looks of things, the poachers used the guise of legal star traders to cover their illegal XT poaching and transporting.

Del considered his next move. If the Garther Ape was really inside, he could simply reach up and close the hatch door, trapping the star creature inside. But, having not actually seen the beast in the compartment, and with the LS still silent, Del didn't know for sure that the predator was inside. If he waited outside, then he placed himself in a very vulnerable position—discovery by the poachers, or worse, the thing could charge through the door unexpectedly and catch Del unaware. Del remembered very well how quietly and rapidly the ape moved in the corridor.

Del leaned against the smooth bulkhead. Beads of sweat dotted his forehead. He licked his lips as he recalled his harrowing experience with the stalker in the preserve. He looked over his shoulder into the huge compartment, and thought, *not again.*

Del wiped his brow with his sleeve and crept around the edge of the hatch and into the cargo hold. He decided to leave the compartment door open since he might need to make a quick exit and didn't want his escape route blocked. As he moved stealthily next to the bulkhead wall, Del used several stacks of shipping containers to mask his movement. He stopped every few meters to listen and had reached the corner of the compartment when two sounds made him stop.

Behind him came the unmistakable sound of the hatchway closing shut. And, almost immediately after from the center of the cargo hold came the unmistakable scratching sounds of sharp talons on metal.

Del had no illusion about the latter sounds. It was the Garther Ape. He looked at his LS, saw the display indicator window softly blink. But because of the high metallic content of the bulkheads, which bounced and fragmented the biosignals into several parts, the LS was having a hard time locking in the beast's signal. The range and direction indicator jumped all over the scale.

Del thought about it for a moment and concluded that it would be almost impossible for the LS to distinguish one signal source as the true target. He quietly put his LS in his torso vest. Obviously it was not going to do him any good. Del slowly backed up and retraced his steps to the cargo hold entry. Squatting next to the access-way, he reached up to press the release button.

Nothing happened.

Del tried again, but the door wouldn't budge. Del pushed the button hard several times more, but the hatch stayed tightly closed. Del looked at the hatchway in consternation. There was absolutely no way he was going to kick the door out. You didn't kick or punch out 5 centimeters of tri-alloyed modenium. He was trapped inside the cargo hold with the Garther Ape!

Del heard the scratching sound again. It was coming his way.

He controlled his initial urge to burst into headlong flight and backed away from the hatch towards the near corner of the cargo hold. He knew he was in a desperate situation, but the last thing he needed right now was to let his mind go into panic mode.

He remembered the ScoutMaster saying, "Each creature has inborn strengths and weaknesses. Consider both to understand how to deal with it. Either trait, a strength or a weakness, may be the key. Even a supposed strength may be used against the creature and turned to your advantage."

As Del crept to the corner, he tried to analyze

what he knew of the beast, and what he could use as a counter. Nothing short of a d-gun or maybe a stunner came to mind as an effective reply to the creature's power.

Near the compartment's hatchway, Del heard the scratching sound. He looked to his right and decided to try to reach a cluster of shipping containers that might provide better concealment within their boxed enclosure. He also decided this was far worse than the jungle pursuit on Terra, but he took grim pleasure in thinking that it couldn't get any worse.

He was wrong. It got worse. The lights in the cargo hold went dead.

Del stopped cold in his tracks as the lights dimmed and then completely blacked out. He reached out to find the wall and eased his back against the bulkhead. That and his long-knife were the only protection he could give himself.

Del knew it was only a matter of time before the ape found him. His only hope was that maybe the poachers would mount an armed search of the cargo hold and get the lethal creature before it got him. Right now, even the sight of the interstellar renegades would be welcome.

As he thought about his situation, he decided he would communicate to the team and tell them the beast's location. He wouldn't tell them of his situation, however. More likely than not, they would try to mount some silly rescue operation that could get them all killed.

He was just about to key his trans-comm open when he was startled to hear Shanon's voice through his ear-piece. "Del, listen carefully but do not answer. I repeat, do not answer in any way! Do not key your communicator!

"We've found TJ. She's okay and awake. We told her about the Garther Ape. She described her experience. Del, I'm convinced that it has supersensitive hearing. But, more than that, it may beable to hear in the electromagnetic spectrum. Its ears may be specialized organs to pick up audio and radio waves. Don't transmit! Your trans-comm will lead it right to you."

She stopped and then said, "I know how we can counter this beast and we've rigged a little surprise. We're headed aft. We overheard one of the poachers say the ape is in a rear cargo hold. Since you're back there, I'm assuming that it's in your vicinity, so peel off and move forward now!"

Crouched against the wall Del felt a trickle of sweat course down his cheek from his perspiring forehead. The adrenal rush was making his heart race and his metabolism soar. He considered for a moment Shanon's explanation of the creature's ability to detect sounds. Shanon was without doubt the smartest on the team, and what she described made sense.

His problem however, was very simple. He couldn't link up with his teammates because he couldn't get out of the locked cargo hold, and if he radioed or shouted for help, the creature would instantly know where he was. His only option was to keep moving and hope that either someone opened the hatch door, or he found another way out of the hold.

For another minute, Del crept along the bulkhead, his hand softly sliding along its smooth metal. His one hope was that he was keeping plas-containers and machinery between him and where he thought the ape was.

He stopped to listen and heard the slight scratching sound again, this time much closer, which caused Del to come up on the balls of his feet, ready to run if the creature suddenly loomed close. He ran his hand over his torso vest and thought that there was one thing he might do to help himself. He could get his infrared snoopers out of his support vest. The problem was that in doing so he might make just enough noise to alert the creature to his presence.

He decided to risk it, and slipped his hand down to the vest pocket that held his IR headset. He hardly breathing, Del lifted the set out, and stopped in midair as the clawing noise came again. This time there was no doubt that the beast was drawing closer. It must have heard him undo the flap.

Del fitted the IR gear on his head and decided it was time to move further away from the hatchway. Taking two steps along the wall, Del heard a noise behind him and spun to face the alien with his long-knife in hand. There was nothing there. Abruptly, the noise came again and Del immediately understood as he looked up. The IR eyepieces bloomed in full color as they outlined the creature leaping down on Del from atop the plas-box containers nearest him. Del had only a moment to react but he was too slow to bring his knife into play.

In what seemed like a microsecond of blurring speed the creature pinned Del in a crushing hold, its claws painfully pinning him to the wall. Del struggled fiercely, but it was useless against the powerful beast. With a shock, Del felt a pointed object against his head. The creature must have slid his claws to Del's neck and was slicing into it! In moments the razor-sharp talons would cut through the flesh and slice open the carotid artery, leaving Del to bleed to death.

Del felt a slight tingling in his body and felt weak and dizzy. He realized that he was losing consciousness. But even as darkness closed on his mind he became aware that the lights had come on in the cargo hold. Dimly he realized that there were people shouting and screaming. Something made the loudest noise Del had ever heard. The sonic booms were so powerful that they actually hurt his eardrums, adding to the pain of the creature's claws.

With no effort, the creature lifted Del off the ground, and as if in a terrible nightmare, he looked into a monstrous, gaping mouth full of dagger fangs that opened wide as the beast came at his head.

Chapter 11

The Queen Bee Crash Dives

Through a blurry consciousness, Del heard the murmuring of far-off voices but he couldn't make out the words. His ears felt as if they were full of cotton wads, drowning out all sound. He felt someone raise one eyelid and a sharp, bright light pierced the eye. He raised one limp arm to try and block the hurtful light, but someone pushed his arm back down.

"He's coming around," a voice said.

He understood that. He forced his eyes open and shut several times before finally willing both to stay open. The renegade female poacher stood near, cold eyes fixed on Del, her mouth curved in a deep frown. There was no doubt she wasn't pleased with the situation. From the look of the room, he was in the ship's dispensary. Next to the female was a lean, tall man Del hadn't seen before.

"Can you hear me?" she asked. Del managed to nod, though when he did, the room whirled and he saw spiraling comets race across his vision.

"Good. Now listen. No funny stuff." The woman leaned closer and venomously said, "I'm Bianca and you're in my ship, the *Queen Bee*. We call it that because I'm the queen boss around here and not only does my ship have a nasty sting but so do I."

She drew back and glared at Del. "A very nasty sting. We've got you and your friends, scoutee, and we're in no playing mood. You've cost me the equivalent of a Polaris RimStone and I intend to get my ducats back one way or another. Understand?"

Del took a breath and muttered, "Guess so."

"Sit up."

Del felt stiff and sore as he raised himself up. Rubbing his eyes, he was grateful to see his teammates unharmed, sitting against a near wall, shackled at their wrists. Their torso-vests, knives and their communicators were gone. His own gear was missing as well.

As he took stock of his injuries, Del was surprised to find that he wasn't badly hurt after the rough treatment by the ape. His arms had several small puncture wounds on them, but someone had dabbed ~~heal-crème~~ ointment over them. They were too small to be even worth a medi-bandage.

In a sullen tone Bianca said, "You are one lucky honcho. You should be dead, but if you're going to wrestle with a Garther Ape, you had impeccable timing."

She cocked her head toward the team, "Thank your friends for getting you away from the beastie. That was a pretty smart idea they had. I'll have to remember it for future use."

Del didn't understand her at all. Seeing his quizzical look, Bianca gave a little laugh and said, "Don't understand, do you?"

Del shook his head weakly and said, "No."

She reached out and pressed her finger on Del's neck. Del winced a little from her touch. The spot was painful and tender. "Hurt?" she asked in a mocking tone. "It should. It's where the G-ape tagged you. It was gonna save you for its next meal."

She saw that Del still didn't understand. "Don't they teach you scoutees anything?" She sarcastically said, "A Garther Ape is a voracious hunter-killer, and likes its food alive or freshly killed. But it had just recently eaten when it came across you." Del raised his head at that and his stomach turned. The poacher Mula!

"That," Bianca went on, pointing to the spot on Del's neck, "Is where the ape injected you with a paralytic poison. Keeps the victim alive, but totally immobile. It then conceals or buries its prey and comes back later to feed."

The look on Del's face made her laugh loudly. "Nice thought, huh? I understand that on humans it goes for the intestines first."

Del tightened his jaw, raised his face and looked the poacher square in the eye. "Okay," he said, "You can stop with the bedtime stories. We're not children."

Bianca laughed again. "Sure thing scoutee, have it your way. But you're not out of the woods yet . . . you see . . . you've got a little problem on your hands."

She nodded toward the four scouts. "Your friends saved you from the ape. They figured out that it was extremely sensitive to sound energies. They rigged up an air horn, using one of the mini-oxygen tanks and a tri-sone diaphragm from sick bay. Ingenious, I must say. The noise from the horn, amplified in the confines of the hold must have been pretty painful to the ape, because it dropped you and backed off. But not, unfortunately for you, before it injected you with its poison."

Del reached up to his neck, remembering the

sharp sensation in his neck when the Garther Ape grabbed him. Bianca pushed her face close to Del's and darkly said, "*X* marks the spot."

She pulled back and smiled sardonically. "About the time your friends came to the rescue we arrived, stunned the ape, and took you five in tow." She shook her head, her short hair bobbing as she did so. She put her face even closer to Del's and almost hissed, "You should've stayed on Earth instead of stowing away on my ship! You've bit off far more than any one of you can chew."

One of the other renegades took a step forward. "Space 'em Bianca?" he curtly asked.

Bianca gave the poacher a disgusted look and snapped, "Are you out of your mind! Shut up and go help Marty with the biospheric synchronizers!"

As the man sheepishly left, Bianca turned squarely to Del and coldly said, "I forgot to mention one other thing about the ape's venom. It's not only paralytic ... it's toxic as well. You ... my young scoutee ... are ... dying."

Del returned Bianca's stare and said slowly, "What do you mean?"

Bianca shrugged, "The ape's venom is a neuraldegenerator. Breaks down the cell's in the body's nervous system. In about twenty-four hours your muscles will start twitching, and then they'll start to spasm and cramp. Your eyesight and hearing will fade, eventually failing completely in a few days. Your major organs will start to deteriorate, and your heart muscle will go arrhythmic. You'll start to lose consciousness and then go comatose. You'll be dead in a week."

There was a rushing sound in Del's ears and he almost missed Bianca's next words. "Fortunately for you, Stinneli over there was . . . um, shall we say in 'medicine' before he decided to enter a more lucrative practice. Just so happens he's familiar with the venom's toxic properties. Before we grabbed the ape, he managed to produce a small amount of an inhibitor for the venom. Not a cure, but an antitoxin that will counter the effects of the venom—for a short while, anyway. He injected you with just enough to counter the venom's effects so that we could have this little parley. But not enough to counter the effects of the toxin for very long."

Del looked from Bianca to his teammates who stared back with unbelieving eyes. "How long will the full inhibitor work?" Del whispered.

Bianca shrugged, "With luck, three, maybe four weeks." She managed a half-smile as she said, "And we don't have more of the ingredients in our little dispensary to whip up another dose."

Bianca gave Del another little evil smile and leaned toward him. "Not exactly what you had in mind when you joined up to go explore the Almighty Firmament is it, scoutee?"

Del had had enough. "Listen, I'm not a scoutee, but a Junior StarScout . . . poachee!"

Bianca patted the laz-gun holster at her side. "Ooh . . ." she taunted, "Isn't he the brave one?" She whirled on Del and whipped out the laz-gun. She pointed it up and said, "And this . . . scoutee . . . lets me call you anything I want and reminds you to keep a civil tongue in your head."

She breathed hard as she waved the laz-gun back and forth. With a scowl she holstered the weapon. "Enough chatter! Here's the deal. I should space you for what you've cost me. I lost several of my crew thanks to the ape, so we're short-handed. We've got a couple of jobs coming up and I need a full crew. I don't have the time to go recruiting so you're going to take their place."

She laughed a little and continued, "The jobs are small, but with easy pickings. In fact, they're actually legal so you won't be 'aiding and abetting' as the magistrate is fond of saying.

"You play it smart, don't give us any trouble and after the jobs are done, I'll set you down on one of the LeClare Colonies. They'll have the medical facilities to take care of your . . . problem."

"How do we know you'll keep your word?" Shanon asked in a clipped tone.

Bianca frowned while saying, "You don't. But that's the chance you're gonna have to take."

"What are the jobs?" Sami curtly asked.

Bianca considered his question, and then shrugged as if it didn't matter. "First, Stygar 6. We've got a lead on some quadro-diamonds. We do a little prospectin'. If the diamonds are there, we pick up a load. Stygar 6 is an open planet. No Confederation mining warrants needed.

"Then to the Eagle Nebula. Wealthy bidder wants to add Sand-Diggers and a Sea-Panth to his private gardens. We've even got federation permits for harvesting the XTs . . . perfectly legal."

Del considered her proposal. Both activities were indeed legal, but the idea of helping known poachers still left a bad taste in his mouth. But he also had to face the stark realization that he didn't have much choice. He could of course choose to disbelieve Bianca about the Garther Ape and its venom, but the painful site in his neck was enough to convince him that it was true.

Del glanced sadly at his teammates. Though he was team leader, this was one decision he couldn't or wouldn't make for them. It would have to be an individual choice. Del turned to Bianca. "Could we talk about this alone?"

She shook her head. "No, but I'll give you some space." She motioned with her head and Stinneli and the other poacher retreated outside the infirmary door. Bianca backed to the far wall, crossed her arms, and leaned against the bulkhead.

Del huddled with his team. "I can't ask or tell you to do this. This goes outside my authority as TL. These are criminals. I don't know what legal considerations this may have with Scout Command and I don't want to jeopardize your standing. If you choose not to . . . I'll understand."

Shanon looked him in the eye and asked, "What are *you* going to do?"

For a long moment Del hesitated, then dropped his eyes. "I'm going to have to go through with it. The choice is a little different . . . for me."

"I don't think so Del," Shanon softly replied. "What would you do if it were any one of us sitting there instead of you?"

Del looked at Shanon with a half-smile. "Not fair," he said, "You know the answer."

"Yes, I do," she said. She looked at the scouts sitting on each side of her. "Roll call."

"TJ?"

"I'm in."

"Nase?"

"Check."

"Sami?"

"Ach lassie," Sami began. "So you'll av' us dance the devil's jig wih'ya, wellll now . . ."

"Sami!" Shanon said darkly, "this is serious."

"You're darn tootin' it is," Sami said, dropping the accent. "We'll probably either get zipped by these guys, or some Confederation battle-cruiser will blast us out of the sky! I say . . ."

"Sami . . ." Shanon began menacingly.

"Ok, ok," Sami said, as he looked up at the ceiling and let out a big sigh, "I'm in."

Del looked at his teammates. "Thank you," he said gratefully.

At that Bianca slapped the door control and said sarcastically, "Very touching . . ." She waved Stinneli in and motioned toward the scouts, "Undo them and give him the antidote."

Stinneli freed the scouts, grabbed Del's forearm and air-injected the antidote just under the skin. Del winced just a bit, the liquid burned as it hit subcutaneous tissue. Bianca gazed at the weary scouts. "I'm putting you in one of the empty cargo holds. You'll stay there while we make the n-space transit to Stygar 6. It's about a twelve-hour run. Remember, no funny stuff. We go through the drill, get the job done and your friend here gets to a medical facility."

She cocked her head toward the door. "Aft and outboard. Move."

A few minutes later, Stinneli directed the young scouts into a small, empty cargo hold. Inside, the five looked at each other, laughed slightly and almost as one, leaned up against the wall and slid to the floor. The adrenaline rush of the last several days was wearing off and they were bone-tired.

Too fatigued to even break out an s-ration to eat, though his stomach was growling like a Gon-wolf, Del closed his eyes and began to drift off. Then a thought hit him and he became alert again. He turned to Sami, "Sami," he began, "Need to ask you some questions."

Sami raised a hand and said, "Give it a rest Del. I'm too pooped to pop any more ideas."

Seeing that Sami wasn't cooperative, Del turned to Shanon who was curled up next to him on the other side. "Shanon . . ."

The young woman mumbled, "Yes?"

"Answer a couple of questions for me."

She yawned. "I'll try . . ."

"How did you guys find me?"

"Process of 'limination," she murmured. "Knew you were aft, just kept opening doors till we found you."

"You were able to open the hatch door in the hold I was in?"

"Of course," she said. "Couldn't have gotten in

otherwise." Del stared at Shanon with a questioning look. The hatch was frozen solid when he'd tried it, but it didn't make sense that the controls were inoperative only from inside the hold and not from the outside. Finally, he half-shrugged and said, "Well, I do thank you for the rescue. That was a slick piece of work."

"Welcome," Shanon replied sleepily. "Team effort. Too bad the poachers showed up when they did. A few more seconds and we would have been gone. Nabbed us just as we were grabbing you."

"Yeah, too bad, "Del said. "But, the only alternative might have been to play hide and seek in that dark hold with the ape again, and that's not something I recommend."

"Wasn't dark," Shanon sighed. "Lights were on when we blasted the ape."

Del started to ask another question, but Shanon was deep asleep. He slid down to get more comfortable and put his hands behind his head for a makeshift pillow. As he studied the smooth ceiling, his eye lids became heavier and heavier. Sluggishly he considered Shanon's remarks. He didn't remember the lights coming on, but it must have been just after the ape grabbed him and he lost consciousness. He looked over at the sleeping scouts and thought how lucky he was that they managed to get the door open when they did. A few more seconds and the ape would have . . .

Del jolted awake. The G-Ape had grabbed his leg! Reaching for his absent knife, Del sat upright, ready to strike out at the star creature. "Hey Del," Tala was saying, "Wake up!" She slapped his foot again. Del smiled sheepishly. "Sorry . . . must've been a nightmare."

She smiled impishly at him, "Well, I hope I wasn't the mare giving you the frights."

Del shook his head no and sat fully up. Around him the others were starting to sit up, stretching out sore muscles. As she stood, TJ stated, "We just came out of n-space." Del shook his head, trying to clear it of cobwebs. N-space? Then he remembered. Bianca said the run to Stygar 6 would be twelve hours. Twelve hours! They had slept twelve hours!

He was about to get up when the cargo hold door slid back revealing two of the crew. Both wore laz-guns but didn't have them drawn. One of the men threw in a net-sac containing five ration cubes and said, "You've got ten minutes to eat. We'll be back," and closed the door.

Sami read the cube label, "Delicious, ready-to-eat. Contains all essential nutritional ingredients. Serve hot or cold." He made a face at Nase, "Give me your boot; it'll taste better than this."

A few minutes later the door slid open and the same two crewmen motioned them out. A short march later and they entered the large round compartment that marked the astro-bridge, the ship's operational nerve center. Del was a little puzzled as to why the poachers would want them there.

As his eyes adjusted to the subdued lighting, Del could see numerous consoles that lined three-fourths of the curved wall. Several crewmen sat at the consoles monitoring various activities of the ship. The forward part of the wall held a large vis-screen for external views of neighboring space.

Del saw that they were approaching a rust-colored planet that seemed to have tiny freckles on its face. Sami leaned over and loudly whispered, "A planet with a bad case of the zits . . ."

Bianca, who had ignored them to this point turned and said, "Those 'zits' are an asteroid field that surrounds the planet. Sometime in the distant past, a sister planet, or moon of Stygar 6 shattered into countless fragments." She pointed to the on-coming planet. "Somehow, those fragments ended up in multi-orbital planes around the planet."

She busied herself at her monitor before continuing. "As you might guess, Stygar 6 doesn't get many visitors. The asteroids are too close to the planetary mass for a ship to use full grav-disruptor. In fact, a Confederation survey ship, the *Bridger* crash-landed about two years ago. Their disrupters overloaded and shut down . . . the ship took several major hits and crash-landed. No survivors."

She let the information sink in. "However, that's not going to happen to us. There's a way to get in . . . a bit risky, but doable."

As Del looked at the planet, he had to question Bianca's judgment. If the *Bridger's* gravity disrupters failed to safeguard a large survey ship, how did she think her smaller ship could make it through the field?

Del had had basic physics in high school and understood the principle behind the apparatus. In actuality, *grav-disruptor* was a misnomer for the device that protected the ship and its crew from the enormous acceleration forces of hyper-drive.

In addition to giving the frail human beings that inhabited the ship a steady earthlike gravity, the machine generated a powerful energy shield that provided a protective screen. The screen was similar to the bow-wave of a sea-sailing ship. The buffer either pushed aside or vaporized any matter that came in proximity to the ship as it plowed through n-space.

The device worked in direct inverse proportion to the velocity of the ship: The greater the velocity through n-space, the more condensed the shield. At slow planetary speeds the grav-disruptor's protective shield properties lessened considerably. In fact, for planetary system transits most space-faring captains relied on maneuverability to avoid masses rather than the grav-disruptor.

As if reading Del's mind Bianca explained, "Turns out that there is a hole in the asteroid field at both planetary axis points." She frowned for just a moment and continued. "Actually, hole is a bad description. Let's just say it's a place where there aren't as many big rocks flying around."

She turned to face the scouts. "We may have to do some pretty fancy maneuvering. Might even lose the internal grav-field. Didn't want you poor scoutees to get smashed up back there in your nice comfortable sleeping quarters. I need you later when we land. So you'll ride down in style. Grab one of the grav-seats and buckle yourselves in. Tight."

With that, she walked over to another console and scanned the digital readings. Del caught Sami by the elbow and steered him over to two empty seats near one of the outlaws and silently sat down. Bianca walked over and spoke to the nearby poacher in low tones. She turned and said, "I suspect you two are a bit curious about how we're going to get the *Queen Bee* down."

"Eternally curious, believe me," Sami muttered.

Her mouth curled up in a tiny smile. "Dan, give them a quick run through."

The man nodded toward the console. The monitor showed a 3-d view of the planet, tilted toward them at a 30-degree angle. Tiny pinpoints of light, like miniature fireflies spun around the globe. There were so many that the planet looked like it was encased in a cloud of sparkles.

He tapped with a finger where it showed the top of the planet's hemisphere closest to them. "The computer says that there's an 80 percent chance of a thirty-second window that opens about every ninety minutes over this pole. It's not a completely debris-free space, but compared to the rest of the planet, it's virtually empty. Only about five or so fragments per square kilometer."

The poacher ran his hands over the console controls for a moment and changed the view so that they looked directly down on the planet's pole. "Before it crashed, the *Norman Vaughn* sent out the data it had collected on the asteroid's orbits."

At the mention of the *Norman Vaughn*, Sami gave Del a sharp look and started to speak, but Del shook his head to stop Sami. He had caught it too. Bianca said the Confederation survey starship *Bridger* crashed, not the *Norman Vaughn*. Del wondered if it was a slip of the tongue or something else. For some reason he felt it important to find out which ship had really gone down on Stygar 6. But obviously he would have to bide his time until he found a way to answer the question.

Not seeing Del's quick head movement, Dan

[Handwritten margin note at top: "I have a hard time believing these terrible characters would willingly (and almost nicely, or at least conversationally) give all this information to the Scouts. If they are trying to scam them it needs to be way more obvious."]

continued, "We fed their data into our computer, and with the long-range sensor input we've got, we should have a pretty good picture going in. Still, it's going to take a bit of piloting to hit the window just right. Here, let me show you."

Adding a few more commands to the program he pointed to the monitor. A tiny green spot joined the whirling pinpoints, a minuscule replica of the *Queen Bee*. "We'll hit the window just as it starts to expand," the man said. "We can't back down or glide in because of the limited time.

"So, we dive through the hole, and this is the tricky part: The computer says the hole will start collapsing inward from the top, sort of like an inverted funnel that starts to squeeze together at its uppermost end-point. Because of that inward collapse, we're going to do a high-g dive straight down, because the funnel is going to be collapsing right behind us as we head for the surface. Once we clear the debris cloud, we'll do an inverted J roll out of the bottom of the funnel."

Sami pursed his lips and said, "Doesn't sound too hard . . . "

The man stared at the young scout for a moment

and as if to say, *you have no idea.* Instead, he said, "Considering that we'll be going about ten kilometers a second when we hit the tail-end of the J and we'll come out about forty kilometers above the planet's surface . . . no, it's not hard at all."

Sami raised his eyebrows, eased back in his chair and started whistling the refrain from Mandelknay's *Ode of the Lost Scout.*

Del thought the man's statement of a 'bit of piloting' was an understatement. Each of the junior scouts had dozens of hours in various planetary StarScout craft, but the maneuver Dan described was about the riskiest he'd ever heard of. "Who's the pilot?" he asked.

As he stood, Dan said straight-faced, "Me," and walked to where the pilot and co-pilot chairs sat in the forward part of the compartment. He buckled himself in as another of the crew slid into the co-pilot chair. "All hands, stand-by. Yankee stations!" he called over the ship's intercom. Immediately, the other crew members pulled shoulder straps tight. A few minutes later, the *Queen Bee* began her dangerous dive through the massive careening asteroids that guarded the planet.

Chapter 12

Gadion Faction

McCarel rubbed his red-rimmed eyes with his fingertips and blinked through sleep-deprived eyes at the detailed holographic image that floated above the imaging device. The hologram's three-dimensional view displayed ten star systems in the Eagle Nebula. He turned back to his computer and wearily began to re-read the StarScout mission reports displayed on the large-screen monitor.

McCarel knew from the record that several of the star systems held a planet where StarScouts were listed as *missing and presumed dead*. If SOG were correct in its postulation that the cause of the StarScouts disappearance was the *Gadion Faction*, then there should be some evidence, some link between their activity and the scouts.

His intense scrutiny of the documents was to find evidence of their involvement, but so far that goal eluded him. He was beginning to think that old reports were not going to be much help, that he needed to actually get on the ground, go Out There and see for himself.

Out of the corner of his eye McCarel saw Shar Tuul walk into the office. He turned as Tuul waved a hand in greeting. Tuul looked at his thumb chronometer. "Know what time it is?"

"Early morning, I suspect." McCarel said as he stood and stretched his back. "Better question is what day is it?"

Tuul laughed mildly. "You're obviously fitting in with the J2 staff. That's a pretty standard line around here." He intently studied the holographic image and said, "It's a little after 0400 hours in the morning and once again you've been up all night. And that," he said, pointing at the hologram, "is the same star-field you were poring over yesterday. How's it coming?"

McCarel motioned toward the three-dimensional image as he stood to stretch his legs. "It's not," he began as he leaned over and waved a hand at the hologram. "The mission descriptions are good, solid reports but there's nothing in them that really substantiates what happened to the scouts. There's no evidence, no witnesses, nothing. There's only two common denominators that I can see; a loss of communications between the team and base camp and the fact that all the missing scouts on these planets were operating in standard five-person teams when they disappeared."

He sat with a shrug and said, "I understand that the SOG evidence is pretty solid and you and the general are buying into it. But I'm still not totally convinced. Too many unknowns, too many variables and 'what-ifs' ~~Out There~~ that could account for the losses." He smiled wanly as he went on, "But you're the boss, so I'll keep plugging away. Just hope you're not expecting some miracle."

Tuul laughed and said, "Oh but we do. After all we're StarScouts. The extraordinary we do routinely, the impossible takes an extra five minutes, while miracles just require a memo from the Old Man." He sat his ~~cup of hot cocoa~~ [bottle of water] down and walked over to stare at the multicolored star image. He grunted. "Pretty close grouping. Star cluster?" he asked.

McCarel nodded. "It's called *The Attic*. Don't ask me why. Who knows how galactic cartographers choose these names. This was the cluster that Barkley found when he penetrated the nebula five years ago and set off the wild hullabaloo. Most of our survey reference points for the other star systems discovered so far run off of Laron, the center star of the cluster."

"So what's so unique about *The Attic* that you've spent the last thirty-six sleepless hours holed up in here studying the thing?" Tuul asked.

McCarel looked at his watch. "Thirty-six hours? Has it been that long?"

"More or less. A lot more than less." Tuul said. "So, what's so fascinating about this group?"

McCarel swept his hand across the hologram. "Twelve Terra-like planets scattered among ten stars. But twelve of the most placid worlds you'll find anywhere. Even more so than Terra. Evolutionary pattern concentrated on herbivorous species, with darn few carnivores. Weather patterns extremely mild. Most of the microorganisms are nonvirulent. You'd be hard-pressed to even catch a cold there."

"Sounds like paradise."

"Just about. If there's a Garden of Eden it's on one of those planets."

"Okay. So, what's the catch that you'd give up two day's worth of sleep for?"

McCarel tapped a finger on his computer plas-screen that showed one of the mission reports. "Eighteen scouts missing on six of those planets. Highest ratio of missing, presumed-dead scouts in just this one area. I served with two of those scouts, Peter Johansson and Danielle Sbotha. Superb StarScouts. Proficient, capable, rock-steady and as level headed as they come.

"Eighteen fully trained and veteran scouts missing on worlds where a hangnail should be the most serious injury experienced. Doesn't make sense. It's like they walked out of base camp and poof! They're gone."

He leaned down on his elbows and rubbed his hands together. "But, the cluster also has the high-comms activity that SOG says is the signature pattern for the *Faction*. So, if the *GF* were on the ground I can't prove it, and worse, if they snatched our scouts, I don't know how."

Tuul scrunched his face up for a moment. "What about this loss of comms? Anything we can do with that? Back trace? Beef up our equipment? New standard operating procedures?"

McCarel scratched his face in thought for a second and then shrugged. "Loss of operational communications for everything from short timeframes up to extended periods is fairly routine for our ops. We can look at all of that of course, but actually I was thinking along different lines."

He stopped and looked directly at Tuul and stated, "What if loss of comms was directly correlated to loss of scout?"

Tuul returned McCarel's direct look with his own. He raised both eyebrows in response. "That would be very interesting and possibly very definitive. You have proof?"

McCarel sighed deeply before responding, "Maybe, maybe not."

Tuul snorted loudly, "Spoken like a true intel guy. Always cover your bases." He looked at McCarel and cocked his head. "C'mon Jak. It's just us two. Let's hear what you have."

"Well," McCarel slowly observed, "Two of those suns were at peak magnetic storm cycles so the stellar radiation could have played havoc with communications. But our gear is pretty hardened against spikes in the electro-magnetic spectrum . . . so my gut is telling me that absence of communications wasn't due to that."

He waved at the computer screen, "But 12 team leaders reported lost contact and shortly after those scouts were gone. Vanished. Little or no evidence on the ground of what happened." He handed Tuul several plas-sheets, "Highlighted portions," he said.

Tuul read the sections that McCarel pointed out and then spoke slowly and thoughtfully, "So, a team goes in, there's an unexpected loss of communications where comms was normal before, and then we have a missing scout." He asked McCarel, "You think the Faction has developed some type of energy damper to block our comms?"

McCarel half-threw his hands in the air, "That's a question for your high-priced staff civilian engineers, I wouldn't have a clue. But, if they have, then why not use it all the time? My own experience and the mission reports don't seem to bear that out."

"Go on," Tuul directed.

"Most of my encounters with the Faction were quick firefights, hit-and-run scenarios, that type of thing. Overt operations, not covert as suggested by communications loss. If they can do stealth-type of operations without us knowing it, why confront openly? Wouldn't make sense."

Tuul was silent for several seconds as he digested McCarel's analysis. He looked at the star cluster hologram. "Alright," he said slowly, "I see your point. Doesn't jive does it? Why come out in the open what you can accomplish secretly, which would be more their style."

He pointed at the hologram, "So how do we explain the correlation between loss of comms and loss of scout?"

McCarel snorted this time as he stood to say in a frustrated tone. "Ask me to explain a quark plasma field; I can do both about equally well." He grinned crookedly and said, "But thanks for saying *we*." He ran a hand over [through] his close-cropped hair. "I can't explain it. All I can tell you is that it appears to be happening."

Tuul laid a hand on McCarel's shoulder, "Easy Jak. No one is expecting you to have all the answers."

McCarel took a deep breath. "Sorry. It's just that this is still so unbelievable to me. The *Faction* [No italics] coming after us I mean."

"I know," Tuul replied. "It took me a while to accept the idea." He looked across the board at his grizzled teammate. "Jak, sometimes the general has hunches about things. I've found his instincts are better than most people's logic. I think he put us together because of how we approach a problem. I'm an intelligence guy and so I think in terms of future events, what-ifs, statistical probabilities, that sort of thing. You're an operations guy and you think in terms of day-to-day plans and missions, beans-and-bullets, practical stuff."

He tapped on the board with his finger. "You smell a rat here so let's see if we can find the nasty critter. But let's change our perspective, leave the comms loss aspect for now, I'll take that over to Research and Development; see what those smart lads and lassies can do for us. What else do you have? Particularly on the operations side. What about your encounters with the Faction?" Tuul asked, "Anything we can pull from that?"

McCarel bobbed his head animatedly, "Actually, I think so. Most operations where we encountered the Faction were battalion surveys, topo or mineral, some seek, locate, and catalog missions," McCarel explained. "But once on the ground we almost always broke down into typical five-scout teams. We'd go into an area to work—next thing you know GF teams would hit us and a firefight would ensue. The skirmishes were almost like a meeting engagement between two forces. Totally unexpected. Sometimes they would slug it out for a few minutes, but most times they'd just melt away after the opening volleys."

Tuul bent to peer at the star system image. He could see that McCarel had added digitized wording under several of the planets. He studied the various symbols and notes assigned to each planet. They identified the StarScout unit designation, date-time of the incident, and what occurred. Most of the notations were *missing-presumed dead* and the number of scouts lost.

Tuul jabbed a finger at the hologram. "And here? Same thing?"

McCarel nodded. "Pretty much. Typical five-person teams operating independently. Nothing unusual, but thinking like the operations guy you say I am, it does bring up questions."

Tuul swung around to say, "Such as?"

McCarel turned his chair to fully face the hologram. "We send scouts out to do specific missions," he began, "Would it not be a fair assumption that the Faction does the same?"

The intelligence officer spread his hands and replied. "Sure. And from what I've seen, those missions appear to be well defined, limited in scope, and have a definite objective."

"I agree. And my contact with them leads me to believe that they're unwilling to take on a large force because they're operating in small teams. I suspect they can't afford the losses that would occur in a big engagement."

"Hmmm." Tuul mused. "Interesting, go on."

McCarel looked directly at Tuul. "And, could be that they're more concerned about capture. Hence, they break off before you can grab one."

Tuul nodded in understanding as he said, "Dead men don't talk, prisoners do. And it's much easier to extract a small team from a fight than a large force."

McCarel nodded grimly. "The smaller the unit, the easier for command and control. So, a five-person StarScout team is fair game but they probably have standing orders to avoid contact with anything bigger. That would explain why they bug out so fast."

He paused and then said, "They probably stay around just long enough to determine that they're up against something larger than a five-person team and then split."

Tuul walked around the hologram to look at it from another view. "Okay, let's assume that we've got a pretty sound working hypothesis that the *Faction* won't take on anything larger than a team. That's a good first step."

McCarel nodded. "And we can at least make one recommendation to the general. No more independent operations lower than battalion or company size. Safety in numbers."

Tuul poked a finger at the hologram and sketched a line from one planet to another. "I agree. But that's only one fix, and means a real change to our organizational structure and operational doctrine. The real answer lies in knowing what they're trying to accomplish. What is the *Faction's* purpose, their objective Out There? If we knew that, then our counters would be more effective."

McCarel smiled half-heartedly, "Don't happen to have an undercover agent with the *Gadions* that we might be able to spend a few minutes with, do you?"

Tuul grinned back. "Nope. Maybe SOG does, but if they told me they'd have to deep space me without a p-suit right after."

McCarel stood and paced off a few steps. "All right, let's review the bidding. From your intelligence findings we're pretty certain that the *Faction* aren't renegade colonists, they're not an interstellar corporation trying to kill off the competition, or a planetary system that's declared war on the Confederation.

"SOG says they're a shadow terrorist group that's highly organized, and very sophisticated. They've done everything from assassinations to robbery to kidnappings. They've never gone public with any demands or stated aims. SOG says those are random acts, no pattern."

He stopped and ran a hand through his gray-brown hair. "Random acts, no pattern," he repeated. "But that doesn't make sense, does it? Everything we've seen about them shouts organization and purpose. I've been in several firefights with them. They weren't some disorganized fighting mob. Their actions were controlled and disciplined. At a guess, almost militaristic, trained professionals.

"We know their communication systems; their equipment is top-notch. And they have a good intelligence collection operation as well." He looked around and spoke quietly, as if the walls had ears. "Good enough apparently to plant a mole right under our noses. All of that suggests to me an organization with a goal, not some ragtag, loosely organized pipsqueak gang."

He scratched his chin making a raspy sandpaper sound as his hand crossed his unshaven face. "Shar, you ever see an *angler fish* catch its prey?"

"Can't say that I have."

"Interesting creature. About half a meter long and as ugly as my first drill sergeant at the Academy. Looks like an underwater rock overgrown with green moss. But it has this tiny tongue that looks just like a dancin' worm. Jiggles the thing right in front of its open mouth.

"Little fish comes along to eat the worm, and the angler pulls the tongue-worm back and leads its prey right into its open mouth. Jaws close fast as lightning, couple of chomps, and swallows the fish. Never moves, just stays in one place all the time and wiggles that tongue."

Tuul cocked his head sarcastically. "Okay, thanks for my daily zoology lesson. Now, what's your point?"

McCarel grinned and held up his hand in the wait sign. "Got another lesson for you. When I was a kid, my Dad would say, *the sun doesn't always rise in the east.* We lived where the morning sun always rose in the east. Never understood him until I did a mountain training exercise on Denali in Alaska. At that latitude at summer solstice, the sun actually rises in the northeast because of the angular tilt of the earth's pole. So he was right, there are places on Terra where technically the sun doesn't rise due east. Took me a while before I finally understood what he was trying to tell me."

Tuul put his hands on his hips and shook his head. "Sorry. You've lost me; I don't see the connection between tongues and sunrises."

"Look, ever since that SOG briefing we've assumed that everything they've fed us is correct. So we've been looking at the data basically from SOG's perspective. And their viewpoint is strictly political. To them the *Faction* is a threat to the political foundation of the Confederation. Right?"

Tuul answered slowly. "Yes, and from their position that's a reasonable assumption . . . ah, I see your point. To SOG the tongue is a tongue whereas it may really be a worm. They may not be seeing the true anatomy of the beast. And they've tilted the analysis to shore up their institutional leaning towards a political threat. In other words, for them, the sun always rises in the east, it's always a political threat."

"Exactly. And add this to the list. When a small unit is pitted against a larger force an axiom of battle strategy is to misdirect the superior force away from your objective. You use feints and ruses to cover your real intentions in order to accomplish your mission and to conserve your own forces."

McCarel animatedly tapped the computer board with his fingertips. "Let's turn this thing around on its head. The SOG thinks the *Faction's* objectives have to do with the Confederation as a whole. Hence, the terrorist activity on populated worlds. But what if—"

"Their primary objective lay outside explored space," Tuul finished for him. "Then you'd use activity in explored space to draw attention away from your real plan."

"Exactly. And, what if this isn't some political or religious, fanatical, terrorist group bent on political overthrow? What if they are exactly what we've seen, a well-organized, trained mercenary force whose objective is to stop exploration of deep space, or perhaps the exploration of a particular piece of interstellar space?"

"Whew!" Tuul interjected, "Slow down, Jak. That's a pretty tall order you've described. Do you realize the organization and financing that you're talking about here? Just to mount the forces and logistics necessary to do that for even your *Attic* here is immense."

"Yes, but not an impossibility. If it's a tightly controlled, very organized group, with very simple lines of command, it wouldn't take that large an organization." He peered intently at the hologram. "In fact, there may not be as many *Gadions* as we think there are."

Tuul shrugged and answered, "Okay, you've got the floor. Convince me."

McCarel pointed at the floating star field. "Let's assume it was the *Faction* that took out our scouts. How many *GF* teams do you think it took to hit our squads?"

"I would think they had attack elements on each

planet, with some type of command-and-control cell nearby." Tuul answered, looking at the hologram again. "Probably somewhere in the neighborhood of six teams . . . maybe a few more."

McCarel shook his head. "An unfair question; you haven't read those reports as many times as I. But no, not six hit teams. I think they had one, maybe two at the most." Tuul looked doubtfully at McCarel. He bent over slightly to get a better look at the hologram and one by one pointed at the star dates of each incident.

He glanced sharply up at McCarel. "The incident dates are successive. Two or three days apart."

"That's right. An easy hop for a medium-range transport."

Tuul slapped his palm down on the board. "Of course! Our mole!" he exclaimed. "They knew the locations of our teams knew exactly where to go!"

McCarel slumped wearily into his chair and nodded. "I think so. And that probably explains at least some of the other incidents. But it doesn't answer the basic question of why?"

For several minutes both men were silent. Tuul stared hard at the star-field before he turned and paced off a few steps. Suddenly he spun around ~~as if an idea had struck him~~. "All right," he began, "I've got one for you. Where did you buy your last sky-car?"

"What?" McCarel said in an irritated voice.

"Just answer the question," Tuul pressed, "It's your turn at the blackboard."

"Easy Eddy's. A Magnum V AirWing. Why?"

Tuul whistled at that, "A Magnum Five! You have been out in the boonies for a while haven't you? Not even Methulasah's Grandmother would remember one of those!"

"Do you have a point here or are we going to discuss my lack of support for the Confederation economy?"

"Sorry. So . . . why Easy Eddy's?"

"Wish I hadn't," McCarel growled, "Forgot to read the fine print. Still paying off the so-called deferred interest payments."

"Okay, okay. Let me rephrase the question. Why didn't you just build your own airmobile?"

"Can't. Mechanical idiot. Wouldn't know a torque from a dork."

"So like me, you go to a dealership because they sell airsters that we know are professionally built, will run, and generally last for a while. Whereas if we tried to build one, it would take literally years of training, time, and resources to get an equal product."

"Go on, I'm listening."

"Jak, what if you were looking for something on an alien planet and you needed to find it quickly. Who would you hire to help you? The best quality, most professional?"

McCarel shrugged. "Me, I mean, us. StarScouts. But we're not for hire. Besides everything we do is public knowledge. There's nothing that we don't share or divulge to the general populace."

Tuul stopped pacing and looked intently at McCarel. "That's not entirely true, Jak,"

McCarel glanced up and started to question Tuul when he suddenly understood the man's statement. He rubbed his hand over his unshaven face and grimaced slightly. "You're right. How could I forget that? Bone-tired, I guess . . ."

McCarel nodded thoughtfully as he contemplated what Tuul was implying. The past spoke for itself. Ever since the Froma IV incident, and the whispers of a Kolomite theft, all Kolomite discoveries were handled strictly through command channels to the High Council. StarScout had standing orders that once the report of a Kolomite find was made, the team was to depart the area and let the civilians or the Sci-Corps handle the rest. StarScout did not want a repeat of the supposed disaster that stained its name.

McCarel stood back up and spread his hands against a nearby plotting board. This was uncomfortable country for him but one they had to explore. He breathed deeply and said, "Okay, but how often is that? In twenty years Out There I've never seen one Kolomite hit on a mineral survey and I only know of one find in the last five years. You know darn well that mineral surveys are pretty low on our priority list. The Sci-tech crew usually does most of that."

Tuul looked at McCarel sharply. "You must be really tired. You're forgetting those two fields found right outside our base camp on Faller's Planet. A red-letter day for Rakin's Raiders."

McCarel stared at the hologram. "You're right, I'm pretty tired. Things are a little fuzzy." There was a moment of silence before he asked, "You think it's

Kolomite?"

Tuul shrugged, "There have been many more discoveries than you're aware of. The information doesn't filter down through the ranks. For obvious reasons, it's pretty close hold. But if I were going to look for Kolomite on an alien world and I needed someone to cover my back or do the actual search—yes, you're right, I'd want a StarScout."

Neither man spoke for several minutes. Finally McCarel broke the silence. "A few significant finds of Kolomite would certainly go a long way in financing an organization. Give them the means to buy weapons, star ships, supplies, and people."

Tuul walked to McCarel's computer to look at the report framed on the screen. "Jak, were there any reports of Kolomite finds on these planets? Were the scouts operating with a Sci-tech team?"

"No to both." McCarel replied. "Or I should say, it's not in the mission report."

"I wonder . . ." Tuul murmured and began rapidly tapping in commands to the computer. After several minutes, he sat back and said, "According to this, the SciCorps has had a threefold increase in the last ten years of missing, presumed-dead technicians. And look at this."

McCarel bent over to look at what Tuul pointed to. After reading for a few moments, he softly whistled. "More than half of their missing are from mineral survey missions, after our StarScouts reported possible Kolomite finds."

"Let's look at one other thing." Tuul said. In a few moments he brought up another data field and seconds later the computer correlated the information. Both men read it and then just looked at each other. "It matches." McCarel said simply.

"It surely does." Tuul nodded. "StarScout reports possible Kolomite find. We pull back to provide cover for the SciCorps gang as they go in. We get hit, they get hit, or vice versa. But that doesn't matter, because the common denominator is the Kolomite."

McCarel thrust his hand toward the star field hologram. "But that doesn't explain *The Attic*. No Kolomite. No techs."

"No," Tuul half-sighed, "It doesn't. And that I can't explain. But at least we have this piece of information to work with. So how do we find out if this is indeed the case?"

McCarel walked over to the work surface and

picked up the folder that contained the listing of junior scouts. He hadn't opened it since the night of Teng Rhee's visit but he had been giving it a great deal of thought. He had an idea of maybe protecting at least some of those scouts and now was a good time to bring it up given the nature of their conversation.

He straightened back up and took a few paces, holding the folder in his hand. Abruptly he stopped and turned back to the intelligence officer. "There might be a way . . ." he began, holding the folder up, "To help with this problem, and to get some answers as well."

Tuul met McCarel's eyes. "Careful Jak. We've been down this road before."

"I know. And I'm not suggesting that we do anything that would jeopardize intel sources. You and the CG have made that perfectly clear. But what I am suggesting is that we consider taking a little time out of the mount and conduct some much needed field evaluations of training and other related topics. And we don't need a big staff team. I'm thinking that maybe just two staff officers would fit the bill nicely. In fact, the fewer, the better."

Tuul stared at McCarel for a long time. His underlying implications were clear enough, but a little on the disturbing side. Finally he said, "You're thinking of turning the tables?"

McCarel shrugged, "As they say, do unto others—"

"Pretty risky. Way outside our mission statement. We're not in the business of hunting humans, you know. Wouldn't sit too well with the High Council."

McCarel pulled at his ear and laughed lightly. "The HC wouldn't necessarily have to know. After all, what do they really understand about our day-to-day operations? If we happen to stumble across some lost *Faction* buzzards Out There and bring them home to roost, who's going to know?"

He scratched at his chin for a moment and then said, "And if those buzzards just happen to be circling in the neighborhood of the Assembly President's daughter while we're doing our inspection trip, so much the better to justify to the council."

Tuul pursed his lips and cocked his head to the left. "Pretty thin ice, Jak. The general would have to know."

McCarel nodded. "Agreed. The general would have to know."

"Alright," Tuul sighed, "I'm not particularly sure I like it, but I'm in. I have to see the Old Man in about a half-hour anyway, you come along and we'll add this to the brief."

McCarel nodded and replied. "Sounds good. Mind if I use your 'fresher?'"

"Help yourself. I'll take care of some items with my staff."

"Check. Half an hour. I'll meet you at the CG's office. What else are you briefing him on?"

Tuul held up some plas-papers. "Latest edition of the JS No-Notice list. You know ScoutMaster's, they giveth and taketh away at will. In this case they've added a couple names that are politically connected and meet our potential target criteria."

"None of the others taken off?" McCarel asked.

Tuul shook his head, "No. But these additions widen the field. The bar keeps getting raised and who knows, your idea might prompt the CG to mount a couple of very innocent-looking operations that might offer some protection, but . . ." he held the plas-papers out in front of him . . . "he would have a devilish time trying to cover all the bases and not tip off our mole or compromise SOG."

McCarel nodded in understanding. Rosberg walked a very fine line trying to provide additional protection to his endangered JS's while at the same time making it appear that his orders were simply routine directives. He nodded toward the list, "Mind if I take a look, might be able to make some tactical recommendations to the CG if he decides to put together some field ops."

"Certainly. I'm sure he'd appreciate the help. Bring up the list and I'll meet you there."

With that, Tuul was off. McCarel picked up the list to read Tuul's highlighted portions that named the scouts and their tactical assignment. He went down the front and flipped to the backside.

He had barely gone down a third of the page when a shock ran through his body. His eyes riveted on one name. He stopped and reread the name several times. His hand reached out to squeeze the top of the sim-leather chair. Though he was indoors he felt like a great wind was roaring through his mind, stripping away every thought but the name on the page.

Tuul came back through the portal, "Sorry, forgot something." The look on McCarel's face stopped him. "You okay? You look like you've just come face-to-face with a Sirkian Gas Ghost."

McCarel nodded slowly as he looked up at Tuul. He clutched the plas-paper so tight his knuckles turned white. His voice was hoarse as he answered, "Yes, I'm fine. In fact, I feel better than I've felt in a long time."

He glanced once more at the inscription on the page. It read, *Del Baldura, Denali Vista Academy, ScoutMaster Tarracas.*

Chapter 13

To Swim with Human Sharks

"Gentlemen," General Rosberg stated gruffly, "your evidence is as thin as interstellar oxygen and so are your conclusions. I could probably drum up half a dozen scenarios to fit your findings. I wanted answers, not more questions and conjectures; I've got enough of those already."

McCarel and Tuul shifted uncomfortably in their seats. The general's office, large and spacious before, now felt like a tiny closet. Rosberg wasn't one to mince words and would shear your head off at a straight plane if he thought you were wasting his time. At that moment McCarel wondered how his neck looked without anything above the Adam's apple.

"Sir," McCarel started again, "We realize that this isn't exactly plas-steel hard, but we strongly feel it's enough to at least pursue the operation we've described."

The general snorted. "And one that'll probably get you either killed or listed as *missing-presumed dead*, and me up in front of the High Council trying to explain you two renegades."

Rosberg lifted himself from his chair and paced a few steps away to stare at the holo-cinema in one corner of his office. The constantly changing scenes that floated midair showed exotic animals and plant life from hundreds of distant starworlds where StarScouts had tread. Just at that moment it glowed with the blazing lime-colored light of Aldura's trio of suns as they shone on the exotic flora of that far-off planet. McCarel could see that the general's eyes were on the vista but he was deep in thought and his mind on something far different than Aldura.

After a moment the general officer turned back to his desk and picked up a single plas-sheet that rested on the gleaming black surface. He glanced at it for a moment before handing it over to Tuul. "This came in just a few minutes before our meeting began. You two might want to look it over."

McCarel peered over Tuul's shoulder at the plas-sheet. It was a terse communiqué from the Sector 11 Commander. McCarel looked up sharply at Rosberg as he exclaimed, "Six scouts!"

"Boss," Tuul sadly commented, "we cannot sustain losses like this week after week."

"I'm well aware of that, Colonel. We also lost two scouts on Seta 4 this week."

"Seta 4?" McCarel asked, "I'm not familiar with that planet."

"Newly discovered, Helix Nebula. Coupla of months ago, Barkley's Battalion found a string of g-type stars leading into the outer edge of the center quadrant of the nebula. No Terran-style planets but analysis of the gravity lines and gas flows indicated a high likelihood of emerging g-stars deeper in the nebula. Barkley took his command through the nebula's outer envelope and found a small cluster of g-stars. Seta's one of the stars with a Level 1 M-type world in its planetary system."

McCarel shook his head. Under other circumstances the loss of two scouts in a week would be normal. But given the rate of overall loss over the past months, the loss of even two was significant.

The general spread his hands on the desktop and leaned forward. His voice was full of frustration. "The Helix has taken eight of my scouts in this week alone. My instincts tell me to pull our units out of there, but the Confederation politicos won't allow me to pull out. Too much at stake. The number of habitable planets and the level of natural resources are astounding."

Grim faced he looked at the two. "The politicians and corporations are literally drooling at the prospects, and don't really care what it takes to explore that space."

McCarel almost exploded from his chair. "And we're paying for their wealth with our blood! Sir, there's not a scout Out There that's unwilling to down-planet just to see what's there. That's why they joined this outfit, to explore, and share what they find . . . but to do it just so some corporate CEO adds another billion Confed-dollars to his credit account is not in our mission statement!"

"Colonel," Rosberg said, his tone brusque and cool,

"You don't have to remind me of what our mission is. I seem to be wearing the Scout Arrow as well."

McCarel's face turned slightly red. "Sorry sir," he apologized. "But ever since that briefing with Rhee, I, well, the truth is I think we ought to either pull out of these sectors and let the politicians deal with the problem, or we have the Navy and Space Marines interdict the whole area and provide overwatch so that we can just do our work."

Rosberg raised his eyebrows at this outburst from McCarel. Both started frankly at each other before Rosberg spoke, "Colonel, this touches a raw nerve with all of us, but I doubt seriously if the Confederation is going to pull the Nav Fleet off its ops schedule to interdict the Helix. No, we're pretty much on our own, just as we've always been."

A strained silence followed his comments. McCarel shifted uncomfortably in his chair, wanting to speak, but not knowing exactly how to respond. Tuul spoke up, interrupting the tense silence. "Sir, I have to agree with Jak. This is beginning to look more like an armed conflict than StarScout exploratory operations. If it's the *Faction* as we suspect, then we've got to either get out of the nebula or bring in the military forces."

Rosberg snorted and sat down heavily. "Didn't you hear what I just said? First off, the fleet doesn't have the resources for a total interdiction of the nebula as you're suggesting. Secondly, how do I explain to the High Council that the StarScouts, the most highly trained, skilled, able-bodied group of humans to ever set foot Out There can't protect themselves against a bunch of hooligans? Our people face dangers ten times worse than the *Gadion Faction* and come out unscathed, but you want me to tell the council that we can't face up to a group of political terrorists."

McCarel grimaced and looked down at the floor for a moment. To him the answer was crystal clear. You didn't waste StarScouts to further political ambitions, and he personally didn't care if any of the corporations found another quadro-diamond, or a seam of quartzite, or a metro-bale of Vega leaves. But he wasn't a politician and had little desire to understand the intricate machinations of Confederation politics. In all honesty he had to admit that he couldn't answer the general's questions, and if it were him having to face the High Council he wouldn't have any explanation for them either, other than a plea to let them pull back and re-group.

Tuul looked at McCarel and shrugged. He didn't have a ready reply either. "All right, sir," McCarel said slowly. "I understand your point and no, I don't have the answers for you. But that's why we proposed you let Colonel Tuul and I run this one single operation, with just the two of us to at least test this one hypothesis and hopefully get just what we need . . . some answers. [use a dash here if you want to be dramatic.]

"We know it's risky and a long-shot, and outside our normal mission parameters," Tuul interjected, "But Jak and I can handle this. And remember, you didn't want any others in StarScout involved. So that logically means that it has to be just us two carrying out the operation."

Rosberg scratched his chin and stared hard at the two of them with his penetrating blue eyes. He grinned lopsidedly as he spoke to Tuul. "Shar, you haven't been Out There on a live mission in four, maybe five years. McCarel would have to spend more time watching over you than . . ."

"Begging the general's pardon," Tuul interrupted in a light tone, "but who placed in the top five the last three years running in the staff round-robin scout skills test? And who, as I recall, got lost in Patagonia in last year's exam and nearly lost his posterior to frostbite?"

"I still say someone sabotaged my geo-compass to bring me down in the standings," Rosberg answered darkly. Then with a sharp laugh he said, "All right, point made. I withdraw my objection."

"How will you explain your absence to your staff? It's going to look very odd for the StarScout intel chief to be out in the field. It's not your normal place of duty, for obvious reasons."

"Aw," Tuul quipped, "I'll just tell them I got tired of flipping paper clips into the trash vaporizer and just had to walk the trail one more time. Actually, I'll come up with a cover story. Something to do with a new 'staff field study' or some sort of usual staff nonsense that you personally ordered. That's why we're doing it and not lower ranking staff."

Rosberg gave a short laugh. "Pretty flimsy. I doubt if it'll fool anyone, but go ahead."

He spun his large computer monitor around to face them. "Want to show you something. I've been thinking about our problem as well. You're right, this thing's getting more like an armed conflict, so I decided we needed to give our scouts a little more firepower. This is my first idea."

They leaned forward to look at the image of a standard scout landing craft used on most planetary missions and nicknamed *scouters*. The model on the screen was the new SLC-31 but its outline looked odd. The slight oval shape of its undercarriage now framed two small bulging protuberances, one on each side of the craft. The stubby nose was outfitted with a large bulb-like apparatus. And the craft looked larger than a normal SLC though the overall design was the same.

McCarel reached out to point at the craft's undercarriage. "What . . ."

"SupraMark IX torpedo canisters." The general explained. "One port and one starboard. That bulge in the nose is an ion-cannon . . . has enough charge for about 6 shots. We extended the length five meters and put in a Hartbeld star-drive to make it interstellar capable. We have four prototypes in testing on Luna even as we speak."

"Pretty heavy firepower for StarScouts!" Tuul said, impressed by the new design and armament.

"Not an easy decision for me," the general replied.

"We've always kept our weapon needs to the very basic and let the military develop and handle the big stuff. But I believe, for obvious reasons, that our units now need a quick reaction force with sufficient firepower to meet the threat.

"So, it was either bringing in the Confed fleet and conduct joint operations with them as our overwatch and reaction force or develop something in-house. For now, I choose to go this route."

He drummed on the top of the desk for a moment before going on. "I've code-named the prototype *Zephyr*. Sorry to say none of them will be ready for your mission or I'd send one along with you. You'll have to make do with a troop transport or some such. So J-deuce, who will be your replacement while you're on this uh, 'temporary duty'?"

Without hesitation Tuul answered, "Witte. She can handle it."

Rosberg registered surprise on his face. "She's pretty junior on your staff isn't she?"

Tuul shrugged as if that didn't matter. "Yes, Adner and Cormack are senior, but Nan's progressing extremely well, good head on her shoulders, smart, very competent. Adner and Cormack are good, but their analytical and people skills fall short."

Rosberg spread his hands out to signify acceptance. "Okay. I'll inform the Chief-of-Staff of the change. He'll want to know why, but I'll use your so-called staff study cover story." He paused for a second. "Evaluation of training would normally come under the J3, but I'll make up some cock-and-bull story about wanting a neutral evaluator so I'm sending you two. Won't set well with the operations staff." He grumped for a moment, "I'll have to smooth some ruffled feathers . . . make some promises, that sort of thing. They'll get over it."

He looked at the two and said, "What planet are you proposing for your operation?"

Tuul looked at McCarel. "Your call."

McCarel hesitated, scratched his chin as he spoke, "I thought that we'd try around Conner's Cluster, but the loss of those two scouts on Seta may be just the opening salvo in that area."

He bit his lower lip and locked eyes with Rosberg, "We've actually got several no-notice teams heading in that general area." He took a deep breath, "We could use that as part of our cover story . . . evaluating those ops, trainers, training plans, that sort of thing."

Rosberg considered McCarel's suggestion for a few moments before he wagged a finger at him, "Tread lightly there, you know the score. Don't advertise. Make it strictly covert. Understood?"

McCarel and Tuul nodded in response. Rosberg went on, "You've got their flight plan?"

"Yes, in fact, one team has an op planned in the Helix. Little unusual to go out so far, but in this case it works to our advantage. Just so happens the team has several of those JS's whose families are listed in the SOG report."

The general nodded and brusquely said, "Okay. Before you leave, give me your planned route. Make your departure prep look like a normal outbound staff mission. Keep it low-key and aboveboard, but try to shoot out of here as quick as you can before anyone starts asking questions."

He paused for a moment, "Umm . . . I'll have Maggie arrange transportation from here to Luna, provide her with your expected departure time. She'll speak with our Luna liaison for a transport as well. Once you get Out There, send me an open n-space message with a fake staff report. That'll be my alert that you're on-planet and ready to start. That cover it?"

McCarel looked at Tuul and then at Rosberg. "This means you're giving us the go-ahead?"

Rosberg nodded. "Yep. Frankly, I'm not entirely convinced that your plan has merit, but, you're right, we need some answers so I'll buy off on this one attempt. Just don't get yourselves killed. Not that I'm particularly fond of either of you, but I'd hate to have to train a new J2. It's taken me a couple of years just to get Shar trained to a mediocre level of competency."

Tuul laughed at the general's remark as both men stood as the general finished. Gruffly he said, "Well, good luck. Scouts Out!"

"Scouts Out!" the two echoed. Tuul turned to fast-pace out of the General's office, obviously not wanting to give him a chance to change his mind, but McCarel hung back. "May I have a moment of the general's time? A private matter."

"Certainly." The general replied. Tuul excused himself and exited the room. As the door slid shut Rosberg held up his hand and said, "Before you get started, you know I wouldn't have brought you back to headquarters unless it was essential. I just don't have anyone on staff with both your tactical expertise and experience with the *Faction*. We're getting hit pretty hard by these slime-balls. This is for StarScout."

McCarel nodded understandingly and replied, "I know. Actually, it's almost providential that I'm here. May I use your computer for a moment? There's something I want to show you."

The general pointed to his desk's built-in console. McCarel tapped in several commands and then turned the monitor toward Rosberg. "See the highlighted name? It's off the latest list." McCarel said. The general glanced at McCarel and nodded. McCarel bent down and tapped in another command. "This is his school record. Read the last paragraph of the commentary."

Rosberg read for a moment then jerked his head up. With an amazed expression, he looked at McCarel. McCarel bobbed his head in assent. His voice caught for a moment as he said, "It's him."

Rosberg sank into his high-backed chair. For a moment he was speechless and then let out a long-drawn out sigh. "After all these years . . . where were they all this time?"

McCarel pointed at another line on the imaged document. Rosberg half-grunted as he read the information. "No wonder. Space knows you looked everywhere, but that's about as far away and isolated as you can get and still be considered in civilized space."

He pointedly looked up at McCarel. "Have you...?"

McCarel shook his head sideways. His eyes misted over as he said, "Couldn't."

He tapped on the monitor screen. Rosberg looked at where McCarel pointed, nodded his head and said, "Ah, I see." He looked up at McCarel, "There are exceptions to policy. Under the circumstances I would be willing to override the no-contact rule."

McCarel shook his head emphatically. "Before I came up, I spoke with his ScoutMaster. He felt that even under these extraordinary circumstances that it would be better that we wait. The distraction would be enormous and might mentally and emotionally jolt him too much.

"The ScoutMaster thinks he's peaking at the right time and should make the grade. Given that he's worked so hard for this opportunity, I think I can wait a little while longer before we meet."

Rosberg again shook his head in amazement at the incredible coincidence of timing. Another thought struck him and he looked up sharply. "His mother?"

McCarel replied, his voice choking. "There is a death certificate on file. Over a year ago."

There was a long moment of silence before Rosberg softly said, "I'm so sorry."

McCarel didn't answer for a long time as he worked to control his emotions. Finally, he said, "Thank you sir. I appreciate that, and everything else that you've done for the McCarel family. I just wanted you to know before I left."

Rosberg came around the desk and laid a hand on McCarel's shoulder, "I appreciate that." He shook his head as if still thinking about this extraordinary occurrence. "Who's his ScoutMaster?"

"Tarracas."

Rosberg looked at McCarel for a moment in stunned silence. "How . . ."

"I don't know," McCarel began, "My guess is that his mother told him and he requested the assignment."

Rosberg ran his hand across his mouth. "Do you think she told him everything?"

McCarel took a deep sigh. "I don't know and I didn't press Tarracas, for obvious reasons. But the fact that he's using his mother's maiden name makes me suspect that he may know at least some of the story. I'm sure he's seen his own birth certificate."

"Well, he couldn't have a better ScoutMaster," the general said. "The kids who make it through his program are top-notch." The general ran his hands through his graying hair and mused again, "After so many years."

He then gathered himself and became businesslike again. "Colonel, thanks for sharing this with me. It's put some bright light into an otherwise dark day. Now, it's time we both got back to work. You've got a mission and the clock's ticking."

"Yes, sir." McCarel said as he stood. "Thanks for listening."

Rosberg nodded and said, "One last thing, colonel." He tapped on the screen. "He's in good hands. He'll be fine, just has to do his part and keep a level head. You, on the other hand, are about to go swimming with a bunch of human sharks that bite and bite hard. Don't let this throw you for a loop and forget what you're doing Out There. You and I both know that preoccupation with the wrong thoughts has cost many scouts their lives. Keep yours on the job at hand."

"Aye aye, sir!" McCarel replied as he snapped a sharp salute and headed for the door. As the door dilated [Closed] behind him, McCarel reflected that the general was pretty accurate in his description of the *Faction*. They were indeed becoming like sharks with blood-scent in the water. Vicious and uncaring as to whom they attacked.

A sudden chilling thought came over him. Yes, almost certainly he would soon be swimming with blood-crazed sharks, but it was very possible that so would a very special junior scout. And there was nothing that McCarel could do to protect him.

Chapter 14

Omega-Epsilon

The spinning current pulled the one-person kayak closer to the cliff's pinnacle wall, if the scout couldn't stroke his way out of the maelstrom he would most certainly be sucked under. Spotting the tiniest of breaks between foam-covered waves, the man dipped and flipped his twin-bladed paddle expertly, powering the kayak forward, using the rush of the raging flow and his own powerful strokes to sprint his way past the churning explosion of water.

Seconds later he shot out of the frenzied rapids as the narrow canyon widened on each side, the towering sand-colored walls lowering noticeably with tiny white beaches checker-boarding the sides of the muddy river. The scout leaned back and let the now lazy current carry him along.

Blasting the rapids in this particular river was one of the true pleasures he allowed himself, though this trip was more than just a vacation. He was on business as well; and very serious business at that. If he didn't find some answers soon, the violent vortex that he had just escaped from would seem like a cushion-float down one of the placid streams that fed this mighty river.

He soon spied the particular beach he was looking for and paddled forward, sending the kayak's nose into a tiny inlet and grounding it on the soft sand. Sitting uncomfortably on a small boulder just above the shoreline was a small, swarthy man who glanced anxiously from side to side. He kept reaching up to nervously pull at his right ear lobe. Though the sun shone brightly overhead and it was a warm day, his sallow skin looked pale and cold. Obviously he didn't see sunlight very often and the fact that they were meeting in the outdoors wasn't appealing.

"I don't like this," he fairly hissed as the senior scout walked up. "There are a lot of people up on the rimrock trail; someone could have a soundscope on us, listening to our conversation."

"Nonsense," his companion replied, "No one knows we're here, highly doubtful that anyone followed me or you, and those people are too far away to hear us. Besides, if someone did have a soundscope on us, you've certainly piqued their curiosity now, don't you think?"

"We should have met in *the mount*, like before," the tawny man said in a dark undertone. "Put up audio and visual blocks. No one would have seen or heard us."

"No. We've met like that too often. It's time to change. I don't want anyone getting suspicious. Everyone knows that this is what I do to relax so it's perfectly natural that I'm here. By the way, if you pull at your ear one more time, it's going to fall off into the river and become fish-bait."

He took a water-ball from his hip-pouch and popped it into his mouth. He swallowed the cool liquid and asked, "You have what I asked for?"

The nervous man picked up several pebbles and finger-rolled before answering, "And my—"

"The usual, with a triple bonus if you deliver."

"Not good enough,"

'What! Listen, you little—"

"No, you listen. I have information. I have some wonderful information. In fact, this is so good, that you'll be more than happy to give me what I want."

The senior StarScout looked around for a moment before answering. "Alright, but I'll need some proof of this wonderful information that you have."

The dun-colored man nodded. "Fair enough. Three little letters. S O G." He threw one of the pebbles in the river where it made a tiny splash.

The scout had started to pop another water ball but it never reached his mouth. His hand with the ball hung suspended in mid-air as he demanded. "SOG? What are you talking about?"

"You know who and what SOG is?"

"Of course I know what SOG is. I'm not some idiot "

"Easy, easy," the swarthy man snickered, waving his hands upward to the ~~crystal~~ blue sky, "Calm down, remember, we're tourists enjoying the beauty of the great outdoors."

"I'm calm. Now explain."

"Not until I see some coins in the kitty. Big coins." [what?]

Glaring, the scout reached into the kayak to bring out his day-pack. He took out his bancmachine and punched in numbers. He showed the display to his companion. "Nice, for a start," he replied and hooked up his own machine to the scout's to receive the transfer.

"What if I told you that your very own J2 was hooked into SOG's communication system and they were talking to each other?"

"I would tell you that you're either inventing this or you haven't a clue how StarScout works. That is totally impossible."

"Oh," the small man replied, "Then try this. Two comm calls. First call: your logistics section. Find out if a Spartan Five hyper-modulator, with co-synch and beta oscillation was ordered for the J2's computer. Second call: lower level guard post. Ask the sergeant to check the log to see if two civilians were admitted to the mount five days ago, specifically around 0600 hours. Who authorized it, who escorted them, what security access, and their nature of business."

The scout frowned skeptically at his companion but activated his trans-comm and made the two calls. After the last, he slowly set down his communicator and demanded, "Alright, explain."

The little man grunted and started, "The Spartan 5 is *the* top-of-the-line encryptor and decoder. Ultra, ultra sophisticated. StarScout doesn't use them. Too high-grade for your systems and very expensive to maintain and support. To requisition one is no big deal as the military uses them so they're in the system. But for a StarScout system to talk to a SOG system takes a very, very special program before the two systems are language synched. And to program the Spartan requires at least two cleared individuals. From SOG and only from SOG."

He grinned crookedly, "Let me guess. First call: a Spartan 5 ordered and delivered several days ago to the J2. Second call: Two civilians. Nature of business:

personally cleared by General Rosberg so nothing entered in the log. Escort: Tuul. Security access: anything they wanted and then some." He leaned over to slyly whisper, "How am I doing for guesswork?"

He chunked another stone in the river before continuing. "Now, you can believe what you want. But, that Spartan 5 became active at the same time that those two civvies were in the mount; ergo, they were from SOG. No other explanation fits."

The StarScout felt his disbelief melt away into astonishment. Before he could speak the smaller man said, "Now being the smart man that you are, your next question to me is, what are they talking about over that very sophisticated device?"

The scout took two steps to half-sit on a large boulder, shaken at this news. Finally he growled at the man, "You're right, I am smart and that was the exact question I had in mind."

"And a good question it is. But the answer is going to need another throw into the pot." He slid his own bancmachine over to indicate what was needed next.

The scout clenched his fist repeatedly, he hated working with this nauseating character but he knew he had to because of the man's skills and abilities. He was a genius at what he did but their association was a devil's pact. He punched some numbers in and showed the man the display.

"Good, but not good enough." Angrily, the scout stabbed at his own machine and held up the display. "Excellent." The man chuckled and said, "Given your earlier reaction and the fact that we want to appear to be having a delightful conversation about this and that, I suggest you take a deep breath and use all of those stress reducing techniques that the StarScouts teach."

"Go on," the scout sputtered, "My patience is wearing very thin . . ."

The swarthy man shrugged and said, "Your J2 is tied into the SOG's Omega-Epsilon system."

The scout used every means at this disposal to remain calm, but the man's casual statement rocked him to his very core. Neck muscles taut, he sucked in a breath and demanded in a fierce whisper, "Omega-Epsilon? He has access to OE? You're absolutely certain of this?"

"Absolutely certain. There's no doubt."

"How do you . . ."

"Know?" The smaller man said matter-of-factly. "Anybody worth their salt has tried to hack OE. The code is very distinctive. You see it once, you never forget. When I tapped the J2's computer it was right there." He rocked back and forth several times, grinning crookedly as if he had told a wonderful joke. "Oh yes, he's got access to OE."

The StarScout had to practically will his legs to stand firm so that he didn't slide to the soft sand at this feet. He was totally dumbfounded, speechless at this revelation. The Omega-Epsilon system was the nerve center for SOG; the literal center of the vast intelligence network that SOG commanded. He only knew about it because of his high place in StarScout Command. But his knowledge was not of the practical variety as it was absolute standing policy that StarScout did not cross into the political and governmental arena and therefore no information from SOG was ever passed to them, even to the Commanding General of StarScout Command.

His mind raced feverishly until he croaked out, "Do you know what . . ."

"He's passing to them and vice versa?" The scout nodded emphatically in unspoken reply. The thin man looked at his bancmachine wistfully and said, "If only I could, then you'd be adding a lot more zeroes to your last deposit for the information." He smiled wanly, "So—yes and no."

The scout looked puzzled and said, "What do you mean?"

The little man sighed and said, "There is a gatekeeper sub-routine in the Spartan 5. Controls incoming and outgoing data. Must've been a microsecond burp in the electron flow because I found one file that was partially encrypted but not totally. Somehow the fact that there was an encryption failure wasn't caught on either end." He reached inside his jacket and pulled out several sheets of plaspaper. "Doesn't look like much of anything to me though."

The scout roughly snatched the sheets and started reading. A few minutes later he turned to the last page. His eyes found the now familiar pattern, *Alstar, Laron, Sega IV, Simbards Planet* . . . Then his breath caught as he saw a new name, *Froma IV*, on the list.

He had been wrong about Tuul and McCarel. They weren't working on some project against the organization. Most of this data wasn't about the

Gadion Faction. In all the information there was only one real common denominator. Him.

The unexplained changes in orders, mission and personnel switches, misappropriation of resources, false reports . . . the incriminating evidence was all there. He had always thought it was buried too deep for anyone to find. But as he looked at these few pages, he now realized that with the right questions and computer data correlation it was possible to bring it to light.

He nervously ran his hand over his forehead and felt tiny drops of sweat bead upon his tanned brow. He hadn't felt this stomach tightening constriction since his last real mission Out There when he came face to face with an Arkkar Beast.

And now he understood why Rosberg had kept this away from him from the very beginning and only met with those two. Rosberg suspected him. What had tipped him off? He didn't know, but it was clear that they were suspicious of him and had carefully isolated him from their true activities. Fortunately he had his own sources or he would have never known what they were up to.

He placed another water ball in his mouth. *Froma*

IV. The suspicion had probably begun with *Froma IV*, he thought. That had been a bad decision. He'd had to do too much explaining, too much cover-up and now the trail had come full circle.

The swarthy man stared intently as the scout paced the beach. With a crooked grin he spoke, "I was wrong. The way you're acting it must be pretty hot stuff," he said, "I think I should charge you after all."

The scout cut him off by reaching out and roughly grabbing his arm. "You're absolutely sure there's no way you can get in and see what else Tuul is passing to them?"

With obvious disdain the swarthy man pushed the senior scout's hand away. "I'm sure." He laughed as he said, "If I had SOG's resources, I could, but not with the stuff I have."

The scout walked to the water's edge and studied the river for several minutes. He made a decision and whirled around. "Head back. I'll be in touch in a few days. You'll get what you need." The little man sat transfixed for a moment, his mouth slowly opening in amazement. The scout held up a hand, "No questions, not now, and definitely not later." He pointed to the man and said, "I want to know what Tuul is up to, that's all you need to know. Understood?"

Rising, the man brushed at his clothes before answering in sullen tone, "I understand," and headed up the arroyo trail that led to the top of the canyon. The scout paced on the tiny beach as he searched for answers. The real question was how close were they to the actual truth? Did they know all or were still putting the evidence together? His instincts told him that they didn't have it all pieced together or he wouldn't be standing on this beach. That meant he still had time to act.

He would speak with his contact in the organization to let them know of the situation. They would help him. They would . . . he stopped in mid-thought. A cold wind seemed to blow across his body even though he stood in the midst of a hot desert.

His mind chilled as he stopped to think through what the organization's reaction would be to his news. What would they do if they thought that he was compromised, that he was no longer an asset but a liability? That not only was he under suspicion by the Confederation, but worse still, that maybe through him Confederation intelligence could tap into *Faction* operations?

He savagely kicked at the water sending a ruddy spray skyward. No, that was *not* the answer. As long as he was clean, he was an asset and could expect appropriate rewards. But let even a hint that he was under suspicion come to the *Faction's* attention and

Abruptly an audio signal came across his communicator. He instantly recognized the tone as Rosberg's personal signal. He took a deep breath and opened the comms channel.

"Sir, Major Tomas here, I have a message from General Rosberg for the General Staff."

"Go ahead," the scout responded.

"Yes sir. The message reads: *On my personal orders, Colonel Tuul and Lieutenant Colonel McCarel will conduct a staff study of joint intelligence operations in Sector 11. They will be out of garrison for approximately 2-3 weeks. Major Witte is Acting J2 effective immediately and temp promoted accordingly. Additionally, I have left garrison and will be inspecting the Ganymede training site and observing academy cadets conduct liquefied ammonia training on Europa. I will be off-site for 5-7 days. My normal staff brief is cancelled until I return.*

Rosberg."

The senior scout grew deep in thought. *Joint intelligence operations.* What in the world were joint intelligence operations? Joint with whom? And for what purpose? The more he re-ran the message in his head the more questions came to his mind, especially in light of what he had just discovered. He finally came to the conclusion that Tuul's and McCarel's mission were part of their investigation and this was Rosberg's attempt to cover for their real assignment.

A dark idea came to his mind that he at first dismissed but which persisted until he finally came to terms with its evil intent. Maliciously it wormed itself into his thoughts until he not only accepted it but embraced it as his only alternative. For just a moment the light from the Scout honor code and oath broke through the darkness, but he consciously pushed it aside. He knew that he had stopped being a true StarScout a long time ago and became someone and something . . . else.

He made another comm-call and heard, "J2, duty officer Kurkhof." He quickly identified himself and said, "I just received the general's message," he began. "Has Tuul left yet?"

"'Fraid' so, sir," the woman replied. "Booked out of here about an hour ago." She paused for a moment as if checking something and then said, "I believe he's catching the 0100 hours shuttle to Luna, but he said he needed to take care of some personal business first. I can page him."

The silver-haired scout thought quickly. "Er, no. If he hadn't left I was just going to touch bases with him about the upcoming Castor and Pollux operation. The last report showed some severe gravity fluxes in the deployment area."

The woman agreed, "Yes, he mentioned that to me and we've already got a series of survey drones enroute. I'll run the reports up to you when the analysis is completed."

"Good. That will be fine." He hesitated a moment as if another thought had come to him. "You know the general must have ordered them to deploy so quickly that I didn't see anything on their route and destination. Did Tuul leave an itinerary behind by any chance, for contact purposes?"

"Sir, he blasted out of here pretty quick. Stopped in my office long enough to give me the news. Said that if I really needed to get hold of him to query the

CG, he'd know. Nothing posted."

He arched his eyebrows at that. "That's very odd. Any idea why?"

"Just a hunch. The J2 has been looking at quite a bit of stuff concerning Barkley's Battalion out in the Helix. It's no secret that they've been having significant problems so I think the CG is sending Tuul and McCarel out for a surprise inspection on Barkley. Beggin' your pardon, but I don't think the CG wanted anything posted so as to not tip off Barkley."

The darkly tanned scout blinked a couple of times. Unwittingly, her assessment tied in perfectly with his previous discovery. Yes, the chances were more than good that Tuul and McCarel were headed to the Helix. If he were them, that's where he would head.

He nodded and spoke firmly "Thank you. If I need to find them I'll send the message through channels to the general. Out." The conversation had settled the question in his mind and solidified the only course of action he now had.

He paced a few steps down the small beach to the edge of the silty river. The water pulsed and gurgled as it flowed downstream toward another narrow canyon. Currents within currents pushed and pulled the water in different directions. Tiny flows merged into larger ones then broke apart as the flow hit unseen underwater rocks. For a moment the scout felt as if he were the river, being pushed and pulled by currents that were out of his control and by events that were becoming a maelstrom of deadly chaos.

He looked downstream at the next bottle-neck. The channel narrowed to mere meters between the cold rock walls. The towering rapids within were dubbed "The Liquidator" on his park map. At this moment he had the intense feeling that if he didn't take care of Tuul and McCarel and the organization found out he was compromised, a watery death would be far more preferable than what he faced from the master of the *Faction*.

He had no choice. The fury of the storm was upon him and he had to act. He opened his trans-comm. Seconds later his daughter responded and he spoke softly, "You wanted to do something about McCarel? It's time."

Chapter 15

Finger Lakes of Acid

Del watched as the two pilots artfully worked the pilot and navigation controls. He judged that at the *Queen Bee's* speed coupled with the orbital velocity of the planetary debris, an impact would send the rock fragment slicing through the ship like a blistering blowtorch cutting plastic. A hit in a critical part of the ship would spin them out of control to a fiery crash on the planet's surface.

Del heard Dan speak to his co-pilot, "All right, Karm, I've got the helm. Disengage auto-pilot."

"Auto off," the co-pilot replied. "Pilot has the helm."

Seconds later she said, "Trajectory locked for tip-over. Deceleration at eight gravities. Approach path is nominal, all systems reading green. Altitude, 30,000 kilometers. We have two bogeys portside at 16 degrees to attack angle axis. Tracking computer says they'll pass astern and above."

"Roger," Dan said in clipped tones. Both pilots' voices were calm but Del could feel a tenseness fill the bridge as the *Queen Bee* entered the debris cloud.

As the seconds trickled by Del kept his eyes glued to the vis-screen. The screen's lower half showed a crescent slice of the ruddy planet, while the upper still showed the starry firmament of deep space.

"We're at fifteen seconds to reverse attitude. And ten. . . . nine . . . eight . . seven. . ." Karm began to softly chant, counting the seconds down to tip-over, the point at which Dan would push the ship's nose straight down toward the planet.

". . . one, execute!" she exclaimed. The crescent section of the planet on the screen slid upward to fill the whole display. Del could clearly make out distinct features on the surface, a mountain range, large flat spaces that looked like long-dried-up lakebeds, a jagged, winding canyon.

Dan's hands flew over the control board, constantly adjusting their downward plunging path. "Anything forward?" he tensely asked.

"Clear, skipper," she replied, then hesitated for a second before continuing, ". . . wait, we got one on the edge . . . computer's tracking . . . okay, it'll pass ahead and outward by a 1000 meters."

More seconds trickled by. Karm's readout of the computer display picked up speed as they dove deeper into the asteroid cloud. "Two at 30 degrees port, passing astern two kilometers, another at 40 degrees—this one's close, skipper, passing ahead at five hundred meters." She paused, and then said, "Computer readout is going wild with targets behind us . . . the window starting to close down."

Dan ordered. "Concentrate on what's ahead and any vectoring close to us from either side."

"Check." the woman replied. "I'm on it." More seconds trickled by. Karm's voice tensed up. "Okay, we got one . . . cripes, skipper, this one's got our name on it! Intercept course, eight seconds to impact . . . 20 degrees portside!"

Frantically, Dan jabbed at several of the controls. With the internal grav-field on, Del couldn't tell what the pilot was making the craft do, but he had the impression that the *ship* had accelerated.

The tension in the room was thick enough to cut, then Karm let out a breath, "It's sliding . . . off . . . passing behind."

The tension ratcheted down a notch. Del noticed that he'd gripped the armrests of his chair so tightly that he left indents in the cushion when he removed his hands. He leaned forward to watch and listen as the two pilots maneuvered the speeding spacecraft down to the surface.

"Time to invert?" Dan demanded.

Karm quickly replied, "Twenty seconds."

"Forward screen?"

"There's one crossing in . . ." Karm began but just then the vis-screen erupted in brilliant streaks of orange and red colors. One of the spheroids had entered the planet's atmosphere directly in front of the plunging craft. The pounding impact of gaseous molecules on the rock fragment turned its surface a fiery cherry red as it sped downward in its death plunge.

"Pretty," Dan said grimly. "Hope that's not us in a few seconds. We're coming in faster than we programmed. The flight surfaces are going to take a beating when we rollout." He paused for a second. "Give me the count at five, Karm."

"Roger." For a few more seconds there was silence in the astro-compartment, then Karm started the count, "And five . . . four . . . three . . ."

Suddenly she screamed, "Skipper, inbound! Intercept course . . . impact in five seconds!"

Dan slammed his hand down on his pilot console.

A wailing sound erupted throughout the ship as a robotic voice intoned, "All hands! Collision alarm! Repeat, collision alarm!"

Over the sound of the robot's repeating voice Del heard Dan shout to Karm, "Going into the J now!" as he worked the *Queen Bee's* controls.

The ship lurched side-to-side. Half a dozen red lights blinked incessantly on the pilot's console, but the vis-screen showed them plunging downward toward the planet. Del had no problem picking out the craggy peaks of a mountain range that was centered in the vis-screen.

"Where did we get hit?" Dan demanded.

Karma started reading off the damage, "Port-side fuselage punctured, compartments 5-delta and 6-echo. Ship's stores. Compartment 7-foxtrot breached. Hydroponics." She stopped for a moment and then said tensely, "Port aero-wing . . . structural failure on forward edge!"

"Okay," Dan said as he stroked his flight controls, "How much of the wing did we lose?"

Reading her display, Karm replied, "About 10 . . . no, 15 percent it looks like."

Dan nodded, "She's still flying tight so let's hope

we don't lose any more surface or we'll start corkscrewing through the atmosphere. The thrusters can't help at this speed."

Del understood all too well. As Dan brought the craft through the inverted phase of the J maneuver, he was hoping that the deceleration forces wouldn't rip off any more of the ship's wing surfaces. The stub like wings jutting from each side of the *Queen Bee,* along with control thrusters, provided maneuverability during the final phase to set-down. Loss of either would be catastrophic.

Del could see that Dan was barely touching the controls, his fingertips deftly running over each display that controlled the myriad aspects of the craft's attitude, bearing, and speed. Dan slowly brought the craft into level flight a mere thousand meters above the planet's surface. At the speed they were going, that distance was less than a second away from impact, but in doing so he saved the remaining portion of his port wing and ensured that the *Queen Bee* would fly another day.

Dan turned to Karm. "I don't think we should try for the set-down spot. Do you concur?"

"Yes. The sooner we set down the better."

Dan spoke over his shoulder to Bianca. "With the damage to the wing, our landing site is unattainable. We'll need to set down at the first likely spot."

"So ordered," Bianca replied.

"Going to S curves to slow us down, start looking for a landing site!"

"On it, skipper!" Karm returned and brought up a topographic view of the planet's surface on her display.

Slowly rolling the craft to the right, the pilot began a series of side winding maneuvers that would provide atmospheric braking to the craft. Judiciously applying forward thrusters, Dan slowed the craft even more. For approximately a minute, the ship turned in a long shallow arc to the right, and then Dan rolled the ship as he repeated the maneuver to the left.

He nodded at Karm. "One more to the right. We've stretched our luck enough for one day."

"Check," she replied. "On the swing-back, come to heading one six zero . . . dry lake bed, ten kilometers distant. Looks pretty good."

"Anything looks good at this point," Dan grunted. A few moments later the forward vis-screen showed a white glare that outlined their landing site. Coaxing her down, Dan softly grounded the craft, the four main landing struts firmly planted on the hard-packed ground.

"Power down sequence." Dan ordered. A few moments later, Dan announced over the intercom, "Secure from off-planet stations. Begin on-planet protocol."

Dan rose from his seat and spoke to Bianca. "Port wing got hit pretty bad. I'll take O'Kelly out with me for a look-over. We're several hundred kilometers short of our intended site. Couldn't be helped. Either I landed her or we all sprouted wings and flapped down that last kilometer."

Bianca shrugged. "It was the right decision and a nice piece of flying, Dan. We'll just alter our, uh, operations to accommodate."

Bianca turned to Del and spoke crisply, "Get your scouts moving. Aft to main cargo. Remember, no funny stuff!" Del unbuckled himself from his gravseat and with his eyes gathered up his teammates to follow Bianca. For just a second he looked at the vis-screen that showed a dusky multicolored alien landscape. Del shook his head in bemusement. They had finally made it to the stars as scouts. To be Out There, but as the captive hostage of renegade poachers! Not exactly what he or his teammates had pictured for their first planet-fall.

[marginalia: ← not a complete sentence]

A few minutes later Del and his team trooped into the main hold behind Bianca. Del's eyes widened perceptibly when he saw six planetary survey craft lined up neatly in the hold. As the scouts walked up to one of them Sami quipped, "Hey, this looks like the one I plowed into old man Klotz's greenhouse on my solo qualification exam!"

"In that case," Bianca dryly commented, "We'll make sure that you don't lay your hands on the pilot controls." Del couldn't help but smile at her snide comment. "Your team trained in these models?" Bianca asked.

Del nodded, "Close enough. These look like 30 models—we did most of our flying in 29's."

"Good" Bianca replied, "We picked these up cheap as Fed Navy surplus. Was such a good deal that we didn't even try to steal 'em." In a brisk tone she ordered, "You'll help on the preflight." She pointed at Nase and Shanon. "Lima 1 with Hannoh. You," she said to TJ, "Lima 2. Clarkston will tell you what to do."

She turned to Sami and ordered, "Since we want to keep you far away from the pilot controls, you check the latrine systems on all six craft. The technical inspection checklist is in the preflight manual. Make sure the catch tanks are drained and flushed before liftoff, which is in two hours."

"Hey," Sami sputtered, "Wait a minute. I qualified on my solo, it wasn't my fault that the stabilizers cut out on my set-down. Ask any of them, they'll tell you I qualified." Del lowered his head and bit his lower lip to keep from laughing at Sami's plaintive appeal.

Bianca was unmoved, and hooked a thumb toward the craft. "Latrines."

Sami glared at Del and crossly muttered under his breath, "The things I do to save your hide . . . you owe me, Baldura."

Bianca jabbed a finger toward Del. "Lima 3. All the preflight maintenance and ballistic checks are complete. Finish the life support and stores inventory."

Del trotted over to Lima 3 and looked the little airship over. The "scouters" were the mainstay planetary survey craft in StarScouts. He wasn't particularly surprised that the poachers were able to purchase these at a surplus lot since new models came out almost every year. The outdated, older craft would almost certainly go to surplus sales.

The machine was essentially just a flying platform covered with a tough sylcron shell. The upper half from the pilot's pod to the access hatch was a composite see-through sylcron layer. At that point a two-meter-wide titanium metal strip cross-sectioned the craft and held the one main hatch with its air lock on the starboard side.

The Jonson nucleonic engine and fuel pods were sealed aft. The little craft had two decks; the main deck held the pilot's pod in the nose, a small passenger compartment directly behind, and a service compartment with a spartan hygiene area, repair locker, medical cubicle, science station, and a one-person mess area. The cramped lower level served as a cargo hold.

Normally, StarScout assigned two of the craft to a team of five. The couches in the passenger compartment served as flight seats and as fold-down beds. As a home away from home it made the most austere of ship's quarters seem luxurious. As a flying base from which scouts, or in this case poachers, could operate, the craft was tough, easy to handle and had proven its worth many times.

Entering the craft, Del headed for the service area to the inventory list. As he started aft he noticed that the hatch leading to the small cargo hold was up. As he approached the square opening he heard a small cough from below. He knelt and called out, "Ahoy, the cargo bay!"

There was a sudden grunt and the sound of something metallic hitting the deck. A man stuck his head up and growled at Del. "What are you doing here!"

"Bianca said to finish the preflight inventory. Need some help down there?"

"No!" the man snapped, obviously agitated by Del's presence. He opened his mouth to speak, and then apparently changed his mind. "Go over to Lima 6 and do the store's inventory. I'll finish up here with what's needed. Don't worry; I'll square it with Bianca. Now, go on."

As Del stood he noticed the man turn away from the hatch and pick up what he had dropped. It was a calibration pic used in repairing or replacing the landing strut seals on the craft. The telescoping struts were withdrawn into the belly of the ship when it was airborne or when it ran submerged. The strut's inner and outer seals prevented atmospheric or fluid leaks into the ship.

The only reason Del recognized the pic was that he and a maintenance tech once replaced all the seals on the trainer model at school. The pic was a specialized tool designed specifically for strut seal repair. Del thought it odd that the man was working on the seals. Unless the craft had seen a lot of action, which he doubted, the seals should be fine for a long time on this new model of scouter. Mentally shrugging off his thoughts, he strode over to Lima 6 and got to work.

Two hours later, just as Del finished the last of his inventory checklist, someone stuck his head inside the craft and shouted, "Finish up. Out-bound briefing in five minutes!" Del finished storing the last of his items, closed the med-locker and hurried from the craft. He joined his teammates in the small crowd that gathered in front of the first survey craft.

Bianca waited until two others joined the semicircle and began. "Because we landed short of our primary landing site, we're going to alter the original plan."

She held up a large mosaic still-photo of the planet's surface and pointed to a white-looking area in the midst of the more numerous tans and reds. "We're here. We originally were going to this line of volcanoes, but considering fuel consumption and distance from the ship, we'll head instead to this smaller chain of volcanic mountains. They're two hundred kilometers out and approximately planetary north from the *Queen Bee*."

On the mosaic Del could clearly see the familiar cone-shaped outline of a number of volcanoes that ran along the equivalent of this planet's east-to-west axis. He could also see that directly south of the volcanoes was a series of what looked like finger lakes, but Del was quite sure that this planet didn't have liquid water of the type found on Terra.

Bianca pointed to the volcanoes. "Unlike our original destination, this chain appears to have very high seismic activity. It's unlikely that an eruption will occur, but the possibility of ground movement, slides, and falling rocks is very real. There are numerous fumaroles along the flanks. Stay away from them! The escaping gas from the vents is highly pressurized and extremely hot.

"The data indicate that these volcanoes are just as likely to have quartzite deposits as the other chain, but because of the seismic activity, it may be just a little harder to find.

"Stygar 6's atmosphere is rated at three hundred millibars." She stopped and looked straight at Sami, "That's about one-third of Terra's atmosphere at sea level."

Sami grumbled under his breath, "I know what a millibar is . . . I used to go dancin' in one every Saturday night."

Bianca ignored the snickers and continued, "Oxygen content is less than 1 percent, with the rest of the atmosphere composed of trioxide, ammonia, and sulfuric gases. In other words, it's flex-suit country. Once we upload in the scouters, everyone suits up and stays suited until we return.

"Scan your suit! Make sure there aren't any microscopic tears that might widen under the internal pressure load and blow out." She shrugged and said, "Remember, it's your skin . . ."

Seeing that she had everyone's attention, she

continued, "Surface gravity 6 percent higher than Terra, so you'll have to exert a bit more effort in your work. Watch your food and water intake to compensate for the extra labor. No solo work outside, pair up in buddy teams!"

Shanon, standing next to Del, leaned over and whispered in his ear, "Sounds almost like a mission out-brief from the ScoutMaster."

Del nodded silently. Bianca was very precise and detailed in her briefing and much more explicit and professional than he expected from an outlaw leader. It was evident that Bianca was very much in command of this renegade group and handled them in a crisp, efficient manner.

As he mulled this over he almost missed Bianca's next comments. ". . . and since this will be a short hop, we'll let our guests pilot us out. We'll just see how well our education tax dollars are paying off." Several of the poachers in the group guffawed loudly.

"Craft assignments," she went on as the laughter died down. "Ry and I will take Lima 3 out. Gant and Aron in Lima 1, Josep and Stevon in 2, Matt and Pat in 4." She spoke directly to the scouts, "You two," pointing at Del and Sami, "In Lima 3 with me." She assigned Shanon to the number 4 craft, TJ to craft 2, and Nase to Lima 1.

"All right, up-ship in ten minutes," she ~~crisply~~ ordered and strode away. Just then, Dan came into the hold and motioned to Bianca. The two walked a short distance away so that they couldn't be heard and began talking. Standing near Lima 3's open hatch, Del noticed that both of them had worried looks on their faces as they spoke in hushed tones.

It didn't take much guessing to figure out the topic of the conversation. Dan had been outside inspecting the damage to the ship. From the looks on the two, Del surmised that the damage was severe, maybe bad enough that the *Queen Bee* couldn't power off the planet.

Del considered this possible new development. If they couldn't up-ship, the outlaws would almost certainly have to call for help. Renegades normally didn't have support organizations, so that meant that if they sent out a distress call it would either be the Confed Navy or StarScouts that responded to their hail this far out in deep space. And one look in the *Queen Bee*'s cargo holds by either of those would-be rescuers and these characters would wind up in the ship's brig.

He liked the sound of that idea. He would alert his teammates, start making plans for their own escape if the authorities showed up. He winced as another thought hit him. If they were indeed grounded and didn't get rescued soon . . . the effects of the poison inhibitor would wear off.

Del shook his head vigorously. It wouldn't do any good to mull over that particular thought. He would deal with each situation as it arose. Bianca had a last parting word to Dan and walked briskly toward Del. She cocked her head toward the ship. "Load up! We've got work to do." As the two entered the ship's passenger compartment, Bianca turned to Del. "You'll pilot us out." She smiled sarcastically at Sami and said, "And if you're a good little boy, I might let you bring us home."

Sami scowled but remained silent. Laughing, Bianca nodded toward the back of the little ship and said to the two of them, "You'll find your vests and trans-comms back there. Suit up."

Surprised, Del and Sami went aft and found their scout equipment hanging next to flex-suits. Both scouts were well versed in using the suits. Intensive training excursions to Luna, learning how to be human flies on the craggy rim rock walls of craters or effortlessly racing across the tranquil dust-seas of earth's moon taught them the intricacies of the simple but rugged suits.

They donned the protective clothing and slipped their scout vests over the glossy-skinned suits. They applied skin-glue to their cheeks, set their microphones in place and inserted ear receivers. After running pressure checks to ensure the suits were airtight, they flipped their soft helmets back and went forward. Del was about to do a comm check with Sami when he was startled to hear in his earpiece, "You two scoutees all wired up? If so, get moving. I don't want to be tail end Charlie."

Del was surprised to see Bianca and Ry, the second poacher making up the team, wearing scout trans-comms. Seeing his expression, Bianca said in an exasperated tone, "What's the matter? Did you think that StarScouts are the only ones to use personal comm-links? Well, think again. We've been using them ever since I got in the trade. We use them on every . . . umm, transaction."

Del didn't respond and slipped into the pilot's pod.

They know what she is, there is no need for her to attempt any cover up with them.

He understood the poacher's preference for the little comm devices; they were excellent communicators for field operations. Bianca ordered, "Power up. Let's go." Nodding, he ran his fingers over the controls and began to bring the little ship to life. Bianca eased herself into the co-pilot's chair and watched as he energized the ship's systems.

As the others buckled themselves in the passenger compartment, Bianca said to Del, "We're the command ship, so you'll be talking to the bridge and the other craft. The *Queen's* your reference point, so set a course of 16 degrees and speed at two hundred knots. Altitude 300 meters."

"Yes ma'am," Del said. Reaching over to the console he clicked open the craft's ship's comm-link. "Lima 1, 2, 4," he ordered, "Report your flight status."

"Lima 1 is go," intoned Nase.

"Lima 2, we're ready."

"Lima 4 has a green board."

"Bridge," Del reported, "this is Lima 3, all Lima craft are ready for ship egress."

"Roger, Lima 3," a voice from the bridge replied. "Stand by for hold decompression and atmospheric match."

Several seconds ticked by while the earthlike atmosphere inside the hold was exchanged for Stygar 6's thin atmosphere. "Lima 3, this is the bridge, atmospheric exchange complete. Hold doors opening. You are clear for lift-off."

"Roger," Del said. Overhead the large cargo doors arched open. With a thin atmosphere, Stygar 6's sky was a velvety purple. Although there was a glare from the giant red sun that rode high in the sky, a few of the brighter neighboring stars twinkled against the dark backdrop.

Deftly touching the controls, Del raised his ship through the overhead doors and set course over the desert landscape toward the distant mountains. Behind him, the other craft rose from the *Queen Bee* and followed. Bianca, seeing that Del had the ship on course, rose from her seat and went aft.

A few minutes after the four craft left the mother ship, Del glanced at his radar screen. In a neat row, the other three craft followed. However, just as he was about to turn his head away, he caught sight of two other blips sliding off the scope in a westerly direction. Puzzled, he looked again at the display. For a few moments he watched as the two blips, obviously the two ships that remained behind, shoot across the screen at a high rate of speed. They were going somewhere in a hurry!

Del was about to turn and make a comment about the other craft when he heard Bianca enter the pilot's pod behind him. "Ok, Baldura," she said, "Activate your topographic display. We'll line out your course settings and flight altitude." Del pressed the control that brought up the topographic map on the pilot's monitor.

Scanning the multidimensional display, which charted out his current path over prominent terrain features, Del saw that Stygar 6 was not a flat, featureless planet. Large, rolling hills intermixed with sharp valleys were pockmarked by various sizes of impact craters. Many of the orbiting asteroids were pulled to Stygar 6's surface in a fiery dive, burrowing deep into the planet's crust, leaving a crater as their death marker. Several of the giant craters had huge debris swaths, with plume like sprays of ash, rock and boulders extending tens of kilometers from their rims.

"Stay on this course and speed," Bianca said, tapping on the display. "When you get to the beginning of this finger lake, peel off and head up the lake to this point." She pointed to a spot where a cluster of three volcanoes formed a rough triangle. "Look for a landing spot near the base of this mountain, but I don't want to go too high on its flank. Once we head up the lake, the others will peel off and proceed to their designated landing sites. Any questions?"

Del shook his head, forgetting to ask her about the other two scouter craft he had seen on the radarscope. With the craft on autopilot for now, he was absorbed in what he was seeing out of the large sylcron windows. From his position, Stygar 6 looked like a barren, lifeless world; nonetheless, it was Del's first alien planet as a junior scout and that made it tremendously exciting.

An hour later, Del could see the volcano range looming over the horizon. Shortly after, an orange, almost red hue in the landscape materialized just ahead and below. Looking at the topo display he realized that it was the beginning of the finger lake. Del called, "Lake coming up!"

"Check," she replied as she came forward. Sticking his head into the pilot's pod, Sami looked at the landscape and said, "What's in those lakes? Certainly not good ol' H-two-O?" [H₂O handwritten correction]

Bianca shook her head and replied, "No, no water down there. The name is a bit misleading. These aren't lakes with liquid water. They're more like trenches or catch basins for a highly corrosive mixture that resembles hydrochloric acid. From our spectra-analysis on the way in, the acidity level of the stuff is off the pH scale."

"Terrific," Sami muttered. "And we're flying over a whole lake of the stuff."

One corner of Bianca's mouth lifted in a slight smile. "The basins have cliffs that are several hundred meters high. Since they sit just below the volcano string, it's possible that the acidic liquid is spewing out from underground vents."

She glanced over at Sami. "If for some reason we lost power and landed in the slop, even if totally immersed, the ship's titanium-syclron frame would withstand the corrosive effects of the liquid. But a few drops would probably eat through your flex-suit." With a little laugh she said, "It's not the kind of place you'd want to hold a beach party."

She gestured toward the upcoming lake and said

to Del, "All right pilot, we're coming up on our divergence point." She turned to Sami and said, "Take the copilot seat. I'll be aft catching a few winks." She looked at both and then said with a slight upturn to her mouth, "With one hand on my laz-gun . . . and I sleep very lightly . . . and shoot without hesitation . . . understood, scoutees?"

Del and Sami looked at each other and nodded solemnly, both very sure that she meant every word. Sami settled into the co-pilot's chair and glanced aft for just a second, "Whew," he said quietly, "That is one tough lady," he offered.

Del snorted, "Wouldn't exactly call her a lady," he countered in a half-whisper, "She's female alright, but I don't see many lady-like qualities in her."

"Guess that depends on your perspective now doesn't it amigo? From where I come from, she'd be one very desired lady . . . and I do mean lady. With her on your arm you could walk-the-walk and talk-the-talk and nobody and I mean nobody is going to mess with your house."

Del cocked his head in disbelief, "You're kidding, right? I'll grant you she's tough, but she hasn't any sense of loyalty to anyone or anything other than herself. If I had her on my arm I'd have my other hand holding a cocked laz-gun on her just waiting for the knife thrust in my side."

Sami glanced sideways at Del, "Loyalty a big thing with you Baldura?" he curtly asked. Del was momentarily taken aback as he thought loyalty was a given among StarScout members.

"Yes, of course," he began before Sami interrupted him.

"Me, I think it's pretty much over-rated."
Del was confused, "Wait," he said, "You told me that where you lived you were a member of a gang and that you . . ."

Sami stopped him with a several shakes of his head. "Fake loyalty Baldura, you did what you did because if you didn't you'd find yourself without ears or other body parts . . . it's called survive at all costs . . . absolutely nothing to do with loyalty."

He smiled sardonically and stated stoically, "My father taught me well . . ."

"Your father? I don't understand . . ."

Sami shrugged one shoulder and frowned. "He sold me to the *Garden Hill Diablos* when I was ten." Sami looked over at Del's stricken face and laughed hard, "Don't get all pious on me Baldura, pretty common where I come from."

Del swallowed for a second before asking, "But your mother . . ."

Sami's hands had been playing across the controls, slightly adjusting trim and attitude, now they slowed and finally stopped. He gradually sat back in his seat, and stared out through the cockpit windows. His eyes seemed to light up as he fixed his gaze on some distant point.

He spoke carefully as if to measure out each word. "She would have fit your definition of a lady . . . every bit of it and more. My father was gone most of the time and there wasn't much support from him, so she had to work very hard to support us. She was tired all the time, but never too tired if one of us needed a book read, or a good night story . . ."

"She had one night off a week, but she made sure that on that night it was our family's night . . . we had the best meal of the week, play games, and she always made our favorite treats . . ."

Sami shook himself from his reverie. "But the work was too hard, for too long . . . just wore her out to where she couldn't take care of us . . . so the almighty, we-know-better-than-you authorities took us away and gave us to our oh-so-caring father . . . and, well, you know the rest."

"What happened to your mother?" Del asked sincerely.

Sami looked over at him for a second and then looked down at the controls. "Don't know. Went back once to the old place. It was on the third level of *The Underground*, but the whole place was empty. No one around even to ask."

Both were silent for a long time. Del realized that for whatever reason, Sami had shared something that was very deep and very personal for him. He also realized that Sami was displaying a measure of trust in him for allowing Del to see a part of Sami's life the he was quite sure few, if any, of his teammates knew about.

He thought about what Sami had said and then turned to his teammate. "For what it's worth, your father may not have shown loyalty or love, but I think your mother demonstrated the highest sense of both . . . she lived strictly and utterly for you . . . even to the point where her body couldn't sustain her . . . but her spirit never failed loving you."

A hard lump formed in his throat, "I lost my mother too . . . and before that my father . . ."

For just a second, the two locked eyes. A tiny smile crossed Sami's face and he bowed his head toward Del, a gesture of understanding between the two. In that moment Del felt that he and Sami had found common ground that hadn't existed before, and a feeling of comradeship that hadn't been there before. It was a good feeling.

Del began making course adjustments and informed the following craft that he was arcing off the flight path and starting his run to their landing site. One by one the others acknowledged and started their own course changes.

Flying over the acidic fluid, Del could see that its color ranged from a light orange near the base of the cliffs to a deeper orange, almost red color in the lake's center. Streaks of shimmering yellow and red swirled through the liquid in constantly changing patterns.

Sami asked, "Wonder how deep the trench is?"

Del shook his head, "Don't know, but I'm more interested in knowing if there's alien life swimming around down there."

"In that stuff? It would need armor plating two

meters thick . . ."

"I know, I know. But remember what the ScoutMaster said, that the chance of life in any environment is possible, if life is given a chance to survive in any possible environment."

He looked again at the noxious lake. "I have no idea how life could survive in such a devil's brew, but life has evolved in the harshest of climates on other worlds, so it's possible."

"Yeah, well, you're not going to get me to do no Seek and Locate in that goop."

Del laughed as he said, "Not to worry, the only thing Bianca is interested in are her quadro-diamonds, so I'm sure we're not going to take a dip in the lake.

"But," Del observed, "There isn't any reason why we can't drop a bit lower, just in case something does pop its head out of the liquid." With a grin he said, "Who knows, maybe this is the real hiding place for the Loch Ness monster."

"Uh huh," Sami grunted, "And not only would the Scots be hopping mad that aliens abducted their monster, but you best hope that Missy Nessie doesn't rise up and swallow us whole."

Del grinned and guided the craft down until it was just meters above the swirling eddies. He locked in the altitude settings and put the craft on autopilot while he scanned the flat, waveless surface. Minutes later a red light blinked repeatedly on his control board and the robotic voice of the autopilot sounded loudly, "Adjust altitude, adjust altitude! Safety zone violation, safety zone violation!"

"What the . . ." Del began and turned his attention to his pilot controls. Sami was already checking his side of the control panel, looking for signs of trouble. When Del had set the craft to autopilot, per normal operating procedure, he'd programmed the computer to alert him if the craft dropped to within five meters of the surface. The blaring voice was the computer's way of getting his attention. Looking at his height-above-surface display, he saw that the scouter had lost several meters of altitude in just a few moments.

"That can't be . . ." he started when Bianca stuck her head into the pilot pod.

"What's wrong!" she demanded.

Shaking his head, Del replied, "Nothing really, I set the autopilot at ten meters altitude with five meters as the safety alert mark. According to the instruments we lost almost six meters and the alarm started sounding. But I didn't feel a thing when we dropped."

Bianca motioned Sami out of his seat and slid in behind him. She looked over the instruments for several moments. The craft was flying smoothly, nothing seemed amiss. Shrugging her slim shoulders, she said, "I didn't feel anything either. Get some altitude and run a diagnostic."

"Roger," Del replied and brought the nose of the little craft up. As he leveled off at fifty meters above the lake, Del swiftly ran a computer diagnostic on the flying and navigation controls. He turned to Bianca. "Computer says everything checks out, nominal parameters."

She ran her hand through her short hair for a moment and nodded thoughtfully. "Never known one of these ships to give a false alarm; they're usually very dependable craft." She looked over the instruments again. "It's possible that the alert was correct . . . that we actually lost those meters of height, but not from the scouter dropping in altitude, but from the other way around."

Del looked at Bianca. "You mean the surface

rising five or six meters?" She nodded in reply as she deftly ran her fingers over several of the instrument displays. Del cocked his head at the thought and then said, "But I didn't see a wave and I was looking forward the whole time."

The young woman pursed her lips for a second and replied, "The computer wouldn't have alerted you for a passing wave. The data off the forward-scanning radar would have to show a continuous rise in elevation over a set linear distance before the alarm goes off.

"The computer would have read a wave as a non-threat unless it was high enough to actually hit the ship. No, either the whole lake surface rose several meters which I doubt, or more likely we flew over a large upwelling bubble. Large enough to trip the computer's altitude safety criteria."

Del thought about that for a moment. "Is it possible for the whole lake to rise?"

Bianca tilted her head, "It's possible. Darn near anything is possible Out Here. On Terra there are documented cases of large rises in the water level of farmer's wells and small lakes prior to major earthquakes. We're talking Terran geology, which is not a particularly good model to use in the OutLands. No, most likely it was a huge gaseous bubble that surfaced just as we flew over."

With a twinkle in her eye she said, "Or maybe it was a giant Gorp fish that just burped after finishing its meal . . ."

Sami quipped from behind, "More likely Nessie the Loch Ness monster according to Baldura."

Bianca turned a baleful eye on Del. "You're not serious."

Del looked over his shoulders at Sami, and muttered, "Thanks Sami." With a small laugh, Bianca returned to the small passenger compartment and settled into one of the reclining couches.

Ten minutes later, the volcano string towered directly ahead. Del brought the craft up over the high cliffs that marked the end of the finger-lake and began to look for a suitable landing site. He spotted a likely-looking candidate and put the scouter into a slow glide toward a flat, boulder free spot that sat low on the volcano's craggy flank.

"You want to check this out?" Del asked Bianca as the poacher poked her head into the pilot's compartment. Del pointed to the relatively smooth gray-black landing site.

She nodded approvingly. "Looks good. Set'er down, pilot."

Cautiously, Del brought the little craft closer to the surface, using his belly and nose thrusters to hover a few meters above the gritty terrain. After giving the ground a final look-over, he eased the ship down, telescoping his landing struts downward. Moments later, he had three steady green lights on his control board indicating that the landing struts were reading terra firma.

Del powered the ship down as the scouter settled itself on the volcanic grit. Bianca ordered, "Sami and Ry will do the first survey. Baldura and I will take the second shift."

Sami nodded at Del as he stood to slide his helmet up and over his head. "Baldura," he said, "Log the exact second that I step out on the surface, will ya?"

Puzzled, Del asked, "Okay, but what gives?"

Sami laughed. "Little wager between TJ and me. She bet that she would be the first to set foot on an uncolonized alien planet. I said I would. Looks like I'm going to win the bet."

With a chortle Del asked, "And what's the payoff?"

"If she wins, I sing '*You're the Only Fiery Comet I'll Ever Need*' at graduation."

"And if you win?" Del inquired.

"She sets me up with a date with her younger twin sisters."

"Not bad," Del smiled, "Which sister?"

"Not which," Sami said, "Both. Same date, same time, just me and the twins."

Del and Ry burst out laughing. Bianca growled, "Knock it off. You can socialize on your own time. Right now you're on mine. Sami, check the hatch airlock, test-cycle it manually. Check the seals, disinfectant spray and blower. Baldura, man your pilot board and monitor ship's systems. Ry, break out the collection kits."

Del sat back down in the pilot chair and looked over the terrain where they landed. Three volcanic peaks loomed directly above, while off in the distance two more peaks thrust upward. Still further Del could see the coned outlines of several more as the string marched toward the horizon. The two flanking peaks of the nearby threesome had thin columns of cloudlike smoke steaming upward, while the cratered summit of the center mountain appeared silent and dead.

Close to the scouter, Del could see wisps of smoke and steam wafting out of the dark gravel. In some places, small mounds like craggy pimples dotted the flanks of the smoking mountain. Del was about to adjust one of the controls when he felt the tiny ship rock from side to side. "What was that?" he heard Sami ask.

"One of those earth shifts that Bianca told us about," Del replied, thinking it would take quite an earth movement to cause the ship to pitch that much.

A moment later, Del heard Ry say over the trans-comm, "I'm cycling through the air-lock, stand by for outer hatch opening." A red light appeared on the console indicating that the outer hatch door was now open to Stygar 6's elements. After a few seconds the light went green as the hatch closed and the air-lock reset for a new cycle.

Del heard Sami say, "Stand by for outer hatch opening."

Del looked out to see two figures walk across the desolate landscape toward the upward incline. One of the figures turned and waved. Del could see it was Sami and waved back. Del heard Ry say to Sami,

"Let's get down to business. We're looking for obsidian-like material interlaced with white flakes. The mineral integrator will read between plus four and plus six on the carbon scale."

"Got it," Sami replied. "Hard, shiny black rock with white freckles."

For several minutes Del watched the two as they struggled up the steep flank of the mountain, occasionally losing their footing in the gravelly soil mix. They criss-crossed the slope until they were fifty meters above the landing site. Suddenly both men lost their footing and began sliding downward. At the same moment, Del felt the craft lurch from side to side and sharply vibrate.

It took Del only a moment to realize that they were experiencing a strong earthquake. The ground rolled from the motion of seismic waves coursing through the soil. As the movement subsided Bianca yelled out, "Ry! Sami! Are you okay?"

"Check," Ry replied, "Just knocked us down."

"Yeah," Sami replied dryly, "Ry's fine, since he rode out the quake sitting on my chest."

Bianca ignored Sami and said, "Del, inject a ground motion sensor through the number one underbelly port. We need to monitor this seismic activity. That was a pretty strong jolt."

"Stand by," Del said. He entered the commands into the computer and fired the super hardened sensor into the ground. Using a high-pressure candium ram the sensor would penetrate the hard earth to a depth of approximately three meters. From there it would constantly monitor the ground's motion, giving the team some idea of what was occurring deep below their feet.

Moments later, the first data scrolled across the computer's digital display. "What are the readings?" Del heard Bianca ~~briskly~~ ask from directly behind him.

Del scanned the alphanumeric figures and replied, "Fairly uniform tremor harmonics, up and down the scale, and constant in duration. One stops, another starts almost immediately. Looks almost like a pulsating event."

"What's the depth of the activity?"

Del studied the sensor report, "Pretty close to the surface. Less than five kilometers."

Bianca started to speak when Del quickly said, "Whoops! Hold on, here comes another one." The sensor alerted him to another large pulse heading up through the ground just before it hit. For several seconds the ground swayed, as did their landing craft. Del, watching the data stream as the sensor recorded the subterranean motion, saw something that caused his eyebrows to rise. As the motion tapered off he said, "Bianca, the computer is reading that these events have a double, perhaps even a triple oscillation."

Bianca leaned forward to stare at the readings. The sensor's report indicated that there was more than one deep source of the seismic activity. Multiple points below Stygar 6's surface were convulsing upward. Even as they watched, the intensity scale of the tremors rose markedly higher.

"I don't like this," Bianca began, "The amplitude and frequency readings are increasing exponentially and the activity is way too shallow. We may have landed on a ticking bomb."

Del nodded. He, too, had seen the ever quickening pace of the underground jolts. With a fierce grip Bianca clamped her hand down hard on Del's shoulder. "The lake rise!" she almost shouted, "I'm an idiot!" Slamming her hand down on the communicator button, she fiercely ordered, "Ry! Sami! Get back to the ship now! Move!"

"Roger!" Ry answered. "Get the ship powered up," she barked. "Emergency out-flight! As soon as they're in the air-lock, get us out of here, directly away from this volcano line, full thrust!"

Without speaking a word, Del turned to his board, his hands flying over the console as he programmed the ship to jet them away at a single command. Bianca hadn't said, but it was obvious to Del that the renegade leader suspected the volcanoes were more active than originally thought. She didn't want to be around if they erupted. Which from the sensors was a very real possibility.

Del glanced up at the mountain flank. He could see Sami and Ry scrambling down the steep slope, their vapor-barrier boots sending up sprays of dust and gravel with each lunging step. As he turned back to his control board, his eyes swept momentarily across the seismic activity display. What he saw caused him to start to shout a warning but the words never left his mouth before the devastating temblor rocked the ship violently.

Del was pitched sideways, his head cracking

against the side sylcron window. Dazed for a moment, he clung to the console board. The earth movement overpowered the ship's gyroscopes, sending the scouter gyrating in different directions. For long minutes the ground rolled and heaved as if a gigantic caged animal struggled to free itself from a subterranean prison. Del thought he could actually hear the ground moaning as if in pain from the violent and painful shaking.

Slowly the movement quieted to just an occasional sharp tremor. Righting himself, Del looked out toward the towering volcanoes. "Oh no . . ." he softly said. A giant mushroom cloud ascended from each of the two flanking mountains. Yellow-bright lightning flashes streaked within the clouds as they roared upward into Stygar's stratosphere. Looking at the volcano closest to them, Del was relieved to see no such billowing cloud expanding upward from its cone.

Del scanned the slope for Sami and Ry, and saw both of them lying face down about ten meters away from the ship. Even as he watched, one of the figures stirred and tried to rise from the ground.

Del hit the comms with a fierce jab, "Sami! Ry! Are you okay?"

In a pain-filled voice Ry replied, "Sami's out. I may have broken my arm or wrist."

"Okay," Del answered, "Hold on, I'm coming out to get you!" Just then, Del heard a moan from behind him. As he turned he saw Bianca stagger to her feet, one of her hands holding her head. Del slid out of his chair to steady her. "You all right?"

"Think so . . ." she began. "Got thrown against the bulkhead pretty hard. What happened?" Del quickly explained about the eruptions. "Ry's hurt, and Sami's unconscious. I'm going to get them."

Bianca shook her head and pointed a finger at Del. "No. You stay here, I'll go out. I want us power-boosting out of here the moment that air-lock is sealed!"

"But," Del started to argue but Bianca cut him off. "I'm in charge here, scout," she commanded. "Now move, I don't have time to argue!"

With that, she raised her helmet up, clamped shut the neck seals and strode over to the air-lock. With taut face muscles Del watched her enter the hatchway. Turning on his heel he climbed back into the pilot's pod. As he did so, he noticed a blinking red light indicating a problem with the number three landing strut.

Running through the diagnostic program, Del looked at the report. It wasn't good. The inboard seal on the strut was approaching failure point. When it blew, they would lose cabin integrity, letting Stygar 6's poisonous vapors enter the ship. The hard jolt must have cracked the seal. There was nothing he could do about it, and as long as they remained in their flex-suits, being exposed to the outside atmosphere was the least of their problems.

Del looked outside and saw Bianca determinedly climbing the slope toward the two hurt men. He also saw that the flanks of the mountain now spouted numerous fumaroles, their gasses spewing upward with violent pressure. Del didn't like the looks of that. Just minutes before, except for the furious shaking, this mountain had been relatively quiet.

He turned back to his pilot board and rapidly ran over the flight sequence again, making sure that craft's flight path was locked into the on-board computer. He looked out the window again to check Bianca's progress. She had just reached the two figures. Slowly, she and Ry got Sami to his feet. With a staggered step, they started to slip and slide back down the slope.

Del stopped as his eyes widened in disbelief. A fissure line was opening up right behind the struggling figures on the slope. Like a zipper opening up the ground, the fissure cracked the slope wide as it raced downward.

"Behind you! Look out!" Del yelled into his communicator but the speed of the opening crevice caught the three before they could jump aside. As if a monstrous hand swatted them, the force of the gaseous geysers threw the three up along with boulders and dirt and flung them skyward.

Del started to rise out of his seat when, without warning, the whole back end of the scouter reared up like a bucking horse. Del was thrown forward into the pilot's console. As he righted himself he knew exactly what happened. A fumarole vent erupting directly under the engine compartment was pelting that section with pressurized gas and rock.

Del looked at the pilot's console which had a dozen or more red lights blinking incessantly. The computer voice was squawking, "Hull breach! Hull breach! Compartment one-alpha, portside, number three landing strut!" The force of the fumarole's eruption under the ship had cracked the strut seal! Stygar 6's toxic atmosphere now leaked into the ship.

Del scrambled up to look out the window. He yelled, "Bianca! Ry! Sami! Report your status!"

He didn't see the three anywhere as he surveyed the slope, nor was there a reply on the communicator. Del could hear an ominous deep rumbling coming through the walls of the craft. Looking upward, his eyes widened as he saw a deep-gray, almost black cloud envelop the top of the closest volcano. He raced to the air-lock. As the device completed its exchange cycle Del grunted as he pushed the slow-opening hatch door open and squeezed himself through.

The young scout sped down the short ramp and skidded to a stop at its base. Around him was an inferno of spewing and shrieking gases. Rocks and gravel rained from the sky, thrown upward by the erupting fumaroles. In the dust and blowing smoke he finally spotted an arm and leg draped over a large blackened rock near the rear of the craft.

He dashed to the prone figure and carefully turned the person over. It was Ry. Nearby, another figure lay wedged up against a large boulder. A few meters further, Del saw a figure struggle to stand on wobbly legs. Through the clear faceplate he could see it was Bianca.

"Bianca, can you hear me?" Bianca nodded groggily.

"Yes. Help me with these two. We've got to get out of here."

"A double roger to that," Del replied. "This mountain is about to blow. Help me get Ry up, I'll carry him to the ship, then come back for Sami. When we get back to the ship, stay buttoned up, we've lost cabin integrity."

"Got it," she said through clenched teeth. With Bianca's limited help, Del slung the semiconscious Ry over his shoulder and clumsily maneuvered him into the air-lock. He cycled through and laid the renegade on one of the passenger couches. After tightly buckling in the young man, Del went back outside to find Bianca desperately trying to drag Sami toward the ship. Del grabbed her shoulder and spun her around. "Get in the ship! I've got him!"

She signaled okay and stumbled her way toward the craft. Del staggered behind with Sami half-draped over his shoulder. The ground swayed and rolled beneath their feet several times.

At the ramp-foot she stopped and doubled over. "Get him in first," she said through pain-clenched teeth. Del knew they didn't have the time to argue so he trudged up the ramp and into the air-lock. Cycling through, Del pulled Sami to one of the couches and buckled him in. For several seconds he waited at the air-lock door to help Bianca when she came out, but the small cubicle remained in *ready* mode. Something was wrong.

As he went back through the air-lock and outside, he found Bianca crumpled halfway up the ramp. Del's respect for the renegade leader rose perceptibly. The poacher must have realized that she was in danger of passing out, and had sent Del and Sami through the air-lock first. If she had lost consciousness inside the airlock, the computer would not have allowed the outer hatch door to open, trapping Del and Sami outside in the inferno.

For a split-second a dark thought crossed his mind-to leave the unconscious poacher and her shipmate at the mercy of the impending eruption. After all, she was the cause of his team's misfortune and woes. If it weren't for her they would still be on Terra or more importantly on their No-Notice, and not held in bondage. He could easily explain that she and Ry were caught in the open by a fumarole's blast and he and Sami had just barely made it to the ship and safety.

On whatever star paths I stride and worlds that I visit, I will respect the sanctity of life, taking life only in the defense of my own or for those I hold responsibility.

Del shook his head as he recalled the Scout Oath. These poachers had threatened his life and the lives of his teammates, so why should he respect their lives? No, that wasn't right. If he did what he was thinking, he would just become one of them and that was no aspiration of his. With a firm shake of his head, Del dispatched the malevolent thought of leaving them behind. That wasn't him, and that certainly wasn't how a StarScout would act.

Grasping Bianca under her armpits, Del dragged her into the air-lock. Moments later Del half-carried the woman into the ship and buckled her in one of the seats. He peered through her face-plate for any obvious head injuries and as he did so she moaned and mumbled several words. What she said caused Del to momentarily stop what he was doing and gape at her in amazement. But only for a second—they were running out of time.

Del made sure Bianca's helmet was securely sealed and then slammed himself into the pilot's seat and pulled his shoulder straps tight. With a quick jab he punched the flight buttons on the console. From the rear of the ship came horrific noises as the severely damaged ship's engines raised the crippled ship slowly. Meter by meter the little craft gained altitude and velocity but it was evident to Del that they had scant power to speed them away.

With a backwards glance, Del could see that the two flanking volcanoes were now in full eruption, with sun-hot lava boiling upward and over their glowing cones. Several vents on each mountain were spewing out jets of liquid rock hundreds of meters into the sky.

The little ship almost groaned in agony as it lifted away. To save power and pick up velocity, Del kept the ship at a level altitude just meters above the surface. Skillfully manipulating the controls, Del squeezed every ounce of energy he could from the engines. In moments they passed over the cliffs and were above the glowing orange of the chemical lake.

Satisfied that the scouter was holding its own for the moment, Del flipped open the ship-to-ship communicator and urgently intoned, "Lima 3 to any Lima craft, respond."

Immediately a voice said, "This is Lima 2." In clipped tones, Del described their desperate situation. "I'm inbound at Mark 260 degrees from the *Queen Bee*. Request immediate assistance."

"Understood, Lima 3," the voice crisply replied. "Maintain your course heading, we're the closest to you, we're on our way."

"Thank you Lima 2," Del replied gratefully. A small sound alerted him to a presence behind him. A hand came to rest on his shoulder as Bianca spoke softly, "Thanks for getting us out of there, scout. How bad are we hurt?"

"Haven't had a chance to check Sami or Ry. The ship's in pretty sad shape. We've lost three of the four main thrusters, and the last one is operating at about 50 percent, just enough to give us some altitude and thrust. There's several breaches in the engine compartment and the seal on number three strut is gone so we've lost cabin integrity."

"Okay," Bianca replied, "Keep her going. I'll check

Ry and Sami."

"Better check yourself too," Del replied. "You passed out on the ramp."

"I know, and I will. And I do thank you again, for myself and Ry."

"You're welcome," Del replied, surprised at the gentle tone in the poacher's voice and manner. As Bianca turned away she gasped out, "Look!"

Del half-swiveled to look at where Bianca pointed and immediately knew their good fortune had run out. Directly behind them a growing mushroom cloud appeared. Then in one monstrous detonation, the whole mountain exploded in a raging maelstrom of blazing lava and fiery vapors.

Del only had to take one look to know that the supra-heated cloud of house-size boulders and shrieking, flaming gases rushed at them at a far greater speed than their damaged craft could manage. In seconds the frothing black hurricane would strike and rip apart the wounded ship, hurling Del and his comrades into the acid lake below.

Chapter 16

Acid Maelstrom

Bianca spun toward Del and commanded, "Max speed!"

"The thrusters are red-line now! We've got less than 10 percent left in the power packs!"

Bianca stared at the roiling, black cloud. "Can we get above it?" she demanded.

"No!" Del stated emphatically. "Not enough thrust, I'm barely able to keep her from heeling over and going in the drink."

"Okay," Bianca replied coolly. "We can't outrun it and we can't get above it. So that means we'll have to get below it."

Del looked at Bianca sharply and shook his head. "Bianca, the strut seal is gone, remember? We go in the lake, that seal will rupture! We'll be swimming in acid in minutes!"

"Understand," Bianca crisply replied. "But we've got to buy ourselves some time until help gets here. Hit the Search and Save button and start over pressurizing the cabin! Now, hard over, scout!"

Del turned to his board and slapped the Search and Save switch. There was no need to try and contact the other ships. Once the S and S distress call sounded on their monitors, there would be little doubt that Lima 3 was down.

Practically at the same time, Del commanded the computer to increase the atmospheric volume in the ship. He understood Bianca's idea, to use the built-up pressure to stem the flood if the seal blew. Del needed to keep the craft airborne as long as he could to allow the vent ports to suck Stygar's thin molecules into the cabin. But with the speed of the advancing maelstrom he didn't think they had enough time for the pressure to build up sufficiently to prevent the seal blowout.

Normally, to submerge the craft the pilot simply used the under-belly thrusters to settle the ship gently into the water. Not this time. Del's only option would be to stay airborne until the very last second and then nose-dive the craft into the thick liquid. Del didn't have any idea of the fluid's viscosity. As far as he knew he could be slamming the little craft's nose into liquid cement.

"Bianca! Give me a count!" Del didn't want to lose his concentration on piloting the craft by looking back at the churning cloud. He needed every second before diving the ship straight down.

"Seven! Six! Five!" Bianca yelled back.

At "Three!" Del heeled the craft sharply over and pointed the stubby nose at the glaring red liquid. He watched wide-eyed as the lake seemingly leaped straight up. The ship hit the ochre broth with a thundering splash. The sudden deceleration wrenched Del violently forward.

Behind him he heard Bianca yell and then a loud thud against the forward bulkhead. Shuddering from the sudden braking forces, the craft plunged downward into the dark abyss. The red-orange light from Stygar's primary disappeared and everything turned black. Del instinctively knew that the eruption cloud was passing overhead, blotting out the sun. Though groggy from the jarring impact, Del fought to right the ship before it imbedded itself nose-first in the lake bottom.

Del couldn't see the lake's surface, but knew that the superheated cloud would probably vaporize the first few meters of the acidic fluid, so for now he would keep the craft deeply submerged. Using the ship's thrusters Del leveled off the craft, grateful that he still had some power left for propulsion. He flicked on his outboard lights, but they couldn't penetrate the thick ooze. He glanced at the sonar and saw that the craft had righted itself just a few meters above the dark lake bottom. To each side the sonar displayed the craggy outlines of tall pinnacle-like rock formations.

Del brought the craft to a halt and satisfied that it would hold this position, put the scouter on autopilot, unloosened his shoulder belts and hurried into the passenger compartment. Ry and Sami were firmly strapped in, but Bianca was wedged in a corner of the compartment and unconscious from the impact. Pulling the slim woman onto a couch, Del snugly belted her into the reclined chair.

He was about to go to the med-locker when he heard an increased whine from the rear thrusters. Del felt the ship start to move backwards as if it were in the grasp of a giant Altari suction-fish. He slid into the pilot's seat and checked his controls. The thrusters to propel the ship forward were operating at maximum level but the ship was sliding rearward.

"This can't be," he muttered to himself. He looked out the window and from the lights could see liquid streaming past the nose rearward. He raised himself slightly off his seat, "What is going on...," he began, then stopped. A peewee light above the sonar began to blip.

The craft was losing buoyancy and sliding toward the rocky bottom. Unsure of what was happening, Del increased the power to his midship thrusters but without full power the scouter settled downward. Del could feel a thunderous vibration penetrating the ship's bulkhead.

Del snapped his head up from looking at his controls. He understood! When the volcano exploded it must have blown one side of the towering mountain into the lake. Tens of thousands of metric tons of rock and dirt thundered into the frothing soup. As if a giant hand slapped the aqueous concoction, a monstrous wave must have splashed upward and outward.

Compressed by the basin's tall cliffs, the huge crest sped down the shallow lake. As it did so, the forward edge sucked up not only the liquid but everything else on the basin's bottom. Del realized that he and his craft were caught in that suction and were being drawn into the violent backwash. Del hit his controls to put the little craft on autopilot. ← already auto on pg. 410 from

Del could literally hear the roar of the monstrous wave through the ship's hull. For just a second all of the liquid disappeared from around the ship and Del was looking at Stygar's sun, then just as quickly the forward edge of the wave seized the craft in its whirling vortex.

Gyrating madly, the scouter spun through the thick liquid. For long seconds the little ship tumbled and tossed, the autopilot fighting to keep them on an even keel but failing. Just as it seemed the worst was over, a giant boulder, either picked up by the powerful suction action of the wave, or flung outward from the exploding mountain crashed on top of the wounded ship. The force of the collision propelled the craft headlong toward an enormous rock pinnacle.

As if the boulder were magnetized to the scouter's roof, the massive weight of the huge slab drove the ship toward the underwater spire. With a jarring crash, the craft smashed into the craggy tower. Unable to free itself from its giant rider, the ship slid down the pinnacle to the boulder-littered bottom. The ship landed upright but tilted upward and to one side. With thrusters at full power, the autopilot labored to free the pinned craft from the grasp of the giant rock.

For several seconds, except for the muted whining of the still operating thrusters, there was silence within the craft's cabin. Del tried to focus his jostled brain. For a moment he sluggishly examined his surroundings, and then with a start he remembered his whereabouts.

As he sat upright, he scanned the control board. Like tiny strobes, red lights blinked on every panel. Cabin and hull lights intermittently flickered, giving Del glaring snapshots of his surroundings. For a moment he couldn't understand why the ship wasn't moving. Glancing upward, he saw the dark shape of the massive slab sitting on the scouter. Outlining the rock, he knew that the damaged craft would not be able to free itself from the gigantic pressing mass.

Del slapped at the controls to shut down the thrusters. There was no need to waste what little energy remained in the power packs. Ensuring that his three unconscious charges were still snugly strapped in, Del checked the tiny craft. Incredibly, the upper part of the ship appeared intact with no hull breach. He doubted that they would be so fortunate with the lower compartment.

Del raised the hatch and shone his hand-light into the small cargo hold. The orange-red fluid roiling below confirmed his fears. The over-pressurization hadn't been enough to keep the caustic fluid from leaking into the ship. Del knew it would be only a matter of minutes before the fluid pushed what remaining atmosphere remained in the ship out and replaced it with the liquid acid.

For a moment Del hesitated, unsure of what he could do. Then he remembered the ScoutMaster saying, "Nothing terrifies a team more than a leader who cannot make a decision. Decide now to never terrify your team when you are the leader."

Considering his options, Del inched down the small ladder and stopped just above the rising fluid. In his hand-light he could see the locker which stored the crew's extra flex-suits. For now, the locker was above the rising tide, but to get to it, he would have to wade through the caustic brew. He had absolutely no idea if the ply-crene material would withstand the chemical's searing touch.

For a moment he hesitated, then resolutely stepped into the aqueous material. With the liquid just below his knees, Del hurried as fast as he could, being careful not to slip and fall into the corrosive broth. He reached the locker and pulled the spare flex-suits out. Only able to carry two suits at a time, he waded back to the hatch and flung the suits into the upper compartment.

Once more he went to the locker to grab suits. As an afterthought he snatched a repair kit and bundled it up with the suits. Standing on the ladder, Del stamped his feet to get the last drops off and hurried up the ladder. He flung the extra suits aside and sprinted to the decontamination cubicle. He closed the hatch, and hit the emergency decon button.

A powerful series of needle sprays showered his entire suit, washing off the remaining liquid and sucking it into the decon tanks. Where the suit had made contact with the acid he could see tiny pits. That answered the question of whether or not the protective suit could stand up against the corrosive power of the acidic solution. A few more minutes and the liquid would have gone completely through the ply-crene and seared his flesh.

He shoved open the thin door and grabbed the extra flex-suits. He was in a race against time and the seconds were ticking away. As he reached his shipmates, he activated their suit's emergency homing transponder which would transmit a distress signal to any would-be rescuer.

Next, hindered by the deadweight, he laboriously put a second flex-suit on each of his unconscious charges. From the repair kit he grabbed the aerosol insta-seal canister and began spraying the three still forms. The insta-seal was normally used to seal small leaks or rips in a flex-suit. In this case, the aqueous ply-crene solution solidified on contact with the suit surface and provided another protective layer.

Once finished, Del bolted to the pilot's pod. He jabbed the communications button and rapidly said, "Lima 2, this is Lima 3. Do you read me?"

He waited breathlessly for an answer but none came. Again he repeated, "Lima 2, this is Lima 3—respond." There was no answer but he could see that the Search and Save distress call was still transmitting. He sprinted back to the lower hold hatch cover and eased it up. No orange liquid oozed out so he lifted the hatch up completely. As he shone his light down he was disheartened to see that the caustic liquid was less than a meter from the bottom of the hatch.

Del closed the hatch and firmly tightened it down. Their time was about up, it would be but a matter of minutes before the caustic acid ate through the hatch seals and flooded the main compartment. And after that it would be but a few minutes before the caustic liquid ate through their flex-suits and began dissolving their flesh. He needed to buy them more time! But how?

Del rushed back to the pilot's pod and once again transmitted a verbal distress call but there was no reply. He was about to call again when he faintly heard, ". . . 3, this is Lima . . ."

Del practically yelled out, "Lima craft, this is Lima 3, we urgently need help, do you copy?"

Seconds later Del heard, "Lima 3 . . . say again . . . breaking up . . ."

The craft overhead was having trouble hearing him, probably because his communications equipment was damaged and couldn't send a strong enough signal through the thick liquid. His hope was that, even with his short message, they would get an approximate fix on the broken ship's location. Help was on the way but would they get there in time?

His momentary elation was severely dampened

when he saw small smoke wisps coming up from the lower hold. The acid was dissolving the hatch seals! A few more minutes and the caustic brew would flood the main compartment. Del looked around the ship. His eyes settled on the decon unit. It was the only other sealed compartment on the ship. Normally it was only big enough to hold two people at a time and even then it was a tight squeeze. Could he fit four? ~~He would have to!~~

Del grabbed Ry and dragged the renegade into the decon unit and literally formed him into a misshapen ball on the floor. He next lifted Sami on top of Ry and finally Bianca on top of the human pile. He made sure that the weight of the other two did not smother the unconscious Ry.

He sprayed the remaining spare suit with the insta-seal solution and hastily he pulled the suit on. Just as he finished with the last of the spray he felt rather than heard a soft pop and turned to see the orange liquid oozing up from the lower hold. They were out of time!

Moving awkwardly because of the hardened insta-seal on the double flex-suits, Del backed into the decon unit. Carefully he shoved arms and legs into awkward positions to keep them from jutting out and pulled the metal door closed, just as the first tongue of the acidic brew lapped up against the bottom of the hatch frame.

In the cramped tightness, Del took a deep breath to steady himself. They were safe for now but it was only a temporary safety. The decon hatch seals were tougher and stronger than the lower hold hatch seals but Del was certain they wouldn't hold forever against the acid. He knew there was only one more option. He also knew he would take that chance when the time came.

Gingerly, Del somehow squeezed himself around his inert companions to where he could reach the outer hatch door controls. The tiny unit's lights flickered on and off so he switched his vest lights on and scanned the door hatches, waiting for the telltale sign of melting seals.

Minutes later, he caught the first faint puffs of gray smoke rising upward. It was time to go. Taking a deep breath, Del manually opened the outer door. A stream of the ochre colored liquid spewed into the narrow confines of the cubicle. It didn't take long for the fluid to fill the decon unit.

Not hesitating, Del grabbed Bianca and pushed her out into the thick chemical soup. Slowly she began to rise. Struggling to keep his balance, Del grabbed Sami and shoved him, followed by Ry. As he guided himself out, Del could see the outlines of Sami and Ry in the semidarkness. He grabbed the two unconscious figures by their belt straps and kicked his way toward the surface.

Small, pearl-like bubbles covered Del's helmet. Looking down he could see the upper torso of his suit was covered with the tiny foamy globes. He immediately knew why. The devil's cauldron he was swimming in was melting his protective layers. The bubbles were the result of the reaction between the ply-crene suit material and the acidic chemicals of the lake.

Del kicked harder to get the three moving upward. Luckily the viscosity of the chemical brew was light enough that the air in their suits gave them some buoyancy to lift them toward the lake's surface. For what seemed an eternity Del struggled upward until finally he could see a lightening of the dark shadows. As he broke the surface, he shook his helmet to clear the acid off. Dark clouds roiled against the lake's surface, but Del knew there was a scouter out there looking for them.

Praying that his trans-comms still worked, he gasped, "Lima craft, this is Baldura!"

Almost instantly, he heard TJ exclaim, "Del! I've got you! We've got your suit transponders too. Keep transmitting so we can get a better fix!"

"Okay, we're floating on the surface. I've got Sami and Ry! They're unconscious. Bianca is somewhere close but I'm not sure where." Del said between breaths. "Hurry! This stuff is eating through our suits!"

"Got it! Keep transmitting! We're using your suit transponders and comm signal to triangulate your location!"

"WILCO!" Del replied and began reciting the Scout Oath.

Del let go of Sami to see if he would float. Satisfied that there was enough air inside Sami's suit to keep him afloat, Del released Ry as well. Swimming in tight circles around the two, Del looked for Bianca in the murkiness of the thick smoke. He was certain she was nearby on the surface.

Suddenly a bright spotlight shone through the

clinging haze. The scouter!

Del yelped, "I see you! Come right about twenty meters!"

For several seconds the scouter side slipped toward Del. Then he heard TJ say, "Okay Del, we see you! Stand by for the sling basket!"

"Check, but I can't find Bianca, do you see her? She should be on the surface!"

"We're looking," TJ replied, "Standby. Here comes the basket!"

Del looked up to see the rescue basket settling toward him. Holding onto Ry, he waited until the basket splashed down and then towed the immobile form to the metal cradle. Swinging the basket under Ry, he made sure that the outlaw was secure and then yelled, "He's in! Up!"

Del watched for a second as the basket ascended toward the belly of the scouter. Swimming strongly, he reached Sami and held onto him tightly in the liquid poison. Just as the basket started lowering, Del heard a new voice over the communicator, "Lima 2 this is Lima 1."

"This is 2, go ahead Lima 1.

The voice replied with just a hint of tenseness,

"Inbound to your position. What is your status?"

The voice from Lima 2 rapidly outlined the rescue operation. For a few moments there was silence and then the voice said, "Lima 2, we are passing over a tsunami wave. Estimated height is fifty or sixty meters. At current speed it will arrive at your position in ten minutes. I don't believe you want to be around when it reaches you."

"Roger that, Lima 1. Thanks for the information. We'll start tracking on the Moving Target Indicator. What is your estimated time of arrival?"

"Looks like we'll beat the wave only by a few minutes. Sorry. Don't think we'll be much help." Lima 1's voice said.

Del put two and two together. Lima 3 indeed had been caught in a mammoth wave caused by the titanic eruption. That wave had sped the length of the finger-lake, crashed against the huge cliffs at the far end, and the rebound splash caused the second tsunami headed their way.

Del knew that it was almost miraculous that they had ridden out the first wave in the scouter; to be caught on the open surface when this immense breaker hit would mean certain death.

As he watched the basket lower, Del called, "Lima 2, this is Baldura. Do you see Bianca?"

"Not yet Del," TJ quietly replied. "We're all looking though."

"What about her transponder?" Del asked.

There was a moment of silence before TJ responded, "Del, your three transponders are showing up on the S and S display, but not Bianca's."

Del shoved Sami into the rescue cradle. "He's in!" he yelled. The basket was yanked from the liquid and soared toward the rescue craft. The young scout looked at the tattered pieces of his suit arms. His outer flex-suit was disintegrating allowing the caustic soup to begin its deadly work on his inner suit. Del knew he had but minutes before the first lesion in the suit opened up allowing the acid to ooze inside to scour his flesh.

Without hesitation he said, "All right, listen up, this is what we're going to do. Lower the basket. After I climb in raise it a meter off the deck. Start a slow sweep of the area. I know Bianca's close. When we spot her, I'll get us both in the basket and then you climb out of here! Got it!"

The unknown voice from Lima 2 said, "We've got

less than five minutes before that wave hits. I'll need some time to get us above the crest without popping you out of the basket."

"Understood," Del said, "Let's do it."

The basket dropped into the drink and Del clambered in. Swiftly the little basket was raised above the orange liquid. Del balanced himself on his knees and intensely peered through the wisps of smoke into the liquid's dark depths. Seconds pass by without any sign of Bianca.

The voice from Lima 2 said, "We've got the wave on the MTI radar. ETA is two minutes."

"Check," Del nervously answered. "Swing over to the left about ten meters and use that as your circle point." The basket quickly swung over to the designated spot. Del tried to scan as much of the surface as he could. Looking over his left shoulder he was about to turn back when he saw a discoloration in the water that looked different than it surroundings.

"Bring me left about five meters!"

As the craft moved the basket toward the darker spot in the liquid, Del's heart jumped. It was Bianca! For some reason she was floating just below the surface!

Del shouted, "I've found her! I'm going in!"

"Del!" TJ said, "Wave ETA is less than one minute!"

"Got it!" Del grimly said. Waiting for the right moment, he dove back into the deadly liquid, right above Bianca. His downward momentum carried him far enough that he was able to grab Bianca. Kicking upward, he pulled her to the surface and furiously stroked for the basket. Del was almost to the metal frame when the basket started to slip away. Del shouted to the hovering craft to keep the basket steady. With a start he realized that it wasn't the basket moving, it was he and Bianca!

He knew exactly what was happening. The oncoming tsunami is again literally suctioning up all the liquid in front of it and he and Bianca are caught in its overwhelming grip. Before he could shout for help, the basket swung toward them. Frantically reaching out, Del grabbed the metal frame. Faster and faster the liquid sucked them toward the giant churning surf. With fading strength he pushed the unconscious Bianca into the cradle.

As he tried to pull himself into the basket, Del

heard TJ's frantic voice, "Del! We've got to lift! The wave is here!"

"Go! She's in!" Del yelled, desperately clutching the sides of the basket as it started to rise above the now onrushing torrent.

As the basket lifted higher, Del's hands kept slipping off the slimy metal bars. In desperation, he tried to whip one of his legs up over the edge, but it too slipped off the basket frame. Del knew that his rescuers were winching the basket upward as fast as they could but the open hatch in the craft's belly seemed light-years away. Del didn't know if he could hang on much longer.

For a moment the smoke and haze cleared. The basket rotated and as it swung around Del's eyes opened wide. Through the lessening haze he could see a monstrous dark shape surging toward him. It was the giant tidal wave. And they weren't high enough yet to clear its crest!

There was nothing Del could do but watch as the massive wave roared closer and closer. The seconds trickled by. Del saw that they were going to barely clear the liquid mountain's top. Looking up he could see that they were but meters away from the safety of the rescue craft. For just a moment he relaxed slightly.

Whether it was some fluke of the wave's foaming structure or his miscalculation of its height, Del would never know, for at the very moment the monstrous wave crest passed underneath, a hand like column of liquid shot skyward and caught Del full in the chest.

Ripped from the basket, he fell helplessly, tumbling over and over toward the waiting acid.

Chapter 17

Luna, Armstrong Bay Naval Station

Using the passageway's grab-hold as an anchor point, McCarel slung his kit bag down the tunnel, watching it slowly arc upward and then downward to the gray metal floor. Rolling several times and bouncing slightly in slow motion it crawled to a stop twenty meters down the corridor.

He smiled as he turned to his companion. "Ain't one-sixth gravity great? I envy fleet sailors. The Confed Admirals were smart home-porting the fleet on Luna. With all the heavy work that the fleet ships require, to do it in Luna's gravity field makes a lot more sense than Terra's."

Tuul just nodded his head and grimly moved ahead, using the grab-holds to steady himself in the weak gravity. McCarel smiled as he looked at Tuul's face. There was no doubt that Tuul hated weightlessness or anything resembling no-gravity.

Tuul tartly replied, "My stomach is doing more rollovers than your kit bag. Ever since we matched gravity fields it's reminded me constantly of why I joined StarScouts instead of the Confederation Navy."

McCarel smiled even broader in reply. Up ahead he could see a waiting committee of two figures. Since he and Tuul were the only passengers on the inbound fleet shuttle that had docked at Armstrong Bay Naval Station, McCarel assumed that the two individuals were waiting for them. It surprised him since they hadn't requested an escort, though he was aware that Tuul, as the StarScout General Staff J2 for Intelligence was entitled to one.

As they got closer and could make out the waiting figures, McCarel broke out into a big grin. "McDougal!" he yelped, "You broken-down space dog, what are you doing here?"

Half-scowling, half-smiling, the tall StarScout saluted his superior and said, "I'm er' because of you, ye dark-hearted heathen. Lost my left knee in a tiny bit of a' accident in the Wasatch Cluster. Docs wouldn't certify me for trail walkin', so your mates on the J3 staff decided I needed to be StarScout Liaison Director on Luna. Yanked me from my troop a month ago and put me on this ~~gosh-awful~~ sterile world. Ye should be ashamed of yourself, lad. It's not a fittin' end for a loyal scout!"

[handwritten annotation: "Please, no more Utah references"]

McCarel guffawed for a moment and held up his hands. "Whoa, Mac. Sorry about the leg, I didn't know. But I'm not with the J3. I'm working with Colonel Tuul here in the J2. Besides, you know such decisions are routine business for the general staff."

McCarel introduced McDougal to Tuul and settled his hand on the StarScout's shoulder as he said, "You know the rules. If the medicos won't certify, then you can't do deep-space operations."

"Aye," McDougal replied, sighing deeply. "I know the rules as well as the next scout, but it breaks me heart not to be with the lads Out There."

There was silence for a moment and then McDougal said, "I beg your pardon, Colonel Tuul, you've got business to attend to and here I stand blabbing away like some academy plebe."

Tuul waved a hand, "No, no, it's alright, I just need to get some gravity under me soon." He stopped for a moment and said, "Your leg, you've had the usual prosthetic regimen I assume?"

"Aye, sir," McDougal replied, "And that's the rub, the micro-circuitry and nano implants haven't imprinted well enough into my neuro-skeletal system for the docs to certify me deep space fit." He smiled thinly, "I guess I'm just a slow learner."

Tuul nodded knowingly as he replied, "It'll come, sometimes it just takes a while for the body and mind to adapt . . . that's all . . . trust me, I know."

McDougal smiled in return. "Thank ye sir. Well, enough about me. You have work to do. We'll have ye dispatched and off this rock in less than an hour." He motioned to a young StarScout lieutenant who had stood quietly nearby while the three senior scouts talked. "This is Lieutenant Lengley. Fresh caught from officer training. He's assigned to Desmond's Brigade, but the medico's had him in quarantine for the last two weeks. Picked up a blood parasite on Vega Five during his last training mission.

"Noticed your flight plan when we received your transport request. Says you're outbound for Sector 11. Colonel Desmond's moved her headquarters over to Sector 11 and I've got the coordinates. Next routine shipment for her brigade isn't for two weeks and thought that maybe you could give the LT a lift."

McCarel looked over at Tuul who shrugged okay. He asked the lieutenant, "Medically certified as fit for duty?"

"Yes, sir," the young man said. "Medics say all systems are go."

"Fine," McCarel said, "Grab your kit and meet us at . . ."

"Berth three," McDougal finished for him.

"On my way, sir, and thanks," the young scout replied and loped away.

"Thanks, Jak," McDougal said. "If you hadn't taken him, as I said it might be another two or three weeks before I could've transited him out."

"No problem. We'll just work in the detour. Just do me one favor though. Don't mention this specific little stop if anyone asks, okay?"

McDougal gave McCarel an odd look but answered congenially. "Sure, consider it done. It's the least I can do. Not that everyone from the general staff is so accommodating, I might add."

"What do you mean by that? Still sore over your assignment?"

McDougal waved his hand. "No, no, water under the bridge. I'm talking about when I dispatched Captain Simur from the staff earlier today. She filed an open flight plan but I saw her pull up Sector 10 and 11 star charts. So I figured she was headed out that way. When I asked her to drop the youngster off at the Sector HQ she got pretty uppity and said no. Just flat out refused."

Tuul slowed to a walk and asked, "What was that name again?"

"Simur." McDougal replied. "Dispatch orders had the chief-of-staff chop on them."

Tuul pursed his lips for a moment. "Were there others in the party?"

"No, just her."

"Headed outbound with no flight plan you said?" Tuul asked.

"Correct," McDougal returned. "Quirky dispatch. She took one of the prototype Zephyr Six craft. Fully armed at that. We hadn't even had time to put Fleet markings on it but that's the one the orders specifically read for the out-run."

McCarel stopped. "Fully armed? I thought they were still in testing?"

"Aye," McDougal gestured with a hand. "They are. The R&D crowd just started evaluating the weapon systems five days ago. But so far everything worked beautifully. The testing team parked two here at liaison and had the other two on the weapons range. They were going to switch out tomorrow. The two here carry fire-and-forget torpedoes, and fully charged ion-particle cannons."

Tuul glanced at McCarel as he said, "Sorry that anyone on the general staff was rude to you. As a junior officer she obviously needs some training in protocol and manners."

McCarel looked at Tuul out of the corner of his eye. He knew that look and tone of voice. Tuul's mental wheels were spinning faster than a proton star. Something was wrong, but since Tuul wasn't saying anything, he would wait for privacy before asking what.

McDougal sniffed and said, "Thank ye, sir, it's bad enough being stuck on this lonely outpost without

bring first name up sooner.

you staff types treating us as if we're pariahs."

To divert McDougal's attention from the subject, McCarel slapped him on the shoulder and quipped, "I know, Ian. With ten thousand fleet sailors around but only five StarScouts, Luna is a lonely place. Okay, let's go. Colonel Tuul and I have work to do."

After a quick stop at the liaison office to complete the dispatch orders they made their way to berth three. Lengley was already on board and stowing his kit when McCarel and Tuul clambered aboard. The small ship normally carried a platoon complement of sixteen StarScouts and was crowded. With only the three of them it would be roomy for the out-bound trip.

Saying goodbye to McDougal, the two scouts went to the pilot's section and began preflight preparations. McCarel slipped behind the pilot's command console and swiftly went through the preflight sequence as Tuul programmed the ship's master computer with the necessary flight data.

Minutes later McCarel received permission from Luna Control to slip the magnetic holds from the ship and begin their slow ascent over Luna's cratered surface. For several minutes he was busy vectoring the craft away from Earth's moon and placing them in the right attitude and bearing for their jump to hyper-light speed.

After lining up perfectly for the jump, McCarel turned the craft over to autopilot and watched as the countdown sequence began to tick off.

McCarel looked over at Tuul, "Okay, what gives? Back there with McDougal. You weren't saying anything but your alarms were blasting."

With his eye on the flight displays, Tuul said slowly, "Everyone that works on the general staff has to have a security clearance. As the J2 I know everyone's security clearance in *the mount*. I review that roster every day to ensure their clearances are current and match their duty billet. It's one of the few routine things that I do myself. Helps me to track personnel and duty status.

"There is no Captain Simur on the general staff. I've been at the mount for almost five years. I've known everyone who's come and gone. There has never been a Captain Simur on the StarScout General Staff during that time and there certainly isn't one now."

"But," McCarel returned, "The orders were signed

by . . ."

Tuul turned a grim face to McCarel. "I know. The question is why the Chief-of-Staff would issue bogus orders."

McCarel returned the same grim stare. "That's a pretty serious charge. If true, he's not just risking his career, he's breaking the law. Why would he do something like that?"

"Don't know," Tuul replied, shaking his head in consternation. "And I'm not totally certain that he did. While you and McDougal were in pre-flight, I looked over those orders. The signature and order code look correct. It's possible but highly improbable for a forgery to occur with all of the safeguards. He has the authority of course to dispatch the craft, but why do it under a false name?"

McCarel asked, "Do we alert someone in the command?"

"Already did," Tuul replied, "This is something strictly for the CG, but he's out of the loop for a few days. Contacted Maggie Tomas. She'll beam him a message first chance. She's also checking the duty roster. See if she can spot who left the command at the same time as our Captain Simur.

"In the meantime, McDougal gave me that Zephyr's transponder code on the pretense that if we caught up I would personally admonish Simur on her manners."

He paused as the chronometer finished its countdown to zero. "You and I are going to catch up with our so-called Captain Simur . . . but we aren't going to talk about manners . . ."

Chapter 18

Gadion Faction Lair

Del sat with his hands pressed hard against tightly closed eyes in what seemed an endless time later. Tsunami waves of pain coursed through his brain, one after another. He was so intent on the hurt that the voice speaking to him uttered unrecognizable words. He felt pressure in his arm and a slight burning sensation.

Slowly the intense pain eased. After some minutes he cracked his eyes open and gingerly looked around at his surroundings. The poacher medic, Stinneli, was leaning over, studying his face.

"That's better, how do you feel?" he asked mildly.

Del massaged his head. "Head feels like a nutomic explosion detonated right behind my eyeballs." He peered at Stinneli and half-smiled, "And surprised to be alive, I think."

Stinneli grunted in return and said, "Understandable, what do you remember?"

Del thought for a moment. "Lost my hold on the basket . . . started to fall . . . then I hit something hard." He paused for a moment, "Um, things are a little blurry after that . . ."

Stinneli nodded and said, "You had quite a fall. Didn't quite knock you out on impact . . . but you were very lucky. Believe it or not, you actually only fell about ten meters, but you had the good sense to fall at exactly the right instant."

Del rubbed his eyes. "I don't understand."

"The scouter was moving in the same direction as the wave. When you lost your grip, your forward velocity was about the same as the wave . . . actually pretty slow. You landed on the backside of the wave, bout' halfway down the crest. You literally slid and surfed your way down to the bottom of the swell."

He looked at Del with an amused expression.

"Remember anything of that wild ride?"

Del rubbed his forehead and replied, "Not a bit of it. I just remember getting smacked by the wave, losing my grip, falling . . . and then splat!"

Stinneli grunted. "Let's just say that given the wave's speed, if you had dropped one second sooner, the wave's front trough would have caught you and churned you to pieces. If you had dropped one second later, the wave's crest would have passed completely by and you would've dropped about sixty meters straight down. No surviving that impact. As I said, you're lucky."

Stinneli paused for a moment and eyed Del. "Say, you don't play poker do you? Cause if you do, I'll stake you for half your winnings. You are one lucky space cadet."

Del half-smiled and said, "Sorry. I don't gamble."

Stinneli was about to speak when the door opened and Bianca walked in. One wrist was tightly bandaged and the other arm was in a sling. Otherwise she didn't look any the worse for the adventure. Scrutinizing Del, she asked a little sarcastically, "And how is our junior hero doing?"

Stinneli looked Del over as he said, "He'll live. A

good-sized lump on the head, slight concussion, terrific headache and too many bruises to count, but otherwise okay. I gave him an injection of Exediene . . . it'll relieve the headache plus negate the effects of the concussion."

He squeezed his hands together and finished, "Otherwise, he'll be pretty sore for a couple of days. Give him twenty-four hours of quarters and he'll be fit for duty."

"Good," Bianca replied. She nodded her head toward the door. Stinneli took his cue and eased out the door. Del sat up, swung his legs over the slim bed and asked, "Sami, Ry?"

"Ry has a fractured leg and bruised ribs, but he'll live. Sami's fine. Just knocked cold from that explosion. He's outside with the rest of your team. They've been holding vigil ever since we got back." She frowned slightly and asked, "Tell me what happened after we hit the drink. As you might guess, that's about the last I remember."

Del recounted in detail what occurred after the ill-fated scouter nose-dived into the deadly lake. Finishing, he said, "I remember bits and pieces after my fall, but not much."

One side of Bianca's mouth lifted in an approving smile. With just a touch of admiration she said, "That was an extraordinary piece of work, Baldura, getting us out of there like you did."

She skewed her head slightly to the right. "Hate to say it, but I guess I owe you one. I'll remember what you did. For now, for what its worth . . . thanks . . . for Ry and me."

Del shrugged in return and said, "You're welcome. Sorry that I lost the scouter, but the slab's weight was too much for what little power was left in the engine power-packs."

Bianca held up a hand. "It was worth the price. We can replace it."

"Well," Del went on, "Things would have gone a lot better if that strut seal hadn't blown out."

Bianca nodded and said, "Accidents happen. It's the nature of the beast working Out Here."

Del looked at her for a moment. He was tempted to tell her about the outlaw he saw working on Lima 3's seals just before they boosted. He reconsidered and decided to keep it to himself. He wasn't sure if the seal blowout was truly an accident or not. But he had no proof that it was sabotage and to claim such in a ship full of outlaws was a dangerous gambit.

"Yeah," he muttered, "Accidents happen."

Bianca gave Del a puzzled look but didn't respond. She walked to the sick bay door, turned and said, "Okay, you're on quarters for twenty-four hours. After that, it's back to duty. Understood?"

"Got it," Del replied.

The poacher leader opened the door and motioned for Del's fellow junior scouts to enter. Once the five were together she looked them over, shrugged grudgingly and said, "We struck out on any quadro-diamonds, but considering all things, you fulfilled the first part of our bargain. Just do as well with the rest and I give you my word that I'll hold up my end."

With that she closed the door behind her. Edging up to Del, Sami said in a conspiratorial whisper, "Nice going, Del. Now we've got them right where we want them. Our bravery on the high seas, saving El Capitan's life, methinks the crew will be voting you in as Captain and giving the ol' heave ho to Madam Bligh there."

Del gave Sami a sour look and said pointedly, "Sami, what do you mean 'our' bravery? As I recall you slept through the whole thing."

Sami sniffed. "I was there in spirit, urging you on to ever greater..."

"Be quiet, Sami," said Shanon. "We've got more important things to talk about."

"More important! What's more important than..."

Shanon's death-look cut Sami off and she said, "Nase, go ahead."

Nase leaned up against the bed. "First thing is we boosted off of Stygar about four hours ago."

Del raised his eyebrows at that. "That was quick repair work. I was under the impression the *Queen Bee* was hurt pretty bad. Bad enough to maybe not fly."

Nase nodded. "Thought so too. But not too quick considering they had help."

Del cocked his head toward Nase, "What do you mean?" he asked.

"Drone supply ship." Before Del could say anything at that announcement, Nase held up his hand and went on. "But that's not all. I was back in the hangar hold retrieving your gear. I don't think anyone realized I was there. A scouter landed, I think it was Lima 6. They started unloading and I was going to give them a hand. Then I realized what they were bringing out and changed my mind. Made myself small in the scouter and watched."

Del waited a second and then blurted out, "Well, what was it? They couldn't have been poaching; they said that Stygar 6 had no alien life."

"No," Nase slowly exhaled. "They weren't poaching. Body bags. I counted twenty."

For a long time there was silence in the room. Then Del spoke softly. "They were bringing the bodies back from the crashed ship. But why?"

No one spoke for a long moment and then TJ said softly, "To sell."

"To sell!" Del exploded. "What do you mean to sell? Sell to who?"

"To their families, Del."

Del looked aghast at the pretty young woman. "You're not serious," he said.

TJ gave Del a nod. "It happens. Del, these are outlaws. They work outside the law, outside the normal values of civilized society. To you and me those bodies are the remains of honored comrades. To this bunch, they're a way to make easy money. The families of that ship's crew will pay a premium to get their sons and daughters back to a final . . . and suitable resting place."

Del rubbed his forehead. The XT poaching, TJ's kidnapping, blackmailing them into helping the outlaws was bad enough, but this—this made Del feel unclean, sick to his stomach. Was it true?

"So that's where those ships were going . . ." he breathed.

"You saw them too?" Shanon asked, "On the scope just after we up-shipped?"

Del nodded. "That's why they were in such a hurry. Wanted to get back from their grisly mission before we did. Hide the . . ." He stopped, not able to go on with the thought of what the poachers had done. For a long moment Del said nothing, then as he looked at the expressions on his teammates faces asked, "There's more?"

Nase shook his head and started again. "Shortly after they began removing the bodies, another scouter landed and started unloading Holett patches."

Del shook his head, "Whoa, what's a Holett patch?"

"It's plating made up of a composite of titanium,

loridium and plas-steel," Nase replied. "You use it to repair the outer skin and interior framework of hyper-speed deep space craft."

"Okay," Del said slowly, "I'm listening but I don't think I understand your point."

"Holett patches are top-of-the-line repair kits and very, very, expensive. There are other, less costly ways to repair a ship like this, but if you've got the resources, Holett patches are first choice. Plus it practically takes a Ph.D. in structural engineering to apply correctly. It's work normally done in a civilian or military space dock, or a Confederation repair ship. It's pretty tricky stuff.

"If it's not done right, in the first moment of hyper-speed, the patch shatters and with it goes a good-sized chunk of surrounding fabric. In other words, you get a much bigger hole than you had before. But, if done right, it'll hold at practically any hyper-light velocity and is extremely durable.

"Other patches you have to replace fairly quickly or get to space dock and have permanent repairs done. A Holett patch gives you flexibility . . . the payoff and advantage being that you can transit at hyper-speed for quite some time before you need to go to space dock."

Sami interrupted with, "How do you know about this stuff?"

Nase gave Sami a bored look and stoically replied, "I read."

Before Sami could retort Del said, "So you think that they had these patches delivered by a drone supply ship and hauled them back in the scouter?"

"Yes," Nase replied as if that explained everything.

"And someone had the technical expertise to repair the damage using the patches?" Del asked.

Nase held out his hands, "Obviously. We didn't implode when we jumped to hyper-speed."

Del rubbed his mouth for a moment as he said, "Just before we lifted, Bianca and Dan were having one serious powwow in the hanger. Dan had just come in from his inspection. I thought he must be telling her we couldn't lift off. Obviously my assumption was totally off-base."

Shanon gravely spoke to the group, "Given how bad we were hit, wasn't a bad assumption Del. But now, the real question is how and from whom do a gang of renegades get a drone supply ship to resupply them with such a sophisticated repair system as a Holett patch? And who among a group of deep space outlaws has the expertise to make such high-tech repairs?

The team looked silently at each other, searching for an answer. Del saw something in Nase's eyes and asked, "Nase?"

Nase looked down and then back up. "Other than the major deep space corporations, and the Confederation itself, there is one other organization that I'm aware of that has the resources and savvy to make major repairs this far off the main star routes in interstellar space."

Nase again down for a long time, before TJ pushed at him and demanded, "Who?"

Nase had a very shaken and uncomfortable look on his face as he answered, "We haven't been shanghaied by a bunch of renegade poachers..." He looked around and caught all their eyes, "We're right in the middle of a nest of *Gadion Faction* mercenaries!".

Chapter 19

Great White Shark

Adiak Peller was angry enough to take on a 1000-kilogram Protosaur by himself, no matter the eight pairs of ripping claws and double-set of 20-centimeter long canines. Of all the things to happen! On his way back from the luxury resort planet RioJan 3, a plasma flare caught his ship, frying computer and electronic circuitry and casting them adrift. It was six days before help arrived.

Six days without communications with the organization, without knowing everything that was going on was more than he could bear. In frenzied haste he entered his palatial home and headed to his secret hideaway. Hands trembling from anger, he punched the code into the security device. He literally tried to push the heavy metal door to make it open faster. He was like a drug addict going through withdrawal, except his drug was pure unfettered control and power. And six days away from having complete and utter control and power was more than he could stand. Luckily, no one saw him in this state for it was far different than his normal serene and calm exterior, which masked the ravenous craving for power that lay just below the surface.

He slammed into his console seat and rapidly opened various comms channels to his most trusted lieutenants. One-by-one he made contact and regained his sense of perspective on the *Faction's* doings, which caused his anger and almost panic to slowly subside.

Hours later he eased back, confident that all was well in his dark and loathsome world. A nagging thought came to mind. He was forgetting something, but what? He mentally retraced his steps, his actions, unable to pinpoint what was left undone. Then he had it, and chastised himself for letting the matter slip, but rationalized his forgetfulness because of the urgency of other matters.

He punched in the comms code and waited. Long minutes went by without a reply. Irritation set in though he knew that the man couldn't always answer immediately. But the last several days had made him that much more short-tempered and even this small delay was irksome.

Finally the screen lighted up, "Ah, there you are," Peller smoothly said. The senior scout looked at

Peller but wouldn't meet his eyes. Peller instantly went on the alert. He had come to know this man very well over the years and his whole body language screamed out that something was amiss.

"What have you learned since we last spoke?" he asked, intently watching the man.

For several seconds the man hesitated, and then spoke slowly, "I tried to contact you but . . ."

"Couldn't be helped!" Peller quickly retorted, and without further explanation said, "Go on." This man knew something, and from the way he was acting it was either damaging to him, or he'd done something that he wasn't sure that Peller would approve of. Or both.

The scout started over, "I was able to obtain some information about McCarel . . ." he trailed off for a moment and then abruptly changed his tenor. "It looks like you're right. I'm sure McCarel's presence here is tied in with his brother's disappearance and the Kolomite."

"I knew it," Peller triumphantly crowed. "Go on," he ordered, pushing aside the fact that just moments before the man had been so hesitant to pass along what obviously was excellent news.

"McCarel and Tuul are working together on a project that centers on Froma IV. A few days ago they left on some phony mission out to the Helix – 'joint intelligence operations' they called it. We've never done anything like that before. I think they're going to link up with Dak McCarel."

"Where?" Peller demanded, "You have the coordinates?"

"No," the man returned, "But don't worry, I took care of this myself."

Peller turned cold. "What do you mean you took care of this yourself?"

There was a long pause as the StarScout officer struggled with what he was going to say. Then, inexplicably, as a child would try to explain a misdeed to a parent and seek forgiveness, the man rushed through the events of the last several days. The scout quickly detailed his daughter's mission and location and that she would report back to him with what they needed to know.

Peller sat stone-faced for several moments staring in total disbelief. His mouth worked but no words came out until he finally hissed, "Idiot! There are better ways than this. Call her back!"

"I . . . I'm not sure I can," the scout admitted, "I've tried communicating, but the nebula must be blocking the messages from getting through . . . or she is not responding."

Peller slammed his fist down on his desk, his anger erupting as he pointed a shaking finger directly at the man. He leaned forward until his whole face nearly covered the screen. The veins in Peller's face bulged from his boiling wrath. Like a striking snake Peller stabbed his finger toward the screen, "No! I said get her back! Get her back now!"

He stopped to venomously say through clenched teeth, "You call off your daughter—this minute! Take care of it personally. From here on, don't do anything regarding this matter until you've talked to me first. You get your daughter away from McCarel, or so help me . . ."

The scout paled at the unspoken threat. He looked wildly around as if looking for some place to escape. Finally, he sputtered, "I'll go out there myself. Stop her."

"That's right, and now!" Peller screamed and cut off the transmission. He sat down in his chair, the sounds of his labored breathing filled the normal stillness of the room. His hands shook from the violent anger that flowed through his body and mind. He slammed his fist down on the console surface. There was no doubt the man's handling of the situation was totally wrong and inexcusable.

His usefulness was at an end and the sooner this was taken care of the better. And if his daughter had to suffer the fate of the father . . . so be it. Peller was past caring if innocents were hurt; after all, he was the one that was important . . . not them.

He immediately opened another channel. In seconds he was looking at a hard-faced man whose eyes showed absolutely no emotion. If ever there was an arch-stereotype of an assassin, then this man fit the picture perfectly. But Peller knew the ruggedly handsome features masked a sterile conscious whose actions mirrored the vicious attack of a Great White Shark.

Peller took great pride in that. He had personally seen to this man's training since his youth and now as a human killing machine there were few, if any, who were his equal.

"Get your team," Peller ordered, "You're going to the Helix Nebula. There are two people who will need your special, personalized attention . . . and I do mean your personalized attention."

Chapter 20

Deep Space Distress Message

Bianca was making a last entry in the ship's log when she heard a light tapping at her tiny stateroom door. Her ship now sped through the darkness of hyperspace, two days out from Stygar 6. "Enter!" she ordered briskly. Dan stuck his head just inside the door. "Sorry to intrude skipper, but Kreg just notified me that we've got a priority message and it's an *Eyes Only*."

Bianca eyed her second-in-command. "Are you sure? We're off the normal channels; we're not supposed to be getting traffic."

Dan shrugged, "Thought so too. But Kreg needs you down in the comms shack with your half of the decoder. It's a Priority One message."

Bianca scratched her head and said, "Okay, but I don't understand." She slipped out of her chair, closed her logbook and followed Dan back down to the communications area of the astro-bridge.

"Ok, Kreg," Dan said to the comms tech, "What do you have?"

Kreg nodded his head toward his lighted displays and began, "The bells and whistles started going off about five minutes ago. Message must be pretty hot because there is a priority boost and send code group in the routing header for the interstellar relay stations between us and Earth. Somebody wants to talk to us pretty urgently about something. That's about the fastest I've ever seen an n-space message get Out Here."

Bianca gave Kreg a puzzled look "Are you sure it's for us?"

"Yes ma'am," Kreg replied. "The address code-header has your personal alpha-numeric identifier and the ship's recognition set. That and the address router are in general code, so I know it's for us. However, the text is in command mode and I need your and Mr. Busly's code key for the computer to decipher the rest of the message."

The young woman shook her head and reached into her sealed waistband to bring out the mini-disc that contained her codes. Dan already had his out and handed the disc to Kreg. With a practiced hand the technician inserted the two discs into the console slots and programmed the computer to decode the communication and bring up the plain-text message.

He pointed to a nearby secure and secluded console and stated, "I'll punch it out over there." The two renegades sat down in front of the screen and watched as the display filled with the message's wording. For long moments both of them stared at the short communiqué and then looked at each other. Dan rubbed his hands over his chin and grunted.

"Well," he began cryptically, "I would say that this takes us a bit out of the way and certainly skewers the flight plan, doesn't it?"

Bianca nodded and replied softly, "That it does, that it does."

After a few moments of thoughtful silence she turned to Dan, "What about the ship? Can it make the haul to the Helix and back on those patches?"

Dan thought for several moments before answering. "Standard operating procedure calls for a thorough diagnostic to check for microscopic stress fractures in the patches and seams within three hundred flight hours of the repair.

"We've already put 50 hours on them so that means we need to get to a space dock or repair facility in about ten standard days and have those patches checked. Right now our internal diagnostics indicate everything is holding together. But we don't have all the evaluation capabilities that a dock or repair station has."

For a moment he looked at the message again and began pulling up various star-charts on the computer. He studied them for several minutes before turning to Bianca. "The original plan was for your team to down-planet on Kanab 4, which was okay as that's a two-day run to Interplanetary Emergency Station 12 Bravo.

"It's a full-capability deep space emergency and repair station, has everything we need, but it's the only one that does in this part of the sector. But with this," he said, pointing at the message, "if we go there, we're talking about a whole sector jump to the station. That would place us at about the limit, but it's doable."

Bianca reflected for a moment before speaking. "So what you are saying is that we can't do both, Kanab 4 and this destination."

Dan considered carefully before he went on, "I believe the patches will hold and we can do what they're asking of us. But yes, you can't have both, the Helix and Kanab 4. The two runs combined would almost double the allowed flight time on those repairs. So you're going to have to choose one or the other . . . I can't give you both, and at this point it doesn't matter to me, the Helix or Kanab are almost exactly equidistant from here."

He sat back and pointed again at the message, "Either way, if you do this or go to Kanab 4, after your operation we'll need to make immediately for the closest dry-dock . . . or we shut everything down, call for help, and try to explain why we're twiddlin' our thumbs in deep space."

Bianca laughed just a bit. "We certainly don't want to do that . . . bad choice all the way round." She drummed her fingers lightly on the console surface. Finally she shrugged and said in an exasperated tone, "It's a little hard to believe that we're the only ship in the area that can handle this, but I guess we can't buck city hall. Okay, Kanab 4 is out. We'll just have to adjust our plans."

For a moment she chewed her lower lip and then

directed, "Head to Sector 11. The scenario for our *guests* is that we've received an n-space distress message. We'll say it's either a star liner or freighter or perhaps a private yacht and we're going to lay claim for salvage."

She laughed mirthlessly, "Which isn't so far from the truth this time."

Chapter 21

The Hunter is Hunted Down

Alena drifted weightless in the ship's pilot pod, her stare transfixed on the incredible starry array that spread out and around her. She loved deep space and understood clearly her mother's love of being Out Here, among the stars. They beckoned her with a silent, serene call that numbed her mind like a powerful narcotic. Sometimes she felt almost compelled to open her tiny ship's airlock and launch herself out into the heart of the firmament, to drift forever among the celestial lights. At just that moment, the reason for her being Out Here would pull her back, her dark thoughts matching the blackness of surrounding space.

Her ship drifted slowly, its engines shut down. What little trajectory it had left would carry it into the Helix Nebula . . . in about ten-thousand years. For now though Alena was satisfied just to let the ship drift as she was waiting for her quarry to arrive, then she would pounce and the deadly game would be on. By lying still and motionless, the effect of shock and surprise would give her the advantage, and she intended to use that edge to its fullest benefit.

Her StarScout uniform lay crumpled and disheveled in the back of the craft. It was one of the first things she had done, to strip if off her body and fling it aside. What it stood for had never meant that much to her anyway, never had, never will. She played the charade for one reason and one reason only, and now there was no need to continue the fantasy any longer.

For just a moment she mentally squirmed with the thought that her mother would be ashamed of her actions, but she pushed the thought aside. What she was doing was for her mother, to right an awful wrong that had been visited on her. To bring some justice and a sense of closure to her unwarranted death.

She smirked as she thought of how her father used to call her his 'little angel.' Well his 'little angel' had grown up and was now an avenging angel with a terrible sense of righteous pent-up anger that would consume the McCarels.

Her father had set her free to do what she must but for her mother's sake she wouldn't use the facade of the uniform to do so. For a moment she let her eyes close in rest, the silence deep around her. It was peaceful and calm, soothing on her churning, fitful mind and soul.

The chirping of the communications console startled her from her almost trance-like state. Highly surprised, she swung around to look at the tiny blinking light. *This can't be!* She thought to herself. No one but her father knew she was out here and he wouldn't have any reason to contact her. Or would he?

Maybe he needed to communicate some update to the situation, make sure she had the latest information. Or worse, a change in plans ... even perhaps to stop her from carrying out ... For long seconds she hesitated, her natural wariness preventing her from acting ... and more so to prevent her father from trying to call her off what she absolutely had to do . . . for both of them.

Finally, she decided that prudence was the better course, particularly if it were her father on the other end of the comms channel with information that she truly needed. She reached over and opened the channel. Without identifying herself, she uneasily said, "Go ahead, I'm reading you."

"Roger," the voice returned, "Please turn your vu-screen on. I have a message from your father. It's important that I speak with you." A little shocked at hearing an unknown voice bring up her father, Alena began, "You must be mistaken . . ."

"Alena," the voice interrupted, "I have a message from your father that I am to deliver to you personally but not via comms as this is an open, unsecure channel."

Alena reached down and turned on the vu-screen. Instantly, it filled with the image of a handsome man in a StarScout uniform. He nodded and said, "I understand why you're a little cautious, but let me assure you, we're on the same side. You're not the only one who hates the name of McCarel."

Alena couldn't contain her gasp. She calmed

herself and said, "The message from my father?"

"These are my coordinates," he began, "I'll vector to you and do a ship-to-ship so that we can talk. My orders are to deliver the message in-person." He looked aside for just a moment and then went on, "Alright, I have you locked in. ETA is 30 minutes." With that the vu-screen went dead.

Alena stared at the gray-black rectangle for several seconds. Her mind whirled with astonishment and puzzlement. A small part of her was uneasy though, as if something were slightly wrong with the whole situation. But the scout knew where to find her . . . and incredibly . . . knew exactly *why* she was Out Here. There was only one other person who knew all that . . . her father. It was totally unexpected and astonishing that her father would bring someone else in on the plan, but there must be a reason of supreme importance that he would. With that thought, she pushed her doubts aside and waited patiently for her unexpected visitor, confident that he must be part of her father's plan to deal with the McCarels.

A little more than 30 minutes later the other ship was off her starboard bow and the two vessels were joined by a small diameter trans-ship tube. Minutes later, the StarScout cycled through the decon unit and entered the ship. Alena faced the man with hands on hips and demanded, "Alright, what's my father's message. Make it zip, mister, I've got work to do."

The man smiled pleasantly as he brought up his weapon and said, "As do I—" and fired point-blank.

Chapter 22

Ambushed in the Double Helix

The Stoner Beast viciously grabbed McCarel's foot in its bone-crunching jaws. He lunged for his long-knife and was about to come up in a slashing uppercut when he heard, "Colonel McCarel! Wake up, sir! Wake up!"

It was a moment before his sluggish senses adjusted to the fact that he was in the middle of a nightmare fight. He shook his head to clear the fog and saw Lieutenant Lengley wisely standing a full meter from the foot of his bed.

"Sorry to wake you, sir, but Colonel Tuul needs you on the command deck. We've got an emergency distress call coming in on the n-space communicator."

McCarel sat straight up and swung his legs over the bunk's edge. As he reached for his boots he said, "Got it LT. Please inform Colonel Tuul I'm on my way."

The young scout turned on his heel and made his way forward. McCarel splashed some water from the small water dispenser onto his face to help him wake up and buttoned up his forest-green StarScout tunic. He slipped through the small portal and strode toward the command flight deck.

As he slid into the pilot's seat, McCarel asked, "What've we got?"

"Sorry to wake you," Tuul began, "But this started coming in on the emergency distress band a few minutes ago. Unknown ship's auto-distress, no verbal transmission. Their comms might be knocked out. Haven't heard anyone respond, so we're probably the closest craft. The signal's identification code doesn't register in our data banks."

McCarel grunted at that, "That's odd. We've got all of StarScout, Confed Navy craft, plus registered civilian ships in those banks."

"Could be brand new," Tuul suggested, "And just

hasn't made it to the system-wide records pool." He mused aloud, "I doubt seriously if any outlaws or the Faction would transmit an open distress signal."

McCarel nodded and started to run his hands over the computer keys, fine-tuning the reception on the distress call. After a few moments he said, "I'm reading it at Mark 125 point 3. The Doppler oscillation is tight, so the signal source is ahead and not behind."

Tuul nodded, "Same as mine." He gestured toward the stellar map on the computer display. "That reading puts it almost dead-center of the middle quadrant of the Helix. There are no star systems along the signal's path on this side of the nebula so it's doubtful they've made planet-fall. With the energy distortions caused by the nebula, my guess is that they're either just inside the outer envelope of the cloud or in the hollow core."

McCarel studied the star map for a moment. "I do believe you're right Colonel Tuul . . . I do believe you're right."

For several seconds he considered the situation. "If it's a civilian job, they're way off the beaten path. The civvies don't like to mess around in uncharted nebulas until we've established a route into or through the cloud—too many bad things seem to happen. Well, I would've preferred to crack the Helix's outer envelope in company with Barkley's gang since they've got a charted clear path in the upper quadrant. But, a distress call is a distress call.

"Okay, send an n-space that we're on our way. ETA ...mmm, make it three hours. They may not be able to transmit, but maybe they can hear."

Fifteen hours earlier they had slipped over the invisible boundary between Sectors 10 and 11 and just inside that line was the spectacular Helix Nebula. It was one of the largest nebulas in the galaxy, covering several thousand light-years in diameter. The Helix was famous for its giant columnar projections that protruded from its dark-green core. The projections looked like giant cloud-puffs shot out from titanic cannons.

The nebula was almost totally unexplored except for parts of its outer fringes and the small inner portion that Barkley's Battalion now investigated. And until Barkley penetrated its writhing outer envelope no one suspected that there was an immense cluster of stars hidden within its core.

To go blindly through a nebula's turbulent gaseous outer skin was risky business and not for the faint-hearted. The thick particles of the nebula were electrically charged and sometimes played havoc with a ship's navigation and control systems. In addition, McCarel and Tuul would have to carefully feel their way through the nebula, hoping that there were no unseen dark masses or proto-stars in their flight path. A chance encounter with one of those would be catastrophic.

McCarel brought up a star-chart of the Helix's mid-quadrant. Both men studied it closely for several minutes. McCarel ran his hand over his mouth and said, "I suggest we drop out of hyper-speed about a million kilometers from its edge and go sub-warp for entry and transit."

Tuul nodded thoughtfully in reply. "Sounds good," he said, "You want to take the helm? I'll take stellar sensors."

"Okay," McCarel answered. Since McCarel was the more experienced pilot, Tuul's idea made perfect sense. "Scout Lengley!" McCarel shouted.

"Yes, sir!" said the young man from the compartment hatchway.

"We're taking a little detour," McCarel explained. "That distress call seems to be coming from inside the nebula. We'll penetrate the outer envelope in an hour. As they say, batten down the hatches; make sure everything aft is ship-shape and securely stowed. Going in we can expect hitting heavy gravity waves. I don't want stuff flying around, including you, if it starts getting rough."

"Roger," the youngster replied and turned to begin checking the trim little craft's interior.

"Gravity waves, huh," Tuul grunted. "Never actually rode through one."

McCarel smiled as his hands played deftly over the flight controls. "Learned about their destructiveness the hard way. Was on the old *Chinook*, a troop transport bout' ten years ago. Flight plan put us close to the Crab Nebula. Navy captain decided that instead of an arc transit around the Crab, he'd take a shortcut and slip through one of the Crab's thinner filaments . . . at hyper-speed.

"Gravity waves started pounding us just as we hit the strand. And of course the hyper-speed harmonics intensified the pressure fields of the waves. Just about shook the old *Chin* apart before the captain could drop us down to sub-warp. As it was, we lost most of our flight controls. Knocked the grav-disruptor out . . . damaged the n-space drive. We limped along at sub-warp in weightless conditions before a Nav repair ship showed up. Half the scout contingent was constantly puking because of the weeks of no-weight, but at least we were alive."

Out of the corner of his eye, he could see Tuul shudder slightly. He had no doubt as why—the thought of spending weeks without gravity. Tuul turned his head toward McCarel. "Maybe we should slow to sub-warp now," he suggested. "Just to make sure we're far enough out."

McCarel chuckled. "We're fine, Shar . . . I've calculated more than enough safety margin."

Thirty minutes later, Lengley reported, "We're secure aft, sir."

"Roger, LT," McCarel replied. "Strap yourself in tight—n-space emergence in five minutes."

At the time mark, McCarel powered down from hyper-light velocity to a speed of one hundred thousand kilometers a second in order to give them a wide safety margin from the force of the nebula's gravity surges. Ahead of them the massive walls of the gray-green nebula stood like mighty ramparts. For long moments the two StarScouts watched the forward viewer as the enormous swirling gas cloud loomed ahead.

"Ten seconds to contact," McCarel said quietly.

Seconds later the craft slipped through the first wispy entrails of the cloud and into the dense dust and gas particles. As the minutes passed everything was quiet on the little craft as McCarel skillfully wove them between thick columns of interstellar debris. McCarel turned to Tuul, "Almost through the outer envelope . . . looks like you're still not going to meet your first grav-wave."

Tuul nodded firmly, "I could go my whole career and not be ashamed to say that that's one thing Out Here that I haven't experienced."

McCarel smiled and was about to reply when the ship shuddered and rocked from side to side. Once. Twice. Three times the craft rolled from the pounding of the nebula's intense gravity waves before the vessel settled down and was quiet. Then, as if a giant interstellar curtain had parted, the little ship shot through the last vestiges of the nebula's wispy cloud wall and into clear space. Directly ahead shone a bright, yellow sun. McCarel leaned back, the tension ebbing out of his body as they now shot through clear space.

"See?" McCarel stated, "That wasn't so bad."

Tuul was about to smile a reply when the craft heeled violently to one side before righting. The command console had numerous red alarm lights demanding attention from damaged systems.

"What the . . .!" McCarel shouted, "That wasn't a gravity wave!"

Lightning quick, Tuul reached out and hit the acceleration control. The ship jumped forward like a racehorse from the starting gate. "Ion cannon!" Tuul shouted. "Look at the aft vis-screen!"

McCarel turned slightly to scan the aft viewer. For a moment he could only register surprise. Closing in on them from behind was the unmarked Zephyr 6 craft!

Before McCarel could react the Zephyr fired another volley from its forward ion weapon. He had just enough presence of mind to heel the craft over just before the full ion stream hit the ship. As it was, a sliver of the powerful blast caught them amidships and just forward of the engines. More red lights appeared on the command console.

McCarel opened the universal comm channel, "Zephyr 6 craft! Cease fire! Cease fire! This is McCarel, StarScout command! I say again, cease fire!"

In answer the attacking craft fired another salvo from its ion cannon. The blast caught the unarmed StarScout ship near the portside n-space antenna array, effectively preventing McCarel from transmitting any further n-space messages. With that blast the two senior StarScouts just looked at each other. They knew that the crew of the other ship was offering them no quarter. It was a battle to the death.

"Can we outrun them?" Tuul asked tensely.

"No," McCarel said as he put the craft through a series of evasive maneuvers. "The Zephyr's got more boost juice than we do. Sooner or later it'll close the gap and we'll be sitting ducks for that cannon."

"What about going to hyper-light?"

McCarel snapped out, "We can't! Look!"

Tuul looked at where McCarel pointed and slapped at his armrest. "We're venting from the drive! Must've got us with that first shot."

"I have to give 'em credit, these guys are good," McCarel said through clenched teeth, "Knew exactly where to hit us first, the drive, the n-space antenna . . . which means . . . ." He looked up as if hit with a sudden idea.

"Lengley!" McCarel yelled, "Get up here!"

In a moment, the young scout, looking wide-eyed, said, "Yes sir!"

"Check the escape pods, all of them!" McCarel ordered. "Make sure they're undamaged and ready to discharge." He heeled the craft over again in a wild turn as he gunned their velocity to just under lightspeed. "We may be using them in just a bit."

"Aye aye, skipper," The young man replied. He spun on his heels and headed amidships to the four escape pods that sat snuggled in against the ship's outer bulkheads.

"We gonna jettison?" Tuul asked.

"Can't," McCarel grimly replied. "After they finished this ship off, they'd just home in on the escape pod's transponders and blast them apart. No, we stay and ride this one out. But as my Uncle John Paul Jones once said, we don't give up without a fight."

Just then an ion blast caught the little craft's stern, slinging it sideways from the powerful blast. McCarel didn't have to look at ~~this~~ the command console to know the damage. It was evident from the way the little craft had stopped accelerating.

In answer Tuul eyed McCarel and said, "Well, at this point, I'd much prefer you had an Uncle Houdini, I think we're going to need one amazing escape."

McCarel nodded in agreement as he sucked in air. "We've lost the port engine! Even if we wanted to chance hyper-speed, we can't now."

"LT!" McCarel transmitted over the ship's communicator, "Report!"

"Checking the last two pods now sir," the scout replied. "Starboard one and two all secure and operational."

"Roger that," McCarel said. "Shar, how close are we to that G-star?"

Tuul shook his head. "Hard to tell . . . the instruments are going haywire. Best guess, two, maybe three hundred million kilometers."

"Okay, are you showing any nearby planets on the sensors?"

Tuul nodded. "One. Make it Mark 238.15, down

six degrees from the plane. Uh, call it a little under five million kilometers."

"Got it." McCarel replied and quickly programmed the navigational controls to head for the nearby planet, coaxing every bit of velocity out of the engines as he could.

"What's your idea?" Shar asked as the little craft gyrated wildly through the darkness of space.

McCarel was silent for a moment before replying, "We can't outrun them. The nebula's out, the ship's barely holding together, one tiny grav-wave would rip us apart. If they hit us full bore again with that cannon, well, same thing.

"So, we make for that planet, maybe it's got a moon or two that we can use to play hide n' seek or at least put some rock between us and that cannon. In the meantime," he bleakly said, "I've got an idea. It's not much, probably won't work and could get us all killed, but there's always a chance that'll buy us some time..."

Just then Lengley stuck his head into the command compartment. Breathlessly he reported, "All pods secure and operational sir!"

"Very good!" McCarel replied. "Strap down tight

back there, it's going to get a little rough around here in a few minutes."

For several minutes McCarel pushed the StarScout ship as hard as he could, trying to stay one jump ahead of the Zephyr. But the distance between the two craft closed steadily and they knew it was only a matter of time before the attackers would strike.

The nearby planet loomed closer and closer with every passing second. It would be perfectly obvious to the Zephyr what they were trying to do. McCarel lifted his head to take a quick visual peek at their destination. For just a second he thought he was looking at Mother Earth. The verdant greens, blues, browns, and tan coloring were remarkably similar. Even the white cloud-like formations that skirted the surface reminded him of Terra. Shaking his head, he tore his view away from the captivating scene and back to the business at hand.

His fingers played across the flight console, trying to maintain the best velocity he could while not letting the Zephyr draw a clean bead on them. But with only one working space drive the best velocity he would get would bring the Zephyr practically on top of them in mere minutes.

"Shar! Anything nearby we can make a run for?"

"Working on it, Jak," Tuul coolly replied. Seconds trickled by. McCarel could see the distance between the adversaries narrowing quickly. He knew the Zephyr wasn't going to fire their remaining ion cannon shots until they had the scout transport dead center with no possible way to escape their final broadside.

Tuul spoke up. "Two small moons Jak—not much bigger than a bread basket. Doubt if they'd do much to hide us. The nearest is at Mark 162.85, three degrees above the plane. At our current speed, about five minutes away."

McCarel sighed audibly. "We haven't got the minutes," he muttered, "So we go with the alternate plan."

He took a quick look at the vis-screen that now tracked the pursuing Zephyr. "They've fired that ion cannon quite a bit. I'm sure it's drained a lot out of their power packs. I think their next shot is going to be with one of their Foxtrot torpedoes. But they want to get a little closer yet before they fire. So this is what I propose we do."

In clipped tones he outlined his idea. Tuul and Lengley listened attentively. When McCarel finished, Tuul looked at him with one eyebrow raised and said, "That's pretty imaginative, Jak. And you realize that if it doesn't work, we'll be more than sitting ducks for their next shot. We'll be smack in the center of their bull's eye."

McCarel nodded. "I fully realize that, sir. Do either of you have a better idea?"

Tuul looked at the young scout. "Now's the time to impress us youngster. Any ideas?"

The young scout gulped. "Sorry, sir."

Tuul shook his head and said, "Okay Jak, looks like it's your show."

"Check. Plaster yourself to that scope Shar; I need to know the exact instant they fire and the torp's course."

"You got it, boss." Tuul replied crisply and turned to the sophisticated moving target indicator radar. The radar's ability to track speeding objects was a critical element in McCarel's plan.

McCarel looked at his own screens. "They're closing," he said. The seconds trickled by. The tension in the compartment thickened perceptibly. "Okay, gentlemen," McCarel said softly. "Stand by for emergency deceleration and a 180 degree come-about . . . and won't they be surprised . . ."

McCarel softly counted to himself, "Five . . . four . . . three . . . two . . . and . . . one!"

With that the StarScout hit the command emergency stop. The ship shuddered for a moment as it flipped over and blasted at full thrust in the opposite direction. In seconds the ship came to a full stop and then leaped forward in a burst of speed, heading directly for the renegade ship.

McCarel could just picture the stunned look on the attacker's faces as they saw their prey speeding directly at them. It was those moments of hesitation that he was hoping for. With both ships hurtling towards each other at a tremendous speed, the distance between them closed almost instantaneously.

Seconds later Tuul yelped, "They've fired! One torpedo! Straight down our throat at Mark 268.77!"

"Got it!" McCarel yelled as he cut the ship's engine thrust, and tilted the craft over so that its starboard side faced the speeding torpedo. With a quick jab of his finger, McCarel stabbed the command control to fire both starboard escape pods along azimuth 268.77. With a slight jolt both pods exploded from their bays and rocketed toward the onrushing deadly projectile.

McCarel rolled the craft again, this time so that its portside faced the oncoming attacking craft. Counting silently to three, he repeated the command sequence and fired the two portside pods toward the speeding Zephyr.

Knowing that he had done what he could, McCarel flipped the ship with its nose toward the M-class planet and hit the acceleration thruster. If his plan didn't work, they would still make a run for the planet but it probably would be a very short race.

Seconds later there was a bright flash of light that illuminated the space around their craft. Tuul punched his fist in the air and yelped, "Gotcha!" He slapped McCarel on the back, "Scratch one torpedo! Great job!"

"What about their ship?" McCarel demanded.

"Still coming on . . ." he started when a flare-like light flash lighted the space behind them. "Whoa," Tuul said, and then laughed out loud, "They're decelerating . . . One or more of the pods hit'em dead-on and . . ."

With a pounding jolt, the little troop ship was punched sideways and electrical sparks flew from the control console. "Ion cannon!" McCarel yelled, "We're hit!"

The ship began to gyrate wildly, its flight and navigation controls obviously gone. In moments, it was out of control and plunging headlong toward the onrushing planet.

Chapter 23

ALPHA PRIME . . .

"Listen up!" Bianca ordered. "We've got a job to do." Looking around, Del could see that the assembly in the hangar hold was basically the same group as on Stygar 6 minus Ry. From Bianca's posture, they were about to get their marching orders and pre-mission tasks.

"We've got a lead on a downed civilian craft. Could be a rich merchant freighter or maybe a passenger star liner, with lots of fat, wealthy passengers. Either way, easy pickings for us if we can beat the Confederation to the ship.

"We just popped out of the outer rim of the Helix Nebula and are headed toward what appears to be a G-type star with a Class M planet. Our best guess is that the shipwreck is on that planet but we don't have a precise fix yet. So while the astro-bridge gang is working on a good locate we'll ready the scouters. Anyar will take Ry's place in Lima 6 with me. And Stinneli will go in Lima 4."

She made quick assignments to the crew, including the junior scouts. Del's tasks teamed him with Shanon running a series of diagnostics tests on Lima 1. As Del worked underneath the command console checking wiring and laser linkage, Shanon began flight and navigation simulations on the master computer.

Shanon poked her head under the console. "Del, do you think Nase's right? Are they really Gadion Faction?"

Del lowered his laser-tip and looked up. He scratched his cheek as he answered. "Nase is pretty smart about such things." He stopped for a second and then said, "Nase's not an alarmist, I don't think he would say what he did without being pretty sure."

Shanon pursed her lips, causing a dimple to

appear on her right cheek. Before we were dealing with common outlaws, but the Faction—that's a whole different story. Where does that put us now?"

Del didn't speak for a long time. Shanon was right. Before, he had felt some hope that they would somehow get out of their predicament. But now it was difficult to have the same feeling.

Del let out a sigh as he spoke. "Shanon, I honestly don't know. I guess we just keep going . . . keep trying . . . and hope that somehow we'll find a way to escape." He stopped and lowered his voice, "Or at least you and the others can escape."

Shanon sat back up and for several minutes neither said anything as they worked. Shanon broke the silence by saying, "Del," she began, "Back to Nase's idea, if he is right, it would explain a number of things; crew organization, sophisticated equipment, deep-space support."

Del nodded gravely, stopped what he was doing and leaned back against the bulkhead. "It would," he admitted and then said, "But would it explain everything?"

"What do you mean?" she questioned. He rubbed his hands down his legs before answering. "Well, to be honest, I don't know that much about the *Faction*. But, have you ever heard of the *Faction* actually being on Terra for instance?"

Shanon opened her mouth as if to answer and then slowly closed it. "Come to think of it, no."

"Neither have I." Del returned, "Especially as star-beast poachers. I've only heard about them being off-world and frankly the poaching thing and the quadro-diamonds seem awfully tame from what I've heard about them."

"Maybe they need to do this to finance their operations?" Shanon offered.

"Maybe," Del answered, "But I'm not so sure." He looked around to make sure no one was within earshot and lowered his voice. "But if that's the case then answer me this." Quickly he set out his observations and finished with, "And when I laid her on the couch she said . . ." and repeated what Bianca uttered in her semiconscious state on Stygar 6.

Shanon's eyes grew large as she incredulously asked, "Are you sure that's what she said?"

"Yeah. Granted, things were pretty screwy right then, but I know that's what I heard."

Shanon sat back in her seat and ran her fingers

over the flight controls. "That doesn't make sense, Del," she began, but then snapped her head towards his, "Unless . . ." she began, and then breathed out, "Unless she's a crossover." She stopped and then gushed out, "Think about it Del. Look at how she bosses this crew, their organization, how they operate. Even why some of their equipment is the same. If she's crossed over, it would explain a lot about her and this gang."

She tapped on the edge of the seat with her forefinger and then said, "I've heard of such things of course, it's just hard to realize that anyone would turn traitor, especially a StarScout."

Del didn't respond to her comments as the conversation struck too close to home. He bent his head down so that Shanon couldn't see him biting down hard on his lip. Shanon spoke again. "Del," she began, "have you noticed that the poachers stopped wearing their d-guns? They're only wearing personal stunners."

The change in conversation caught Del off-guard. He thought about her comment for a second and realized she was right. He poked his head out from under the console and said, "No, I guess I hadn't really noticed, but come to think of it, you're absolutely right."

Shanon bobbed her head as she continued working the computer. "I think they made the transition couple days ago. I didn't really see it at first myself. I've gotten so used to them carrying weapons on-board ship. But it caught my eye when I was with a work party moving stores in one of the lower deck cargo holds."

Del rubbed his chin as he answered. "I guess they don't feel a need for the heavy hardware."

Shanon bent her head down and looked Del squarely in the eye. "Del, unless I'm mistaken, that Garther Ape is still on board."

"Don't remind me," Del answered dryly, his experience with the beast still fresh in his mind.

"Sorry, but why would they go to all the extra precautions earlier to protect themselves and not now? I don't see how the conditions have changed to warrant lower safeguards."

"Maybe they've got the ape so well contained and sedated that they don't feel personally threatened anymore."

Shanon just looked down at him sweetly. Del could

see that her mental gears were running full speed. And he knew that he would be smart to pay attention. "Okay," he said, "I see you don't buy it. What's your idea?"

She raised her eyebrows and sighed. "I don't have anything solid to go on, so that's why I'm going to go snoop in the life-form holds. I want to see what they've done with that ape."

"Hold on, Shanon," Del hastily said. "That's pretty risky. What if you get caught? Bianca could get pretty nasty."

Still running her fingers over the computer input controls, Shanon replied, "Yes, it's chancy. If I get caught I'll simply tell them that that's what I'm in training for and I was curious about the thing. After all, that's a big part of what we do. Seek out new life, observe it, study it . . . etcetera, etcetera, etcetera, as Instructor Scout Smythe would say."

"Shanon, I'm not sure it's worth the risk."

Shanon bent her head down and said firmly, "Del, you get your hunches—well, I get mine. I've got a notion there's something not quite right here. I'm not sure I buy into your cross-over theory. [not Del's theory, it was hers] And for some reason I think that we need to get a good look at that ape."

Del could see the fire in her eyes and knew there was no use in arguing with the strong-willed young woman. "Okay, okay," he replied, "But I'll go look. You stay here and keep working."

"Hey!" she protested, "My idea!"

"Certainly was," Del replied, "And if anyone asks, you'll get full credit. But if you get caught, your cover story is pretty flimsy. Mine, on the other hand, makes more sense. In the meantime, if anyone comes looking for me, tell them I'm down in parts getting a replacement modulator . . . which I'll actually visit, but only after a little detour."

He was about to stand, when unexpectedly, she reached out and gently took hold of his arm. "Del," she began in a soft voice, "Please be careful."

He looked up at her and couldn't help but notice her luminous and lovely green eyes or how perfect her soft pink lips were. The isolated farm life-style that he had lived on Randor made Del's experiences with girls practically non-existent. He knew he liked girls, a lot, he just didn't know how to act around them in a social sense.

Shanon returned his look with warm, soft eyes.

She brought her face close to his and looked at him expectantly. Not exactly sure what to do, Del drew back just a bit.

Shanon laughed lightly and said, "Del, I'm a girl, not some Battaurian Death-Wasp."

Del didn't answer but turned to the modulator that he had pulled from under the console deck. His heart pounded so loudly in his ears that he almost didn't hear Shanon slyly ask, "Say, don't tell me that on your planet boys don't like girls?"

Del vigorously shook his head, "No, Randorian boys like girls just fine."

"And you?" she coyly asked.

Del's hands were cold and the conversation had turned decidedly uncomfortable, "I like girls just fine . . ." he began defensively, "Just never had much time for them. We lived pretty far out from town and there weren't any girls close by . . . and my chores and school pretty much took up most of my day." He shrugged his shoulders, "So there wasn't much reason to really pay attention."

"So it's true with you," she teased, "The old adage about sweet sixteen."

"What do you mean? I don't know what you're

talking about." He had to admit he really liked her melodious laugh though he would prefer not hearing it as she poked fun at him.

"You know," she began, "Being sweet sixteen and never been kissed."

Del's ears burned with embarrassment as what she said was pretty much on target. Not that he had ever made any attempt to kiss or get kissed by a girl as what few opportunities for such things never seemed to come his way. But for some reason getting teased by Shanon about this was almost as bad as when the Garther Ape grabbed him in the spacer's hold. Or, maybe worse, much worse.

He looked over at Shanon, and noticed that there was something different in the way she looked at him. Her eyes and face had grown soft, and she wore a look of expectancy on her face. It hit him like a thunder-bolt that her teasing small talk was actually an invitation. He laid down his tools and the modulator. Slowly he moved his face closer to hers, and noticed that he was breathing faster—but so was she.

Just as their lips were about to touch, a voice blasted over the ship's internal communicator,

"Lima 1! Report status!" the disembodied voice demanded.

Del pulled back from Shanon, who laughed out loud and rolled on her back. Del angrily hit the comms-switch, "Moving along quite well until you interrupted," Del snapped out.

"Good," the voice replied, "What about the attitude modulator you were to check?"

Del sighed in frustration. "Pulled, the diagnostic shows it's running about 2 degrees off-center."

"Don't try to repair it yourself, run it down to parts, get a new one and install it right away."

"Roger," Del replied, glancing over at Shanon who dimpled slightly, shrugged, and raised herself to sit in the cockpit chair to begin running another series of flight control tests. Del lightly hit his fist on his knee, knowing that the magic moment had passed. In an exasperated tone he replied to the nameless voice, "I've got a few other things to check first before I head to parts."

"Understood, but make it fast, we're on a tight time-line here."

"Okay, okay." Del muttered as he picked up his tools. There was a long moment of silence before

Shanon rolled her head and shoulders down and said gently, "Sorry Del."

Del shook his head, "It's okay," he laughed, "I guess I'm still sweet sixteen..."

Her face turned serious and she asked, "Del, what story are you going to use if you get caught?"

Del grabbed the broken modulator, stuck it in his waistband and grimly said over his shoulder, "That I'm going to try and milk some poison from that ape and concoct my own antidote."

Minutes later, Del moved in the passageway leading to the cargo holds that held the extraterrestrial life forms. He ignored the first and headed toward the last hold. If he were the poachers, he thought, he would place the ape as far away from the crew as he possibly could.

Walking silently toward the last metal hatch, Del stopped several meters away. He was certain that the poachers had the ape sedated, but less certain if the crew had set up a surveillance system to watch the deadly beast. Quickly he surveyed the entire area around the cargo hold but nothing spoke of an exterior observation system. The bulkheads and ceiling were completely bare.

With a deep breath, Del walked forward to stand before the hatch and placed his ear against the metal door to listen for several minutes. The air was still and quiet, ~~nor could he feel any~~ there were no vibrations in the metal that indicated something large moving inside the room. He stepped back from the door and reached for the access controls.

Del steadied himself. His idea was that as the door opened, he would take one quick look inside and then shut the hatch before the ape could react. His plan would work as long as the creature wasn't silently waiting in ambush. Carefully Del reached up to the door panel. With his hands readied in attack position, he pressed the control device. As the door slid open he stuck his head quickly in and was about to jerk back when he stopped.

The Garther Ape lay unmoving on the metal floor of the cargo hold. Del remembered the first time that he was this close to the creature. Then it was sedated and confined in a stasis sleep chamber. Now it lay totally free, unfettered by any restraints. Nor could Del see any drip tubes indicating the beast was receiving tranquilizers.

He peered intently at the prone figure and at first

thought the creature was asleep or dead. He considered for a moment that the creature was in hibernation. For long moments he carefully watched the body. There was no upward movement of the chest indicating breathing. No sounds coming from the mouth or nose. The beast was still and lifeless.

With the hatchway left open, Del cautiously advanced one step at a time toward the extraterrestrial killer. The wicked talons lay outstretched on the cold floor, the fanged mouth open. The eyes were closed and the accordion-like ears folded under the head and shoulders.

Del stopped two meters away from the still figure and scrutinized the unmoving beast. His instincts told him that something was terribly wrong. He took the last few steps and knelt near the creature's head. With a slightly shaking finger, he reached out and touched the beast. It didn't stir.

His heartbeat thudding in his ears, Del lightly placed his hand on the creature's chest. The body was cold and lifeless. It was dead. Del bent down to minutely inspect the extraterrestrial. He didn't know what he was looking for, didn't know what Shanon's hunch was telling her. But he trusted Shanon's instincts, her innate ability to formulate solutions to complex problems.

Del began at the beast's head with his careful examination. Moments later he bolted upright, his eyes wide, his heart racing. He stifled an exclamation as he bent back down to look at his discovery. "Well, I'll be . . ." he softly muttered. He looked at the beast's prone figure as he whispered to himself, "If this is a . . ."

Just then the ship's intercom blasted out, "All hands, report to stations! Landing party, stand by your craft on the flight deck!"

Del fought an emotional battle over his find. One part of him demanded that he confront Bianca with his discovery. Another part urged caution. This latest find increased the questions and the mystery. For a moment he wavered, then made his decision. He would share this with his teammates, but sooner or later he was going to have his answers.

He strode out of the hold and closed the portal door. He quickly made his way to the electronics shop and hailed the crew member on duty. "We're about to up-ship and I need to replace this circuit board on Lima 1." The outlaw took the circuit board, found its replacement and handed it to Del. With quick steps, Del entered the flight deck and caught Bianca's glare at him as he joined the assembled group. As Del slipped next to Shanon, he whispered, "What did I miss?"

Shanon barely shook her head. "Nothing. She's been pacing like a hungry Maw-tiger. If I didn't know better I would say the lady is a bit anxious about something. Did you find it?"

"Yeah." He leaned over, cupped his hand against Shanon's ear, and whispered his discovery. She practically stopped breathing, gaped at him for a moment and then turned around. They both knew that they needed to discuss this revelation, but now wasn't the time.

"We've cleared the nebula and got a fix on the distress beacon," Bianca began, "It's coming from an M-class planet directly ahead. There's nothing in our data banks on the planet. Completely uncharted and unexplored, so we'll be going down cold. But our sensors indicate its atmosphere is Earth-like and surface gravity is at 98 percent of one gravity. So we won't need protective suiting."

She stopped for a moment to ensure she had

everyone's attention. "However, remember what I just said, this is a totally new planet; nothing whatsoever is known about it." She stopped and purposefully looked right at the scouts, "When we get on the ground, watch where you put your hands and feet, if you don't, you might be missing one or the other by the time we're through."

She again paused for a moment to let the message sink in and went on, "The good news is that we've got an identifier code on the downed ship. It's the *Celeste T,* the private yacht of Mr. Samuel Theodore Pinkins."

For a moment there was silence, then Bianca jutted her chin toward Sami and asked, "You savvy Samuel Pinkins?"

Sami looked back at her and replied with, "Uh, the Confederation sector Governor?"

Bianca rolled her eyes and said, "Do the names Galactic Express, Stellar Cruises, Galactic Mining and Exploration, Interstellar Outfitters to name a few, ring a bell?"

Sami looked at her for a moment and said, "Well, sure. IS makes a dynamo mega-hertz stereo woofer. You can bounce-sound or do a singular . . ." Sami trailed off as Bianca glared at him. Several of the renegades laughed out loud. Next to Del, TJ tried hard to stifle her own giggles.

Bianca darkly said, "Samuel Pinkins runs those deep-space corporations plus about twenty others. He personally owns two planets. He is undoubtedly the richest man in the Confederation."

"Oh . . ." Sami said meekly. "That Samuel Pinkins."

"That Samuel Pinkins," Bianca retorted. "So if he's down there, it means we've hit the jackpot." She glared at the five scouts. "So remember the deal, and no foul-ups!"

She shifted her weight and continued. "Here's the plan. Dan will take the *Queen Bee* down to a hundred thousand meters and do a Heerdon maneuver. The scouts will pilot the scouters to the surface. I assume they've all done at least one Heerdon.

"The bad news is the distress beacon transmitter appears to be damaged because the signal is intermittent and extremely weak so we don't have a good lock on the *Celeste's* precise location. Once we clear the ship we'll spread out in a standard *V* formation. I'll be the lead ship."

She stopped and pointed at Sami. "You'll pilot

Lima 6. Lima 1 will be on my left wing, 2 on my right. Lima 4 and 5 will trail. Three kilometers apart. Once we locate the *Celeste* wait for my orders. Any questions?"

No one raised a hand so Bianca ordered, "Man your craft. Egress in 20 minutes." Quickly the Lima 6 crew entered the craft and Bianca said to Del and Sami, "Your gear is in the back, suit up."

Moments later Del and Sami had their StarScout gear on and came forward. Del's jaw dropped when he saw that Bianca and Anyar wore comparable StarScout equipment over their forest-green and earth-brown outfits. Sami and he eyed each other silently, not knowing quite what to say.

Bianca quickly ordered, "Sami, pilot seat. I'll copilot. Baldura, take the third seat in the pilot pod." She reached down and handed Del and Sami their scout-knives. "Just in case," she muttered. Quickly the two slid their knives into respective scabbards.

Del made his way forward to the pilot's compartment and buckled himself into the jump seat after Sami and Bianca slid into the pilot's command chairs. For several minutes, Sami and Bianca went over the preflight sequence, carefully checking their flight controls

"How many Heerdons have you done?" Bianca asked Sami. "Plenty," the young scout replied nervously. Seeing Bianca's skeptical look he shrugged. "One."

"One's better than none. You remember the routine?" Bianca asked.

Sami nodded. "Wait for the flip-over, we go static and I hit the boost button. A cinch."

Bianca blew a small puff of air that lifted her bangs slightly and turned back to her flight checks. Del, listening to the conversation, was more than a little mystified that Bianca ordered the junior scouts to do the fly-out.

A Heerdon maneuver was a boost-out stratagem in which the mother ship, inverted, would come to a dead stop relative to the planet's surface. With the open flight bay facing the planet's surface, the scouters would shoot out like bees from a hive and head for the planet's face.

Del knew there were potential catastrophic problems to the maneuver. As the transport ship hit dead-stop, there would be a short period of weightlessness. Experiencing the distressing twin aspects of negative g's and vertigo, the scouter pilot would then have to fly the craft in those conditions out of a very confined space. The slightest misjudgment and the pilot could easily slam the craft into a side bulkhead or overhead ceiling.

The second problem concerned the *Queen Bee*. If there was engine failure and the crew couldn't restart the main engine, the big ship would spiral down in a death-fall to the surface.

But the maneuver was the most economical method for placing the scouters directly over their target and drastically shortened their time to land on the surface. Del could only assume that Bianca was willing to take the risk to the Queen. As he mulled this over, the ship's communicator came on. "Bianca," Dan said, "We've got a little problem."

"Can we discuss it in the clear?" Bianca replied looking at the two scouts.

"Roger," Dan replied back, "Telescopic sensor images coming back from the planet show heavy storms directly over your target area. I think you're in for a pretty rough ride going in."

Bianca considered this bit of news for a moment before asking, "Any idea of their magnitude?"

"Best guess from the images, I think you're looking at a six on the Kamuchi scale."

Del silently whistled to himself. A magnitude six storm would knock the little scouter around like a stone bouncing down the side of a mountain. Dan's 'rough ride' was a bit of an understatement. The scouter was rated airworthy in a magnitude six storm, but anything above that would be very risky.

For several moments Bianca digested the information, then she replied, "All right, Dan thanks for the information. We'll continue with the plan but work the edges of the storm until it dies out or we ascertain we can navigate through."

"Check. Five minutes to roll-over."

"Roger." Bianca turned to Sami and ordered "Get a status check from the other ships and let them know of that meteorology report."

Sami nodded and relayed the storm message to the other craft over the ship-to-ship communicator. He then directed, "Lima ships, status checks." In sequence, all ships reported as flight ready. "Very well," Sami intoned. "Stand by for roll-over and boost out." Then to the astro-bridge crew he said, "Bridge, Lima 6, all Lima craft standing by."

Karm's voice came back in reply, "Roger, Lima 6. One minute."

Sami and Bianca finished with their final checks. All pulled their shoulder straps a little tighter and settled back to wait for the countdown from the bridge crew.

Seconds ticked by before Karm's voice came again. "Lima craft, stand by, bay door opening." Overhead the great metal door slid back to reveal the black of space turning purple and then blue as the *Queen Bee* dove through the planet's atmosphere.

Seconds later, Karm said, "Beginning roll-over, prepare for dead-stop." Above them, Del could see the sky start to swing through the giant skylight. A large arc of the planet's green and brown surface swung into view.

Karm's voice came again, "Dead-stop in ten seconds, prepare for boost out." Then she counted down, "and five . . . four . . . three," Sami poised his hands over the flight controls. "Two . . . one! Ship at full-stop!"

Del felt his stomach try to crawl up his gullet as full weightlessness hit. At the same time, Sami punched the thruster control and skillfully shot the ship cleanly through the bay opening. In moments Del felt full weight return as the little craft rolled over to point its nose downward. Behind them, the other craft slipped away from the confines of the mother ship and followed Lima 6 downward toward the waiting planet.

* * * * * * * *

why are there here?

Once all of the scouters cleared the bay, the transport flight crew fired up the main engines and lifted up into space. From the command deck, Dan directed that the ship go into a high synchronous orbit above the scouters' intended landing site. Twenty minutes later, Karm reported to Dan, "Locked in orbit, forty thousand kilometers out, velocity matched to the planet's rotational period."

"Very good," Dan replied and turned to Wentz, his comms technician on duty. "You have a bead on them?"

Wentz nodded. "Aye, sir. Followed them down to the surface, looks like they've just started the . . ." He was about to finish his description when his console display started scrolling data. As he read it, he yelped in surprise and said, "Sir, you better come see this!"

Dan took the few steps over to the communications console and read the message. As he shook his head, he muttered, "What next?" He reached over to open a comms-channel to Lima 6.

"Lima 6," he began, "This is the *Queen Bee*."

"Go ahead *Queen*," Bianca answered.

"Six," Dan grimly said, "We've picked up another distress call. Very faint. Looks like it's about ten, maybe fifteen kilometers planetary north of the *Celeste* beacon."

There was a moment of silence and then Bianca said, "Is it a second beacon from the *Celeste*?"

"Negative. This one registers as a StarScout Save and Rescue call. Scout platoon ship. Designation Yankee One-Niner."

There was a long moment of silence. When Bianca didn't answer, Dan asked, "Six, did you copy my transmission?"

Bianca replied slowly, her voice clearly showing incredulity, "Roger, *Queen*, I copy scout Save and Recall ten kilometers planetary north of *Celeste* beacon."

"That's affirmative. Please advise on your intentions."

"Standby," Bianca replied.

Dan nodded in understanding and was about to reply when Karm screamed out, "Sweet galaxy, where did that come from!"

Dan whirled from the console and took several steps to stand behind Karm. She pointed at the moving target indicator. "Captain," she said excitedly, "We've got a bogey on a collision course! Closing fast! It just appeared out of nowhere! We need to maneuver and now!"

He could clearly see the computer's projected trajectory for the incoming mass . . . it was headed right at them!

"Evasive maneuvers!" he ordered, "Full boost now!"

Karm began hitting the flight controls, calling up emergency power to rocket them away from the deadly mass. For a moment she let her eyes go to the forward viewer. As she did so, her fingers stopped in midair. Unbelieving she choked out, "Captain! Forward screen!"

Pivoting toward the forward vu-screen, stood

riveted on the command deck. Around him there was complete silence except for a few gasps. The image of the alien spaceship as it filled the viewer transfixed the crew.

A giant geyser of sparkling blue light spewed outward from the on-rushing alien craft. Wide-eyed, Dan watched as the expanding blue globe headed toward his ship. He spun away from the viewer and barked to his comms tech, "Get a message out now! Do it!"

Wentz bent over his communications console. In seconds the message sped toward Earth. It simply said,

ALPHA PRIME ... ALPHA PRIME ... ALPHA PRIME ...

Chapter 24

Footprints in the Forest

"Whoa!" yelped Sami, "Just lost our nav beacon with the *Queen Bee*! Disappeared right off the scope!"

"*Queen B*ee this is Lima 6, do you copy?" Bianca spoke firmly into the communicator. She waited several seconds but received no reply. Tensely, she repeated her message but with the same result. Speaking into the comms unit she asked, "Lima ships, any contact with the *Queen Bee*?"

Each craft responded that they, too, had lost all navigation and communication contact with the *Queen*. Del looked at Sami, who shook his head and arched his eyebrows. For all the craft to lose contact in the middle of a transmission could only mean trouble. Catastrophic trouble.

"Orders, ma'am," Sami asked quietly. For a long moment, Bianca was silent and then spoke ship to ship. "Lima 2, come to a heading of 030 degrees and begin a series of 'S' sweeps. All others, stay with me, same course. Our primary target is the *Celeste*. Exercise caution. The met-Doppler radar registers heavy thunderstorms. Several are in the supercell category. Do you copy?"

"Roger Lima 6," came TJ's reply, "Breaking formation."

Del spoke up, "What about that scout distress beacon?"

In answer, Bianca raised her hand to quiet Del and said sternly, "You heard my orders."

She spoke into her trans-comm. "Anyar, we're

going to set down on a high point close to the distress beacon. If we haven't raised the *Queen* by then, break out the wide-band transmitter and the portable sky tracker. Soon as we land, get them set up. We need to find out what happened to her."

"Roger," Anyar replied from the passenger compartment.

Del's eyebrows rose. The sky-tracker was a sophisticated piece of equipment used by Confederation forces, such as the StarScouts, to track and communicate with overhead orbiting spacecraft. That this group would have such a device only added one more piece to the puzzle.

As Sami guided the craft toward the surface, Del could see towering cumulonimbus clouds reaching upward. Over and over, clashing lightning strokes seared the dark innards of the swirling cloud masses. Del appreciated Bianca's orders to steer clear of the storms until they dissipated. Sturdy as these little craft were, it was wise not to underestimate the titanic forces of t-storms.

Sami steered the scouter clear of the thunderstorms and they were able to get a good look at the terrain. Del's first impression was a series of three kilometers equidistant.

Moments later, Del heard TJ say, "Lima 6, this is 2, we've got the *Celeste* pinpointed. We're approximately eight clicks from you on an azimuth of 160. Looks like we'll have to set down several hundred meters from the crash site. It's too heavily forested to get closer. We're not able to see much from the air, too much vegetation and we've got heavy rain showers moving through."

"Understood," Bianca said, "Report when you reach the ship. We're going to land and try to raise the *Queen*."

For several more minutes Sami wove the craft lower, looking for a suitable landing site. He pointed out several possibilities to her but she wasn't satisfied with his choices. He was about to point out another to her when the ship-board communicator erupted to life, "Lima 6, this is Lima 2." Del didn't immediately recognize the voice.

"Go ahead," Bianca instantly responded.

"We've almost reached the crash site. No sign of any crew." For a moment the voice paused, then said, "But this is really odd, the ship is . . ." his speech trailed off. Suddenly the voice exploded in urgency,

"Lima 6! Lima 6! We're under . . ." then the communicator went silent.

Bianca waited for a moment, then crisply said, "Lima 2, you broke off! Say again!" Several seconds went by without reply. Bianca urgently repeated her message into the communicator but there was only silence. Practically growling she said to Sami, "Turn us around, now! Head for the *Celeste* site!"

Sami sputtered, "But what about . . ."

"Do it, scout!" Bianca tensely commanded, "We've got people in trouble back there!"

Sami heeled the craft hard over, bringing the scouter on a beeline for the *Celeste* and increased his speed. At the same time, Bianca ordered the other craft to follow and to close formation.

Minutes later, while the other craft held station higher up, Sami brought his ship down into the narrow valley where the Lima 2 craft and the *Celeste* lay. It took only moments for them to find Lima 2's landing site in a small clearing. Hovering above the craft, Sami skillfully circled the ship. As Del scanned the small meadow he couldn't see any indication of life or any sign of TJ.

Bianca jutted her chin toward the upper reaches

of the valley and grimly said, "Move on to the *Celeste*." Sami heeled the ship over and shortly was in a tight flight pattern directly over the *Celeste*. The canopy from the towering trees made for extremely poor observation but it was obvious there was no movement on the ground.

Del studied the downed craft that lay partially on its side. A series of splintered tree trunks outlined the path of the craft as it crashed through the trees, and then slammed against the valley side-slope before it slid to the valley floor. Several large trees lay criss-crossed over the ship preventing a really good look at the downed spacer. But something about the craft struck Del as odd.

Del spoke to Bianca. "You want me to rappel down?"

Bianca kept looking at the *Celeste* as she said, "No, we're going to land and go in as a body. I don't want you alone on the ground." She gestured to Sami. "Hold this position." With that she got up and went into the passenger compartment. She motioned to Anyar and pulled him over to the port vu-pane. For several seconds they held a hushed conversation with Bianca pointing several times at the *Celeste*.

They broke off their conversation as Bianca came forward and slid into the co-pilot's chair. "Head up the slope; I want to set down on that ridge."

Surprised, Sami said, "You don't want to land near Lima 2?"

"No," Bianca said, her mouth set hard. "We need to get the tracker and transmitter set up. I need to talk to the *Queen Bee*. Now."

"You're the boss," Sami replied, and running his fingers over the controls moved them quickly upslope. A few moments later Sami pointed down and to the left at a small plateau that cut the sharp ridge line. "There?" he asked.

Bianca nodded. Opening the communicator she said, "Follow us in. We're setting down."

Carefully, Sami eased the craft down to the landing site, moving off to one side to allow enough room for the other scouters to land. With a soft bump the craft settled down on its landing struts.

Within seconds the other scouters set down and the group gathered around Bianca near Lima 6. She gestured to her poacher crew saying, "Let's get a three-sixty around the scouters. Anyar, get the transmitter going." She pointed to the four scouts.

"You four stay put."

Precision-like, the group peeled off and set up a defensive perimeter around the grounded scouters. Off to one side, Anyar worked feverishly setting up the sophisticated transmitter. Bianca pulled at her lip as she studied the junior scouts for a moment and then said, "All right, you know the score. Something happened to the Lima 2 crew. I don't know what, but we're going to find out. Now listen carefully. This is not some training preserve on Terra. It may look and feel like Earth, but it is NOT! The chances of this planet having a completely terrestrial environment are statistically nil. The dangers here will be real, and possibly lethal.

"You're going to want to act like six-week-old puppies, sticking your noses in everything. Don't! You literally know zip! Be suspicious, trust nothing! That purple bush over there may be just a purple bush, or it could be this planet's equivalent of a Portuguese Man o' War. That tiny insect-looking creature may be just that, or it could be a flesh-eating parasite just waiting to burrow into your body. That pretty rock you want to pick up may not be a rock. It could be an organic life form just waiting to latch onto your skin and suck your life blood out. That branch you're about to step on may not be a branch, but this planet's equivalent of a poisonous viper."

She stopped to take in a deep breath and then with conviction stated, "Trust me. I know what I'm talking about!" With that she turned and walked toward Anyar who was assembling the last components of the sky watch.

Del somberly nodded. He clearly understood her message. Except for a slight green tint to the sun, so far most everything on this planet looked remarkably Terran. Even the air tasted like Mother Earth's sweet mixture. The remarkable similarity could lull them into a false sense of security, a dangerous complacency. It would be easy to assume that because the environment looked Terran, that the ecology would be similar. But that would be a foolish and potentially fatal assumption.

Del remembered a lesson from ScoutMaster Tarracas, "Out There, assuming that all is well can be a deadly mistake. On an alien planet, an ill-advised or ill-conceived assumption can kill you just as quickly as the strike of Marsten's Viper. Assume if you must, but if you must assume select your next footstep most carefully."

Sami leaned over and sarcastically whispered, "Trust her? I wouldn't trust her if she swore on her father's grave. But I must admit, I didn't know she cared so much."

Bianca whirled and opened her mouth as if to speak but then stopped. Instead, she took a deep breath and said, "I don't Sami. But I need you four to help me find that sky-liner and my missing crew—and that's all!"

As Bianca strode over to Anyar, Sami leaned over and whispered, "Wow, I didn't know she had such great hearing either."

Shanon softly commented, "It's called 'mother's hearing' Sami."

Sami half-snorted, "Her? A mother? I don't think so, and heaven help us if she's breeding!"

Shanon shook her head, her brown hair swishing slightly, "It's just a saying." She replied in a low voice, "A new mother's senses are heightened so that she's aware of even the tiniest sounds her infant makes." She stopped for a moment with a funny look on her face and then said, "Same thing happens to us when we're extremely concerned or worried about another person." She looked around at her teammates, "Or in this case, persons."

Del rocked slightly forward in sudden understanding of Shanon's observation. Given everything else it certainly made sense, he thought, as he watched Bianca stride over to where Anyar operated the transmitter and sky watch. Curious, Del edged toward the two. As he did he overheard Anyar say to Bianca, "There's absolutely nothing in synchronous high orbit ma'am. We'll have to sit and monitor for about sixty minutes to see if they're in low orbit."

Bianca shook her head. "We can't afford to stay here that long. Run a remote relay over to the edge. Make its line-of-sight straight down into the valley. Carry a monitor with you. Start doing a comms check every five minutes." For a moment she hesitated and then said very quietly, "And, have it start sending a distress call. Put it on automatic mode. You know the code."

Anyar somberly nodded. "Will do, ma'am." The young man grabbed one of the relay devices that would allow the team to be hooked into the main transmitter. Setting it down near where the ridge started to slope downward, he lined up the laser settings in the two devices. As he finished, he nodded at Bianca.

Bianca spoke up so that all could hear, "We're going to leave the scouters here. With no comms with the Queen Bee and the loss of the Lima 2, I feel it best to do a search from the ground rather than the air.

"Mount up. Team by craft assignment. Craft commanders are team commanders. If I go down, Gant is in charge, Anyar has the point. Trail formation until we can spread out. Pat, rear overwatch, and as soon as you can, put out a flanker to each side."

She looked around to make sure everyone was ready. "Move out," she ~~curtly~~ ordered

Anyar quickly moved forward to slip over the edge of the small plateau, picking his way carefully down the brush-filled slope. Seconds later, standing at the lip, Bianca turned to Del, "Break out your LS. Free search for now. Sami, team overwatch."

With that she turned and followed Anyar. Del wasn't too surprised to see Anyar pull out a Life-Sensor and begin scanning as he made his way down valleys, some large and open, others steeply V-shaped, broken by sharp ridges and high irregular hills. In the distance he could see the hills trailing off into a large flat plain. Deep within the valleys he saw an occasional glitter as sunlight struck water. In places, the blue-green forest canopy was so thick that it completely hid the valley floor. As they dropped lower, Del saw that some of the trees rivaled Terra's giant redwood sequoias in size.

Sami glanced over at Bianca. "If the crash-site has trees like those, you want me to set down?"

Bianca shook her head. "No... We'll get as close as we can. If we have to, we'll hike." Del understood Bianca's thinking. Technically the scouter could push through the thick trees, but with the loss of communication with the *Queen Bee*, Bianca was being extra cautious.

For several minutes, Sami put the scouter through a series of figure eights as they waited out the storm. Finally Bianca said, "Okay, met-radar is showing the storm system moving off. Ease her in."

"Check," Sami said and began maneuvering the craft closer in to the disappearing cloud wall. The other scouters took up station on each side of them, slope.

Though it rained just hours ago, the soil quickly absorbed the water and Del found his footing remarkably firm on the steep incline. As Del carefully threaded his way, he kept one eye on his footing and the other on his Life-Sensor.

His muscles and stomach were tense as he realized that this was his first truly alien world that might have extraterrestrial life. This was what he had trained so hard for, and now he would find out if he was truly prepared to face the joys and the dangers of finding that life. He was also tense knowing that something had happened to Tala, but he didn't have a clue as to what.

The steepness of the sharp incline forced the group to do several diagonal switchbacks and delayed their progress, but after thirty minutes of steady marching they neared the valley floor and entered the forest. On the way down Del could occasionally see the flicker of light on water as a shaft of sunlight pierced the forest canopy.

Overhead, small flying things flicked rapidly through the tree branches and leaves. They appeared benevolent and left the encroaching humans alone.

Del could see that instead of one set of wings, these creatures used a dual set to maneuver through the trees.

They had landed late morning and now the sun was nearing its zenith. Shafts of yellow-green light pierced small openings in the canopy to spread small pools of light across the dark undergrowth. The temperature was high enough that Del's forehead started to glisten with tiny drops of perspiration.

His LS display showed several life-form readings, but they were all in the low-band range. The flying creatures had lighted up the sensor several times. Once he got a midrange spike on a life-form. But the display registered only for a moment and then vanished as if the creature had sighted the humans and sped away in the opposite direction.

Ahead Del saw Anyar abruptly stop. With his back to the group, he raised his arm up ~~in the age-old traditional sign~~ the others to halt. For a moment he stood stock-still. Then, kneeling he turned and motioned for Bianca's group to come forward. At a half-lope, Del trotted to where Anyar focused on his Life-Sensor.

Bianca knelt and asked, "Contact?" Anyar nodded. "Multiple hits. Most in the low range. But I think we might have a hunter . . ."

"Where?" Bianca asked as she rotated around to look into the forest.

"Front and to our right. It's paced us for the last five minutes. Fades in and out on the display but the last two times it's come in a little closer." He looked at Del, "Beta scale, four point five bandwidth."

Del nodded, "Got it. Saw it a while back but never registered again. Did you get a visual?"

Anyar shook his head. "No. Stays in the undergrowth." He turned to Bianca. "Saw some bushes move, think we're looking at a creature the size of a large dog or wolf."

Bianca nodded in return. "Ok. We'll tighten up a bit and shorten our intervals. Baldura, lock your LS on this signature and track it. Anyar, keep your LS on free search."

She keyed her trans-comms and explained the situation to the rest of the group. "Pat, pull in your flankers to five meters."

She lightly slapped Anyar on the arm. "Let's go." The four stood and began moving through the leafy brush. Del intently watched his Life-Sensor for any appearance of the unseen creature. The trees prevented any wind from disturbing the plant growth, so the forest was still and serene. For several minutes the group moved quietly, listening to every small sound the forest made, watching every tiny movement in the undergrowth.

Del's Life-Sensor lighted up with the creature's distinct signature. He hit his communicator and yelled, "Right flank! It's coming right at us!"

Instinctively, Anyar and Bianca dropped to one knee with their stunners at the ready but the creature was too fast for them to even get a shot off. With a lightning lunge out of the bushes the creature charged Anyar. Only catlike reflexes saved the youth as he managed to hurl himself out of the way at the last possible moment.

As it whirled sideways to attack again, Del got a good look at the alien creature. Its head reminded Del of a Terran snapping turtle with huge jaws that crunched together as it lunged. Four wickedly clawed appendages propelled a large oval body with melded skin-plates. Its underside was leathery, almost lizard like in appearance. A sinewy long tail ended in a heinous looking barb.

Anyar scrambled feverishly on the ground to avoid

the creature's snapping jaws. Without hesitation, Bianca joined the fight, firing her stunner point-blank at the beast's head. Del and Sami sprinted toward the melee, forgetting that neither one of them had more than their long-knives.

For a moment the beast slowed, then in one ripping lunge, clamped its jaws tight on Anyar's booted foot. Without thinking, Del grabbed an arm-sized dead log. Charging the beast he slammed the branch into the creature's mouth. The thing shook Anyar's foot back and forth but Del's gambit paid off as the animal let go and clamped down instead on the branch that jutted inside its mouth.

Freed from the visor-like jaws, Anyar rolled free. Del hung tenaciously onto the branch as the creature snorted and twisted. With a loud snap the branch broke sending Del stumbling backwards from the sudden release. Out of the corner of his eye, Del saw a hobbled Anyar get to his feet.

Screaming like a banshee, Sami raced between Del and the hulking brute. Momentarily confused by Sami's darting dash, the beast stopped dead in its tracks, allowing Del time to clamber to his feet. Spinning, the beast charged the wounded Anyar.

Again Bianca closed on the creature and fired directly into its armored head.

The stunner's effects slowed the reptile-like thing, allowing Sami to grab Anyar and push him behind one of the giant tree trunks. Deprived of its main antagonist, the creature whirled on Bianca. Backing while still firing, Bianca tripped over a log and went down hard.

Unmindful of his own safety, Del sprinted by the dazed creature and pulled Bianca to her feet, shoving the woman away from her attacker. Just as he did so, the creature whipped around, sending the cruel barb on the frenzied animal's tail, squarely into Del's lower back.

A shot of excruciating pain shot up Del's spine. For a moment he thought he had caught a disruptor's blast full in the back. He staggered and lurched away from the creature, searing pain matching each step. Behind him he could hear muffled shouts as the others joined in the fight, the sharp sounds of numerous stunners piercing the forest stillness.

"Don't move, Baldura!" Shanon and Stinneli were at Del's side, pushing him to the ground. Stinneli turned Del over, pulled up his tunic, took one look and grabbed his med-bag. In quick-fire succession the poacher medic injected Del with neuro- and hemo-med-sprays. As the other junior scouts gathered round, Stinneli checked Del's vital signs. He said to Shanon, "Vital signs are stable. Keep his head higher than his heart, and no liquids. I'm going to check the others."

"You heard the man," Shanon ordered as she eased Del's head in her lap. Del smiled up at her, "These orders I can handle." Shanon dimpled back at him.

A few moments later a slightly limping Anyar and Sami slid to a sitting position next to Del. "How're you doing?" Sami asked.

Del rubbed his eyes with his hand. "Except for some back pain and a thousand killer bees in my head, not bad. How bout' you?" he asked Anyar.

Anyar bobbed his head as he said, "Thanks to you and Sami, doing good. The foot and leg's a little tender where that thing clamped down on me, but the soreness will work out in a day or so."

"Speaking of that thing, where is it?" Del asked.

Anyar pointed. "Over there, took about twenty shots to finally put it down. Never saw anything so resistant to a stunner. Its brain and primary neural system must be armored-coated."

Bianca and Stinneli came up to the group. The outlaw medic bent down on one knee and began examining Del again. "Numbness or tingling in the hands or feet?" he asked. "Spasms? Cramps?"

"No," Del responded. "Back's sore, but okay. Bad headache. That's all." Stinneli asked Del a quick series of questions and then stood up, seemingly satisfied with Del's answers and condition.

"Well?" Bianca asked. Stinneli looked down at Del and replied, "Give him fifteen more minutes, then it should be conclusive."

"Hey," Sami sharply said, "Remember Del? The pin-cushion guy? Maybe he'd like to know what's going on."

Stinneli smiled ruefully and said, "Sorry." He hooked a thumb toward the now still beast and spoke to Del. "The barbs on our friend over there appear to be a delivery device for what I'm assuming is some type of poison. When I examined your back, I found a white liquid draining from three small puncture wounds. Matches the liquid I found seeping from the thing's fleshy spikes.

"However, without a field lab, I can't tell you what type of poison. So I injected you with two sets of hemo anti-venom and neural anti-venom. Plus Stop-Shock, and a universal antibiotic."

He paused for a moment before going on. "Since you don't seem to be showing any major ill effects, either your natural immune system is handling the poison, or the med-sprays I gave you are working. So, if you don't turn purple in about fifteen minutes . . ."

Del held up his hand, "Got it."

Sami looked down at Del and shook his head ruefully, "What are you? A human collection site for poisons of the galaxy?"

Shanon glared at Sami. "Sami, you've got a big mouth."

"Matches my intellect," Sami retorted, "I was only . . ."

"Enough." Bianca ordered to the two. She looked down at Del. "Nice work, Baldura, and thanks. I guess I owe you another."

Rubbing his forehead to relieve some of the pain, Del said, "Just put it on the tab."

Sami snapped his fingers, "Say," he began, looking at Bianca. "That's not a bad idea. Seems to me that we've pulled your chestnuts out of the fire several times. Don't you think a little payback is in order, like maybe, releasing us?"

Bianca snorted and sarcastically said, "What do you mean 'we' Sami?"

"Well . . ." Sami began but trailed off as he saw Bianca shake her head and walk away.

Bianca put the group in a defensive circle around Del, with all of them keeping a watchful eye on the sleeping creature. Anyar made his way over to take his place in the ring, his limp noticeably less. Del and Shanon were alone. Del looked up at Shanon and very quietly said, "For poachers, they move through the woods as if they were on a Seek and Locate, don't they?"

Shanon glanced around before answering in a low tone. "Yes, and they're very good. I think this about confirms what we discussed. Do we tell Nase and Sami?"

"If we can do it without Bianca and the others hearing. Maybe later."

"Got it. Now be quiet, you're supposed to be lying still, remember?"

After several minutes, Del found his headache

lessening and the pain in his back gone. Stinneli checked his vital signs one last time. "Well, no major purple splotches to speak of. I guess you're going to make it, Mr. Scoutman. You can get up now."

As Del stood up, Bianca came over and looked at Stinneli. Nodding he said, "Fit for duty."

"Good!" she said and softly clapped Del on the shoulder. "Has Sami done point work before?"

Del nodded. "Best in our class. I know he babbles a lot, but he's a born woodsman. Great instincts."

Considering that for a moment Bianca turned to the others. "Form up. Same trail formation. Double point. Anyar and Sami up front. Let's go."

As he adjusted his vest, Del said to Shanon, "Thanks for the lap pillow. It did a world of good."

Shanon winked, smiled, and softly said, "Anytime, Del," as she strode off to take her place with her team. Del didn't know if the warmness coursing through his body was the after effects of the creature's poison or Shanon's smile. Either way it made him feel so good that he was willing to go another round with the beast just so he could lay his head in Shanon's lap again.

"Okay, point, listen up," Bianca spoke softly in her

trans-comm, "The noise from our little fight may have alerted predators. Stay sharp. Keep five meters apart and start a double weave. Sami, you begin the first out pattern." Almost in unison the two young men acknowledged Bianca's orders. Del smiled to himself when he heard Bianca order the weave; it was a common StarScout field tactic for a forward point patrol. In a few moments, the group moved off through the woods, leaving their once frenzied foe sleeping peacefully.

After a few minutes of steady pacing, Del noticed that the vegetation was thinning out, actually opening out into true clearings. The loss of vegetation allowed them to see further and lessened the possibilities of an unseen attack from ground level.

Del knew they were getting closer to the stream since he could hear the gurgling of water as it splashed against rocks and boulders. Moments later he heard Anyar say over the trans-comm, "Okay, we've hit water. Turning upstream."

"Roger," Bianca acknowledged. Moments later, Del and Bianca approached the fast-moving stream and turned left. Del could see that the water was clear and slightly green-blue in color. He estimated its depth at half-a-meter.

Up ahead he could see Anyar and Sami approaching a line of low bushes that intersected with the stream. With a snap Anyar whipped his hand up. Instantly, Bianca and Del sprinted forward. As they came up, Anyar had his stunner out and was pointing at the bushes. Something grunted within the latticework of leaves and branches.

For several seconds the bushes rattled as the unseen animal moved rapidly away. Breathing a collective sigh of relief, the four relaxed. As Sami looked at the bushes, he quipped, "Noisy neighbors in these parts. I definitely shall not recommend this planet to Galaxy Tours and Cruises for rest and relaxation."

"Enough." Bianca said curtly. "We should be two, maybe three hundred meters downstream from Lima 2. When you sight it, do not approach, set up overwatch before we close. Understood?"

The two nodded. "Let's move," Bianca ordered. Twenty minutes later, Anyar said quietly over his communicator, "We've got Lima 2 in sight. No movement."

Bianca organized the group into two overwatch

teams with stunners at the ready. The two teams speedily took up a defensive semicircle around the scouter. Bianca, with Gant and Aron covering her flanks, stealthily approached the scouter. She entered the airlock and slipped into the ship.

Moments later she reappeared. "Empty," she announced. "Move out. Short intervals on trail formation," she ordered, "Extreme care in approaching the *Celeste*."

Moving slowly, alert at every sound and movement, the small group cautiously headed toward the next ship. Bianca directed them away from the stream, afraid that its constant gurgling would drown out other sounds. For several minutes they eased through the intermittent bushes and trees. The vegetation was thick enough that they couldn't see more than twenty or thirty meters ahead.

They had gone perhaps a hundred meters when Sami blurted out over the trans-comm, his voice catching, "Team leader, I think you should come forward and see this."

Bianca motioned for Del to follow and jogged forward to where they could see Sami standing. He was looking down at something on the ground.

Bianca, Del, and Anyar surrounded the young scout as he pointed at the ground. There were several sets of boot prints in the soft soil.

Del looked at the ground and mirrored Sami's amazement. Intermixed with human footprints were dozens that obviously weren't human.

Chapter 25

"I will Return with Honor"

All four stood perfectly still, each looking at the other. Finally, Bianca cast a baleful glare at Sami. "Did you make these? We don't have time for pranks like this!"

Sami raised both hands, "Hey, this is not my doing and not my idea of a practical joke. I'm much more creative." He pointed at Del, "He'll tell you."

Bianca muttered something unintelligible and keyed open her communicator. "Stinneli, Gant, up front! Bring Lia with you. On the double!" Within seconds, the three burst through the broadleaf bushes. Bianca pointed down at the footprints. "What do you make of that?"

For several seconds, they looked down at the

deeply imprinted marks. Almost as one, they knelt and began to minutely examine the footprints. Bianca crisply spoke into her communicator, "Everyone move up. Pat, form a defensive perimeter." She said to Del and the others, "We'll be overwatch for these two. Spread out and keep your eyes peeled."

For several minutes, the three moved from print to print, quietly comparing notes. Del couldn't hear what they were saying. Finally, they got up and slowly strode back to Bianca, careful not to disturb the prints or the surrounding ground. All wore deep frowns.

As they walked up Del heard Bianca ask, "Well? Lia you're the expert."

Lia shook her head and said in an unsure tone, "It's either an elaborate hoax, or the real thing." She knelt on one knee near the closest of the larger prints and made a sweeping gesture in the air above the ground. "We've got human footprints mixed in . . ." She stopped and put a hand over her mouth for a second before going on. "Mixed in with what appears to be non-human prints."

She took a deep breath and exhaled, "There is a distinct depth variation with each set of prints suggesting different mass and stride. If someone were doing this deliberately as a cover or a joke, most likely there would be less of a noticeable variation in the deepness of the track. And, you probably wouldn't find each print to be anatomically consistent throughout the set.

"But here, there is complete consistency . . ."

She pointed to one which was obviously much larger than neighboring prints. "This suggests a biped with a large, toed foot, narrow heel. In humans, the foot length is typically 15 percent of the person's actual height. If we extrapolate that the same criteria apply here, then by the size and the depth of the tracks, I would say it stands anywhere from two to three meters tall."

"Three meters . . . whew." Gant muttered, "Must be Goliath's long-lost cousin."

Lia glanced over and said, "Cousins. Plural. Appears to be several of the large sets." She crab-walked to the side and said, "This one," pointing to a smaller track, "is bipedal as well. Again, it appears to be toed, and the outward angular aspect of the frontal portion suggests the foot is wide at the front and narrow at the heel. Couldn't say exactly web-like, but very wide at the toe in proportion to the heel. I would say no taller than a meter, perhaps a meter and a half, if that."

She dusted the dirt off her hands and concluded, "Doesn't look like there's as many of the smaller prints, maybe three . . . four at the most." She hesitated and said, "Mmm . . . I think you actually have two different parties . . . the larger prints following the smaller."

She stopped as if struck by another thought and looked at the surrounding forest as she said, "Or pursuing . . ."

Del was listening intently when he suddenly felt very uneasy. Looking around, he noticed that Sami was nowhere in sight. Del's guard immediately went up as he said to Bianca, "Something's wrong, Sami's missing!"

"Wha . . ." Bianca began before demanding thru the comms link, "Lenz, where are you!"

"You said to spread out, so I spread out. Twenty-five meters to your front and off your right quadrant. Near a really big tree."

Dryly, Bianca commented, "They're all really big trees Sami."

"Yeah," Sami replied, "But I'm talking a really *big* tree. You can't miss it. And I was about to call you. I think you should come see what I've found."

"On our way. Hold in place." Bianca ordered. She motioned for the group to follow and trotted forward and over the small knoll. As he came over the crest behind Bianca, Del immediately saw Sami's "big tree." Even in the midst of a grove of large trees, this was a giant. On Terra it would easily dwarf even the greatest of the sequoias.

As they trotted up, Sami said, "Came over to look at this big guy and stumbled across this." With that he pointed down into a large notch in the giant's tree roots.

Del glanced down and saw what "this" was. Lying under several protruding roots in the short almost moss like grass were a number of unidentifiable but distinctly odd looking pieces of equipment. Three slender gray-silver belts each with an assortment of attached gleaming cylinders and oblong shapes, lay strewn against the tree's thick roots. Around the base of the tree were a cluster of the small bipedal footprints. Del could see that they circled the tree and then made for a meadow-like opening in the woods ahead.

Del was not an ET expert, but as he looked at the objects, the hair on the back of his neck raised up because to him, there was no doubt that he was looking at alien artifacts.

Bianca motioned for Lia who carefully stepped on the roots and squatted down to look at the objects. After bending over for a moment to look at the belts, Bianca straightened and said to the others, "Overwatch while she does her work." She opened her trans and ordered the other teams into defensive positions as well.

For several minutes, without touching them, Lia examined the artifacts. Finally she stood and rubbed the back of her neck. Del was close enough that he could hear Bianca ask, "These and the footprints? Authenticity?"

Lia opened her hands, "Sorry. No better than fifty-fifty. It could be an elaborate charade." She looked squarely at Bianca. "If it's a hoax, why is anybody's guess and this would be a heck of a place and time to pull a joke. And this certainly wasn't part of the scenario."

She looked over at the objects and said, "Without

> I don't understand why they think it could be a hoax.

metallurgy diagnostics, and a host of other tests, your guess is as good as mine if they're XT. But you know the protocol—don't' touch, move, or disturb. Notify upper echelons to send a properly equipped assessment team."

"Which . . . we can't do," Bianca rejoined. She stared again at the tree roots and surmised, "I think they stopped here, perhaps for a breather . . . perhaps to meet up with another party. Someone put those things in there for a reason."

Lia ventured a guess, "To hide?"

Bianca nodded as she looked up at the Paul Bunyan of a tree. "If I were dumping stuff and wanted to later identify the site . . . this would make one heck of a cache marker."

Lia nodded thoughtfully, "With the idea to come back later and recover the items?"

Bianca returned the nod, "Probably. To me this looks like a temporary cache. Whoever did this didn't even try to bury the stuff, just dumped it among the roots. I think that someone was in a hurry, didn't want to waste any time and found this a quick hiding place."

She stared hard at the half-buried articles and

spoke as if thinking out loud, "It would be very interesting to see who comes back for this gear." She rotated her body and studied the surrounding forest. "We could set up a concealed observation point..."

For a long moment she thought and then decisively said, "No. We won't split up. We don't know enough of what we're up against. We'll leave everything as is since we know where it is, and when we can, we'll come back later to recover the items."

For just a moment she practically growled as she said, "Why oh why didn't I issue standard equipment like vis-corders? We could at least have some record of this!"

"Because," Lia returned, "You thought you were on a rescue mission, remember? No need for that equipment, so quit beating yourself up over it."

Bianca called Stinneli, and Gant to join her and Lia. She turned in a full circle as if studying the forest before coming around and stating, "Opinions and options please. Stinneli?"

As if it took a great effort, Stinneli slowly said, "My personal... and... professional opinion is that we need... to stop the evaluation phase and go full-up operational."

He took a breath and spoke faster, "We're out of contact with our support ship. We've lost the Lima 2 crew. And now this. The logic curve is too great; there are too many unanswered questions, too many variables cropping up for us to continue in our present configuration."

Bianca nodded and said, "Gant."

Gant nodded his firmly as he spoke, "Agree. The eval is now secondary, saving our teammates– primary."

Bianca turned to Lia, "Can you give us anything more on what you're seeing here?"

Lia glanced once more at the strange looking objects before saying, "Ma'am, I think that the evidence is too strong to ignore. Call off the evaluation phase scenario, go full-up operational and implement as best can, ET Protocol Level Alpha Prime."

Bianca took a deep breath, nodded and said, "Thank you. You're right. I'd reached the same conclusion. Besides," she continued, looking around, "I suspect that we very much need the additional help at this point."

Sami, who had sneaked in close to the group

without them seeing him, now broke into their conversation. "Evaluation phase? What do you mean evaluation phase? And need who?"

Bianca raised a hand. "You and your teammates. Cool your jets Sami, we'll explain."

She opened her trans-comm. "Shanon, Nase, Pat, come forward and report to me."

Moments later, Nase and Shanon, with Pat at their sides trotted up to face Bianca. She wore a grim look as she began, "Because of—circumstances, it's best that you know the truth about us and what's been going on," she began. "First, we're not . . ."

"Renegades," Shanon finished for her. Bianca's eyebrows went up a fraction at Shanon's sudden interruption. Del looked at Nase who stood with an open mouth and then emphatically stated, "Nor are you *Faction* cross-overs. You're StarScouts."

"Whoa!" Sami began looking askance at Del, "What are you talking about . . ."

"The truth," Bianca finished for him. She swept the four with her eyes and said, "You're right. Your team has been on your No-Notice Final Exam from the moment you entered the preserve on Terra. I am StarScout Major Bianca Ruz. I'm posted with

StarScout Training Command as the Current Operations Section Leader, and I'm also your chief examiner."

"Pretty elaborate setup for a No-Notice," Nase dryly commented.

"Very elaborate, Nase," Bianca replied, "And something that's never been done before. But it's what ScoutMaster Tarracas requested for your team from the training command. You see, we respect ScoutMaster Tarracas highly. In fact, he was . . ."

"Your ScoutMaster." Del replied.

Bianca's face showed shock for a moment. "How did you know that?"

Del smiled thinly. "When you were semiconscious in the scouter on Stygar 6, you mumbled, *Return with Honor, Stripling Warrior.* I suspected that only someone trained by him would know that phrase and have it so impressed on them that they would mutter it while practically senseless."

Bianca made a face as she said, "I'll make it a point to keep my mouth shut the next time I'm woozy."

"Hey!" Sami stuttered, "What about the Garther Ape, the poison?"

"A beautifully constructed Sim-Life," Shanon said to Sami, "There never was any poison."

Stinneli spoke up, surprise evident in his voice. "Wait. When did you find that out?"

"Well," Del began, "Shanon and I suspected some time back that you weren't who you said you were. We had theories but only finally figured it out today...just prior to planeting in fact."

Seeing the look on Bianca's and Stinneli faces, Del explained, "First, we couldn't understand why we were sent up against such a known powerful predator with only long-knives in the preserve. Long-knives can handle most of Earth's predators. But against something like the Garther Ape, it just didn't make sense.

"Second, on Terra, we closed on the beast at least three times to at least ten meters and it never attacked. That went against your explanation of its feeding habits.

"Third, it seemed just a bit too convenient that the beast escaped in your ship. If it was so dangerous that you had to wear d-guns, we postulated that you would have greater security measures and its escape would have been close to impossible.

"Fourth, the way the crew was organized and operated seemed just a bit too professional for outlaws. You used Confederation equipment. Your mission briefs were almost textbook precise.

"Lastly, when you stopped wearing your d-guns on the *Queen Bee*, that really piqued our curiosity. So I did a little recon while we were supposed to be readying the scouters. I located and examined the ape. Found one of the torso side control panels slightly open." He shrugged, "After seeing the micro-relays in the array grid it wasn't hard to deduce that it was a Sim-Life."

Bianca shook her head and asked, "When you went looking for the ape, did you know for a fact it was a Sim-Life?"

Del looked at Shanon and then back to Bianca. He chose his words carefully. "No. As I said, we had suspicions but nothing firm. But we needed answers, so we accepted the risk."

Bianca looked at Del with open admiration. "So, practically unarmed, and after having faced the ape before, you went after it again?"

In response, Del merely shrugged.

Stinneli stepped forward, "My name is Doctor

Troy Stinneli. I'm a StarScout medical doctor but my specialty is macro- and micro-anatomics. I study the anatomy of life-forms, both terrestrial and XT. I was part of the team that developed the Sim-Life ape for training command. It's been in development for about five years. Your team was the first to, uh 'experience' our field prototype."

He turned to Del. "Sorry about the rough handling in the cargo hold, the muscle control compensators are a little out of synch. It wasn't supposed to grab you quite so hard."

"And the puncture marks on my neck?" Del asked.

"Sterile hypodermic needle, the old-fashioned kind. Still keep a few around—never know when you might need them. You actually had a slight contusion on your neck, so I barely punctured the skin and let the bruise mimic the supposed trauma of the ape's venom."

"Hold on," Sami started, "I'm not sure I'm buying into this. Like Nase said, this is all too elaborate a scheme to be just a field test."

At this point Gant stepped forward and said, "StarScout Lieutenant Gant Renn. Sami, let me ask you a question. Did you enjoy your playmates in the jungle? IS Young and I almost gave away our positions laughing so hard when we saw your fire ant dance."

Sami glared darkly. "I didn't see the hill when I lay down. Banana leaf covered it."

With a quick smile, Gant asked, "It was quite a jig, and how are your . . ."

"Fine!" Sami quickly interjected. Muttering he said, "No need to get personal."

Gant spoke to Del. "And that was a pretty close call. You were lucky that there was an overhanging branch. When the Jaguar jumped you, IS Smythe thought you would high-tail it for the trees. He was going to cover you in case the cat closed before you could climb. But you went the other way, toward the water, caught him flat-footed. If the branch hadn't been there . . . well, he wouldn't have been much help at that point."

"So one of the Instructor Scouts was shadowing me!" Del exclaimed.

"Yes," Gant went on, "At first. Smythe was trying to distract you, give you two problems to work on at the same time. But things kind of backfired because he ran you smack into the cat. So he started shadowing you. He felt obligated to cover you since if it hadn't been for him, you and the jag probably wouldn't have tangled.

"And by the way, he sends his compliments. He said that you gave him quite a run; you almost caught him twice. He said that between you and the Jaguar it was a very interesting day."

Bianca held up her hand and pointed down at the objects, "We need to finish this. There is obviously more that we can discuss but we have teammates that are possibly in very serious trouble as well as this situation."

She cocked her head and asked, "Convinced?" The young scouts looked at each other and nodded affirmatively. "Good!" she said, "We need to get to work and I need you four."

"Say, ma'am," Sami slyly asked, "Does this mean we've passed our No-Notice?"

With an eye toward Sami, Bianca said, "Sami, I am not only formally ending the No-Notice Examination of the junior scouts constituting Team Baldura but because of the circumstances, I am going one step further. I believe that StarScout Command will endorse my actions based on our situation."

In a loud whisper, Sami said to Del, "I think that means we're in."

Ignoring Sami's jibe, Bianca raised herself up and in a firm voice said, "StarScout Officers Stinneli, Renn, Grove, and Zowalt, Stand to Witness!"

The four StarScouts immediately formed a single line and stood at attention facing Bianca. She turned to the four junior scouts and commanded, "Junior Scouts, fall in!"

The junior scouts formed a second line facing Bianca and stood tall, eyes front and body ramrod straight.

With a solemn expression, Bianca began, "If this mission had gone to its expected completion, your ScoutMaster was to meet you on Kanab 4 where I would report to him the examination results. However, there is some doubt in my mind that we will reach Kanab 4 anytime soon. As I am empowered with commission and enlistment authority, and having the necessary quorum of StarScout Officers present, I will announce the examination results."

She stopped for a moment and a sad look crossed her face, "Though Junior StarScout Tala Jane Utlander is considered Missing in Action, nevertheless, I am including her in this action as she has earned this right as well."

She took a deep breath, and continued, "I find that each of you has not only successfully completed all examination criteria successfully, I can unequivocally state that you far surpassed the nominal expectations. As such you have earned the right, and I have the great honor to offer to you an enlistment into StarScout Command as a StarScout, rank of novice, with all the rights and privileges therein.

"Each of you must enter into this condition without coercion and of your own free will. If you choose not to accept, there is no disgrace or dishonor, and we will accept you as a civilian under our protection until such time as we can safely place you in the hands of the proper authorities."

She paused for a moment before continuing, "Unfortunately, we don't have the time for you to carefully consider all of the ramifications, and therefore I must have your answer now."

"Junior Scout Lenz, how say you?"

Sami gulped and in a weak voice said, "I do . . . wait, that's for getting married, I mean . . . I accept."

"Junior Scout Ahren, how say you?"

Nase quickly answered, "I accept."

"Junior Scout Hsu, how say you?"

Shanon answered in a firm voice, "Without question, I accept."

"Junior Scout Baldura, how say you?"

Del's knees suddenly felt weak, his heart was pounding, but there was no hesitation in his voice when he said, "I accept!"

Bianca smiled approvingly and then said, "Throughout history, different societies and civilizations developed unique ways to enact oaths and covenants; for some it was the raising of the right hand accompanied by an oral vow or expression, others used both hands, again with some form of verbalization, and still others performed complex rituals.

"We StarScouts have our way too. After we recite the Scout Oath and Covenant, if you accept its conditions, precepts, and the associated code, simply step forward."

Del couldn't help but notice that Bianca's eyes gleamed as all of the StarScouts together recited the oath, but it didn't matter, as his own eyes glistened as well. Del couldn't help but feel that he stood in a solemn and sacred place as the words flowed, not loud, but hushed and reverent.

Of my own free will and choice, I solemnly pronounce this oath and do covenant that;

I will do my best to do my duty at all times, in all places, in all climes, and with all people.

"I will obey all lawful orders of the Terran Confederation and StarScout command.

On whatever star paths I stride and worlds that I visit, I will respect the sanctity of life, taking life only in the defense of my own or for those I hold responsibility.

I will safeguard the lives of my teammates, holding their lives as sacrosanct as I do my own.

I will magnify my abilities by keeping myself physically fit, mentally alert, and morally just.

From my First, to my Last Trail, I will Return with Honor.

As one, the four took a firm step forward, Junior StarScouts no longer, but StarScouts in name and deed.

Bianca stepped forward and crisply ordered, "Scouts, return to your teams and stand by for orders. We have work to do."

She motioned for Del to come over. "I don't have enough for everyone, but I do have at least one for the scout who saved my life." With that, she reached into a vest pouch and retrieved a Scout Arrow emblem and pinned it on Del's right collar.

She grasped his shoulder and said, "Well done!"

She stepped back, looked around and then asked Del, "Ready to go, Scout?"

Del looked at his collar and replied, "Yes ma'am, I've been ready to go for a long time."

Bianca nodded in understanding and said, "Then give the word scout."

Del straightened, looked at his waiting teammates and in a proud, firm voice ordered,

"SCOUTS OUT!"